KT-165-451

red

black

you choose

6

9

10

# TRYING

## About the Author

Emily Phillips' two main life goals have always been: to write a book and to have a baby. As *Grazia*'s Features Director, she's helped change the law to close the pay gap, written on everything from over-committing to egg donation, and interviewed the likes of Amy Poehler and Jane Birkin. Her career highlight was when Jamie Dornan told her (while taking his top off) that his murderous character in The Fall would've found her 'right up his street'.

She lives in London with her husband and two cats. TRYING is her first novel.

# TRYING

EMILY PHILLIPS

HODDER &
STOUGHTON

First published in Great Britain in 2018 by Hodder & Stoughton
An Hachette UK company

1

Copyright © Emily Phillips 2018

The right of Emily Phillips to be identified as the
Author of the Work has been asserted by her in accordance
with the Copyright, Designs and Patents Act 1988.

A CIP catalogue record for this title is
available from the British Library

Hardback ISBN 978 1 473 66380 0
eBook ISBN 978 1 473 66379 4

Typeset in Sabon MT by Palimpsest Book Production Ltd, Falkirk, Stirlingshire

Printed and bound by CPI Group (UK) Ltd, Croydon CR0 4YY

Hodder & Stoughton policy is to use papers that are natural,
renewable and recyclable products and made from wood grown in
sustainable forests. The logging and manufacturing processes are expected
to conform to the environmental regulations of the country of origin.

Hodder & Stoughton Ltd
Carmelite House
50 Victoria Embankment
London EC4Y 0DZ

www.hodder.co.uk

For Charlie, always in it together.
And for my parents, for whom this may be TMI.

# Cycle 18

'MAYBE WE SHOULD TRY SOME *PORN*?' I say lightly into my husband's exasperated face. The flaccid loll of his penis on my thigh suggests the need for subtle diplomacy along with some brute stimulation.

'I've told you this a million times, Liv . . .' he says, rolling his eyes, tugging, then dropping the unresponsive one back to the safe space on my leg to perform a cursory sweep across the peaks and troughs of my hips and waist. 'I don't need porn: I've got you.' Three minutes in and already Felix is agitated with my sexy suggestion.

'I'll switch the lights out then? Maybe it'll . . .' I bat his hand off my prickly thigh and up to a handful of boob (safely seductive, no perceivable hairs), leaving the old boy to develop at his own pace. Felix drops his palm down for a grab of under-bum and I immediately hate myself for cancelling that wax last week in favour of a two-hour row with my mum about us *not* moving to Walthamstow. No level of perfect darkness will protect him from detecting the full coverage of fur. Maybe how little effort I've made is a turn on – I'm so elaborately sexual that I just don't need to give a shit. Except, I do give a shit: I'm just substituting any leg-shaving energy I have for this attempt to make a baby.

I go in to see how he's getting on down there. I'm swatted away.

'It's not ready yet. Just wait,' he says. I'm not doing much to help matters, but I won't blame myself.

We're kissing now like a pair of fourteen-year-old washing machines, while I impress my bottom into his hands in the way I imagine a Kardashian might – contrived and slow, seductive and at just the right angle to keep him away from the patch that's even hairier than everywhere else. No airbrushing here.

I just need to join him in that mood I've cultivated so beautifully. I spin the wheel for myself: Tom Hardy naked (cold, shrivelled, move on). Donald Glover serenading me topless (warmer, oiled up). Justin Trudeau negotiating environmental sanctions (polar ice caps melting). The *Game of Thrones* cast brawling (violently hot). Beards. Tongues. Even moustaches. Hair's clearly on my mind, but I'm losing momentum. Got to keep the tongue going. Must stimulate my husband, the quite stoppable baby-making machine. I go in for another grope below stairs. We're getting somewhere.

'I'm ready!' he shouts, as if I'm not face to face beside him on the one mangled pillow. And I can feel that he at least partially is, as he throws me on my back with cage-fighter agility (*this* is an exciting thought for me) setting to work like a man possessed – or, at the very least, a man in a rush.

There's no real need for me to do anything other than show up and lie back now. The Internet tells me 'cervical mucus helps predict your fertile days', and it also eases the flow when you'd rather be watching paint dry on *Grand Designs* than being dry-humped by the love of your life (even though he's a very attractive man and performing all the relevant manoeuvres).

Having sex with Felix used to be my ultimate pastime. We'd throw each other around the bedroom, up against wardrobes, clinging on to headboards, breaking slats, striking ambitious poses in front of mirrors and windows. We'd *want* to look at each other's crevices. But, as it's nearly midnight on a working Thursday – where today I've eaten avocado on toast at a breakfast meeting, pad thai from the truck on Leather Lane at lunch, *then* fish and chips for dinner, plus an entire airport-sized Toblerone to finish me off – and this is our eighteenth month of 'lucky day thirteen' shagging, I'd rather throw up than watch our missionary efforts reflected back at us.

Because after a year and a half of '*shall we?*' and '*must I muster it?*' and '*quick, the ovulation stick's flashing!*', we're both secretly glad when it's over quickly. I know we are, even if Felix won't admit it. It's a case of good job well done. We've had a productive night. When it's great – he comes, I don't feel the infernal creep of a bout of cystitis – we high five and imagine that this *must* be the time. We'll indulge ourselves and go through what we'll call the little bunch of cells already sparking into life. He likes Abe for a boy (Biblical? Presidential? 'Abbi?'), and Berenice for a girl after his grandma, while I'm for Will (every boy in our family seems to be a variation of William) or Matilda for a girl, so we can call her Matty and she'll be a prodigy. Either way, it appears we're having children with pensioner names. But then they all look like little old men, don't they?

I watch Felix's beautifully toned shoulders and footballer's bum as he pads off to the bathroom to retrieve the loo roll. As soon as he's out the door, I turn on the bedside lamp (requires dusting), wiggle myself up on to the scatter cushions so I can lie with my feet in the air, gather my tangled mess of long brown hair into a top knot, then shroud my exposed stomach and flailing arse with two corners of the duvet.

I hate this bit: the gawkiness reminds me how obviously we're trying and failing. It makes it a thing. Felix does a good job of making it better, sometimes positioning my pyjama bottoms over my feet so I can shimmy them on without creating a deluge, other times quietly bringing me a cup of tea while I lay rigidly with a tuft of toilet paper sprouting from between my legs, appealing to gravity to help us. Tonight he simply slides back into bed and powers up the Apple TV. Laughing helps.

Struggling to keep my toes aloft, I stare at the ornate cornicing on the high ceiling. It's taken me a long time to appreciate it, but my affection has grown for our little two-up-two-down's Victorian proportions. Even if we are stranded out here in ~~Boringwood~~ Borehamwood.

Felix settles in beside me and flicks on an episode of *Catastrophe* we've seen before – as if to reassure us that getting knocked up would probably just be a ruinous event – and I'm thrown back into my East London FOMO.

'That's it, we're locked out here in the burbs for ever!' I've wailed into my freshly purchased Ikea pillow at least once a week since we dragged our heavy boxes (and heavy hearts) over the threshold. I realised our mistake with slow-motion inevitability once we traded our ambitions of getting the deeds to *any* dump with two bedrooms in Walthamstow in favour of getting tangled closer in my parental apron strings in London's dullest outer reaches (ideal only for child care and Co-Ops, of which we have three). This non-existent child has a lot to answer for.

'Our friends will never come to see us,' I cried, ignoring the fact that we do all of our socialising after work in central London. 'Our neighbours are all ancient – we might as well retire now,' I harrumphed, even though that's surely the dream. There's no way a pension could cover our exorbitant Help To Buy mortgage rate. I probably don't even have a pension.

Because, while we took this decision to exile ourselves to the outskirts for one reason, now – twenty-five months after collecting the keys, and eighteen months of sweet unprotected, completely futile love-making later – that reason is still refusing to appear. Two years on, I still wake, sweat-drenched after a dream about our poky rented flat in Hackney, nearby to the over-priced brunches, and the bars and the all-night-noise. I even miss the mould. All I can hear now is the silence of a road unmarked by crime, the cats scratching the door to return to the foot of the bed now we're finished with our 'seven' minutes of 'heaven', and the Apple TV whirring.

'Do you need anything, lover?' Felix says, nuzzling into my side, always hoping I'll take pity on him and stroke his forehead while he falls asleep. 'Water? A comb for those legs?' Bret and Jemaine jump on board and snuggle by his feet, casting only the faintest of disapproving glances up at my unshaven but vertiginous pins (the only time that could ever be said of my little stumpies).

'No thanks, sexy boy, my leg hair is lustrous enough,' I say, running a hand seductively up my shin and bending to kiss him, careful not to upset my cantilever. 'And I've got everything I need right here.'

I just wonder if it's true.

Egg-White          Happy          High Fertility

**THERE'S ALMOST AN ENTHUSIASM** to getting up on Fridays. The workday is one last sticky door to cajole before you crack open the weekend. It's right there on the other side if you just put your back into it. It's also the day when I routinely gift myself a luxurious 8.30 a.m. lie in and pretend I've been at a breakfast meeting. Except, today I do actually have a breakfast meeting. Rachel 'has news' but the walls have ears at HYGGE so she can't tell me over the desk.

As I spot her through the window of Ray's sandwich shop on Albemarle Way, she looks more like the hung-over Rachel of old – hunched like a scrawny prawn on my sofa after one of our indie discos – than the creative professional, head-to-toe in asymmetric Isa Arfen. Her auburn hair is barely formed into a bun, her olive complexion jaundiced and without make-up. Even the collar of her denim jacket is half inside out. She's a travesty. *I should probably take a picture*.

I've known Rachel since university. We were in the same year at what was then called the London College of Printing (before the world abandoned paper) and our Visual Communications tutor vouched that at least 10 per cent of us would become gainfully employed, and someday one of us might even get to *intern* with a Hollywood set designer. It was a heady dream, but it was mine. By the time we had to pair up for a collaborative project in the second year, I'd decided that because my parents would not be gifting me a Georgian town house in Islington for my twenty-first birthday, I'd better buckle up and do something sensible like brand marketing before my only option was a life crafting shaky sets for school plays. I picked Rachel as a partner because she owned a circular saw and had hair that was dark on top, peroxide underneath, with a Debbie Harry fringe – the same as me. We accessorised our matching hair with copious homemade plastic jewellery and even now, the waft of Jean Paul Gaultier transports me back to us hunched over a workbench. I found out later she only picked me because everyone else hated her. Because being entitled *and* talented really doesn't win friends or influence people, especially when all the others are also entitled and talented little shits.

What Rachel lacks in the ability to moderate her insane self-belief, she makes up for with thrilling execution and some artful bullshit bingo when things go wrong. I've lost count of the times she has winged it to create masterful landscapes from the dross of uninspiring worksites. We aced the project and now here we are doing the same daily for a flatpack-merchant, always vying for the same promotion.

Naturally she's turned the same trick with her personal life. There's her husband Chris (handsome, rumpled, nicely greying curly mop, curmudgeon); a photogenic terrace in Walthamstow Village plus a mansion flat in Vesterbro for when she's 'working from Copenhagen' barely two weeks a year ('it's such a great city to invest in!' she tells me); then last year she accessorised with Beckett and Freja, the Insta-famous twins. Imagine how many miniature smug slogan T-shirts I have to avert my eyes from.

When she recommended me for the job of marketing manager eighteen months ago, Rachel (store design manager) sold HYGGE – the byword for cosiness in the Scandi mid-range furniture market – as a dream employer with incredible pared-back warehouse offices in Clerkenwell, Copenhagen and Paris. 'Imagine telling people you work for a *Scandinavian* brand?' she tittered. 'Plus, *everyone's* good-looking. And the maternity benefits are incredible.' She'd only been there six months, but Rachel was already happily twelve weeks pregnant, timed perfectly so she'd get the full package by the time she dropped on her first HYGGEversary.

But while the place *looks* like it's living the dream we're peddling, peel back the mid-century-inspired veneer and the political backbiting is vituperative.

'Sweetheart,' Rachel says, weakly reaching for my hand and side-eyeing my pointy white Topshop boots (she'll have them on by Monday). 'So glad you came. I've ordered us some matcha lattes.'

Her face has taken on a new light: as green as the drinks in front of us. I'd come here calm, thinking she would reveal that all those sly 'doctor's appointments' were actually job interviews, which would leave her seat wide open for a less hostile takeover by me. Now I'm worried she's either going to fire me – which she absolutely does not have the power to do – or projectile vomit on me like the girl from *The Exorcist*.

'What's this news then, Rach?' I say. 'You're not sick are you?'

*Maybe she's only got weeks to live.*

'Oh, it's good news, Liv,' she says. 'Don't look so worried! I'm just feeling a bit queasy.'

*How could I have been so idiotic not to see the early warning signs.*

'I have to tell management today and wanted you to know first . . . I'm pregnant!'

8

LAPPED. AGAIN.

'Oh, wow!' I take a big slurp of my now cold gunge to quell the rising resentment. 'You two must be at it like rabbits! How exciting for the twins to have a little brother or sister.'

The tears are pricking, but I keep them back with an upward glance to emphasise my unbridled joy. *Push it down, Olivia. Keep it together.*

'I know, right? It just sort of *happened*,' she says, clapping her hands on the table in ungainly excitement and spilling our mulch across the stripped wood. 'We weren't even trying! It was like when we fell with the twins. I must be the most fertile woman in the world: one look at Chris and I'm up the duff.'

She is not being purposefully hurtful. *Must remember: she is not being purposefully hurtful.* I've not even told her we're trying. But it still bruises – and the second baby announcements are even harder. We've been at it so long that people have conceived, given birth, allowed their bits to recover, got their sex lives back and then got pregnant again. Our friends' kids will be at university by the time we have one.

'When's it due then?'

A solid, interested question. I'm on board. I'm just your cool friend who's having too many great nights out in Boringwood to even consider a baby.

'I hope for your sake it's just the one this time!' I just can't *quite* contain the snark. 'I imagine the twins took their toll . . .' I eye her crotch for effect.

*Although, if there were four, perhaps we could adopt the runt of the litter like rich benefactors in a Dickens novel. Just without the rich part.*

'Ha, just the one this time. It's due in late October, which is great, because it will be one of the oldest in its year, just like Beckett and Freja.'

*As if you don't have those prime gestation dates pencilled on the inside of your eyelids so you see them every time you screw your eyes shut to have boring sex with your boring husband.* Who am I kidding? They're blatantly swinging ecstatically from the mid-century pendant lights.

'You couldn't have timed it better!' I'm eking out my last bit of sincerity now. 'Bet work will be pissed off, you've only been back a few months.'

*It's OK, they'll give all your work to me and I'll get promoted. Silver linings.*

'They'll cope. They'll have had another year out of me, and Chris will do shared leave again, so I'll only be off six months max. I'm going to work right up til it's due this time too.'

I bet Chris is up for doing shared leave again – he's still bloody on it. Well, officially it ends this month, but he's taken to east London's latte papa circuit like a pig in artisan truffle shit. Tough luck, Chris, back to that gruelling TV producer grindstone for twelve long months before you can return to that terrible sitcom script.

'Oh, we'll have to get the boys out to celebrate – Felix will be so pleased,' I say, knowing he most certainly will not want to play congratulations for their smug faces.

'Maybe we could have dinner at that new Paraguayan place in Hackney? Have you been?'

'Funny you should mention that, love, I actually designed the space on the sly when I was on mat leave . . .'

I wish I was at my desk.

Hey lover, how are you getting on? So that news that Rachel needed to tell me? She's pregnant again. Of course @Kid_n_Play are only just a year and she's having another one. WHAAAAYYYY?! Maybe you should run off with Rachel. She's more creative than me, and her womb is obviously very luxurious. I adore you though, just giving you the option. Xx

Delivered

Hello babycakes, just pootling up to Stoke for this meeting with Andre and the manager. He's on thin ice, definitely getting transferred as soon as the summer starts. Cannot believe Smug and Smugger have done it again. Are they not too tired from having all the babies already? Don't lose heart, darling. Your womb is luxurious – I bet Rachel's is made of moulded plastic like all her work projects. You're my sun and stars. xxxx

**AS SOON AS I'M AT MY DESK,** I wish I were away from it.

'Where've you slags been?'

An unusually warm greeting from Ryan today. His blond-haired, blue-eyed frailty masks an ardent bitch who will never forgive us breakfasting without him.

'It's ten fifteen and you knew that it was my turn for a lie in. I got the full wrath of old Toddler when I got in and there was no one here to cover for me.'

I settle myself with a wry smile: 'Never you mind, slaggy.'

The lack of gossip transferral will be gnawing on his soul; I can see him writhing in his perennial shorts. He doesn't like to rob the world of his beautiful shins.

I give a conspiratorial eyebrow to Rachel who is entering the office five minutes behind me in an attempt to throw people off the scent. She settles herself opposite on the one long desk that houses HYGGE London's thirty-strong creative team. Ryan and I are buffered from bandying arch one-liners about the furniture (and whoever's sitting on it) by about ten completely self-absorbed and therefore blissfully unaware twenty-two-year-olds who manage the website and 'do' our social.

The children in the middle don't care for our desperate, thirty-something vies for power and instead spend every working hour laughing at themselves, making green juices and getting off with each other in the toilets. Of course I'm horribly, horribly jealous.

I look towards the frosted glass and spy the blue-blonde blow-dried bob of doom. Trish Chippenham is pacing behind the firmly shut bi-fold doors of her office. Today, she's showcasing her angry toddle in a black Cos tunic and pointy flats. When one has 'revolutionised' (her word) that many interior businesses, I suppose we must accept that one can grunt around like a British bulldog, unleash withering put-downs without warning and regularly throw a shit ton of work at one's inferiors. She also has five children, which means she shows short shrift to anyone who feels they're 'overburdened'. Her signature move is to pluck obscure, misremembered statistics from the Sunday papers and expect us to stack up some research and re-render all of our retail spaces accordingly within a week. Rachel loves it when she does that.

'Olivia! Rachel!' she yells in her sharp Midlands twang. 'In here, please.'

Trish is known industry-wide for not having a PA. She revels in doing all her own shouting.

Rachel raises her precision-arched eyebrows, alarmed. 'My one-to-one invite is still pending,' she whispers as we walk hesitantly to meet our fate. 'Not a word.'

Things are not as *hygge* as we thought.

'Ladies.' Trish is leaning her miniature rounded form against the beech desk, more authoritarian head teacher than jaunty newsreader. 'Something is rotten in the state of Denmark. They've got it into their heads that we're not *creative* enough. They want to see the London office *originating*. Standing shoulder to shoulder with the Copenhagen mothership. They've been redefining how people hibernate for forty-four years. We can't even seem to be able to get a lamp approved. I've heard through the *vine du vin* that Paris have 3D printed a whole kitchen. What can we do? What is the market saying, Olivia? Rachel, have you seen anything outrageous on the "blogs"? There's a promotion in a winning idea.'

Rachel looks at me, and I look at Rachel. It's Friday and our brains are wrung dry: mine by Rachel's news; Rachel's by Rachel's hormones. And now we're pitted against each other. Again.

'Can we take the weekend to have a think?' I ask, buying some time.

'Sure,' says Trish. 'We've got some new "bigwigs" coming in next month with the Copenhagen management for a "creative conference".'

She's haphazardly air bunny-earsing words for extra embellishment.

'How about you "young things" both put together a presentation of some "ideas" for next week, and if I approve, perhaps we can let them in on how "creative" I assume we can be when we're not out for gossipy "brunches" on work time.'

Trish has risen from her perch to stand directly over us (which at her height means that though Rachel and I are sitting down, we're roughly face to face). Caught red-handed.

'Now get out – and remember I can see your screens from in here, so those big brains of yours had better be gainfully engaged.'

Weekend gone. Rachel will not be sharing her 'joyful' news for a while.

> **Orla**
> Hideous day. Are you about tonight? Gin & Sympathy in Holborn? Thought it sounded apt. Can't take one more minute of this place, but I guess I'm contractually obliged to stick at it till 6. Xxxx   15:42

**I WEAVE THROUGH THE FRIDAY NIGHT** crowds already gathering on the pavements by my office. The Slaughtered Lamb is heaving with twenty-seven-year-olds at peak Tinderability. It would make an attractive backdrop for drinks, so I call Orla to rearrange our venue, but wherever she's picked must be underground so it doesn't even ring. I continue. It's irrelevant where we are, I suppose. I'm having a last hurrah before more self-imposed abstinence for the sake of 'the baby'.

Every month, my teehalfism starts in earnest at mid-cycle. I've read that alcohol can't affect embryos until they implant, which is *at earliest* six days after ovulation. Then I cross my fingers and hope I'll be staying on the wagon for another eight months. I sell evenings like this to myself as last nights of freedom. I've just had one every month for the last year and a half. I can't face being sober full-time just because we want to have a baby. However, telling my mother that drunk women get knocked up all the time – when drunk on the phone to her – means she is now convinced I'm a barely functioning alcoholic. I reckon the very fact I'm capable of this binge/cold turkey switch-up shows I'm nothing of the sort.

Orla is sipping a flute of champagne in a booth of this moodily lit, chi-chi new cocktail place off High Holborn. It's unironic in its lavish use of cream and gold, and the chandeliers match the oligarch-botherer's earrings.

She embraces me in a warm hug, her expensively blonded hair appealingly escaping its pins and tickling my cheeks. She smells expensive and her smoky eye make-up is precision painted around her big green eyes. A new Mulberry Bayswater guards my space as I limbo inelegantly beside her, trailing my H&M bucket bag and cloth tote full of market reports that I hope will miraculously sprout into an idea while I get ginned up.

Orla blends with the booth. She's been a girl committed to a clean white jean since Liz Hurley started wearing more than just safety pins circa 1999. My purposefully ragged-hem skirt is drawing stares like I'm an urchin who's slipped in to beg. There's nothing refined or classic about me: I'll test every unflattering raw-edged kick flare, skater baggy, grunge-wash mom-waister that flits in and out of fashion. But from the moment we saw each other's spotty little faces in our first-form room at Lady Jane Whitmore's Grammar School for Girls (still second best in the country, thanks very much) we clearly thought, 'Hey there, you. Got hilarious Irish parents? Bit scared by all this academia? Favour inappropriately sheer lace dresses for discos with thirteen-year-old boys? We must be kindred spirits.'

Now we're more like those sisters who are nothing alike but share an abundance of history, odd mannerisms and fertility issues. Plus, we live close: she and her banker husband Rich live in a sprawling six-bed manor house just into the Hertfordshire countryside, while Felix and I are sequestered in the servants' quarters down the road in

Borehamwood. We prefer living in close confines. It keeps us warm when our one lump of coal runs out.

'Thank god that's over!' she toasts, pouring me a glass and topping hers up in a way that says she's throwing credit card to the champagne fridge. Or at least I hope that's what it means, because I've got £40 in my overdraft to last until payday, and we could have just gone to that cheapo Sam Smith's pub with the Tinder fodder. 'It's the weekend!'

'It's the weekend for you,' I moan. 'I've got to come up with some sort of creative masterstroke and write it into a presentation by Monday.'

I scan the bar for inspiration. Nothing *hygge* in here.

'Hideous,' says Orla. 'What more does that woman want from you?'

'She was on the warpath today. There's a promotion in it, though.'

'You had your whole Christmas ruined by that rebrand when they dangled a promotion over you last time. You're in a toxic relationship with your job.'

'I bet Rachel gets it this time,' I say. 'She's pregnant again, so they're damned if they do and damned if they don't. And I'm damned both ways.'

The bubbles get up my nose as I take a maudlin swig.

'Again? She's got to be the most fertile woman in the world,' exclaims Orla, beautifully fuming. 'I've come off Facebook; I can't take all the announcements.'

While Orla has taken a retro black-out route with her broody moodiness, I prefer to pick at the wound by constantly scrolling through social-media's bountiful wombs. But then Orla did have twenty of her closest university, work and couple friends suddenly drop-sprog in unison last year, whereas my and Felix's circle have only welcomed five happy arrivals. But friends are like dominoes. Once one falls, they all do. It's only a matter of time.

I decide to change tangent.

'Did I see on the *Guardian* that they're sending auditors in to Children's Circle? Does that mean you're going to get *investigated*?'

If there's one thing Orla loves more than anything, it's unannounced government investigations. It'll be like when she ran away from home over the stress of our German GCSE oral exam. She only got as far as her nan's in Barnet.

'I've been trying to get the truth out of Jemima for months,' she says, resting her line-free forehead in her diamond-heavy hand. 'Today she just locked her door and left me to deal with ten angry teenagers. How can I be communications director of a charity when I can't explain where she's putting the money? I read in one report that they think she's been giving the kids cash to buy sweets with – and then they use it for drugs. I don't really blame them.'

'What are we talking? MDMA?' I say reminiscently for those days when holidays were for festivals and clubbing – and weren't all timed around fertile windows. And when we actually had money for holidays. 'Reminds me of Ibiza.'

'We're too old for Ibiza now,' says Orla. 'Even Ibiza's too old for Ibiza. It's all just yoga retreats now.'

'We're still passable! Maybe less so if we had big bumps.'

'Better than being ejected for being too old . . . Speaking of which, I had a blood test this morning at this fertility place on Harley Street.' At least Orla has the money to fast-forward the investigations on her own. 'Not that I'll ever conceive while I'm this stressed.'

'That's progress!' I say, legit glad that she's performing

reconnaissance for us both. 'Meanwhile, this is our "good" weekend, and Felix is away almost the whole time.'

'It feels like he's away every weekend,' she says, patting my arm.

'Ah, it's OK – he's back tonight. Then off at six tomorrow morning, poor bastard. We just have to make sure we fit it in between. Who knew that switching to being an agent was going to be more intense than just writing about football?'

'At least now he gets to do his "Show me the money!" bit,' she laughs. 'I know it was a sacrifice for him, and the travel's a bastard, but he's done it with good intentions.'

'Baby intentions. And where is that getting us? Anyway, how's Rich getting on at the banking coalface? Still facilitating those mega yacht purchases?'

'He's all right, out with the merger lot at some hoorah dinner in Chelsea. It can't be doing his lazy sperm any good. I've told him that next month we have to go on a detox. We went to McDonald's *twice* last weekend.'

I picture Orla's McNuggets on a silver platter in the grand dining room. You can take the girl out of the suburban high street . . .

'Surely there can't be a correlation between burgers and babies,' I laugh.

'Well, it seemingly hasn't stopped any of the mothers up at Children's Circle! Anyway, tonight's a free pass. Drink up: Rich told me to treat ourselves on him.'

'He's sweet. But I can't have you guys picking up my drinks tab. Christ knows how much it'll be in this place.'

I wonder if Monday me snuck a twenty into the back pocket of my bucket bag for Friday emergencies (she's thoughtful like that). At least then I can buy the shots.

Orla doffs her flute at two burly Euro Sloanes by the bar.

'Well if not, I'm sure those guys will treat us to a couple of cocktails. Who needs sleepless nights with a baby?'

Egg-White    Energised    Peak Fertility

**I'M PEAKING** and Felix is on a train to Bournemouth. And I really need to prepare for a night of renewed passion after killing the mood last night with my champagne vomiting. Orla is such a bad influence. She knows I'm mid-cycle, allergic to rich men's stinky chat, and can't drink on an empty stomach. I must sort my life out today.

---

# *Book A Treatment*

·····································································

### THE STICKY TRUTH – YOUR BOOKING INFO

·····································································

Order reference: 56445992

Time & date:     11:00 am, Saturday 8 April
Employee name:  Wax On Wax Off Borehamwood High St
Guest name:     Olivia Gyamfi

·····································································

| Product: | Quantity: | Price: | Subtotal |
|---|---|---|---|
| Waxing Treatments 1hr | | | |
| Full Leg and Bikini Wax | 1 | £46.00 | £46.00 |

---

**I FEEL ELATED.** I'm a free woman. It's taken me a long time (nine and a half weeks to be exact) to extricate myself, but I've done it. I'm having a wax. Just legs and bikini, but things were so overgrown that the beautician is keeping my wax strips in isolation like some Victorian curiosity. Clearly I'm not too obsessed with grooming, otherwise there wouldn't have been such a delay in tackling the situation, but I do see a direct correlation between my forestry and self-esteem. And trust me, I've read all the feminist books on the matter, and grown everything out accordingly. The seventies big bush I can *kind of* get with: just not the over (and under) growth around it. I even grew out my underarm hair as an experiment. It's wasn't quite Betty Blue's sexy softly tufted pit fur, but I reckon Felix was pretty into it when I become a post-honeymoon free spirit for three months.

I've come to the conclusion that my legs are sort of my own fault. If I'd have just *not* kowtowed to the patriarchy at age thirteen – and refused to shave, epilate, or wax (and been blonde like Sienna Miller in *Layer Cake*) – I'd probably have only the merest of wisps right now. But that's a lot of ifs. And I hate that I care.

I lie back and take the pain, staring at the flickering strip light and breathing shallow breaths to ingest as little of the acrylic fumes as possible. My mind turns to our unborn, unconceived daughter. I hope that when she hits puberty the patriarchy will have toppled, pink razors will be outlawed and all people will be covered in their natural down: like when Cara Delevingne turned up with her slugs and made us all grow out our eyebrows after reducing them to three strand commas for the whole of the nineties and noughties.

I give my newly shiny legs a little inspection to revel in my fur-free state, but remember they're not tanned, toned or long enough to let out in the spring air. I prefer to keep my legs imprisoned in 60 deniers until they sweat like little black sausages, offering them a six-week summer reprieve under various jumpsuits and midis, before returning them to captivity for the rest of the year. It's not like I judge others by my standards. My friend Ada has the most amazingly plush, womanly body and looks like the embodiment of sex. I'm the embodiment of trying and failing: to have self-control, to be healthy – or to even substantiate my body's claim for being this out of shape by becoming a mother.

However, after a long week, last night's alcohol consumption and that less than amorous 1 a.m. display between myself and Felix, I'm girded for a productivity overdrive. Waxing: complete. Now all I have to do is finish (well, start and finish) my big important, *highly creative*, promote-me-now presentation, do all the washing (neither of us have any clean pants and he can't sort the delicates out from Bournemouth), buy a present for Margot's birthday, post a card for Aunty Gloria's seventieth (which was last week: we're in the bad books), get the airbags fixed, sponsor Ada for the marathon, take my cousin Una to the cinema for a 'girly evening' (her words, she's fourteen and I'm working on her), then seduce my returning husband – at midnight. Again.

I hurl the dirty laundry over the bannister – the stair carpet scuffed by Bret and Jemaine's playful scratching – before stuffing the first load into the machine. I wonder what it would be like to have a baby in the middle of all of this. Would it take me longer than my usual allotted 20 minutes to exit the house? Would this washing pile be an insurmountable mountain? Would I require a babysitter to get my nine-weekly wax? Or is it uncouth to bring babies in to hear *you* scream while they scream in their buggy?

*It's not like they haven't seen your vagina before.* Would people let me off late card buying and keeping-up-appearances Sunday lunches? And would I appear more proficient at work for turning in a presentation that I wrote half-asleep while my baby was playing on a colourful mat beside me? Or would that just make me a bad mum? Meanwhile, our house feels empty. A needlessly family-ready home for a largely absent married couple.

I miss how Felix and I used to be. Always laughing, always spontaneous. How he smiled when he looked at me. How I would light up when I saw him. He exuded 'I'm special'. Which he was. Which he *is*. I just assumed he was a bit of a lad – that he *knew* he was special. I was completely wrong.

I remember the very first moment I caught sight of him eight years ago. The width of Regent's Park seemed to narrow in the hazy spring air as he ran towards me, wiping sweat from his face with a corner of his faded football shirt. I saw his stomach first – dark skin, lightly toned, unshowy muscles, a smattering of hair creeping down into the elasticated waistband of his football shorts. Subtly sexy. It was a well-arranged torso even from afar and I'm glad I got to see it. It's just a shame he was concentrating on drying his face with his T-shirt, and didn't see it coming. At that moment, he lingered at the corner of the pitch looking directly at me looking at him. I knew we had a cosmic connection. He maintains his stare was owed to my yellow chick costume and the bat in my hand, and he couldn't establish quite why I was gawping at him. That was until the ball hit him in the face.

He pin-balled sideways, like a ragdoll hit by a sniper, only maintaining his stance thanks to his gracefully flexible neck and slightly shorter-than-average (his admission) midfielder's legs. The legs were even better than the stomach. I only noticed these details as I closed in on him, running, wings flapping, beak bobbing with Mufti, the family Irish wolfhound by my side. A massive chicken and a giant pup to his rescue.

As I made my way across the field, my school rounders ban (for being such a volatile batswoman) flashed before my eyes. Unluckily for this victim, my family weren't aware I was taking my chances to win back extra points for the yellow team with a couple of serious smacks.

I screeched to a halt in the muddy grass next to him, his Sunday league team not even attempting to contain their laughter, as the blue bruise sprouted across what I now realised was a spectacular square jaw.

'Girl, you knocked me out,' were his first words and I exhaled, safe in the knowledge that he was also a fan of Tatyana Ali and didn't hate me. As he rubbed the right side of his face with his left hand, I realised I had injured the most handsome man I had ever seen in my quarter of a century on earth. I braced myself for shouting, but instead got a broad gap-toothed grin, with a slight overbite (I was orthodontically conscious then, having only just stopped wearing my retainers). It was the smile I'd been dreaming of all my life.

'Your face . . . your beautiful face . . .' I said, forgetting myself as I tried to restrain Mufti from doing as I wanted to do: licking him immediately.

'Not so beautiful now!' he chuckled, continuing to rub his sore jaw.

'I'm so sorry, I've never done this before' – *lies*: I knocked out at least three girls in school rounders matches – 'Please tell me how I can make it up to you?'

'Just maybe keep that bat to yourself?' he said, smiling again, and looking over his shoulder at his friends as they dispersed back across the field. 'I'll think of a way to get you back . . .' And with that, off he strode, back to his game and out of my life.

As I returned to my clan, each dressed as various Easter characters – it being the big annual family sports day – I hoped he might indeed hatch a revenge plan so I could see that smile again. I was off my game from then. My egg and spoon round was won by my sixty-five-year-old Aunty Sharon (dressed as a rather scrawny bunny). The three-legged race went to my cousins Una and Paddy (Kinder surprise toys).

I tried not to look over. I was afraid he'd be rinsing me for pitch 'banter'; that every panting roar echoing across the park was at my expense. It was coming near to the end of our games. I had to pull it back for the 400-metre costume-change relay, and derobing from fluffy chick to hot chick took a lot of manoeuvring. Plus, I was now mindful that my change needed to be sexy enough for him to notice long distance, while tame enough that my dad, uncles and male cousins wouldn't twig. And it needed to be done at speed.

As Mum blew the whistle, I began another flappy run, this time rabidly rolling my costume down from my shoulders like a banana peel. I got down to the waist of my Nike vest when I felt it: sweet revenge, lobbed at the back of the head. I tumbled face-first into the dirt, hearing a collective slow motion 'NOOWOAH' as everything turned to black.

That waking moment is the one I think of most often now: opening my eyes to his goofy, fearful face looming over me, topless as he tourniquet-ed my bleeding head with his shirt. It smelled of what I now know to be my safe place: him. Mum tells me she, Sharon and Kathy were taken once they witnessed his wound-dressing skills (Scouts knot-training came in handy), even if he had just knocked me unconscious.

'Your face . . . your beautiful face!' he parroted, as he tended to me there on the ground surrounded by my five cousins, two aunties, two uncles, parents, an eager puppy and an entire panting football team. 'I swear I wasn't aiming to get you back!' His face was one of ultimate horror, plastered with dismay and a growing bruise.

'Boy, you knocked *me* out,' I laughed coming to from my daze to what I knew was my future. 'And now we're even.'

He took me to A&E, us being just a walk from the UCH where we'd coincidentally both been born six months apart. He ribbed me that I was a cougar in chick's clothing because I was older than him (same school year doesn't count, I maintained). I sometimes wonder if it was my parents who had the blow to the head that day, allowing me to be carted off by the topless assailant who'd probably fractured my skull, but they maintained they'd meet me with the car. And as he stopped to buy me peas for the back of my head, and I gave him the top half of my chick to keep him warm in place of his football shirt, I knew that this wasn't just any other day, or any other assailant.

Later, after a five-hour wait – the peas having turned to mush and when I realised my parents had gone home to wait because my dad's too tight to pay the parking even though it was a bank holiday – he took my details like a concerned driver expecting a hefty insurance claim. I was seeing too many stars to wonder if he'd use my address to begin a stalking campaign. Maybe I was just hopeful he would.

But in the days that followed, I'd get note after note in a tiny left-handed scrawl, the first time I'd had actual, non-overdraft-related post since university. They started out as extravagant apologies, developing into funny stories to help me recover from the concussion he'd inflicted. I did my best to reply using various coloured pens to draw him silly pictures to amuse my convalescing self, sending them off with obscure stamps (because natty stamps are a type of self-expression too, yeah?), until one day I just invited him round.

'Why are your notes so tiny?' I asked him, struggling for an icebreaker after a fortnight of missing a man I had met for only an afternoon.

'It's just a habit I got in school,' he said, looking a bit sheepish. 'I would, sort of, get my head kicked in for being the nerd who paid attention. I used to take down notes from a whole class in one corner of my rough book, in a size that no one would be able to read.'

He told me about how he dreamed of being a football writer at *The Times*, how he'd just got an interview after working at the *Croydon Gazette*.

'In the end, all my notes just looked like a series of dots and dashes – and yet I still can't do shorthand,' he laughed.

It reminded me of when I used to write elaborately miniature notes to the tooth fairy. By the time I got to grammar school, you'd get your head kicked in if you *weren't* taking copious notes. My dickheads are all barristers and brain surgeons now. He says his are all in prison, but I know he's just upping the roughness so he doesn't feel silly for being bullied by guys who now work in insurance and advertising sales.

After our meeting – where I laid 'sexily'/comedically prone-in-my-neck-brace on my parents' sofa in East Barnet – he passed me one final note in what he now refers to as 'the concussion confessions'. All it said, in tiny letters was: 'us?'

When I opened it, I let out an emotionally overwrought snort last heard when Emma Thompson received Hugh Grant in *Sense & Sensibility*. I still can't work out if it was sweetly old-fashioned, or just immensely immature for two twenty-five-year-olds to be passing notes when we were in the room together.

It was intense from there. He'd take me to gigs in tiny holes in south London just so we could see some Spanish girl band I'd heard once on an advert and we'd kiss furiously in a corner. We became friends with each other's friends until our friends became friends (in Jack and Ada's case, very special friends) and our Facebook feed was just a melee of *our* people. He'd make me mix tapes, and root out cute T-shirts on American sportswear sites for me just because they were fun. I'd cry reading his football match reports, because they showed me how passionate he was. We'd send emails as long as novellas, and phone constantly because we missed each other's voices. He'd post me hand-written love notes in cards and on scraps of paper and I kept them all in the vintage tin decorated with flowers that he gave me – like all the flowers he'd presented me with over the years – to look back at sometimes. He told me he worshipped me, a person who is completely fine in admitting to being medium in every way (hair: brown, eyes: brown, height: five foot six, size: 12, feet: 5.5). OK, I've got great eyebrows. And pretty decent boobs. And I wasn't actually quite as medium back then, before the work 'n' baby stress eating. Back when I'd get my fringe trimmed by someone other than my dad. Or when I'd wear underwear in a colour other than sludge grey because I knew it wouldn't be on for long enough to start chafing. When we moved in together, it felt like we were cheating the system – how was it *us* who got to be so happy? And then the routine set in.

I slam the washing machine door shut on the thought, and open my laptop to work.

# Five fertility risks you may not have considered about working in an office

Improve your fertility with lifestyle changes such as not thinking about work at the weekend

*Sunday 9 April*

*Click*

'I'VE BEEN DREAMING ABOUT THIS ALL WEEK,' says Felix, stretching out across the bed, his muscular arm around me and the cats play-fighting by our feet. 'I've been proper pining for you.' We relish our first fully free weekend day in three months with a big sloppy kiss. It's after 11 a.m. (our preferred wake-up time) and the day stretches in front of us like a beautiful blank canvas.

'Maybe we could go and see *A Bout De Soufflé* at the Everyman? Or we could just spend the whole day watching Netflix in bed?'

'Or we could do this?' he says smirking and rolling on top of me with unusual interest. Considering we'd normally be forcing ourselves into getting the job done before sprinting out of the house mid-argument, actually having the day to ourselves is working a treat.

'Hold that thought,' I say, rolling over to grab my phone, still holding his penis. 'Let me just ring Mum.' That shrink-rate is incredible.

Why would I choose to be so self-sacrificing just as we

have this pure glorious day of nothingness in our grasp? I can only put it down to Catholic contrition. I can't allow myself a good thing without first paying a penance. Or maybe I'm psychic. As I unlock my iPhone, there she is calling me.

'*Hello*, Mother . . .' I say.

'God, that was quick,' says Mum. 'Sure, you never normally answer me.'

Since my sister Grace left for Turkey last month to photograph the devastation of the war in Syria, I have been on the parental front line. But not before we play five rounds of phone tag. Mum loves an extended voicemail.

'I had my phone in my hand.'

*And a penis.*

'I was just about to call you. Are you all right?'

'Well, y'know. No. Not really.' Her voice is cracking on the end of the line. 'I've just seen one of Gracie's photos of a bombed-out school on the front page of the *Mail* . . . I mean, yay, it's exciting to see she's made the front page of *the paper* . . .'

*I wish she'd read more than that bloody paper.*

' . . . but it's been impossible to get hold of her the last couple of days. Your father stayed up all night watching the news and trying to get in touch with her bureau chief while I was stress-eating away like a madwoman. Then this morning we just get a text with an Internet link to some story and not so much as a smiley face.' I hear gentle Irish weeping. 'You don't think she's dead, do you?'

'Well, she's not sending you links to her work from beyond the grave, Mother. She's probably just asleep after a hard night and too caught up in her own head to put you out of your misery.'

I picture Mum waking up in a panic, face covered in chocolate and Flumps dangling from her long dark hair.

When will my sister ever learn to keep the parents informed that she's still alive? Are photojournalists always innately selfish? Or just ones from East Barnet, escaping a bad break-up and hounded by Maeve and Billy Galvin?

'What's that, Billy?'

I hear my dad hollering something in the background.

'Call you back!' she says, putting the phone down on me.

'Grace is dead again, obviously,' I say, rolling back over to pick up where I left off. We manage one short peck before the phone is buzzing again.

'She's back in Turkey now, so that's a thing,' Mum says brightly as if she was just talking about having bought the wrong milk in Waitrose. 'She said it was a little dicey when they came to the checkpoint but I'm not letting myself think about it. Dad managed to catch her for two minutes on FaceTime, and she says she's got another two days of shooting, but it's just a military coup in Istanbul, so that's made me feel a bit calmer, at least.'

'Oh good. Just the rolling tanks to throw herself in front of, then.'

'Now don't be like that, Livvie, you hear how upset I get. It's important work. Yes, she's got my nerves shot to shreds, but it's just Gracie. She's always been like that. Lucky I have you.'

I can suddenly feel Sunday slipping through my fingers.

'So you know how I've been leaving you alone this week because I know you're both so busy with work?'

My mother clearly doesn't do irony.

'Mum, we spoke ten and a half hours ago, right before I went to bed. *And* I saw you on Tuesday night.'

'Well, yes, but you should always have time for your mother.'

'What is it, Mum? Spit it out.'

'I just wanted to check in to see if you're free today, I know you're probably not, I know you're always booked up. But I thought I'd ask as we might need a bit of help. You know how your dad is building the wall . . .?'

Billy Galvin has been building the garden wall around the back of their pub Molly's for three months. It's a big wall, but he seems to be building it one brick per weekend. Which is especially ridiculous since Sundays are their busiest day.

'Would we be able to borrow you and that strapping husband of yours?'

'You want me to come and lay bricks?'

Felix rolls around on the bed, exasperated. I mouth my apologies. Obviously I'm grateful my parents are close by, but god save us, woman, when do we get to have a life of our own? It's my own fault for picking up the phone.

'Oh no, don't be silly. We don't expect *you* to help with the *wall*, darling. Just Felix, and just for a couple of hours. We can have a roast together afterwards. Maybe you could help me behind the bar, save that back of yours.'

Life is a test. Felix knows there's no escape for me, but I can see from his messages that he's hastily sourcing an escape route.

> Hi Mum, I might be free today after all. Is there anything you need doing? Anything at all, I'd love to be of service Xx
> 11:05
>
> Delivered

Oh lovely boy, that's very sweet of you. But your father and I are going to the Tate Modern, so we'll be out all day. Relax now after your week of travelling . . . <3

Andre buddy, I'm worried about you. Fancy brunch at The Hartley today, on me? Think we need to go over the plan of attack once you're match fit again. 11:10

Delivered

Got Tinder girl round, so can't today. Lunch after physio on Wednesday? The manager keeps calling.

He can't find one, and I'm glad we're in it together. I sigh, heaving myself out of our duvet haven, and raising my eyebrows to Felix. Five minutes of showering to relax the body before the weekend is over.

'When do you need us then, Mum?'

I receive instruction, put down my phone and make for the bathroom. Felix follows me in to passive-aggressively brush his teeth.

'Don't you see that our families are stopping us from having a family of our own?' he froths (all down his T-shirt). He's right. Unless it's just me not knowing how to stop them stopping us?

**MONDAY IS A BLUR.** It's big promote-me-presentation day, and I woke up at 5 a.m. with a vibrating stomach and a clawing feeling in my chest. I ache from the heavy productivity and lack of sleep. Felix was mixing cement until 7 p.m., and by the time we'd eaten our roast pork and Mum's best potatoes (her payment after a day of devotion), it was 10.30 when we got home.

Ironing, lunch-construction, a final sense-check of my presentation and a *Parks and Rec* later and it was nearly 1 a.m. We tried and failed to get the energy up to have a roll around, but tonight is the penultimate fertile day on the calendar.

*Groundhog day. Must get through work. Must have sex. Repeat.*

Why do I do this to myself? I don't have to flagellate myself for HYGGE. And now I'm up against Rachel and clearly her idea will hit just the right note of Scandi cosiness.

Perhaps I shouldn't have discussed my vague idea of a HYGGE Christmas installation with Ryan at the end of Friday. Rachel would have pounced on him immediately, laughing haughtily at my audacity at having an idea, then nicking my concept as her own. It's not Ryan's fault, he thinks she's his friend. But Rachel will never love him like I do. And that's why the idea I planted with him was a ruse to be abandoned on Saturday, to protect him from the espionage. It's just now I'm concerned what I've gone for instead is actually much worse. Is it too late to rewrite a whole Keynote? How many Rescue Remedies can I fit in my mouth at one time? You can't overdose on those things, can you?

Being summoned by Trish Chippenham into Trish

Chippenham's office to give Trish Chippenham a presentation is how I imagine walking on to death row must be like. She is the shouty, pastel-headed guard who will preside over the whole sorry performance. There's a glass wall so everyone outside can witness your demise: death by dry mouth and half-baked idea. And instead of a human rights lawyer interrupting proceedings at the last, I have Rachel wheeling past with what looks to be a perfectly scaled-down, fully lit-up model of a HYGGE Christmas amphitheatre-cum-spaceship, ready to kill me again. Meanwhile, I'm three slides away from boring Trish Chippenham to sleep with a piece of shit film on: 'What a HYGGE family means.'

Rachel's lapped me and now she's going to lap me to a promotion on a wheelie chair.

Orla
Saturday 18:35

So it's basically early menopause. Just got a letter from the fertility specialist. Eggs of a 45-year-old. Fucking ridiculous. Xxxx

Quick look at Instagram before I reply. Will require a long remedial answer. Maybe I should consult Dr Google, asking for a friend.

Oh my god, so sorry I thought I'd hit reply on Saturday! Had to go to a family day with Felix's agency – everyone had kids apart from us of course – and got back late and yesterday I had to go round to Mum and Dad's to help with the wall (again). So I've googled early menopause and you have literally none of the symptoms. Getting a bit warm at hot yoga doesn't count – you weren't even sweating! And those fertility doctors will fill you with nonsense so you'll pay them a million pounds to fertilise you. Don't listen. I bet your eggs are super fresh and feel so youthful that they don't think you're old enough to have a baby. Lots of love xxxxx

Started to feel really hot typing that message. What if the early menopause is catching, like syncing your cycles? Maybe it's just my blood boiling as I enter hell for being such a bad friend.

Creamy    Exhausted

**JUST ONE BABY ANNOUNCEMENT** on Facebook this month. And it was an IVF one, so we'll let them off. It's been a whole week since the presentation to TC, and Rachel's Christmas spaceship is still taunting me as it serves as a temporary uplighter-cum-conversation piece in the corner of the office. Maybe we should send it to Copenhagen for lamp approval.

I'm desperately bridling myself from screaming 'who got the promotion?' at Trish any time she paces past me, flicking

Post-it notes with targets on them in my direction. Instead, I'm channelling all my energies into putting together an *exhaustive* qualitative research report on how changing our Twitter handle from @HYGGE_UK to @HYGGETHEUK has adapted perceptions of the brand. Sample glowing responses include: 'It's all right' and 'Has it changed? I didn't notice'.

Thankfully, I have another distraction. Tingly nipples. Something's definitely different this month. I mean, I know something was definitely different two months ago, and that time just after Christmas when I was knee deep in the rebrand, and indeed the month we started trying, eighteen whole months ago (I was so young and foolish back then). I look back at those moments, when I cried over the first negative pregnancy test, or how I went and bought myself nipple cream on day 24, and realise that wasn't real. But now, this is definitely *definitely different*. I've got this little butterfly feeling in my stomach. That's a thing, right? Like something is happening in there. I've been saying hello to it when I wake up. And this morning in the long planning meeting, I felt queasy (though that might *also* be because I doused my porridge in too much honey at my desk). Plus, now I have a headache. And that's not stress at the presentation fandango. No, it has to be hormones. It's way too early for PMS – it's only day 25 – so it must be 'a thing'. Maybe my boobs are a bit bigger? It's hard to tell, they're already quite big, though just not necessarily in a sexy way. I'd go on a diet if I weren't eating for two.

**ONE OF THE TWENTY-TWO-YEAR-OLD** web-builders just asked me whether there is some sort of anti-ageing cream that could be used on your ovaries to make them younger. He was drunk, the whole team was. I was being good, but then I just couldn't take the pressure of one more person asking why I wasn't drinking. So I cast aside my teehalfism – even though I am at least partially convinced I'm babied – and had two glasses of red (and a couple of mouthfuls of prosecco). Eighteen months in and you've got to give yourself a break. So, cloaked in three-glass wittiness, I suggested that sperm was the only moisturiser I knew of, but that it's more the consistency of those peelable facemasks. He laughed his head off nervously in a way that reminded me that:

a) he's probably never used a facemask in his life.
b) he is twenty-two, so he thinks I'm an old woman and that this was my sad grope at flirting.
c) he is eight years away from googling 'sperm motility' and having a cry in the office loo, so should give himself a break from thinking about ovaries while he still can.

Now as I survey the darkened bar, with the office kids smouldering at each other for Snapchat, I wonder if I need to reconsider Tuesday work drinks going forward. I'm an 'honorary' member of YPNO – they'd never utter the full name, Young Person's Night Out, in the office for fear of letting anyone over thirty know they're not invited – but because I'm the only person born in the early eighties who doesn't have kids, they have me along. These are generation renters though, so my ability to mortgage a tiny terrace in the burbs has me on their hit list, and Zara and Ryan will soon be on borrowed time. I'm still clinging on because I

37

know all this could be over in one flicker of a heartbeat on a sonogram. But is it already over?

**HAVE YOU EVER FELT** like you're on the outside looking in? As I sit listening to the Rhythm Method on my long slog back to Boringwood, I notice how people look at me, staring at the orange lips, or the big blue fur. Who does she think she is? They don't get the joke against the grey of the everyday.

I knew by the age of eight that East Barnet was not where I was meant to be. I could never quite fathom why we were not still in the hustle and bustle of Kilburn with the grand guest houses where Mum and Dad used to live. Why did they move out there with the seventies semis, just so they could have a narrow strip of drive and a patch of yellowing lawn? It's not even real Barnet. Then I got to go to school in Camden, and I saw the goths, and the indie kids and the rastas hanging out on the banks of the canal and I wanted in.

I was never going to be one of those girls with the perfect stripy highlights and the tanned Britney stomach, but there was only so much you could do between Bay Trading and a miniature Topshop to make yourself unique. So, I spent a lot of time rummaging in the Sue Ryder and hiding from the sunshine to make sure I was as pale and interesting as possible. I'd travel up and down the Northern line inspecting charity shops for grandma cast-offs. I hacked up their sparkly cruise-wear – the last bastion of suburban sartorialism – into indie disco dresses, buying scuffed stilettos older than me from second-hand stalls on Camden Market for 50p and dragging Orla (dressed like Edie Sedgwick with her massive bat-winged eyes) to electro nights at The End off Tottenham Court Road.

functional essentials that go otherwise undone if he's there distracting me.

Recently, though, I've had the creeping realisation that if you can't make money out of doing what you love, then it at least needs to become a 'jobby'. *I can't even have a hobby without making it work.* So for a year and a half I've been building things back here, keeping my hand in with any skills I used to have. Tinkering.

I've built some shelves, and on them sit marionette-sized props – clouds and columns and stage surrounds – at various stages of completion. I've made nobbly colour-glazed vases for our mums and begged the local school to let me use their kiln. I've batiked 'backdrops' and then given them to aunties as scarves. I even reupholstered our armchair when the velvet started to wear through. And recently, I've been mucking about with neon sign-making – fashioning this wonky, brightly vacant uterus that had been floating through my dreams. Every time I come in here, it stares me down from the shed wall, unlit.

But now I'm making something for Felix. It's Easter soon, which means it's the anniversary of the day we first met, and the weekend when we got married (because I figured I'm only capable of remembering one date, until I remembered Easter is moveable). He's the only one who's not had to pretend to look pleased with my burnt offerings. As I fire up my soldering iron and begin to play with the neon tube, I hope that this will be the gift where the reaction will be real. That he'll appreciate the bright cerulean squiggled across the clear Perspex (even though my writing in neon isn't quite as neat as in pen); that the word will mean everything. US?

*To my wife, my best friend, my beautiful girl,*
*Can you believe it's been eight years since we met? And two*
*years since you walked down that aisle and made me the*
*happiest man alive? My life is flying at warp speed with you*
*in it. Every day, I wake up next to you and thank that football*
*for getting caught on the wind. This is the first time I'll admit*
*it, but I did kick it in your direction. I honestly only meant for*
*it to land near you so you'd pick it up and come talk to me.*
*Imagine if you had kicked it back: I'd have never recovered*
*from my injuries. I'm sorry I hurt you that day, but I'm glad I*
*get the rest of our lives to make it better. I'm also sorry that*
*I've not been able to give you the baby you so deserve, but I*
*promise this is going to be our year, lover. I can't tell you how*
*excited I am to have a miniature version of you running*
*around. I love you with all my heart. Thank you for being*
*mine.*

*Your husband, Felix xxx*

**WE'RE ON A TRAIN BEFORE 10 a.m. ON A SUNDAY.**
Our anniversary and we didn't even get to stay in bed. Who
has a bloody party at 11 a.m.? Even brunch doesn't start
until twelve, and that's not even a real meal. Don't people
realise sleeplessness is the new cancer? I get that babies
wake up at 6 a.m., but maybe my friends need to train them
into better patterns – perhaps by keeping them up until
midnight, so they'd sleep like teenagers until midday? That
way they could allow us poor childless folk that last bit of
rest while we can still get it. The weekend is not for making
all the friends you *used* to see snaffle round the bushes in
your local park, like some sort of early bird perverts, so

you can vainly reveal the sex of your unborn child. Just WhatsApp me the deets when it's born.

> **Luke**
> Thanks for coming, mate! Did you manage to get home OK? Didn't realise Liv was so wasted, otherwise would have given her the soft bat to bash around with.                                    20:04

'LOVER, HELP ME! I feeeell siiiick . . .' The good thing about early morning parties is that you get home at a regular hour. The bad thing about early morning parties is that you have to be carried all the way home in a triple surge Uber by your deeply embarrassed husband in daylight. So now you're nursing a hangover before dinner. Actually, maybe dinner will help? I need Potato waffles.

We arrived, despite our consciously early uncoupling with bed, nearly an hour late, because both where we live and where they live are without tube. So, after two overground trains, a tube, a rail replacement bus and a half an hour detour (sourcing booze at 11 a.m. on a Sunday morning is tricky when all the shops are independents), we found the park in this hipster outpost Felix's friend Luke and his girlfriend Azi call home. Feeling a bit cranky about our epic expedition, I swore to Felix – who was employing his footballer babysitting skills to keep my morning mardiness in check – that as soon as we got pregnant I was going to invite our friends to troop to some remote field in Hertfordshire at 7 a.m. to pay them all back for this abomination. And by abomination, I mean glorious, fresh spring morning.

With mini quiches and two bottles of warm screw-top prosecco in hand, we orienteered ourselves to the clearing in the middle of the woods and discovered everyone half an hour into a 'clue hunt'. Azi handed us both coloured sashes (presumably lifted from an unsuspecting primary school) and directed us to our teams. I was joining the gender-normative pink team over by the petting zoo (we ladies just *wuv* fluffy bunnies), while Felix headed to the blue team who were hacking through a thicket in what looked like an attempt to retrieve a body from a ford.

I could hear the boys' yelps and cheers as they liberated a big baby-shaped piñata (that contained the gender of Azi and Luke's baby, and hopefully some sweets) from a tree behind me as I approached Camp Mum. I looked over my shoulder to see the boys raising their bottles of beer in celebration, but ahead I couldn't see a single alcoholic beverage (not that I would be drinking in my condition – I must remember to buy a new test). Instead, there was just a sea of children and pushchairs (bar Jackson, who is perennially strapped to Liam's chest).

'Oh Liv, thank god you made it, we needed some adult intervention,' said Hayley, balancing six-month-old Eloise over her shoulder as she rifled through a goat's feeding box for a clue. As she dodged the confused goat's attempts to gnaw at her hand and pulled the token free, the group burst into celebration. And the kids burst into tears. Hayley motioned for me to take a screaming Eloise while she disinfected her hands with baby wipes. I joined Azi, who had somehow managed to wedge her epic bump under a child-sized picnic bench and sat down next to Jen. She was jiggling three-year-old Gordon's pushchair like a power plate (even though Gordon looks like an accountant and should *not* still be napping in a buggy). I tried to avoid eye contact with a gaggle of other women I most probably sat next to during Luke and Azi's wedding. Fortunately, people aren't interested in small talk when crisis-managing toddlers. One mousy woman, fairly featureless in a smock top like everyone else (Luke's sister Katie, maybe?) was calmly breastfeeding amid the chaos. There's always one.

'Only five more tokens to find!' barked Azi, trying to get the energy back up. 'Then we can help the boys with the piñata!' She swigged from a bottle of Shloer like it was moonshine before attempting to swing one leg over the bench and free herself. She swung again. Nope: stuck like a tortoise.

'I'm so fat!' she howled suddenly, mood swinging wildly, unlike her lacklustre leg. 'Who cares if it's a boy or a girl? I'm going to be a bloody whale for ever!'

I was not having this. Eloise still over my shoulder (no muslin required), I took Azi under the armpit and began to prise our host from her plywood prison. Never leave a pregnant woman down.

As I wiggled her back, I lost my own balance and, wary of Eloise landing with me in the mud, kept my arms outstretched thus taking Azi with me. I just invented a new form of baby yoga. I was the support mechanism, Eloise, safely nuzzled up on my shoulder was gurgling merrily and Azi had swapped tears for laughter. I was the only one with a ruined outfit but I *had* saved the day.

Hayley was less impressed. As she swiped Eloise swiftly from my arms, she dragged Azi to her feet, leaving me in the dirt. As the mothers I've probably met before began to whisper at my embarrassment, I stumbled up, and excused myself to de-grime while they all baby wiped for the fiftieth time.

'You're already sanitised,' I sneered as I walked past, nicking a pack from Hayley's no doubt extortionate Jem + Bea python changing bag.

As I walked my filthy self to the zoo loo, I felt that familiar dragging rush of my imminently impending period and quickened my pace. I never anticipated that I would be glad to have the back of my lilac velvet slip dress – a subtle colour nod to the gender-blended future – caked in mud to disguise me now free bleeding on to it. Protest fashion this was not. What came next, I can only describe as a knicker massacre. The pregnancy tests were right. Those two extra days of waiting had built a tsunami flow, and now I was up zoo-loo creek without a tampon. And there wasn't even any toilet roll. There's only so much you can do with a wet wipe, and fashioning a field sanitary towel is not one of them.

I stuck my head out and shouted to Camp Mum for back up. A collective smirk broke out at my tampon SOS, and maybe-Katie came to my rescue (having unlatched momentarily from little whatever-the-baby's-name-is).

'Hi Olivia, sorry I didn't say hello before, I was in the zone.' She remembered me. She must be Luke's sister. 'So we have two options: neither of which are tampons.'

'Oh, anything will do, thanks so much . . . my love,' – hedging my bets in case maybe Katie is not her name – 'it's, um, pretty heavy.'

'Well, you've not seen anything yet, but I have just the thing for you then . . .' she said, digging around and producing what looked like a nappy from the baby bag. 'It's a maternity pad. I had to wear two at once after Amelie was born.' I inspected the mattress in my hand, and enquired casually what option two might be.

'So this one is not the most obvious of options, but if it's not so heavy as a post-birth bleed – which I hope for your dress's sake it's not – a nursing pad might be more discreet?' I backed away with a deeply grateful bow, taking both options, along with a second pack of baby wipes, to return to the stall to figure out which to wodge.

Waddling back with a wet-backed dress and ten togs between my legs, I decided to crack open the prosecco and get involved with the task in hand – *the gender treasure hunt!* Four clues and forty-five minutes later, I was through a bottle on my own. Anaemic, having bled half my body weight and replenished its volume with alcohol, I was also entirely wasted.

We rejoined the boys and I cheers-ed my way through what looked like the crucifixion of the sexless monster baby piñata. Felix subtly strong-armed the second bottle of prosecco from my grasp once he realised I had reached halfway and was stumbling dramatically. *Not quite quickly enough, my love.*

As the jolly baseball bat – covered in blue and pink ribbons – was passed round for us to all take turns swinging at Azi and Luke's piñata progeny, I fell as sullen as the tiring children in their push chairs. *All this will never be mine.* I'll never get to knock the stuffing from an effigy of our baby, or cluck around drinking Shloer with baby wipes in every pocket. I'll just keep on rutting and bleeding and repeating, and Felix will tire of his barren, drunken wife and realise that he's done his time before finding a young fertile thing to give him the babies he deserves.

Mid dark thought, some faceless earth mother handed me the baseball bat. Her mistake. I swung. It felt therapeutic. I gave it another and felt better still.

I clubbed at it wildly, vowing to liberate that bastard piñata.

'Get back here, big baby, I'm not done with you!' I battle cried, whacking it across its papier-mâchéd bottom.

I'm told that this is the part where I started to attack it with the *end* of the bat. Seemingly that was too much. Felix tried to calm me down/restrain his psychotic wife, but I shrugged him off. And bashed and bashed and bashed until the pink papery guts came spewing forth. No sweets, by the way. Not one.

'Isssa gurrl!' I screamed, as Felix led me from the battered carcass. *Happy anniversary, my darling, look at what you married.* Azi laugh-cried at the joyful news, while our friends crowded to congratulate the proud, if startled, parents-to-be. And presumably protect them from the murderous perpetrator.

So, right now, I'm dying. But before I do, I'm having potato waffles.

# Cycle 19

'BABY, WAKE UP,' Felix whispers, stroking my hair as he would the cats' fur: tenderly, slightly patronisingly. 'It's Monday.' His voice is soft but unnecessarily bright compared to the dark fog in my head.

'No, I can't I'm afraid . . .' I say, cracking one eye open halfway. 'Come back tomorrow, please.'

'As much as I'd *love* to bunk off to stay in bed with my super-hot wife,' he says, gesturing at my hair, matted after last night's vomiting, 'we are only ever one missed payday away from living in the car. So we have to get you to work.' He kisses my forehead, and alleviates the thud for a moment. 'Unless you've been squirrelling away a secret fuck-off fund in case of emergency?'

I have not.

I harrumph myself under the duvet and turn to face the opposite direction in protest. Felix has made me a cup of tea as a reward for simply waking up after last night's pre-sleep hangover crisis, where I ran amok crying 'I'm soooo sorry!' in a shrill wail between strategic sick breaks, wearing his precious (and now pebble-dashed) nineties Spurs shirt and no bottoms. I want to cry at his thoughtfulness. Or is it just the prospect of putting my socks on?

'Please, darling, I can't. I'm ill and I'm mortified,' I say ruefully. 'You should just leave me behind and move on.

The cats will look after me for a time, and then they can eat me when they're fed up of my wallowing.'

'Nope, I'm not having this,' says Felix. I look up with genuine tears in my eyes hoping he'll take pity and grant me a fake doctor's note, or maybe even ring work for me. Instead, I find him wiggling around the bedroom in his pants with a wide grin plastered on his beautifully angular face. He's running product into his hair, which is curled tightly post-shower. 'Plus, the cats would never eat you. Bret and Jemaine are your catty protectors for life.' He picks up Jem, the big ball of silky ginger fluff from his blissful slumber at my feet and continues the dance around the bed with him.

'Come on, now, you can't resist this, can you?' He says in a silly sultry voice.

I giggle, defeated. I have lost the power to resist.

'Join us, come on – up and out of there.'

He pulls me very gently from between the covers where I've sausage rolled myself for protection. 'We can conga to the bathroom together.'

'But I'm a barren baby basher!' I wail as I flop back down on the pillow. My brain sludges with the drunken memories: me, bat in hand, dancing around in the piñata baby's entrails, surrounded by terrified faces.

'Nobody thinks that.' He sits back down on the edge of the bed, smile suddenly extinguished. Jemaine runs for cover.

'Everyone knows we're just frustrated. I've spoken to the boys about us trying.'

Tears line the solid dam of last night's encrusted mascara, my face munching at the humiliation.

'I wish you'd told me they knew.' I sob. 'I didn't realise I was being judged.'

*Now everyone knows I'm not able to do as they've done,*

*that my physiology is sub-standard and my heart is empty.*

'So everyone now knows that I've failed you.'

It wasn't supposed to be this way. As we laughed through our vows in Mum and Dad's favourite gothic church, I mentally granted us a six-month reprieve – honeymoon, buy a house, enjoy youth for a few more moments – before I'd come off the Pill and immediately ruin our lives with sleepless nights and fiscal cuts.

That first month, I was so convinced I was pregnant that I ate nothing but pickles for seven days and seven nights. After three negative pregnancy tests, all I was left with was bad indigestion. I blamed the backlog of hormones from a decade of contraception. *Just a couple more months.* Then came 'the black period'. It wasn't a bleak time, just an actual black period, ten days late. In those nine interim days, I resisted every urge to test – I was not tempting fate this time – so I sat on my hands, went for runs, froze my Boots Advantage card in a shallow ice tray. Again, my hackles were up: I must be pregnant this time. No other symptoms apart from the passage of time. When I eventually bled what looked like tar, I began to think I may have developed the zombie plague. I visited the GP 'just to check in.' Admitting you've been trying for four months raises little more than a chuckle from medical practitioners, so I was shamed into silence after that. From months five to nine, it all gets a bit murky. The fun sex wasn't working, so instead, we proceeded with military intent. Except a sergeant-major barking at a flaccid penis – especially when said penis has just moved house and resigned from his dream job at *The Times* to go and earn 'proper money' as an agent – doesn't get major returns. We couldn't even look each other in the eye. After four months of trying and failing to even initiate anything, we wrangled with the sex elephant in the room, settling into the groove we now call home: cycle after cycle of bland sex, blind hope, then abject failure.

'I needed to get it off my chest,' says Felix, raising himself off the bed to stand in front of the mirror, looking at me over the shoulder of his reflection. 'You got to tell Orla . . . And Liam has been so good about it. He asked me one day whether we wanted any of our own and it all just flooded out. It's been such a strain for me keeping it to myself.' He's pacing the room now. 'I'm sorry though, darling, I should have asked you first.' He curls up beside me temporarily and holds my hand. 'Not everyone knows. I just don't want you to feel you're alone in this. We're in it together. I want to be a father just as much as you want to be a mother. And I'm going to look after you every day until it happens. OK?'

'OK,' I whisper, moving my head forward to kiss him and then dredging myself from my bed of pity. I wipe away the tears with the corner of the duvet cover. 'I know I look like a useless guinea pig right now, but we can look after *each other*. I'm sorry I haven't given you the support you need. I didn't realise how hard this would be on both of us.'

**MY HEAD STILL THROBS.** Half a life ago at university, I'd be alive again after a full English and an off-brand energy drink. Now my liver takes an entire week to process my shame and no amount of extra sausage and hash browns helps.

I scroll through Instagram waiting for the 08:38 to leave.

*Shit.* Liam has Boomeranged my deranged piñata bashing. It's racked up 179 likes. I don't think I've even got that many followers. He's thoughtfully tagged me, so at least my drunken idiocy may improve my social profile. But the least he could have done was made it an Instagram Story so my embarrassment could dissolve in a day. This is like my hangover – painful and potentially permanent.

The office goes quiet when I start the long walk down the length of the desk, the kids all huddled round Zara's Mac. I catch my bedraggled reflection between their hyena faces in her desk mirror (positioned on the screen so she can constantly perfect herself, while pre-empting management sneak attacks). As I sit down, a ripple of surely sarcastic applause breaks out.

'What?' I say, heaping my hangover scorn on them.

'Bashing the shit out of social expectations like that,' says Zara. 'Liv – you're a fucking hero, babe.'

Even Ryan is clapping non-ironically (I think), although it's hard to tell while he's wearing a black peak cap lowered over his eyes. Going incognito at his desk.

I burst out laughing: the balloon of my fear pierced with a squeal. The kids follow. Someone brings me an ambiguous green juice to celebrate. Trish Chippenham raises her eyebrows at us all from a conference call in her sealed glass box. I'm the toast of YPNO.

'Rachel, have you seen Liv whacking the baby?' asks Ryan, sidling over, milky legs free though we're barely out of winter.

'A baby? You hit an actual baby?' Rachel's distracted, draping *another* amazing new red vintage duster jacket on the back of her chair. 'Liv? What baby?'

I'm dying inside.

'She's a paper baby *killer*!' Ryan is delighted.

I sound insane; I'm the cult leader who's recruited a band of impressionable youths with an outlandish crime, and lured them into drinking my Kool-Aid. (OK, *they* made *me* drink the green juice.)

Ryan shoves his phone – now loaded with me bashing

on repeat – directly in front of her nose. She screams, but her volume is moderated, so she doesn't make herself look bad. Just me.

'How could you do that, Liv? You look like a maniac!'

'As if, Rach!' I say. 'It's obviously not real. I was drunk. And I was just getting into the gender-reveal festivities. Because I'm an *excellent* party guest.'

*Got to keep it light. No tears, Olivia.*

'Well, you won't be coming to any more parties at our house. Clearly you're not a fan of *children*.' She's not laughing.

Now I'm wounded.

'I love Beckett and Freja, Rach! Check their Instagram: I've liked every picture!'

Their outfits are better than mine, their hair is better than mine, their house is better than mine, their squad is better than mine. Even their frequency of visits to craft alcohol establishments is better than mine. I often wonder: am I taking adult life inspiration from twin toddlers? (#twinspo?)

Should I just tell Rachel what's really going on in this sad mind of mine, or just style it out like a double hard-hearted bitch? Unrequited broodiness, or unrelenting selfishness? I can't admit to my self-hating infertility thrashing while she's pregnant and about to steal my promotion. And yet I hate the idea that someone I've known for fifteen years could believe that I – Olivia Eoife Galvin (or Gyamfi, depending on which email I'm using) – could actually dislike a child. My face feels like a watering can.

'Look, the truth is, Rach . . .' – let's load this mortification right up – 'Felix and I had a bit of a row on the way to the party. So I got a bit carried away on the prosecco and took my frustrations out on the papier mâché. Don't tell anyone though, OK?'

She'll tell everyone.

I give her my best Diana-on-Bashir eyes from beneath my fringe and hope she takes pity on this white-lie life. She already pitied my entire existence anyway, why not throw my marital bliss under the bus? Felix must never hear of this.

'Oh love, I'm sorry, I didn't realise things were bad,' she says reaching across the desk. This is it: sweet reprieve from the smug fertility lamentations that would have been. '*As a mother*, I can't even imagine how hard it must be to look at the depressing expanse of life ahead, *childless*,' she'd say, wiping away one beautiful solitary tear with a ring finger sparkling with push-present diamonds.

'We've sorted it. But he's been away a lot lately. It's a strain.' I can suffer her relationship counsel another time, but now I need to get some reconnaissance on her progress with this project while her guard is down. 'Obviously, now I've got *this* as a distraction,' I gesture at my lacklustre presentation. 'How are you getting on with your . . . construction? Looks flashy!'

'Yeah, Trish was pretty inspired,' says Rachel. 'HYGGE's just recruited a new creative director from some brand in New York and she's very excited to show him *my* plans.'

'Me too, me too,' I concur, although TC has said nothing of the sort to me. 'Trish was all like: "this is going to win awards!" (Not true.) "Let's take it to the festivals . . ." (Not true.) "I can't wait to show it to management."' (Partially true: she *has* to show it to management, because she has nothing else.) 'I've already started casting. I'm calling it *My HYGGE Family*.'

'Oh, mine is called the HYGGExperience,' says Rachel, flicking her blow-dried auburn hair over her shoulder to reflect just how casually she's acing this.

But does she not realise that our brand name is pronounced 'hooger' like an old person clearing their throat? Hoogerxperience isn't a thing. Maybe the hormones are affecting her pronunciation. But then *me* conceiving My HYGGE Family, when I've just gone viral for knocking the stuffing out of a pompous paper baby, is probably just as ridiculous. Cosy families are reputedly my number one enemy.

'Can't wait to *experience* it,' I say, competitiveness seeping from each syllable.

'And I can't wait to see *your* vision of a family,' says Rachel grimacing, not even looking up from the photo of Beckett and Freja I can see she's uploading on Instagram. 'Better get on, actually.' And then, she puts on her headphones to tune me out. They're not even plugged into anything.

---

| 1 MAY | Event Details |
| --- | --- |
| **Dinner at Mum's** | |
| **Mum and Dad's house** | |
| Saturday, 6 May | |
| All day | |

| Calendar | Felivia shared |
| --- | --- |
| Invitation from **Felix** | |
| Invitees | |
| Alert | None |

Notes
Dinner at my mum's? They're going to make jollof because it's your favourite, (but we've got to clean out my bedroom first because all the cousins are coming over from Accra)

---

Can I reject a calendar invite from my mother-in-law? I suppose that jollof is worth tidying for.

Egg-White   Low Energy   High Fertility

**THE WEATHER IS BRIGHTENING.** The mornings are less crisp and there are fewer layers about. The sunshine is not kind to my face, nor my cat-fur-coated black tights. It'll be time to bare arms soon. By Felix's birthday – the one-month financial countdown is upon me – we're usually in the throes of a heat wave, and he'll host London's best attended non-statement birthday drinks. Every bloody ex backdating to his school days will pop by. 'He's just such a lovely guy, it's so great to be friends,' they chime, every year without fail. And I believe them, these various faces of me before me. The skinny one from university. His posh first love. The one with the great style that *just* pre-dates us who wasn't *really* his girlfriend. I hate the unfinished business. The fizz of unmixed chemistry.

Does Felix ever feel a pang of jealousy? He's so relaxed and secure, I doubt it would even cross his mind. He'll sometimes catch sight of Rafe, the boy I dated for about ten minutes in sixth form, on my Facebook feed and do a bit of a skit about my long-lost love, but there's no weight behind it. No pain. It's not like I want him to feel anxious. I just want him on his toes, like I am sometimes. But when your wife has furry legs both inside and outside of her tights, there's not much chance she's on the pull at work.

**EXCEPT SHE IS.** The most aesthetically pleasing man I have ever seen has just entered the building. I'm at the opposite end of the office to the lifts, but I just happened to look up from my screen as the doors parted and a rugged Scandinavian – forty maybe? – took two steps out, raising his eyes to meet mine. In that moment, where time expanded to fill the void between us like an airbag inflating in the slow motion of a crash, he swept his ear-length sandy hair back from his forehead, half laughing and half dipping his (grey-blue?) eyes. The lightly tanned stretch of muscular underarm peeping from the white T-shirt is now emblazoned on my retinas. I am assuring myself that time did not stand still, I am not in a Diet Coke advert, and he will not be removing anything more than his battered leather jacket. He's still in reception. And I really need a wee, but can't make the long walk over there on account of these cat fur tights.

I've casually turned about thirty degrees extra to my left (aiming my *incredibly important* marketing conversation at Ryan, while cultivating an unimpeded view of reception), but can spy Trish Chippenham rearranging her new navy Issey Miyake pleated two-piece. I wondered why she'd suddenly gone directional on us.

She's on the move. And she's got her arms out in front of her, welcoming him, a smile plastered eyes-to-teeth. Her ears might even be smiling, and that neck has never looked so taut (mini face-lift to prep, perhaps?). Prior to this, I've seen little more than resting bulldog face from her. And now, as *he* stands up to greet her, showing off just a little flash of his lower back that I'm ashamed to be excited by, I clock all the other girls in the office have noticed him too.

At least he was mine for a moment.

'MADS, darling! So good to see you!' Trish is on rare form, kissing him on both cheeks and embracing him in a deeply unprofessional, ill-matched bear hug. 'How long has it been?' Even beleaguered receptionist Sue – '*Hullo, Suuue!*' – who's well used to turning a blind eye to all of our nonsense, is watching the show keenly.

And now they're walking this way. On my side of the desk.

'Liv, Rach,' – oh, we're on short-name terms with our *cool boss* for her new friend – 'we're just going to catch up, then do you want to come and show our new creative director your ideas?'

Our new creative director? I've got to present to this man? Now? In these tights? I've got two minutes, a roll of Scotch tape and my trusty, crusty desk lipstick to turn it around. Toilet, now.

**SCOTCH TAPE IS ACTUALLY** surprisingly effective. I de-fuzzed the hosiery, mended the hem of my dress, stuck a bit on the inside of my bra for a perk up and nearly waxed my eyebrows. I pulled my hair into a high ponytail (instant facelift), and gave my glasses a wash with hand-soap. Just a slick of nuclear orange lipstick and I'm pretty much night-out ready. When Zara came into the loo, I begged her to lend me her heels, but she looked at me as if I was mental, so I'm still wearing my flat loafers. I'm going for that insouciant, give-a-shit look that probably appeals to well-travelled creative directors anyway. Don't want to try too hard. Rachel is in the next cubicle cleaning her teeth, but all I have is one slightly soft Wrigley's from my now discarded cardigan pocket.

**TRISH CHIPPENHAM'S OFFICE** is like a rare-animal enclosure now, with every woman in the company (as well as a surprising number of boys) suddenly milling about, hosting impromptu brainstorms so they can surreptitiously stare in. He, as a man of the world, is paying it absolutely zero notice, while no doubt expanding his ego internally.

'Mads Rasmussen—,' says Trish, as he leans elegantly on the corner of her desk, arms crossed, a smile creeping across those beautiful lips while we're sat at knee level (*in the lap of the god*) '—meet Olivia and Rachel our marketing and design managers here at HYGGE UK. Your new remit will probably impact them most directly.'

*His remit can impact me directly any day. Jesus, calm yourself down, woman.*

'Olivia,' he smiles broadly, reaching to shake my hand. 'Rachel,' he says mock-seriously. I stare at their fists, attempting to compare intensity of shakes. Rachel's was a limp, wet lettuce, a fair maiden bestowing a dainty hand to be kissed; mine tough and impassioned, well-matched. Jaunty, perhaps. I think I know who won.

'Now, the girls . . .' says Trish – *thanks for the instant denigration, Miss Trunchbull, we're women* – 'have been working on a couple of very exciting creative projects. We'd love to get your feedback on them now you're fully installed.'

'Great,' says Mads, pushing that tendril of hair back again. Maybe he's cringing internally at us judging his bad hair day. Or perhaps he sets it loose for dramatic impact, like an arrow to ensure we're always looking at him (as if possessing Thor's own face isn't enough). But then, he's said two words to me, I just don't know why I can't work him out.

'Can I say how exciting it is to be working with you, Mr Rasmussen?' says Rachel. 'I'm such a fan of the work you did at MOMA. I flew to New York specifically to check out that new visitor centre you designed last year and blogged about it.'

I cannot believe she has somehow magically pre-empted this lick-ass encounter by a whole year (they probably consulted her on hiring him, she's *so well thought of*). I've never been less aware of someone's work. I cannot believe anyone still has a blog.

'Thanks, that's high praise coming from you,' says Mads, a relaxed Danish lilt muddled with an East Coast twang. 'I've heard a lot about your design work in the London store, Rachel.' She glow-worms to new levels of smuggery. That's it, I'm off. *Ciao, adios, I'm done.*

'I'm afraid I've never heard of you,' I interrupt. 'But obviously I would have spent some time deep googling and setting up an architecture blog had I known you were arriving today.' I punctuate with a haughty laugh. Trish's laser stare burns a hole in my already puce cheek.

'Ah, this one speaks honestly, I see . . .' he says slowly, drawing his shoulders back and placing his broad palms on either side of him on the desk. *Go with it, Olivia.* 'What you need from marketing: the hard facts, and the solutions. I've heard plenty about your excellent campaign work too, Liv.'

I'm on short-name terms. He looks at me, poker-faced. I shall not buckle under the weight of how much I want to lick his face. *Think of something unsexy. Think of ovulation sticks. Think of Felix.*

'We need that MOMA credibility here,' I say, not knowing which direction my sentence is going in. 'HYGGE's cosiness has an impact on how we're perceived as a brand. A hug has no passion. How do we elevate ourselves from that?'

*I almost believed myself there.*

'What I *think* Olivia is trying to say, Mads, is that it's very exciting to have you on board. Your vision is going to transform the brand *significantly*.' Trish gives me some thin-lipped admonishment, while I smile – my best challenging half-smile – directly at Mads.

'I'm very excited to work with you on making some really interesting changes.' I remove my glasses and look him dead in the eye. He meets my stare and his lip curls just slightly.

His fingertips are itching to pull that loose strand of hair back from his forehead, but I have him chained to the chair.

Trish's gaze is ricocheting between our faces like a Wimbledon spectator: two grunting opponents who want to beat each other in straight sex. She won't be allowing us to present in this state. Rachel has regressed into a morning-sickness hunch and is staring at Trish's bin in the same lustful way that I'm staring at Mads.

'Mads,' Trish intervenes, barrelling into the narrow divide between us. 'You must be tired after coming straight to us on the red eye. Why don't you and I head to lunch, and *the girls' – back in your box, Olivia –* 'can present to you when the rest of the Copenhagen team join us tomorrow?'

Class dismissed. Trish drafts Mads out of the office as fast as her toddle will carry her.

In the meantime, maybe I do need to google him. I hate to have to lower myself to Rachel's level, but information is power and I'm not letting her have the upper hand. Plus, I get to look at him again. Rachel's popped to the loo, again – a now half-hourly occurrence (which Trish, while she's in the dark about the baby, must have put down to a serious coke habit) so I've got five minutes to have me some undivided Mads time.

I must be grinning mischievously, because Ryan and Zara immediately skip to my side, bearing witness to my little fingers clicking and my beady eyes scanning every LinkedIn endorsement, *New York Times* review and what's this – a TED Talk?

'I mean where are the thirsty Instagram videos, hun? I don't want to see him presenting . . . in clothes . . .' laughs Ryan.

*Hands off, he's mine.*

'He really is an exceptional specimen,' continues Zara,

with her serious pout on. 'Do we know if he's *single*? Have you checked Facebook for a status, or a ring, or some gross old wife?' She's double screening behind me trying to track down a Dane.

*Seriously, he's mine.*

'Can't you see I'm doing a professional investigation?' I say, turning my head slightly to their distraction. 'I'm not some desperate stalker like you two . . . I can't have a restraining order on my boss, how would I get paid? I only have five pounds to last till payday and those credit cards won't pay off themselves.'

'I reckon he'd be worth it,' says Ryan, sultry now. 'He'd be one of those people who'd get off on it and would strip in front of open windows when he knows you're outside.'

*Save that thought for later.*

I click the play button on the TED Talk: 'Making Brands Sexy'.

'I'M PREGNANT!' shouts the pre-roll ad, my Mac set to loud so the gurgling baby sound reverberates round the office's lofty ceiling. All the social-media children, responsible for getting ads like this in front of idiots' eyes, look at me astonished that I still have my ads enabled. I hide my head in shame, muting and minimising just as Mads takes his spot confidently. On the dark stage, Ryan and Zara are belly laughing at my conspicuous search history just as Rachel emerges from the bathroom.

'Oh, *you* get those ads too?' she grins smugly. 'I thought it was only me because I'm always googling babies, but maybe it's just because we're old . . .'

I've got to take her down. My slides need some serious scotch-taping now I know they're for him. Then I need to smash and grab my way around Oxford Street to find something appropriate (or possibly entirely inappropriate) to present to this MOMA-fucker in.

**THREE WAY MIRRORS** are not my friend now. But as I stand here in the glaring light of & Other Stories tugging at the neckline of a completely career-risking silk cami dress – I refuse to be slut-shamed out of wearing what I want when breaking the glass ceiling – I imagine what it would have been like to meet Mads back when I met Felix. Before the extra stone of stress settled around my thighs, and the black rings around my eyes. When I didn't have to work until 8 p.m., and didn't *need* to have a baby right this second because the egg timer's nearly out of sand. Whether I'd have enjoyed sneaking him in to the changing room with me, like I would have smuggled Felix in back then, enjoying a covert fumble behind the heavy curtains. Letting him press me up against the mirror and rub furiously against me like he was going to take me from behind there and then so I could see it from every angle. His hands tugging at the plunge of the silk: Felix's hands, Mads's hands. The bulge of his arms in that T-shirt, the roughness of his unshaven face making my neck raw. How hot it would have made me then. I don't want to see every angle of this now. *The fantasy is hideous.*

I WhatsApp Felix a shot of the dress, leaning as provocatively as I can in the unflattering light.

> Want to see more? x    19:20

Five minutes, no reply. Paid for the dress, no reply. On the other side of the tube, no reply. What if he doesn't want to see more? What if I've pushed the boundaries too far? It's been at least four years – since we've lived together, thinking about it – since I've sent him even the vaguest of sexts. What if he thinks it's for someone else? I break out into a cold cringe. Have I definitely sent it to Felix? It's not like it's a money shot, just a bit of cleavage. But it's still out of character. A moment of Madsness.

Nearly home, no reply.

Keys in the door . . .

A picture of his hand on his bulging crotch.

I'm in the door and it's on. I drop my bags and he presses me against the living room door, fumbling to get my tights down and off one leg as we kiss enthusiastically against the raw pine. He lifts me up, and I wrap my legs around him (one pasty and free, the other still 60-deniered) and he's unzipped and in within seconds. We've not even spoken. I notice a burbling in the background and realise he's left his conference call on in the background and I'm excited that a single noise would tip them off to our extra-meeting affair. Maybe this will be the time. This would make a good story. Conceiving a baby mid-way through a player negotiation in hot stand-up sex. I writhe against his still-clothed body, gripping his broad shoulders and kissing his beautiful full mouth. What would I want with a scruffy Scandinavian when I've got Felix?

*If only.*

Keys in the door, still no reply.

I'm in the door and he's on a conference call. I drop my bags, and he presses his lips against mine for the briefest hello kiss. I lift the phone up and mouth 'pizza' at him, and he nods, distractedly scanning a contract on his screen as I notice the increasingly agitated voices on the line. A single noise would tip them off to my pizza ordering so I take myself upstairs. Maybe this will be the time. This would make for the real story. Not conceiving a baby after we've tiredly stuffed our faces and hardly talked, we're so worn out from work intruding on our lives, another 'fertile' day wasted. I settle myself on the edge of the bed. What would I want with a scruffy Scandinavian when I've got 'a Mighty Meaty, a Vegi Sizzler and seven chicken wings, please'?

---

*To that beautiful face,*
*Every day you astound me. Today I found you out in the rain*
*tinkering in the garden with a blob of plastic and some wood.*
*An hour later, there you are sitting on a stool you've made. I*
*learn from you every day. I strive to be better so I can be*
*worthy of you every day. Please let this feeling that I have*
*when I look at you, like my heart is going to burst from my*
*chest, only get stronger as it has done since we met, every day.*
*I adore you.*
*Your Felix*

---

TOMORROW IS NOW. Cami cast aside, I settled on an austere button-down midnight-blue denim shirt-dress. It hangs architecturally – and, very key, unseductively – off my less-than-architectural curves. It's pitch perfect, and I can see from across the desk that Rachel is doubting her unusual choice of a puffball skirt and plain black tee. She's dressed for the Christmas party she's about to pitch.

I need visual cues for this meeting, not just the staid Keynote I bored TC with, so I'm casting my film via

Instagram, and putting together a list of HYGGE-worthy influencers who can vocalise what the brand means for families. I want it to be epic in scope, searing in minutiae and perfectly shot. I will direct, but I have a camera-person in mind who will render the project vital and necessary: my award-winning photojournalist and film-maker sister Grace. If I can just lure her away from Syria.

I type #parenting into Instagram and watch photos load of my never-life. Little hands holding big hands. Kids in band T-shirts. Japanorama lunch-boxes filled with baby avocado on toast. Toddlers in galleries. Women like me playing smug mother for the cameras.

The Danes have landed and they are sombre in their well-designed utilitarianism. The meeting room next to Trish's has become a makeshift workspace for them, six fifty-year-old bespectacled Klauses, primed for creative brainstorming with only our jaded mugs beyond the glass wall for inspiration. It's 10.13 and Mads is still nowhere to be seen. Zara – decreed by the office as girl most likely to deputise for a Victoria's Secret model should one pass out from starvation on show day – is also notable by her absence. I scour the shared calendar and hers is simply marked as 'coffee'. She's nabbed him. Oh, the cliché of it. It's deeply inappropriate and I'm going to complain. I refuse to present to a workplace predator.

I'm about to hit decline to the presentation request in whistle-blower protest, when in he saunters. He's wearing a sapphire-blue double-breasted suit with another pristine white T-shirt and box-fresh trainers. I take a long hard tracking stare at his ridiculousness, but maintain my steely demeanour. I will not be put off my stride by this blatant peacocking. Zara is nowhere to be seen. Am I the predator now?

**RACHEL HAS GONE TO PIECES.** She's gluing what look like sparkly pipe-cleaners to the base of the HYGGExperience and it's looking less on-brand with every passing bauble. The puffball nearly reaches her neck when she's sat down. Meanwhile, my mummy influencer list (mumfluencers? Hideous) is looking healthy and I've gathered aesthetically well-matched blown-up shots of them all to show to the Klauses. I've created a Pinterest board of visual references on how the film would look (fully interactive presentation, tick) and teed up some of Grace's more human war reports to give them a feel for tone. I'm going big.

Trish is striding this way. She's clearly received Mads's outlandish memo and is wearing a Barbie pink trouser suit which is part seventies Prada, part seventy-year-old Hillary Clinton. Chippenham's got fashion chops. I'm now concerned my denim button-down is erring on the side of only Klaus-appropriate, which, as I see Zara walk in the requisite two minutes behind in spray-on red jeans, may not be enough to impress Mads. *I need something more.*

I stick my hand across the desk and root around in the shared well of crap in between all our Macs (one day we might urgently need a peptide eye-refresher and dinosaur paperweight).

'Ryan, can I borrow your gel?' I hiss, as Rachel looks up quizzically from her science project. I retrieve my emergency super-hoop earrings and a lipstick the colour of decaying cherries from my drawer selection and head off to my Wonder Woman changing toilet again.

'It's not gel, bitch,' Ryan shouts behind me. 'It's sea-salt-enriched modelling paste.'

*So, gel then.*

MADS IS STUNNED. I can tell, because I'm greeted by silence, and a one-second glance. My side-slicked gothic glamour is overwhelmingly sexy, so he wouldn't be able to disguise how agog he was if wasn't committedly eyes-down into his iPhone.

'My HYGGE Family' sounds ruinously twee coming out of the mouth of a childless faux-cyberpunk backed by a screen rolling with screaming babies amid the crumbling Aleppo cityscape. The Klauses are nodding stoically, but Mads still hasn't looked me in the eye. He is, however, studying the screen behind me conspicuously.

'Can I ask,' says Mads, interrupting me mid-flow, 'what Aleppo has to do with HYGGE, Olivia?' Now he speaks.

I fix a concerted glare on my face and turn to him. How dare he interject? I'm only four slides in and was absolutely getting to that.

'Well, Mr Rasmussen,' I say, firm. 'I was getting to that part. But, in answer to your question, this is our world now. Everywhere we look is heartache and pain. And yet even in places like Aleppo, people continue to have families and take comfort in them. We take our lives for granted. But comfort is an innate human need. I feel that family is the most universal version of HYGGE there is. And I want to get people's perspectives on what that means to them.'

'Very interesting, Ms Galvin,' muses one of the Klauses (his name is Christian). 'I can see how this can have world-wide appeal. We may not be known for our filmmaking, but we are known for the values you set out. Do you propose to make it solely in the UK?'

'I was thinking for starters I could find those stories here, but then use our international reach to pull from all places. And eventually, I'd like to take the project worldwide and use the research to not only feed how we shape the brand, but also to create and focus a charitable project to help families in need of that comfort we offer our customers.'

I've got the room. This was worth the extra time Felix and I spent running through my notes last night. I know he didn't really have the energy after he got off the phone at 9.30. And it meant we didn't have time to even contemplate having sex, despite the ovulation stick saying I was in the zone. Mads is now openly studying my face, but I refuse to notice. I carry on with presenting my research and potential casting. I can do this, even if I can't have a family of my own.

Trish Chippenham's Barbie suit is bursting with the pride of my reflected glory. Rachel's puffball skirt and light-up model is obscuring my view of her face. But I know that after her HYGGExperience ultimately boiled down to a Christmas grotto staff party, she's defeated.

**Felix Gyamfi**
Tonight.
To: Olivia Galvin

Hey beautiful girl,
How did you get on? I've missed you today.
Feel so tired after last night. What time will you be home?
Want to cook for you so we can celebrate you being done
with that crazy presentation and me with this stupid Andre
business. Just saw the pic you sent me last night – I'm so
sorry I didn't reply. I would very much like to see more
tonight, if you're still willing to show me?
Xxxxxx

Felix Gyamfi | Senior Sports Agent | 11MGMT | +44 20 7590 6215

**Olivia Galvin**

Re: Tonight.

To: Felix Gyamfi

Hey darling, I didn't embarrass myself! And the serious Danes seemed to like the charity angle (you have all the good ideas). Dinner and kindness would be perfect. I'm on the edge of a sugar crash, so please can we somehow double carb? Health can start again next week after all of this is out of the way. Also, I thought you'd gone off me when you didn't reply to the picture – or that I'd sent it to someone by accident. But yes, you can definitely see more tonight. Plus, it's the last good day and we need to make it count, because the next one is while we're away with our parents. I am freaking out about having to do it with the entire family in the house (even though I know we are a lot quieter than we used to be). Adore you. xxxxx

Olivia Galvin

Marketing Manager

HYGGE (UK)

+44 (0) 7757406596

As I hit send, another email ghosts its way into my inbox.

**Mads Rasmussen**

Re: Drink?

To: Olivia Galvin

Who knew you were a documentarian . . . Management are going for drinks before dinner and I suggested you join us. Can you make time in your busy life for us?

Mads Rasmussen
Creative Director
HYGGE
+45 (0) 7925 074 053


Haven't they had enough out of me for one day? But I'm rinsed of every bit of fake contempt and am glowing at the prospect of the invitation. It's my time in the spotlight. Rachel has already left to pick up the twins. Having an ineffectual womb can work in my favour, after all. And how could I turn down the chance to mix with the higher ups? Felix wouldn't blame me for taking this opportunity, would he? *He would if he saw Mads.*

**Olivia Galvin**
Re: Tonight.
To: Felix Gyamfi


Darling love! I'm so sorry, but they've just invited me out to have drinks with management. I can't say no, can I? Will you hate me (I hate me)? I'll make it up to you with lots of head strokes when I get in? I won't be out late: they're all super boring and will be eating their pickled herring and head to bed by 10pm. I'll be home by 9.30, promise. Is that ok? I feel bad! Xxxx

Olivia Galvin
Marketing Manager
HYGGE (UK)
+44 (0) 7757406596

**Felix Gyamfi**
Re: Tonight.
To: Olivia Galvin

It's fine. But don't be too late if it's the last good night of your cycle. Work keeps getting in the way. We've got to be better next month, even if it does mean having sex behind a sand dune to get away from our families. No more excuses. x

Felix Gyamfi | Senior Sports Agent | 11MGMT | +44 20 7590 6215

He hates me. But I still can't go home. Another month crossed off the list.

# INTERVIEW 1: HANNAH
## aka @MUMMING

So this is the start of it all. Grace has shown me how to work the two cameras HYGGE have bought for this project so I can self-shoot. I have one for the interview, set up so that they talk across the lens to me as I ask the questions, and one to capture all the incidentals – the real moments. I'm still frightened I'll push the wrong button, even though I've practised on my mum, Orla and Felix (to varying degrees of blurry success). Or will I just develop verbal diarrhoea and confess my infertile jealousy at this woman with 100,000 followers?

Hannah arrives looking as glowy as in her Instagram shots. She's thirty and has three children under the age of five, with another on the way. Despite arriving late with a mid-sized bump and two rambunctious toddlers balanced on the baby's buggy board, her subtly balayaged hair is mussed to perfection, and her slogan tee is ironed, tucked and stain-free. She must have some sort of primp team on her at all times. She definitely didn't get the bus here.

We've got the brood on stand-by next door – cared for by Rachel who is just so bloody adept – so we can have a couple of shots with them together at the end. I've created a kind of HYGGE living room in one of our downstairs studio spaces, and I'm pretty happy with my styling. It's kind of dystopian Scandi: a bit edgy, but still comforting.

I've been following MUMMING on Instagram for more than a year. At first I guess I thought it wouldn't be long until I'd become one of her kind: 'winning at motherhood'. Now I can't unfollow in case it brings me bad luck. She holds pub quizzes in Walthamstow and Peckham in the daytime for women on maternity leave (recently lots more men like curmudgeonly Chris on paternity leave seem to feature on her account too). I daydream about what it would be like for Felix to leave in the mornings while I feed and nurture our child, before opening the door of our Georgian town house in an east London village and rolling off to laugh with other women just like me. No one would raise an eyebrow about our baby appendages constantly suckling. Then I wouldn't raise an eyebrow at the smugness.

**Olivia:** Lovely to have you as our first interviewee, Hannah. What's the secret to looking so good with so many kids? I don't even have any and I look more knackered than you.

**Hannah:** Ha, well it's all about routine. Which is tricky with so many of them. You've got to roll with the punches. Don't be afraid to let them cry. But if you can get their sleep patterns fairly in-sync, then you'll be on your way.

**Olivia:** So when I say 'family' to you, what does it mean?

**Hannah:** Tiredness! It means making mistakes. But for me it's been the best time of my life. I was pretty unfettered before Jed, our eldest, came along. I was 27, playing in a band, doing the odd job working for digital brands, and then I fell pregnant. I really had to think about what I was doing. But I was on a high when I was pregnant – those hormones! – so I think it made me super creative.

I started blogging about the experience and realised there were so many women out there feeling the same as me. Twitter was new and we just formed a really big bond. I think my husband Tom thought I was talking to myself, I spent that much time online at the start of Mumming. So it was just instinctive to keep it going once Jed arrived, and then Arlo shortly after. I got pregnant again when Jed was six months so I was just in the zone I guess. Tom and I always wanted loads of kids.

**Olivia:** And now you're about to have your fourth . . . Can you try and distil motherhood down for me? I know that's a hard question.

**Hannah:** I think firstly, it's *comfort*. You're constantly frightened that you've got this tiny life reliant on you, but at the same time, there's a security you'll never experience in any other part of your life. The bond you have as mother and child is immediate and intractable. I cried for the first three months of Jed's life because I was so consumed by love. And then as you build a family, and they age and change, it adapts every day. You're the ultimate problem-solver. Sometimes it's boring though. You feel like you're just a fixer for mini-tyrants, or just getting through the day with a series of feeds, sleeps and poos. I have made peace with the Eau de Spew. I thought I'd miss it when Missy stopped breast-feeding, so now we're having another one. Yeah, I know I could have continued breast-feeding a bit longer, but when they get bigger, they need you less and less. That's why babies get addictive. Who knows if this will be the last? There's nothing cosier than snuggling up, surrounded by all of your children, especially when they're tiny. Tom joked that I should just become a midwife or something, so that's my next business idea! Remote doulas for when you're in labour, via Instagram Stories or Facebook Live . . .

**Olivia:** Interesting! Family has become the central focus for your work as well as your home life. Why is that important?

**Hannah:** I just wanted to share the process with other parents. It's hard lots of the time. It's lonely. You sort of duck out of normal society. I wanted to set up something of our own. Somewhere we could be adults and mums (and dads!) at the same time. It wasn't always easy when I would be feeding, and doing my emails with one hand. But it's been so eye-opening to meet all of these people and work with so many brands. I don't care if I'm a bit tired here and there. There are times when Tom and I disagree though.

**Olivia:** Why's that?

**Hannah:** He's not into social media. He thinks the kids shouldn't be in the photos with me. But then I show him how cute the shoots are, with them in their mini-me outfits. He'll thank me later when we've got this amazing archive of their lives.

**Olivia:** Do you think you'd cope with motherhood without social media?

**Hannah:** D'you know, that's an interesting question. I'm not sure. It's all I've known. And it's a special support network. I guess I'd spend a lot more time at Monkey Music.

**Olivia:** What's the hardest part of bringing up a family?

**Hannah:** Maybe making decisions for the good of all of you, not just for yourself. I've basically got a baby-business plan. But then when I'm out and about on the streets of Hackney where we live, I see how much harder it could be. The biggest decision I have to make most of the time is which graffiti to shoot against next!

**Olivia:** What change has family made to your home?

**Hannah:** Well, we had to head to HYGGE to stock up! We used to be all about clean lines and spartan living. But now I spend so much time at home. I work at the kitchen table with the kids playing on their mat or sleeping in the bouncer beside me. It's important to make the house as warm and inviting as we hope the Clark family are.

**Olivia:** And, last question, how would you describe HYGGE?

**Hannah:** It's just about really taking the time to make yourself and the people you love *cosy*. It's about hunkering down and being together. But I don't think of it as just a winter thing. You don't have to be tucked up in a fur rug to get *hygge*. You can just have those moments, when you're brushing your child's hair, or dishing up a lovely wholesome meal, and you get that feeling in the pit of your stomach. I guess it's the same feeling as love really.

**Olivia:** Hannah, thanks so much. I'll send you over a cut when we've done a few more of the chats. Shall we bring in the kids?

**Hannah:** Oh yes! I've missed them, where are they?! And can I get a shot of us all for Instagram? I'm OK to post about this if I loop in the brand?

**Olivia:** Go for your life, they'll love it. Just don't say exactly what it's for.

As I go through the motions of adjusting the focus on Hannah's family – Arlo bowling round like a nutter, Jed carefully tending to Missy in the pram – my eyes start to fog up. It's too perfect. It can't always be this easy. They're the definition of *hygge*, but I need the *real* experience if I'm going to make this film work.

# Cycle 20

Sensitive     Egg-White     High Fertility

**DEEP BREATH.** Deep breath. I pull myself up on the railings to take in the restorative saltiness and cast my eye across the sea. I've never been so glad to set foot on solid car park. After what feels like nine hours, three hundred miles, around sixteen family ructions and one aborted Little Chef stop, the whole Galvin–Gyamfi cavalcade – dogs included – has reached Newquay. Scene of virtually every holiday of my childhood. Stag-do capital of the south-west. Possibly a bad idea.

'Oh Liv, we've made it!' says my mother, deadly serious in her mod parka, as if she's going to hop on a moped and speed off along the seafront flicking us the V. 'I swear your father was driving so fast I thought we might die on that last leg!'

I pull her into a corrective embrace. Her inner actress comes out most when she's shaken, the storytelling wild-eyed and the hand gestures even broader than usual.

She's so absorbing, I sometimes find myself wishing we hadn't been born so she could have been the next Julie Walters like she'd planned when she arrived in London in

1978 with big *culchie* curls, ten quid in her pocket and a bag full of leg warmers and extremely high-cut leotards.

'Sure there was no room for a girl with an accent as thick as mine at the Royal Court,' she reassures me whenever I double check she wouldn't have preferred to send us back, than hang up her Repettos and her ambitions after just over a year of giving it a go. Because there was definitely a place for her in the line-up of Hot Gossip (if they just hadn't asked her to remove the suspiciously bump-covering tutu at her audition). My parents' trademark: always silly for themselves, always self-sabotaging. Maybe they're just unlucky. I blame Grace.

'We've already been down to the seafront for a tea and come back to the car in the time it's taken you all to just get here,' she says, forming a sandcastle of Catholic guilt at my feet. 'Then I started to think maybe it was all of you who'd died.' Her round face is as still as a mourner's, but the glint in her eye indicates she's just having us all on. Mona, Felix's mum, smiles and nods in the right places, sensing the immersive theatre we're part of.

'Your eyesight is dreadful, you daft old goat,' I say to Dad, smacking him on the shoulder and taking the role of judge and jury in the skit, so we can all move on with our lives. 'You shouldn't be driving, let alone at speed.'

He laughs, removing his wire-framed spectacles to rub those tired sockets, faux-resigned and exhaling broadly through his silver brushy moustache like he always does at the brunt of Mum's tall stories. 'A hundred miles an hour isn't speeding,' he deadpans.

Everyone thinks he's playing along, but after a childhood wrecked by the fear that we'd meet our end on Cornwall's curly coast roads, I know it's the truth.

'And where's the point in wasting a day as glorious as this, eh?' He levels his outstretched arm at the desolate greyness in front of us with a grin. Dad's jokes, much like his guitar playing, have always been hit and miss. But then he only learned to do both 'so Londoners would stop looking at me like I was over from Derry to nail bomb them'. At least he's enjoying himself. Mufti circles his legs yapping softly considering his burliness.

'Ya poor wee fella,' says Dad, ruffling his furry head and finding the ideal exit to this conversation. 'John, Mona, who fancies a walk so Muttley here can stretch his long legs?'

'And Hippo's little legs . . .' chortles John, Felix's father, as he wanders over with their tiny terrier quietly on her lead.

When we first introduced our families to each other after we got engaged in Berlin, I worried that – as with the dogs – there'd be a groaning gap between our parents' outlooks. Mona, whip-smart and right on, is one of those mega heads of a sprawling Croydon academy. She grew up in Brixton after her parents left Jamaica for London on the Windrush and spent the seventies marching for civil rights. She's what my mum calls – in her serious actorly voice – 'a women's libber'. John's an engineer for Transport for London, which says a lot about his sensible, timetabled existence. When he's had two half pints (the precise amount it takes to get him drunk), he likes to tell people the rags-to-riches story of how he 'started out on the buses fresh from Africa'. Until Mona swoops in to tell them he's never even so much as sat in a bus driver's seat. He's from a very well-to-do family in Ghana and came over to study mechanical engineering at Imperial, which is where she met him at a rally.

They make up for their serious careers with easy humour. Hopefully Mum and Dad won't embarrass us too much.

John rubs his newly replaced knee that has been locked on the accelerator (going a moderate 55mph all the way) for the best part of the day. I feel bad for planning such a long journey for them all. They're all still young for parents (my parents are both fifty-seven, John and Mona are in their early sixties) but the wear and tear is starting to show. Mufti side-eyes their slowness, pulling hard towards the sandy ridge just beyond the car park.

Over by the bandstand Mum and Mona are like two teenagers escaping for a fag, huddled on a bench looking out to the escaping grey sea. Behind us all, Felix's two brothers James and Isaac (not too much younger than us) and their 'pleasant surprise' fifteen-year-old sister Clementine, are awkwardly adjusting to coastal air after so long in captivity.

The tide is far out, as we all prop and bend ourselves against the wind on the promenade.

'Such a stunning view!' says Mona, her dark curls swept away by the wind, but always reliable for a positive spin. Which view of the dank, sagging, tideless flat in front of us is she looking at? The sky is stormy, unnecessarily so for June – doesn't the weather know it's nearly Felix's birthday? – but Mona has a quiet admiration for the non-sunny days, having had enough of her parents harking on about their lost Caribbean glow. Mum pulls her furry hood up around her youthful face, still chill-averse even after her rainy Dublin youth.

Family. Beloved. Abundant. Inescapable. All here in front of my eyes. James and Isaac have got the 99s in for everyone and Clem's in another world of cat memes and gurning

YouTubers. While the boys hatch a plan to go sea-fishing, the matriarchs are on to the tough strategy of which pubs to try first. Mum has devised a crawl of the town's more tucked-away drinking establishments so we don't have to go elbow-to-elbow with all the stag dos, but I wonder if Mona, with her distinguished taste in French reds, is into it, so I throw in that we need to take a drive to North Coast Wine in Bude, and leave them to it.

I did this – booked the house for us all, planned the route, made the itinerary – and yet here I am again on the edges. Only Grace is more peripheral than me. But not in Mum's heart. You can see it in her eyes sometimes: always a missing piece of happiness while Grace is gone.

Felix catches me skulking from beside the bandstand and tries to pull me in close. I'm not having any of it after his 'stop telling me how boring my parents are!' blow-up in the car. I was only trying to express my fears for our incompatible families.

'Liv is going to take us on a tour, aren't you, Liv?' he says, trying to win me round again. 'Show us all her secret places . . .' I stifle a laugh at his innuendo in front of our clueless parents; Isaac's guffaw echoes around the sand dunes.

'Yeah, come on, Liv,' chips in Isaac, 'you can show me the best place to catch some good winkles!' Always lowering the tone. I'm so glad he's here.

'Why don't you kids go on with the dogs and we'll take John and Mona to pick up the keys and get settled in?' Dad's doing the sensible act now, but I know it's a ruse to cover up how knackered they all must be. I'm sure they can think of nothing less fun than a trek to Newquay's highest point, but I can't wait to finally show Felix my favourite lookout (even if he was being a chippy arsehole in the car).

'Come on then, you ugly lot!' I holler, reusing my dad's trusty regimental march for forcing us up the hill when we were idle teenagers. 'We've got a long climb ahead, and no one's going to do it for us.'

'Liv, I think I'm dying . . . I've got . . . altitude . . . sick—' Isaac collapses in a laughing heap on the path (luckily it's dry – for now), and James kicks him gently in the gut as he steps over him. I stand at his head giving him my best stern sergeant face.

'Private Isaac! On your feet, man! This is not a drill!'

Isaac jumps to attention, joining Felix and James as they do a bouncy marching exercise on the spot awaiting my orders. Clem lingers just behind, but I can see she's actually covertly enjoying the three brosketeers' show from over the horizon of her iPhone.

They make a handsome line-up. Felix is a beautiful blend of his parents – his mum's distinctive gap between his two front teeth, his dad's height and shoulders (without the stodgy middle). After Felix, Mona's star rose as a history teacher, so James wasn't born for another six years. He's an exact clone of his dad: sensible, stocky, good with numbers – they even have the same quiet uptight laugh. Isaac arrived a year later. Lithe and athletic like his Jamaican cousins, brash and into everything gaudy, he's the perfect visual merchandiser for Topshop. It was only when Isaac came out aged seventeen that Felix realised his gangsta schtick was all just a ruse, and actually he really wanted to be wearing gold lurex rather than grillz. They understood each other a lot better after that.

And then came studious little Clementine. Isaac had been the golden boy for eleven whole years until she popped out of nowhere. Mona thought she was going through the menopause and actually turned out to be pregnant. 'There's hope,' says Felix, whenever I moan about my biological clock's deafening alarm bell. 'Just look at my mum having babies till she was nearly fifty.' Clemmie's not that little any more, at least four inches taller than me and reed thin, the kind of thin I never was, even when I was a gawky eleven-year-old growing into myself. She's also got their mum's gappy smile, but with a pronounced overbite that should be awkward but actually lends her model-ready cheekbones. Isaac told us she got scouted a couple of weeks ago when she met him for a conversation-free lunch of using his staff discount, but she threw the scout's business card in the bin by Oxford Circus. Clem wants to be a cultural historian (what of, cat videos?) and 'modelling would be too much of a distraction'. Isaac tried to pull the card out of the bin for himself, leaning in while tourists pushed by, pitying the homeless wastrel in his spray-on American football leggings and low armpitted vest. All he got was a fistful of slimy Pret salad and tinnitus from the looming megaphone of the 'God will save us' loony who lurks by the station. I told him he'd definitely make a good hand model.

I need to keep them interested. I can handle the parents not being an exact match, but I don't want the youngers growing to loathe my forced fun (or lack thereof). I start an evenly paced martial run up the steep bit of path round the old Victorian Hotel beside the cliff, singing a song about the legend of a nude beach just visible from the tip of the cliff. Isaac breaks rank and starts running comically for the peak, the dogs following, revelling in their new-found freedom, and Clem just one pace behind with her phone in her hand, acting as Isaac's Snaparazzi. They're racing for the fixed binoculars on the cliff top, and I'm suddenly concerned that the grass might be wet and I'm about to watch a family of lemmings skid off the side. At which point they'll realise they've been duped about the nude beach and that everyone below is actually wearing dog-walking fleeces and sand-splattered jeans. James, solemn as always, closes on them in a risk-assessment jog, leaving Felix to grab me round the waist as the wind starts to whip our faces.

'At ease, *privates*,' I say, making a covert grab for his crotch with a grin, forgiving him the sullen drive. 'This is the place. When I think of us at our happiest in the summers, we were always up here, tucked away in the clouds. No matter if it was raining. No matter if there were tears. We'd always look out at that expanse of sea and our bit of the world seemed so small.'

Felix envelops me in his jacket and kisses my forehead, still trying to win me round, and we look across the cliff top at his siblings messing around. The sunshine is threatening the clouds now, and the sea looks almost inviting from way up here.

I kiss him softly. 'This was where my parents first snogged as eighteen-year-olds, on a church camping trip so all the displaced Irish teens in *County Kilburn* could get some sun on their pasty faces,' I tell him. 'What they *actually* came back with was a bus-load of vest-shaped sunburn and teenage pregnancies.'

'Fertile ground, then,' smiles Felix, staring out to sea. I've never thought about it, but I bet Grace was conceived up here on a return visit – my parents do a lot of giggling when they're up this cliff. And, after that first trip, our family came back every year to 'celebrate where it started'. How naïve to think that they meant their first kiss. I don't want to sully the memories of us taking hours to make our way up this cliff as toddlers with them and the picnic, building blanket forts inside the wind-breaker and being kept on reins until Mum was confident that she could reason with us (for me: three, for Grace: twenty-five). We'd spend time on the beaches too. But up here, looking back towards the little pocket of sand beneath the headland, it seemed too obvious to be building sandcastles when you could be queen of your own fortress. Will we ever have a daughter to feel that way?

I look around to see if there are any bushes that could give us enough cover to give it a try up here. Mufti has his leg cocked against the only thicket and that's not even waist height. Perhaps not while the siblings are loose.

'Who's hungry?' I yell above the wind. Felix goes to round up the troops, while I punch in a secret WhatsApp, before leading the charge back down the hill.

> I can't wait to see you x    17:30

THE 'COTTAGE' IS MORE like a manor house: a manor house that's been left to the dogs. When we get in to claim our bedrooms, my parents have seen fit to put Felix and I in the downstairs room, just off the large open kitchen. Mum seems to have an uncanny knowledge of where I am in my cycle at all times and this being the optimal week, I think she might have done it on purpose. Unthankfully, Mufti and Hippo have decided that *mi casa es dog casa*, and they're having a post-walk spoon on our bed. It's a beautiful scene, if you discount the whole room now smelling of sea dog.

'DAAAD! Who let the dogs on the bed?!' I tip them off

the duvet gently, hollering through the wooden barn door as I attempt to find some new linen to switch over to before the duvet and mattress become completely sodden. *Too late: this damp patch is already substrata.*

I can see through our tiny little frilly pink-curtained window that John, forever pottering, is in the garden inspecting the herbaceous borders, while my dad – still ignoring my increasingly harassed sighs – seems to be 'resting his eyes' in the dark-panelled living room. The rest of the house has also fallen suspiciously silent while everyone has a pre-dinner snooze after the testing journey, lungs full of sea air. Felix shoos Mufti and Hippo, already the best of friends, out the door, wedging a chair under the handle so they can't break in while we fumigate.

'I see from the sign on the door that this room is called The Pigsty,' laughs Felix. 'So perhaps that smell isn't all soggy dog?' He hands me mismatched floral Laura Ashley pillowcases one by one so I can aggressively stuff.

'How is it that even Clem gets a room with an en suite, while we get two single beds shoved together in the old swine pen?' I ask. 'When I was a teenager, I'd have ended up on the sofa bed if I was lucky. Inflatable mattress at best.'

'Still, at least we're away from all their snoring,' says Felix, towelling off the wet mattress and laying down a preventative/stench-insulating plastic sheet. 'Plus, there's plenty of *quiet* for us to get on with our own things down here . . .' He pushes me down on the clean side of the bed, and begins sliding off my leopard-print gym leggings (that haven't seen a workout in at least a year).

'Felix, your dad is right outside the window looking at the bloody borders – I don't need him seeing my bush as well!' I'm not *fully* pausing the moment, however – we must take our chances when we can get them – so I pull up my leggings, draw the curtains, and push Felix down on his back, undoing his flies and attempting to wriggle out of my Lycra as quickly as I can.

And covert *is* a bit of a turn on: for the first time in months, I'm on top, riding away, bawdy as a Carry On character. But just as we're picking up the pace, the chair goes clattering over as Mufti bursts through the door and in two hairy strides is straight back on the bed next to our heaving bodies. My naked bottom is on display to the empty kitchen – and John is opening the back door.

'Felix!' I hiss, as he throws me off him and runs to close the door, his bare appendage narrowly missing his dad's line of sight. Mufti is now bed-surfing next to me, while I, panting, attempt to pick up something, *anything* to wrap round myself. Of course, it had to be the wet towel.

Grabbing at Mufti while attempting to clasp the soggy rag around me, I manoeuvre him out as Felix stands guard at the now latchless door.

'Felix, Liv, are you OK in there?' John knocks, quiet but concerned. 'Are the dogs terrorising you? Shall I come in and help?'

Felix and I, both bottomless apart from the dog-sodden bits of fabric, mouth 'SHIT!' at each other from across the room.

'Sorry, Dad, we were just changing when Mufti broke in, we'll be out in a second.'

Felix is convincing enough, but I can hear his dad chuckling as he goes back out to the garden. I shove Mufti in his direction while I pull my leggings back on and throw him his jeans. 'Get the dog out of here and let's see if we can finish this off quick. Really quickly, please.'

'PADSTOW SCALLOPS ALONE are worth the six-hour drive, I promise you that now.' Dad is applying the seafood hard sell tonight. The Galvins have been coming to this restaurant a bit up the coast from Newquay every summer for nearly forty years. Keeping his audience captivated, he talks them through the specialist fishing practices which make it *almost* as good as his dad's home-caught fare back near Derry. I'm half expecting him to break into a sea shanty.

I watch Mum survey the table smiling, but her eyes search the middle distance, incomplete. She's channelling coastal glamour (striped red top, frayed boyfriend jeans, chic white plimsolls) and is happily sandwiched between Dad and Mona (who's looking like the photos I've seen of her in the British Black Panthers as a teenager, with her weather-appropriate navy polo neck and combed-out afro). But I can see Mum's missing something. Someone. It's already 8.30 p.m., and I'm anxious to get ordering, but I'm letting the table chat run over as I anxiously keep an eye on my iPhone under the table.

| | |
|---|---|
| Ten miles | 19:59 |

| | |
|---|---|
| Five more minutes | 20:33 |

| | |
|---|---|
| Just wait. | 20:33 |

I'm about to give up and call the waiter, when in glides the taller, more striking me with her dark bob and brand new Barbour: the prodigal daughter, Grace.

Mum, intuitive to a surprise-ruining fault, is somehow

already out of her seat before the door is open, in floods of tears at her beautiful daughter's glorious return.

'Gracie!' she squeals. 'How did you know we were here? I thought you were still in the Middle East!' She's shaking with joy. Dad tuts to himself at the spoiled shark-fishing punchline, but stands to greet his long-lost daughter anyway.

'Very good of you to *Grace* us with your presence!' he chortles, squeezing her tightly as she smiles thinly over his shoulder at me. It's only then that I notice the tall, very serious-looking, sandy-haired man in chinos lingering close behind.

'Is he with you?' I whisper into her ear as she leans across the squeaky vinyl-upholstered booth to give me a kiss on the cheek.

'Yes, this one is with me,' she says. 'Everyone, Mum, Dad, this is Henry. He's our bureau chief in Istanbul.'

Henry reaches across to shake Dad's hand firmly. 'Good to finally meet you, sir.' (*Christ, he's proper posh*). Dad's face falls at his suspicious propriety – he's become formal William, not silly Billy.

'Henry, this is Grace's sister Olivia and her husband Felix,' leads Dad in the purposeful, put-on voice he speaks only to his accountant with. 'Then we have Felix's mother Mona and father John, and his brothers James and Isaac and sister Clementine. Let's get two seats added for Grace and her new fella, shall we?' he motions over to the waiter, dropping his guard a little bit.

'We prefer *partner*, actually, Dad. Sounds a little less infantile now we're nearly forty,' Grace says, in her usual aloof manner.

'I'll tell you what's less infantile, Grace?' I joke, forgetting to add a note of humour. 'Bothering to tell your family you've *got* a *partner* . . .'

'It's new, Liv,' she chides me wearily. 'We've only been together about three months, and there have been more pressing things going on in Syria.'

She's weary because, just weeks before leaving everything for the Middle East, she was actually in a very serious, not at all infantile relationship with a guy we all thought she was about to marry. Then, out of nowhere, he left. We never heard why. We just heard a lot of crying and then she got on a plane for Turkey. So actually, *partners* is a bit forward, and no, she doesn't get to withhold good news when all we've heard for months has been dirge.

'Grace, it's so good to see you,' says James, matching Henry in intensity. I always thought James and Grace might make an earnest match even though he's a decade younger than her. 'How did you guys meet?'

'Well, it's a terribly funny story actually,' starts Henry, delighted at having a reason to be involved and avoiding Grace's glare. 'We were visiting a decimated school in Aleppo, and I was meant to be interviewing a teacher. So I began speaking to this woman – I couldn't see much apart from dark hair and pretty thick eyebrows under her headscarf – in Arabic, and she started to reply in English. It was only when I noticed the camera round her neck that I realised she had a pretty convincing London accent.' The pair of them laugh, as if they just told us they hooked up in a Wetherspoon's, and not at the scene of hundreds of children's deaths.

By my calculations of when she visited that school in Aleppo *last trip*, this *partner* might have been on the scene for a bit longer than three months. Will, her sweet engineer boyfriend, clearly didn't stand a chance. Oh, poor Will.

Mum and Mona are enraptured by Grace and her dashing bureau chief as we finally get to taste scallops that melt in our mouths. Does Henry not realise he's on a mini-break with two normal families (and their two idiot dogs) in the surf-and-shag capital of Cornwall? I suddenly feel like a failure. Felix squeezes my hand under the table, and I know he sees it too.

Exhausted

**I'M WOKEN WITH A BUZZ.** It's 6.30 a.m. I wouldn't even be up if I was at work. Why the Christ did I not turn my email alerts off when I got down here? I didn't expect to have signal, let alone patchy Wi-Fi.

**Trish Chippenham**
Re: Report now
To: Olivia Galvin

Olivia, I know it's a bit early, but it's the management all-hands today and I could do with some analysis on these stats that have just landed in my inbox from Paris. I need them by 9.30. Can you do what you do best when you're on your long commute in?

Trish Chippenham
Head of UK Operations
HYGGE
+44 (0) 77235 556 475

**Trish Chippenham**
Re: Report now
To: Olivia Galvin

Just seen your OOO. Can you do it anyway?

Trish Chippenham
Head of UK Operations
HYGGE
+44 (0) 77235 556 475

I'm away for one day and still I can't be left alone. All I wanted was a weekday lie in, but instead, I'm at my laptop at 7 a.m. with Mufti warming my feet beneath the farmhouse table. I type furiously, trying to get this market research into a fit state for consumption before Trish's 9.30 a.m. emergency summit. Despite the shot of anxiety you get from your boss ranting at you in bed *on holiday*, my eyelids lull heavily and my progress is sluggish. I am itching to do anything other than work: make tea, walk the dog, even tidy the haywire, but blessedly still, farmhouse. But I must keep on. Only an hour and a half until my deadline and this analysis needs to be perfect.

**Olivia Galvin**
Re: Report now
To: Trish Chippenham

Hi Trish,
Please see my analysis of the Paris report attached. Hope it helps. Even though I am on annual leave, I should have access to my email for most of the day if you have any questions.

Olivia Galvin
Marketing Manager
HYGGE (UK)
+44 (0) 7757406596

Can't let them forget me after making such a good impression on the Klauses last month.

**HOW IS IT POSSIBLE THAT** three hours on, I'm still the only person awake in this house? I make pointed rattles of pots and pans, but decide against the highest order of passive-aggressiveness – the holiday wake-up call – and instead bid to lure them out nose first. I'm cooking bacon. I am the world's best person, quite honestly.

'Morning, lovebirds,' smirks Isaac, padding in only seconds after Felix, his amazing multi-coloured Kenzo tracksuit unzipped to the navel. Does he wear that for bed? He plonks himself in the middle of my work notes without offering to help, watching Felix toast round after round of bread as I drain eleven weak teabags in the chipped, mismatched mugs on the same cramped work surface. A buttery clump flops into one cup as Felix passes over me – that'll be mine then. I gather three unsullied teas in each hand and carry them precariously to the wipe-clean-clothed table, Isaac knocking them into a wave as he grabs eagerly to take one. My city self is barking at the insubordination, but outwardly, Newquay me is calm, calm, calm.

The old wooden farm door creaks open. John and Dad enter the dim living room laughing and clutching skinny fishing rods with a couple of briny newspaper parcels. They must have been up since dawn on the pier, silly fools. No wonder they look worn out, even on holiday. I've lost all sympathy.

Suddenly, the kitchen is full of bodies. The mums are passing out sandwiches as if they'd been down here crafting them, not upstairs getting beach ready.

'Any more where that came from?' asks James, already knowing the answer. I used five packets of bacon and two loaves of bread, but every crumb has been hoovered up. It's all gone, apart from two sandwiches – the juiciest ones I crafted for Felix (who ended up with a streaky slice of fat in two charred heels). They've been squirrelled away by Mum for Grace and whatshisname. They're still nowhere to be seen. It's 11.15. *Pass me the pots and pans.*

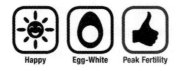

I HATE TO SPLIT THE SEXES, but not one of the girls, including myself, fancied a sea-fishing expedition with the dads. So, after I kissed goodbye to Felix (hilariously tricked out in my yellow mac and Dad's galoshes), myself, the mums, Clem, Isaac and Grace – along with Henry, who's hermetically sealed to her face – are heading into town for afternoon tea, Galvin style. Since we were last here, a cool little boutique hotel has popped up on Fistral beach offering champagne afternoons that wouldn't look out of place in the city. Instead, Mum is fixed on Betty's, her favourite hideaway, a place untouched by modernity since 1976. The chairs are threadbare, the walls are covered in chipped anaglypta wallpaper and the hot drinks come in branded mugs, but their cream cakes have the genteel authenticity of a wartime housewife polishing her front step to a military gleam when she's right next door to a bombsite.

Betty's is usually a favourite with the grey crowd, but today, it's teeming with new mums bottle-feeding their screeching babies while also filling their own faces with fondant fancies. I'm being stalked.

'Oh, look at her beautiful curls,' Mum says, leaning back towards their table, her dainty cucumber sandwich poised to wave at the cutest little three-month-old. She motions at me to join the cooing.

'Look, Livvie, isn't she cute?' she says. 'Don't you think that's what you'd dress yours up in?' Always picking the same scab.

'She's adorable,' I agree. I can't even be bitter. She's a picture, blowing bubbles in our direction.

'I used to love it when they were that small,' says Mona, piling on the pressure. 'Maybe that explains why I went through the baby phase four times across three decades!'

'Yes, Mother,' I say, pointedly. 'If Mona had Clemmie at forty-seven, then I'm hardly a geriatric like you keep telling me . . .'

Isaac's eyes are like saucers at what I'm walking into.

'Oh, you know what I mean, Liv,' says Mum. 'You've just got to get a move on. You want one, don't you? So what's stopping you?'

'I don't know,' I say, the anger rising in my voice. 'My womb? My ovaries? Do you want to do a little scan here on the table so you can see what the hold up is?'

'I'm sure it'll happen in its own time,' says Mona, attempting to cut the tension before I float off into the sunset like a hot-air balloon of rage. 'You both just need to enjoy life as it is now and see how it goes.'

I see my mother's face munching up in disapproval out of the corner of my eye, but she daren't say a word.

'But, sure, while we're on the subject, what is it that's stopping you *really*?' says Mum, not satisfied that I merely *can't*, and probing for why I *won't*.

'You're incessant, aren't you?' I say, angry now. 'Maybe it's because I don't want to spoil my life, like you did with us?' She looks at me astonished.

*You can't unsay that shit, Liv.*

'And you think that's what I did then?' says Mum. 'Ruined myself because I had kids? Yous two were the best thing that ever happened to me. No starring role as a dancing dollybird would have *ever* made up for that.' She's raised herself so she's standing over me, her knuckles white with the energy of keeping her locked to the table.

'Yes, and I think that's exactly why I've left it this long. And it's completely why it's not magically happening for us like it does for everyone else.' I throw my hand out to the room to illustrate and realise that all the mothers are listening as they feed, wildly entertained by our daytime soap.

'I can just imagine that's what your girls looked like when they were babies, Mrs Galvin,' pipes up Henry, who's been checking his BlackBerry unaware of the war breaking out at the table. 'Let's hope it's in the genes!'

I see a silent warning shot fired by Grace towards Henry, although it clearly hasn't made an impact. Isaac does a mock-Scream face at me behind his hands at the awkwardness.

'I'd always hoped I'd be a father by now,' Henry says. She's squeezing his hand incredulously. 'It's just so hard being away, isn't it, Grace? But now I've met your daughter, who knows . . .?'

Mum gasps, beside herself with joy. Maybe I'll catch a break.

'Oh, I don't want kids, Henry,' says Grace flatly. 'I don't know what gave you that idea.'

The bombshell hits. Clem has even paused her YouTuber to peer with raised eyebrows, Mona is possessed, Henry's using his devastation report face and my mum is instantly in tears. Grace's face purses tightly, knowing what she's just done. Isaac and I look at each other in shock that we're no longer the family fuck-ups.

A colicky scream breaks the silence, as if to illustrate Grace's reasoning.

'But . . .' Henry continues, crestfallen. 'But you're so amazing with them.' I think I prefer him a bit sad; it takes the edge off his poshness. 'Seeing you in that school with those kids, you're such a natural. I fell in love with you instantly.'

Big words, Henners. Mum's eyes dart from side-to-side, her head looking like it'll explode over the inner conflict between teary grand-broody devastation, and enraptured happiness at how dashing her daughter's suitor is.

'But look at how those kids have to live,' says Grace. 'This world doesn't need more mouths to feed.' Cold as ice, but she's got a point. Should I be taking this stand too? 'Plus I can't do my job with a baby. It's just not what I want.'

'Gracie, maybe you just need a bit more time to think about it?' reasons Mum. 'It's early days with you two and you're only just set up in Turkey. Maybe the moment will come. You've still got plenty of time.'

*Not what you've been telling me with your 'hurry up' IVF links and your unsubtle 'stop drinkings' ever since I turned thirty, woman.*

'It's just not something I've ever wanted, Mum. Nothing to do with you and your lack of career,' she says. I can't believe it's me who started this. 'It's just not for me.'

'Well, it's Grace's choice, isn't it?' I say, supporting my sister as Isaac nods along effusively (but silently). 'None of us can say what anyone else wants.'

I instantly regret re-heaping all the expectation back on myself, but it's not fair for Mum and Henry to ladle the emotional blackmail on Grace, even if they're newly shocked.

'Maeve, why don't we give you a little bit of space so you can talk about this,' Mona says kindly, hurriedly collecting their beach bags. '*Take me with you*', I silently mouth to Clem, but she rolls her eyes and inserts her other earphone. Isaac squeezes my shoulder and shouts 'Laters, babe!' as he runs desperately for cover.

Mum presides over the table like Queen Mary studying her son's abdication. Henry rests his elbows on his knees and looks aside to the little one on the next table. I can feel the heat of his deep sulk even though his face is turned away. Grace is simply still. After the split from Will she must be giving tears a hard pass. This was the reason he left. This is the reason we didn't get to hear about. And now this is the test of her mettle and of Henry's. He turns back to her and kisses her gently on the mouth, and now it's my turn to look away. Mum touches my arm.

'Liv, you're not going to deny me grandchildren as well, are you?'

**AFTER TWENTY MINUTES** more solemn scone scoffing, I can't take it any more, and pay the bill on the way to the bathroom.

'Come on, Mum,' I say, hoping she's at least half forgiven me now. 'Let's leave these *partners* here to talk and we can go for a little walk along the promenade.'

As I usher her out of the doily windowed tearoom – leaving Grace to inspect the embossments on the walls sourly as Henry touches her arm to implore her – the curly haired baby waves. It could have been a bit of trapped wind, but Mum's in floods of tears immediately at the sacred gesture.

'Sure, now I'll never be a nanny!' she hyperventilates on the pavement outside. 'She's left me for good, she's going to live in a war zone until she gets herself killed and she's found herself a man who'll whip her off to the hoity-toity classes where she'll have no need for her old mother ever again!' Mum's big brown eyes are saucer-wide with tears. Naturally, it's started raining and my umbrella remains on the chair beside the *partners* who are now having a war of gesticulations. I look back at Mum, still open-mouthed and now also soggy. She's too disconsolate to even pull up the hood of her parka. 'And then there's you. You never stop running, you're always out, always working, always drinking, never giving yourself a moment's rest, taking it out of your body. You'll never have a baby because you're too tired! But you never listen! I'm telling you, you need to listen to me, before it's too late. It's all right for Mona, she's got that whole brood after Felix, but I've only got you and Grace and look where that's got me? Can't you see that your father and I are desperate?'

'But why can't you have your own life?' I say. 'Why does everyone's happiness have to rest on a bloody baby?' I wonder whether my own happiness even does.

I guide her along the sea front, even though she's shouldered off my touch a couple of times through the tears. We're dodging the mewling kids on their two-wheelers and the OAP mobility scooter joyriding.

'You wouldn't understand it. Not yet,' she says. 'But you wait until you have one. Then you'll comprehend the kind of worries I go through every minute of the day.'

Have a baby, go direct to martyr, do not pass go.

'I am happy!' I shout. Mum doesn't need to hear I'm basically barren straight after Grace has told her she's strategically so.

'*Are you?*' she asks insistently.

'Mum, come on, now, please . . . Take a deep breath,' I say. 'This is all a shock. It's a surprise just having Grace back, let alone with an unfamiliar forty-year-old attached to her hip.' Mum has Turin Shrouded all of her foundation on to one of those dainty pocket-pack tissues.

'You know what she's like,' I continue. 'Grace has never danced to anyone else's tune apart from her own. How she treated poor Will, this job. You can't have just expected she'd suddenly come back from Aleppo pregnant, join the local NCT and be content with that?' I wonder if I'm making it worse.

Mum takes a stuttering deep breath and takes hold of the crook of my arm with her creamy gold-ringed fingers.

'But she doesn't look happy, does she?' she says. 'Not even doing as she pleases across the world. When will either of you just be satisfied?'

'When will you?' I say. 'You have to give Felix and I a chance. We are trying our best. You think you and Dad are desperate? Gracie came along when you were twenty-three, I'm a whole decade older than you were. It's tough, but I can't give up my whole life just to have a baby.' I get to take a lungful of sea air now, wiping my dripping fringe out of my eyes.

'I know, Liv,' she says, her eyes glistening with blinked-back tears. 'I just worry about you both so much. But Grace might come round if she likes this Henry enough. And you'll be pregnant soon. Just maybe give that fringe a trim in the meantime.'

**'SSHH!' I CLASP ONE** hand across felix's mouth, the other fending the wrought-iron bedframe from scraping against the wall. The bed makes a gnawing creak as Felix clambers on top of me to do what we need to do again.

'I can't be any quieter, I have to breathe!' he whispers angrily, cheerlessly thrusting at a snail's pace for fear of waking the family at 1 a.m. with our scheduled *business time*. My mind wanders to those nights when we were both living at home and in the throes of new lust. Consideration was not an option then.

'Just breathe through your nose and make it quick,' I sigh, lying back and holding my breath.

**I'VE OVERDOSED ON SUNDAY BLUES.** It's our last night, and while I should just be lamenting the end of the holiday, I'm silently dreading the drive home and the fallout of baby-gate in the real world. While we're in Cornwall, everything is in stasis. Nothing bad can touch a big blended family and their tired, sand-splattered dogs on the dappled forecourt of a Walkabout welling with under-clothed teenagers. Mum and Mona are deep in serious but smile-punctuated conversation, the dads are grinning at photos of their prize catches, and the brosketeers are attempting to ingratiate Henry up at the bar between fifteen stags dressed as Justin Bieber (or just their normal clothes?) and three surfers resting their pints on a horizontal board. I send Clem up with our joint account card to get Felix to buy us all a round and watch as she locks eyes confidently with the youngest surfer.

'Grace,' I start, hoping her contained composure at Henry's acceptance means she'll be a bit softer to me now. 'I hope you realise I support whatever decision you make about kids. Don't let Mum put pressure on you.'

She stares at me, shocked. 'I thought you would have known all along that I didn't want them. You must have noticed, no? All those times when you bored on about fertility issues and I would yawn and change the subject?'

'God, all right, thanks, sister dearest,' I reply. She always lashes out like this when she feels like we don't understand her. But it's tricky monitoring someone else's inner monologue when they're only available via satellite link-up. She smiles and suddenly embraces me like she hasn't done since we were drunk teenagers.

'Thank you, Liv. I do appreciate that. I know it's tough having Mum's dreams all on you now. But the burden suits you. You've developed a sort of sexy hunch from all the weight.'

I laugh, because, what else is there to do? And then, as Felix and the boys – Clem abandoned with the inappropriate surfer who I'll rescue her from in a minute – return to the table with our drinks, I pick up my phone.

**Mads Rasmussen**
Re:
To: Olivia Galvin

We missed you on Friday, Olivia. If I couldn't bring Paris to you, perhaps I could bring you to Paris? Next month?

Mads Rasmussen
Creative Director
HYGGE
+45 (0) 7925 074 053

Felix's grip on his pint falters as I minimise the message. *Happy nearly birthday, dear husband. Maybe it won't be so bad seeing all your ex-girlfriends at your party this year.*

# Cycle 21

**I'M EGGY.** What started as a perfectly pleasant team-bonding trip to The Diner has resulted in a bad case of egginess. As myself, Rachel, Ryan and Zara tuck into our delightfully greasy burgers – how they all stay so lithe with the amount they put away, I don't know, Rachel's hardly showing – and as the yolk of my fried egg forms a yellow pool on my chin, I am confronted by my fertility ground zero.

'I know it's a bit TMI, but fuck it,' says Zara. 'I'm having my eggs frozen.'

'I didn't want to say anything, hun,' says Ryan, his usual infernally supportive self, 'but I thought they might be going off.' It was at a volume imperceptible to all but dogs, but Rachel definitely guffawed with smugness.

'Zara, you're five years my junior. And *you* need an insurance policy?' I say, mock sternly to hide my consternation, letting the yolk drip a bit for comedic effect. 'Mmm, tasty amniotic fluid.' The table laughs, not knowing they are ridiculing my actual misfortune.

'Trish was so impressed when I told her,' continues Zara, unfazed. The table is still present in burger eating, but is now completely absent in spirit – Ryan, because he's a man with zero desire for a future featuring anything more labour-intensive than a French bulldog; Rachel, because all her eggs have been fertilised to perfection; and me, because I'm having to stop myself punching her in the ovaries to even us up.

'Trish said she "admires my commitment to the company",' continues Zara, looking Rachel dead in the eye as if to say *because I'm clearly not doing a maternity runner any time soon*. 'They're even looking into whether HYGGE might pay for it.' Why did I not know to ask about these unwritten perks when my eggs were still in date?

'Sounds *amazing*, Zara,' I say, raising a sham toast with my Coke float. 'To chilly eggs!' The waitress slides in to ask if that was a genuine order.

'Thanks, Liv. I've heard it's a bit painful, but, I thought, I can't bank on them not being stale by the time I make up my mind about having kids. I mean it's just not on the agenda now, but in five years' time . . . well I don't want a baby coming out like Benjamin Button.'

Rachel's resignation switches to indignation in a nanosecond, even though she was only two years older than Zara when egg begot babes. I feel a pinch in my belly that surely signifies mine are growing more decrepit by the second: I draft a text to Felix under the table for reassurance.

Felix
Today 13:45

> Darling, should I have frozen my eggs? Zara is doing hers . . . Worried mine are now ancient and would not even be omelette-worthy if found in back of fridge. Should we look into egg donation? Xx

Delivered

He's not going to reply to that. Better send one to Orla instead. Need a second opinion from one who knows such medical scenarios.

Zara's freezing her eggs now . . . Should I just defrost someone else's in place of my ageing follicles? Or should I just nab one of hers before it goes to Iceland? She's twenty-eight and very tall, so good quality, even if the child is likely to come out with her lack of ability to spell? xxx

Delivered

Ask if I can have a couple too. Rich would never notice it didn't look anything like me, and could keep a second one back for the sequel. xx

At least my lunch can count towards some of my daily prenatal vitamins (which I forgot to take again this morning). Burgers are a great source of protein (ignore the grease), as are eggs (which must go some way to enhancing *my* eggs), plus I had a dollop of guacamole, which is basically unsullied avocado (healthy and Instagrammable). The brioche bun and Coke float were just a dietary anti-depressant to quell my anxiety over the egg-freezing bombshell. Something must have had a bit of zinc and folic acid in it. Plus we're only day three, so I've got at least a week until I have to be primed like a well-oiled machine again. Now I'm just well-oily, especially around the face.

I was only really eating such fatty food to line my stomach ready for tonight's long promised Big One with Ada and Margot. We're going drinking *and* dancing, which basically means eating is cheating and they will not rest until I am throwing up at the side of the kerb blaming 'the rich food'. But I'm way ahead of their tequila: following the burger,

I'll also be staging a precautionary pre-drinks at my desk. And my shot of choice will be trusty old Pepto Bismol.

'WHY D'YOU HAVE TO BE SO SLOW, Margot?' I'm already chanting, which can't be a good sign at 8.30 p.m. Though, the fact I'm self-monitoring my drunkenness as we totter across Brixton market means *I'm totally fine.*

'Why d'you have to be such a div, eh Liv?' Margot shouts back tunefully.

I catch sight of the three of us reflected in the darkened window of a funeral parlour – me in my silky shorts, long brown hair drawn in a high pony-tail and way too much red eyeshadow (it's a *thing*), Ada drawing everyone in with her low-cut floral jumpsuit and bronze-tipped afro at maximum volume, and Margot striding like she's seven foot in her chunky black platforms. We lurch a bit in the heels we don't wear so often these days. How is it possible that we look much older than I care to admit, *and* like thirteen-year-olds on the way to their first disco, all at the same time? I laugh maniacally, and a homeless man regards me with fear.

'We just want some dancing!' shouts Ada, beautiful even with her eyeliner all smeary under her eyes. 'Where's the dancing?' Ada is propositioning a gang of pub-goers gathered round a busker one by one. 'Dancing?' 'Dance with me?'

No one seems to know where to go any more. One guy takes her by the arm and starts her swaying to the light reggae coming from the white man with dreadlocks and his banjo on the pavement. The last time I had a proper dance was about five years ago when we went to visit our friend Jenna in a market town in Wiltshire. A pregnant lady drinking blue WKD was getting fingered on the carpeted dance floor. Is the drink embellishing the memory, or was it embellishing her big night out?

'Stop the search! I've got it! Let's go to Frank's!'

Frank's is probably forty-five minutes away from here, but south London is like a different country to me, all melted into one easy-access strip of nightspots in my mind map. 'We could get the bus?'

'Aren't we feeling a bit beyond the bus now?' says Margot. 'As we're now thirty-three and thirty-four, and have jobs that pay over the minimum wage? Maybe we could stretch to an Uber and just save the night bus joy until after the night out is over and we *want* to smell like eau de kebab as we make our way back to the north?'

She is *so* sensible, even after a bottle and a half of wine to herself.

'You win. Ube me!' I prod lavishly at my phone.

*Oh shit.*

I appear to have ordered an Executivemobile to my office. The driver is ringing me. I don't suppose he'll redirect from all the way across London to come retrieve us. Cancel. CANCEL! *That'll have to go on expenses.*

'Perhaps I am more night bus material . . .' I say, swaying off to the bus stop.


**FRANK'S WAS A GRAND IDEA** from me. (I'm always vainer when I'm drunk). I'm prancing to 'Lovers in the Parking Lot' on top of an old multi-storey, which, in my tequila-addled brain, means I am channelling the spirit of goddess Solange. I sweep the dance floor with my right foot and pose one leg askance, arms in a triangle above my head, a seductive performance for myself *and* the crowd of hot guys congregated round the bar. I'm the same age as them, right? They've all got so much facial hair it's hard to tell. We're the only ones drunk enough to dance, so there's a crowd of questionable interested parties.

Ada's already chatting up a bloke the opposite of her Jack – a big rugby sort with tanned tattooed (what I imagine he'd call) guns sprouting from his tightly turned-up shirt. Jack's arms are the colour and consistency of overcooked spaghetti. Margot is shimmying next to a very hot girl, but I think she's got the wrong idea, because there's a guy next to her with his hand planted very firmly on her arse cheek.

Here, babies are positively discouraged. I need to have more of these nights. I've been trapped in a cage of self-loathing and perpetual defeat for so long that I forgot to enjoy being young (ish). What is broodiness anyway? It's just a socially programmed construct to trap us, isn't it? So we can't come to places like this and feel the wind in our hair as we pretend to be Beyoncé's sister while our friends bark up the wrong tree and men we don't know Snapchat themselves drinking shots against the sunset and our writhing. Is this not better than a baby? I let out an exhilarated howl to the sky and everyone turns to stare at me, because I am clearly so ~~inebriated~~ incredible.

'Liv, they're closing up,' says Ada followed by Inflatable Jack and Margot with her new couple friends. Have they pulled? I look around; I'm the only one dancing and have been for some time.

'Where to now?' I shout over the now non-existent noise.

'These guys have got tickets for this soul night at the Bussey Building,' she says, 'so we thought we'd go and see if we could get in?' I'm already on their heels. *Did they think I'd just go home?*

As we emerge from the car park, the queue of expectant faces snakes down Rye Lane.

'I'm sure we can just get in if these guys have got tickets,' I say, sidling to the front of the line, like I used to do back in my Camden days when I was hot and nineteen and knew the door whores (no slut-shaming intended). Confidence is worth more than any QR code from Ticketmaster, surely.

'You, in. Yep, that's fine,' the doorman says, ushering in our new mates. 'Collecting from inside, are we?'

In go my friends. The velvet rope falls in front of me like a guillotine.

'Oh no, I'm with them,' I say, smiling my flashiest grin, trying to keep my eyes focussed on one fixed point.

'I can see that,' he says, turning his shoulder away from me ever so slightly.

'Well, then let me through,' I say, the wine-whine rising. 'I'm picking up my tickets inside too.'

I'm still holding together the politeness, but only because I'm dancing on the thin line of a dangerously drunken lie.

'You're not coming in.'

'There's no need to be *antagonistic*,' I say loftily (because *that's* going to gain me entry). Margot and Ada are standing on his other side now, petitioning him.

'I'm not being *antagonistic*,' he says, mimicking my drunk drawl which has become more grammar school with every gin and tonic. 'You're just not in the right kind of state to come in.'

'I can tell you I am in *exactly* the right kind of state,' I say, pacing back and forth in front of him to steady myself. 'I'm in the mood for fun!' *All right, grandma.*

'You've had too much fun already by the looks of it. And

don't you think you're a bit old for this now? I mean what are you, like forty? Why don't you go home to your kids and call it a night . . .'

'I don't have any kids! And I'm only thirty-three and two-thirds!'

'Well, maybe you need to go home and get a move on with those kids instead of hanging round here pretending to be one then,' the doorman looks triumphant at his kicker. The queue of south London trustafarians is now braying loudly at my expense.

I know when I'm not wanted, but I still have free reign over my phone. So, as my friends beg and plead with him and then tell me they're coming out for me over the velvet rope – they've made no move in my direction, so much for uteruses before duderuses – I prod at my Uber again, stagger across to Rooster's Hut while I wait and fire off a Tweet with a magnificent blurry picture of my face demolishing a chicken strip burger.

*@Busseybuilding RUDE doorman said I'm too drunk/old to dance & should be making babies. Shall be suing for age/ maternity discrimination*

Cue the U OK HUNS.

**FELIX IS OUT AGAIN, SO ORLA IS HERE,** contemplating our living room with beneficent disdain. She's examining our monkey lamp as if he's about to attack her.

He doesn't mean anyone any harm – he's too busy monkeying around with his light bulb. I love that lamp. Luckily the cats have slunk off, as she's very uncomfortable with them sniffing around another new Chloé bag. I wonder if Rich buys them for her to apologise for all the late nights at work and all the lavish parties with his Chelsea mates. She's too proud to admit she's lonely. I couldn't put up with it. *Am I putting up with it?* It's lucky my love don't cost a thing: Felix is as broke as I am.

'It's like every time I go on Facebook there's another one,' she sighs dramatically, picking up her tumbler of prosecco off the floor.

'Who now?' I ask, trying to figure out how many more of her close circle could be about to give birth this year – unless they're doubling round on to their seconds within nine months . . .

'Spence and Rose are due soon and they got married about five months ago. Calypso is having twins. And now bloody Beth's bloody three months in – and the *darling daughter* isn't even a year and a half yet,' she's got her disgruntled voice on now. 'It only feels like about five minutes since she was chewing my ear off about her gross leaking nipples and now she's up the duff again!'

Beth was Orla's housemate after they left Edinburgh, and ever the source of chagrin.

'I mean, she didn't even want that bloody DD in the first place – she was about to embark on an affair with her personal trainer when she announced she was pregnant. And now that'll be two in the time that I've had zilch.'

'And me . . .'

'Oh, yeah, of course. It's just: *two years* and not a jot?! Not a single period out of place,' she says as if I wasn't afflicted in exactly the same way. 'Well, actually, they are getting incrementally shorter – a day per month. In eighteen months I'll be fully menopausal.'

I roll my eyes and laugh.

'As if! We're still young. Beth and Zara and Rachel have got us all wound up about time ticking, but we're fine! I read in the *Guardian* that the fertility cliff is just propaganda so we try earlier and save the NHS all that IVF money.'

'Well, the NHS is going to have to get its credit card out, because my private tests showed that I'm basically on the brink of being an old bird,' Orla says getting whipped up, 'and I want what eggs I have left steamed, massaged, cajoled and fertilised. I am going to chain myself to the gates until I'm pregnant.'

'It won't come to that! And Jemima's been teaching you bad tricks again after that lock-in.'

'Oh, it would have been hilarious if I hadn't been on the *inside* of her office when she did it. Three hours of her inane chat and shit coffee while the police bashed down the door. And she had the nerve to drop the dreaded: "so, do you not want kids?" question. Bloody bitch, doesn't she realise the only reason I've not turned whistle-blower is that I'm holding on tight for my mat leave? She looks like she's pregnant full-time anyway.'

I pour us a big glass of prosecco each and hope that Orla doesn't choose to 'improve' our Ikea rug by tipping it over the floor when she's doing another impression of her boss.

## 'I THINK I'VE GOT GOUT.'

Felix was even drunker last night than I was last weekend when I returned from south London with only one shoe and a party pack of half-eaten chicken wings emptied into my handbag. He's not prone to exaggeration so I check his feet for nobbles under the duvet. I worm back up until my face is poking back out at the top. Gone are the days where I'd stop under the duvet to give him something to ease his hangover by – god forbid he ejaculates anywhere but directly at my ovaries.

'Nope, no gout. But you are going to need some gross super-powered green juice to detox your sperm. It's our first good day again – we need them feeling their best, not hung-over and lying around in their tracksuits feeling sorry for themselves. At least I save my drinking for the days when it doesn't matter . . .'

All right, it probably matters all the time, but we can be saints when it's not sunny outside. And I'm facing a nine month stretch as soon as something actually happens for the good.

'OK, OK, I already feel bad enough, don't ladle on the guilt too,' he says, tiredly. 'You're really starting to sound like your mum . . .'

I throw the duvet off more mardily than was necessary and start choosing something to wear for work. He pulls me back into bed and begins peeling off my lightly clammy pyjama vest.

'Plus, I needed a drink. Entertaining lawyers is *boring* . . .' he's taking off his Calvin Klein sleep shorts in a sex-robot daze ready for some speedy pre-work business time to *Get. It. Done.* 'I just need to get through today and then we can have some *us* time tonight. And, yes, before you nag, that will include some actual sensual seduction – for which I will prepare with many Olympic-banned performance substances throughout the day.'

*Scheduled us time: my favourite time.*

| <29 June – 2 July | Event Details |
|---|---|
| **Sexy times** | |
| **Our House** | |
| Thursday, 29 June | |
| 10pm | |
| Calendar | Felivia shared |
| Invitation from   Olivia | |
| Invitees | |
| Alert | None |
| Notes | |
| We're doing it right this time – no more telling me I don't warn you | |

'MAYBE WE SWITCH the light on for a change?' says Felix, getting racy. 'Give us something visual to work with?'

I surreptitiously wipe the Sudocrem splotches off my face on to the pillow in preparation. Spotty, or spot creamy: my only real options.

'I mean, we don't *have* to,' he shifts himself back away from the precipice of the nightstand. 'I don't want to feel like I'm forcing you into it.'

'Oh no, do it, switch it on,' I say, double-bluffing. 'It's just usually you say it shines in your eyes.'

*Shines my face in your eyes.* I know he keeps it dark so I don't see how he scrunches his eyes shut to fantasise about anything but *this* while he forces himself to come.

'You're right,' he says, discouraged at my subtle reminder that *I know* and withdrawing his hand from the light switch to place it romantically on my left breast. 'Let's just get this done, shall we?'

117

Egg-White　　Happy　　Peak Fertility

**OH, PARIS.** I didn't expect Mads to deliver on his email, but when I returned to my desk from 'the holiday' (if you can call it that), Trish announced that not only would I be expected there in four weeks, but I'd also be staying overnight in a very *chou* hotel along with the rest of management.

The itinerary sounded less business conference, more city break: a Michelin-star dinner at Champeaux, brunch at Holybelly to *faire connaissance* the French equivalents of myself and Rachel. Mads had even been so thoughtful as to put time in my diary to walk me round his favourite structures. Research, *naturellement*.

As I totted up the dates, I knew I should be obsessing over lost fertile moments, and have been planning to smuggle Felix in my hand luggage for fertile shagging in the city of love. But honestly, I just didn't want to. Felix is always away: this was my turn. Maybe absence would make the heart grow hornier, and I could pick up some saucy can-can tips to revolutionise the remaining fertile days when I was back.

Felix's face had fallen into an impermeable frown when I told him, as he looked at his phone calendar to see my demanding reminder that we have sex every day while I'd be across the Channel. I redacted the exquisite ten-course meal and sleeping next door to my flirtatious boss.

And now, as I slam the front door shut to trundle my case off to St Pancras to catch the Eurostar, the silence I leave behind is deafening.

**PARIS IS PACKING ITS BAGS.** As I drag myself, weary but full of anticipation, from le Eurostar (I'm continental now) it feels like the whole of Paris is leaning back to soak up the last moments of summer in the city, take a sip of the milky Pastis, sweat it out. The month of July is barely functional here, people willing on their month's leave like a slow, sticky screw. But I can't afford to sun myself for a month, so I'm throwing caution (and my thick black tights) to the stiflingly warm breeze and my inappropriate cami dress is getting its debut with a collection of dainty gold necklaces and simple flat gold mule sandals. This is my *vacance*. I've also brought an oversized houndstooth blazer for when things get professional, because it's not *that* hot. Yet.

As I roll through Gare du Nord with all the other commuters, on second inspection, this slip is little more than a wisp of silk and completely anti-Parisienne. My arms are free, my legs are free (also, for once, hair-free), and, in this light fabric and crap strapless bra, I'm basically Free the Nipple too. French girls like having their nips on show, right? My hair has crinkled in the humidity of the train, so I've piled it on top of my head in what I hope looks like a 'brunette Bardot' (or at least not a 'brunette scare*crow*'). I hope my red lipstick is still intact because it's a euro to use the *toilette* and I have nothing but my credit card until payday. I remember to be angry with Felix again for giving me the cold shoulder this morning when he goes away every second week.

After a decidedly un-chic morning conference hosted by Marie-Christine the long, wiry French Trish Chippenham (no sign of Mads), I slip out for an early – and what I hope to be *long* lunch – loping languidly out through the Marais to a spot I noticed in the cab. It's a neat gravelly square tucked just behind the pretty church decorated with pea lights near their office. Here I'll sip iced coffee, contemplate how sticky I am, leaf through *Paris Match* and my wanky dog-eared paperback without absorbing a single page, and get my shoulders burnt – all the things a cool Parisienne would never do – blissfully unblighted by my Euro colleagues trying (and failing) to speak to me. That's what brunch at Holybelly tomorrow is for: unlimited 'you're so cute when you try to speak French!' condescension with my coffee. Now is just for me.

That is until I see shoulders. Sweaty shoulders. *Those* shoulders. And a hand rifling through hair. On the bench in the best sunlight. The bench I'd spotted. I don't even share with French pigeons.

I know I could sit anywhere. It's 12.30, so even the small pockets of lawn are *sans* picnickers. But no, I'm determined to take my rightful throne.

'Monsieur, is this seat taken?'

It's unnecessarily formal, given my state of undress, his state of recline and the state of my French pronunciation. I pull at a fallen tendril of hair at the nape of my neck and bring my rip-off gold Miu Miu cat eye sunglasses down just enough to arch a brow. I'm flirting like a repressed

Victorian suddenly faint on her midday constitutional. No need for the sweat of self-contempt; the sun has saturated my summer nightie with a fresh-from-the-swimming-pond dampness. Sweat pools in my cursed strapless bra. *You never support me, you bitch.* It's like a historically infused, feminist take on the wet T-shirt competition. Luckily I've got some muddy slime in a cup as a prop too.

'Oh, it's *you.*'

'Yes, Mads' – I luxuriate in saying his name out loud – 'it's *me.* You remember, the underling you're supposed to be hosting on this trip?' I laugh at my own impetuousness, but I really did convince myself that I'd made an indelible impression on him in London when he was so keen to invite me here. But of course, he's far too *important* to be my chaperone.

He looks up over his perfectly simple tortoise-rim sunglasses and draws his feet in a touch to make room for me. 'I thought I'd just get a few rays before joining you for the boredom this afternoon. But I'm glad *you've* found me. Isn't this spot *smuk?*'

'Smut?' I laugh contemptuously. He must have been out here a while. He's got sunstroke.

'No: *Smuk.*' My face must be less than amused. 'It means beautiful. In Danish. You work for HYGGE – aren't you supposed to speak the language?' And then under his breath, with impeccable timing, '. . . *you schmuck.*'

'So, now I can't tell if you just called me beautiful, or stupid . . .' I reply drily. 'Or indeed, which would be more inappropriate at this point?' I laugh and take in the view. It is *smuk.*

I can see from the corner of my eye that his hair is as dishevelled as it's ever been, several strands dancing precariously in front of his glasses. My hands itch. What would happen if I just grabbed a handful of his hair? Would he bat me off? Would he like it? *What am I, a pigtail-grabbing child in the playground?*

Then, there's that beautiful arching motion of hand to hair again. He can't help himself. With his elbow aloft, we're divided for a moment and I breathe slow and shallow, covertly lavishing myself in his smell. *We're all just animals.* He lowers his arm, resting it behind me on the bench: the classic teenage date move. On me. I'm pleased to see from his sweat patch that he's as wet through as I am at this point.

'So what are you doing here,' I press slowly, 'if you can't be bothered to come inside?'

'I couldn't miss an opportunity to see Paris when it sizzles, could I?' He turns his torso towards the arm draped behind my back, and I can feel the heat of his chest against my pale clammy arm. Why did I not fake tan? But then, imagine the smear it would leave on his pristine white Sunspel T-shirt.

'Or me . . .' I say, pseudo-seductively, but not in control of the words. 'It's bloody boiling here!' *What are you saying Olivia Eoife Galvin Gyamfi? Do not unlock that door.*

'Well, having you here was part of the plan too,' he says removing his sunglasses and staring me right in the face. Obviously while the glasses were on he was staring down my drenched cleavage. I shouldn't be willing that. *But I was.*

'But until then, you're going to have to be my date to this lunch meeting.'

**THE HANDS OF THE CLOCK** are like oars in a lake. Marie-Christine is taking us through the triumphs of the

Paris design team and all their bloody lamps. The virtue of the French working system – regular coffee breaks in their creative spaces to reboot their HYGGE (it's pronounced 'auuge' here, allegedly). Their marketing department talk about brand differences by country – what it is that France wants ('sophisticated *simplicité*'), Denmark ('affordable design') and then the UK ('cheap fuss' – Brexit dig there). Despite my illegally low dress, I've de-jacketed so I don't pass out in the dead heat of the seventeenth-century meeting room. The Paris team are all impossibly shiny-haired, make-up-free, beautiful twenty-somethings, but I notice Mads's eyes have not strayed from my shoulders. By 4 p.m., I try not to trace Mads's path out of the room as he absents himself from the next lecture. At 4.30, I allow my mind to wander to him laughing over aperitifs in a courtyard with a bevy of Bardots. Hopefully it's just the Klauses. Then at 4.45, Marie-Christine gathers her laptop and her neat black handbag and wafts out of the room. The people who had not followed her as close as a shadow tell me that this is the signal that we're free to leave. No 'thank you', no 'goodbye', just turn and go. I need to move here if this is how it works. Back to the park.

*No excuse.*

'STILL A SCHMUCK?' I ask casually, as I approach him from behind, realising he'd escaped to be alone in the sunshine instead of that repressive room, the heat still close around us like a bell jar. The square is empty, the streets around it buzzing with creatives eager to flee their offices, back to their sunshine lives. Bar Mads, who has his feet up on the bench, with my battered copy of *Madame Bovary* and a bottle of Aquavit next to him. I touch his shoulder so lightly, changing my mind as I do and pulling back, but the electricity shoots up through my spine. He turns to look up at me.

'Still *smuk*?'

*Heart stops.*

I sit down as the pea lights suddenly illuminate over Place des Vosges. The five o'clock sunshine continues its reign.

'So, Olivia, can I show you Paris, or am I going to have to see it all by myself?'

*My last out.*

'OK. But don't bore me with the Eiffel Tower bullshit,' I say. 'Show me something I haven't seen before.'

*Point of no return, gone.*

'As if I'd ever give you that,' he says in a lilted mock-Parisian croon, collecting his bottle and my book and straightening out his crumpled T-shirt.

*I want to be sick.*

I look up at the grand baroque cornicing on the various *hôtel particuliers* that emanate from the square. Keeping my eyes on the sky will keep me separate; keep this professional. I nearly run into an attractively greying man in his cool linen shirt and neat navy slacks as people spill out of the quaint bistro on the corner. My new HYGGE colleagues are nowhere to be seen. *Better to be invisible for this.*

'So, Mads, as I didn't ever google you,' – *lies are sexy, right?* – 'I guess you should just tell me about yourself.'

'Well, Olivia, I'm glad you're not a stalker . . . but what is there to say?' He laughs. 'I'm just an ordinary boy from Copenhagen. I lived in New York for fifteen years. All I do is draw buildings and inspect lamps that look the same. Pretty boring, really.'

'Such a man of the people,' I rib. Imagine what he'd

think of Boringwood. We turn into another cobbled street, the sun suddenly obscured by the cool white stone terraces. 'And so committed to making the world a cosier place.'

'HYGGE is a little too cosy for my liking, I must admit. But if you tell anyone, I'll have to kill you.' He winks.

'Too cosy, eh? Your secret is safe with me,' I whisper, moving closer to him. 'So there's no Mrs Mads, or little Rasmussen Jrs sequestered in an expertly designed penthouse in Vesterbro or Brooklyn?'

'Ha. Sequestered – I like that word,' he says. *That's a no then.*

'So has anyone come close?' I'm getting braver.

'One or two. The last was twenty-three, which was a disaster. I should have known. Nineteen years is a bit of a gap.'

So he's forty-two. Nine years isn't as cavernous a void.

'It wasn't Zara, was it? She's not actually twenty-three.' I thought I'd won.

He snorts, and even that is sexy. The cars on the beautiful, wide tree-lined *rue* come between us briefly as we cross.

'No, Olivia, that was just a coffee. Not even a walk.'

*I did win. Ding ding ding.*

'So what do you go for then? Do you like your women like you like your buildings?' *Shut up shut up shut up.*

'What, tall and brutal?' He laughs and runs his hand back through his hair.

We walk through a narrow passageway and he drops behind me momentarily. I bury the thought that he's inspecting my pale legs. Hopefully he can focus on the sprinkling of freckles behind my calves, not the unshaved patch by my ankle.

'I tend to go for challenging women,' he shouts as I pick up pace, laughing again. I notice how his eyes crinkle as I turn to look at him straight. 'Y'know, contrarians who have more going on than googling me.'

I'm choosing to ignore this, to not dance down the Parisian backstreet, because he *is not* talking about me. He's just a beautiful marauder, dangling his attentions to win me round.

'God, looking for a challenge, how *draining* . . . What about getting *hygge* with someone? Settling down? Don't you want that? It's quite nice.'

'Is it now? Well do you want to tell me about your set-up then? Very cosy, I see?' He's teasing me now. *Why are you here really, Olivia? What do you want?*

'Yes, it is cosy, thanks . . .' Felix seeps into my mind, 'but then, sometimes cosy has its drawbacks.'

'Especially in this weather. What you need is a breath of fresh air.'

And then, he blows in my face.

His breath, thick with Aquavit, isn't as fresh as it should be, but it feels like a seduction technique straight out of some old, slightly sexist, movie. If meant as a joke, there were at least three seconds too many where we were simply staring into each other's eyes. *Kiss him, no one will ever have to know.*

We turn the corner on to Rue du Parc Royal, where we're flanked by a gated garden and a hotel carved from a fondant fancy: pretty white awnings like heavy eyelids over every window.

'I always want to eat macarons when I come sit in this square . . .' he laughs. 'I can't think why?'

*I just want to eat you.*

126

'It's the colour my shoulders will be after this walk,' I say, flipping the skinny strap of my dress down to show him the line, but really to reveal even more of my bare chest. 'I've been like caged veal all winter.'

'You asked for my tour and I'm giving you my tour,' he deadpans. 'I can't control the weather. Would you prefer it if we returned to the stifling office? Or maybe I can take you to a museum with all the tourists?'

'I'm sure you've designed a visitor centre somewhere you'd care to brag about,' I say, laughing.

'Well, there is actually this *very smart* new building opening on the Champs-Elysées I just worked on that's just dripping in history? It's where an ancient order of Danish bores realised they could make a killing selling balsa wood and fake sheepskins to the world for very reasonable prices.'

We laugh as we walk too close to one another through the gated garden. We're the only ones in the square, and the blazing sunshine is temporarily blocked from view by the sugared almond building beside us. His forearm brushes mine and we smile at each other, suddenly sheepish. He doesn't bother to fall behind as we squeeze hip-to-hip now through the narrow gate into the opposite side of the square. *Is this how it's meant to feel?*

A buzz sounds from my now sweat-soaked bucket bag.

Felix
Today 19:05

It should be me taking you to Paris, not your manager. I can't believe you said yes to staying there when it's one of our good weeks. That's just our life, though, isn't it? We'll never have a baby.

I minimise the message in a flash, lest Mads discovers my illicit husband. Another pops up in its stead.

Today 19:06

Sorry, that all came out wrong. I'm just frustrated because I'm always away and then you're away and I miss you. I'll take you to Paris and we can do it properly soon. Sure you're just holed up in boring meetings and missing the sunshine. Love you with all my heart, mon amour. xxxxx

*Do I even miss him?*

'Do you want to go back now?' Mads asks, surprisingly tender. He's a warm kind of drunk and he's unscrewing his Aquavit, planning to be more so.

'Nope, I'm all yours' – *no* – 'I mean, I'm all yours for the tour. We're finishing this.'

I grab the Aquavit, take a big swig (and retch a bit), determinedly striding off down the Rue des Francs Bourgeois, Mads tailing me by two steps the whole way, to the foot of the Centre Pompidou.

'A building like you like your women: challenging and colourful. And maybe also a bit brutal?'

AS WE WEAVE OUR WAY through the shaded streets of Le Marais, I spot men easing their ties (and wedding rings) as they drink with inappropriate 'colleagues'. The steamy evening has slowed to such a sloth-like pace that every minute feels like an hour. We steal an ice bucket and two glasses on our way through Rue du Renard and I look at Mads's excessively handsome face, laughing to himself as he pours us tall measures of Aquavit, and wonder if I've fallen into Wonderland. He nudges me, grabs my waist, puts his arm around my shoulder whenever he sees a modern building that he knows the designer of. That's all of them. He touches me constantly now. He's so easy in his skin. We take off our shoes and play in the sand on the fake beach laid out along Quai de Gesvres, sitting down over-dressed amid all the beautiful bodies drinking cocktails by the water, and taking in the view. I grab his hand for the first time as we cross over Pont Notre-Dame, the Seine glimmering iridescent beneath us.

I smile at him and he smiles at me and then Felix's voice dances through the haze of the dream. *'We're so close.'* But what are we close to?

At the end of the bridge, the cathedral casts a long shadow. Its gothic balustrades are just like the church we got married in. As we step into the darkness and turn down the steps, away from people's view, Mads grabs my waist as if to tell me another of his design secrets. Instead he turns me to him and holds me there, my face in his palms. I realise he's waiting for me. Letting me go first. My mouth is magnetised. Every inch of me wants this. I stare into his murky blue eyes: questioning everything.

And then I pull away, and I run.

'WHAT'S GOING ON?' yells Felix, sitting bolt upright with fear in his eyes. I'm an intruder in my own house as I slip into the bed beside him.

'It's just me. I came home early, I missed you.' I detect remnants of the Aquavit as I kiss his forehead gently to settle him. I frightened myself how quickly my guard disintegrated in the sunshine. How quickly *this* was forgotten. Have I been inadvertently keeping myself un-pregnant for my *cinq* à *sept* slot with Mads? But I'm back now and that is never happening again. As I lay my head on the pillow next to my husband, I wonder if he'll find out how many lies I've told today. How work picked up my 300 euro change-of-ticket fee because of a family emergency, how Mads thinks I didn't want him, how Felix doesn't know I came home because I couldn't trust myself to be in the same country as temptation.

Felix exhales relieved, still partially asleep.

'Remember it's one of our good days . . .' I say, moving closer to his warm body beneath the duvet. 'Do you think you're awake enough to take advantage of it?'

'Anything for you baby,' he says, rubbing his eyes in the half-light and pulling me into a well-worn embrace. I'm with him. *But am I really here?*

Exhausted        Sticky

'YOU DON'T REALISE HOW MUCH WE NEED THIS,' Hayley whispers to me like a warning in the kitchen as she warms Eloise's milk through – her parting gift to me before they drop the mic on parenting for an evening and leave us to practise on their children.

'You just enjoy yourselves, we've got it all under control,' I say, taking the bottle (am I clutching the contents of Hayley's left boob?) and standing guard for their escape in the spacious hallway of their Hackney maisonette. 'I want to hear stories in the morning. Don't be boring.'

'Liam can't support his own bodyweight after three pints these days, so we won't be late,' she says, evidently still worried. Do we look that incapable? I realise the bottle's rubber nipple is dripping on their cream carpet. So yes, we probably do. Liam comes down the stairs holding a freshly bathed Eloise, duckling cute in her towelling robe.

'What can't I support?' he says, laughing. He looks smart in his lightly flecked navy suit, his hair slicked back instead of his usual mop. Hayley looks equally hot, in a silver strappy midi as she wipes spilt milk from the worktop. They hardly even look at each other. *Felix and I haven't dressed up to go out together in months, maybe even a year.*

'Seriously, don't make me reverse parent you,' I say, looking faux-stern at them both. 'There's no need for a curfew! Be spontaneous. We can just kip down in the spare room if it gets late.'

Or is staying awake all night a babysitting prerequisite? I thought it was about making six bucks an hour with your boyfriend in the shower, not putting yourself willingly through Guantanamo torture. Maybe we can take it in shifts to have a snooze. It's not like they're paying us.

'Now get out of here!' shouts Felix, looking up briefly from the floor, where he's concentrating on the construction of a Star Wars Lego model with Jackson. It's outsmarting them both. Jackson couldn't be less perturbed at his parents' desertion, but Eloise turns banshee as Liam hands her over, wriggling and rigid.

The front door slams, and suddenly, we're parents. With Eloise struggling on my hip I sidle into the living room to feed her on the sofa. How have we already conformed to the 'boys build things' and 'girls nurture' trope after only five minutes? Not exactly: Felix still can't work out how to fix the wings to the TIE fighter.

At least the milk has temporarily placated Elo. She's soothed into a quiet suckling that makes my ovaries do a flip. I'll put her down as soon as she's done with her nightcap, but it doesn't look like Jackson – wired on coloured plastic – is anywhere close to sleepy.

'Do you think we need to get *you know who* ready for *you know what?*' I mouth to Felix quietly, in case Jackson has become a master sleuth since we last saw him toddling round a petting zoo making the wrong noises at the animals.

'What's *you know what?*' Felix over-mouths, too loudly, in return. Jackson looks up from his model, head cocked.

'B-E-D.' I can't believe I'm miming now.

'Leave him for a minute, he's chilling,' says Felix. 'We're having fun, aren't we, Jackson?'

Jackson looks up at Felix and Felix looks down at Jackson, their smiles mirrored, and I can see why my social media feeds are a gauntlet of smuggery every bloody day. I reach for my iPhone with my spare arm, eyes on Eloise's zombie-sucking, pointing it to capture them just as a jagged handful of Lego bricks fly at Felix's face. Jackson, laughing deliriously, lassos us as he jumps to his feet and goes ricocheting round the room.

'No wings, no fun!' he shouts, waking Eloise from her blissful pre-sleep and unleashing her alarm-wail again. 'No wings, no fun!'

Felix picks the tiny colourful pieces off his shoulders and out of his hair, and tries not to grimace for the camera that's still pointed in his face as I try to protect Eloise's head from the parkour.

'Maybe it's time for the little S.H.I.T. to go to B.E.D. after all . . .' says Felix. Jackson bounces off the sofa next to me, lands two feet on their bouncy footstool and spring-boards on to Felix's back, pommel-horsing around him using his ears as the handles.

'Oi! Jackson . . . That's my hair,' he says, still level-voiced, the dad that won't say no, who wonders why his kid is running riot. 'Liv, help me?' he implores kneeling up with Jackson's hands over his eyes, his strong legs clamped over his broad shoulders, feet kicking his chest. I've dropped the iPhone, but now Eloise has turned beetroot with rage and has thrown up on my vintage mohair jumper.

'Jackson! It's not kind to blind your Uncle Felix!' I say sharply, putting Eloise into her bouncer before I give chase to the two-headed monster, ignoring the milky dribble across my shoulder. *I'll be bad cop then.*

'They've laced his fish fingers with speed to show us up,' I grin as I wrestle Jackson, scissor-kicking and laughing like a deranged hyena taking apart its prey, away from Felix.

Felix looks shell-shocked. I point down towards Eloise, still dolphin flailing in her bouncer: he can assume baby duties while I solve the toddler problem. Jackson's weight is like power-lifting an over-stuffed long-haul suitcase, but I am not putting this child down until I get him into the bedroom.

'Now what happens with naughty little shi—SHIFTY children,' I whisper as I struggle up the stairs under his weight, 'is that they have to go straight to bed with no stories . . .' Jackson's face drops and he suddenly stops his angry twist to listen. 'Now you don't want that, do you, Jackson?'

'No, Aunty Livya.' His bottom lip wobbles.

'Of course you don't. Because having us here is supposed to be fun. But jumping around like a monkey isn't fun, it's dangerous.'

'Dangerous.'

'And throwing things and jumping on your Uncle Felix is very naughty.'

'Naughty.'

'So let's try and have some nice fun now by getting you all cosy in bed, and then we can ask Uncle Felix really nicely if he'll forgive you and come up to read you a story.'

'Story.' At least he's pulling out the key words.

As I stand Jackson on the chair in his room to take off his dungarees and pull on the cosmic pyjamas we bought him last Christmas (which he's only just grown into: such bad size-judges), I feel a wave of accomplishment. He's calm. I did this. I turn on the night light, tuck him under his giraffe duvet and kiss him on the forehead. I close the door and switch the big light off and Felix is waiting on the landing bouncing a now calm Eloise in his arms, his hair standing on end after the altercation. I kiss him deeply, transferring the baby from his shoulder to mine and ushering him wide-eyed into the lion's den. My heart swells at his bravery.

As I sit in the nursing chair with Eloise in my arms, my pride turns to sadness. Will it ever be us, taking it in turns to quell our tired-out little ones? Do I even have the energy for it? I shut my eyes and absorb the warmth of Eloise sleeping on my chest.

'Wake up, baby,' Felix says, his hand on my shoulder, smiling down at me in the half-light. Eloise is still curled in my arms, her light burbles showing she's having as good a sleep as I was. The journey may not run smooth to get up here, but the result is definitely golden.

Sensitive

THE 'WEEKS BETWEEN' are my least favourite. From day 16 to 28, it's just a waiting game: counting the days until the period comes and ruins your world a fraction more. I check my app three times a day, as if I've forgotten how many more days of phantom symptoms there are until I can do a pregnancy test only to raise the nib up to find it covered in blood.

And because this has become a ritual now, and I can't simply leave normal life behind, I revised the list of foods I'm supposed to avoid. I haven't changed the cat litter tray in over a year (Felix is suspicious that 'toxoplasmosis' is just another word for laziness). And I read up on the effect of alcohol in early pregnancy. Delving into some site with a *mummo*-jumbo title, alcohol isn't too much of an issue until after 'implantation' which is actually *seven to ten* days after ovulation. *More drinking time than I originally thought.* So, loosely calculating – given I forgot to do the sticks this month – implantation might happen at around day 21 or even day 24. This means I *could* be all right-ish to drink for three weeks of the month and not do terrible damage to my baby. But then people get drunk when they don't know all the time, don't they?

As these questions go round my head every month in the weeks between, I wonder if I am actually an alcoholic like my mum claims. I probably only drink five or six times a month really, it's just that all the weddings and work socials bunch up. I don't drink in the house unless we have guests; I don't drink on my own. And I certainly don't wake up with a hangover and want to get straight back on it. I don't drink to forget. I just drink so I don't miss out on everything while I'm still missing out on a baby.

But, teehalfism is getting me nowhere. Next month, I've

vowed to myself that I am drinking nothing. I'm abandoning sugar, starchy carbs and caffeine. I'm going to make Felix join me in hell. I look forward to us killing each other in our headache-ridden sleep over dreams of marshmallows. Until then, since I ovulated, not a dribble of drink has touched my lips. It's only tonight with the girls that stands in my way, like a cocktail-lined gauntlet. And I can't say I've got cystitis *again*.

'I'LL HAVE THE' – lean in, hushed voice – '*virgin* BLOODY MARY, thanks.' Don't think Ada heard, so I can get away with it for one round at least.

'I'll just have a lime and soda please,' I catch Ada mid-whisper. So she's at it too?

'Joined AA, eh?' I say with cocked eyebrow, as she's done to me for the last six months of excuses.

'I've got gangrene, actually,' she deadpans. 'Antibiotics for the next nine months.'

'Hang on, are you actually *pregnant*?!' She is looking even more glowing than usual, with her hair teased into braids drawn back off her beautifully round face, all dewy and make-up free. I wasn't prepared for this.

'Ha, I wish. Nah, we're doing this fertility treatment and they've said I shouldn't drink.'

*Phew*.

'At last, a new signing for Barren United!' I say, looping my arm around her shoulder, to offset my insensitivity. 'I thought it was just me and Orla—'

'Oh, there was me thinking you just had cystitis constantly because of your filthy sex life,' she laughs. '*I'm* trying, but Jack is just trying to get the business to work. He's got a meeting in Japan with a massive games company just as

136

I'm supposed to be starting the drugs. So it's a write-off already.'

'What's this?' Margot sidles in behind us, bobbed golden hair side parted and tucked neatly behind her ears, her long lean frame in tight white T-shirt and leather skirt juxtaposed against the roundedness of myself and Ada, conspicuous in our dresses. In her hand is a cocktail sprouting two ironic umbrellas and a little Perspex chimpanzee. 'Have you two finally answered the inevitable call of the tame?'

She's never talked about it, but I think Margot might be like Grace in her child-rearing aspirations.

'And there was me thinking I was so covert . . .' Why was I being covert? I wish we'd had this conversation at least a year ago.

'I mean, the binge-drinking for only two weeks of every month, the super depression at every period and constant obsessing over who else is pregnant weren't *that* obvious . . .' says Margot, tucking a little pink umbrella into my hair and taking me under her wing back to the table she's found. 'It's going to be a boring old night with you dry old slags. Might need to rope in some more drunken company . . .' she says catching the eye of a tipsy hot girl on the next table.

'Or I could just ring Trine?' I return, pretend-sarcastically. We love Trine, but as a couple, she and Margot are just so bloody private. It's like they're in their own secret world. Tonight though, Margot's on lairy form.

'So, what's been holding you back then, slaggy?' I say to Ada, because there is no better bar chat than gynaecology bar chat.

'Not ovulating, am I? I came off the pill nine months ago and haven't even had a period. So given all that sex we're NOT having, it would have to be an immaculate conception if I suddenly dropped a bub.' She looks perturbed, but only slightly, a bit like how I imagine I style these feelings out. 'What about you?'

'Not sure, really. I suppose we should go and see someone. They say you're not supposed to see your GP until it's been two years, so I guess time is up.'

'Two years?! God, that's a lot of sex with the same person to have to put up with . . .' Margot catches the eye of tipsy girl again.

'It's just *pressure*,' I say. 'And it stops being fun. I can't remember the last time we just spontaneously screwed when it wasn't a fertile day.'

'Fertile day? I'd kill for one of those!' says Ada fraught but still laughing.

'Remember all those group trips down the Marie Stopes in last night's heels for the morning-after pill?' I say. 'I was on Dianette from fifteen! Needn't have bothered with any of it . . .'

'And me with that coil which made me put on two stone!' says Ada. 'We might have been popping out sprogs if we'd have been having this much sex when we were twenty though.'

'I was having plenty of sex,' I remember wistfully, 'and never so much as a scare.'

'Not this regulated and rigorous though . . .'

'Boring me to rigor mortis, more like . . .'

'What have you two become? I'm off!' Margot picks up her wacky cocktail and heads to the next table. If she doesn't come back in half an hour, I'll take a picture of them and threaten to send it to Trine.

'But seriously, what *have* we become?' I say to Ada, fearfully staring her dead in the eye. 'Did you ever think it would be like this?'

'All my friends have got two kids,' she says. 'I didn't think it'd turn out like this hormone-shooting shit-show. And then Jack's just burying his head in the sand because he's scared.'

'Felix has taken it really badly. Jack's got loads of friends who don't want kids, but when Fe sees his mates, there are children everywhere. Maybe I'll get him to talk to Jack about it?'

'He needs it. He thinks we're twenty-five, not approaching thirty-five, and it could take me years to conceive if I'm not even releasing an egg. It's not like we're even ever in bed together. All he does is work through the night so he's on Japan time.'

'Let Felix talk to him. They're well overdue a night out.'

Ada grimaces at the prospect. Hopefully Felix can fix their fertility problems at least.

LOVE IS FORMED OUT of strange materials. As I make my way home, I think how different my relationship with Felix is to Jack and Ada's. But it all starts the same way. First, it's physical attraction – I like your face, you like my T-shirt – maybe it's possible to see that you'll get along from some of those visual cues. If I like your T-shirt, then we've got the same taste. If you think I've got a kind face, maybe it's because I've switched my resting bitch face off momentarily because I've spotted you. Maybe we just light each other up. Then comes getting to know one another. The core values come out. The things your parents wanted for you (and the bits that you rebelled against). The way you interact with your friends. How you treat the sixteen-year-old staff in McDonald's. There might be blips. As you go deeper, you might see bits you don't want to see. How the other flirts with people who aren't you. How the other behaves when you become a green-eyed monster and they explain that this is, in fact, just their cousin, and they were *only laughing*. But then further down the line, you'll hopefully arrive at the shared sensibility. This is the best bit. It's one part lust for gossip, one part us-against-the-world. Having common judgements on other people is how you become a unit. Sure, you can still argue about how you feel about each other, but as long as you both agree that Max from university is being ridiculous thinking he can put a picture of him and his girlfriend on Tinder so she'll maybe try a threesome with him, then you *know* you're made for each other. But what happens if you're diametrically opposed on things like this? What, if after eight years in sync, you hit a fork in the road. Like will Felix really want to 'have a word' with Jack to tell him he needs to give Ada the baby she wants? Or, will it ever be safe for Felix and Mads to be in the same room together?

# INTERVIEW 2: LYDIA

We all know a Lydia: she looks like she's blazing through life on a dream. No make-up, curly carefree hair, clothes she just threw on, yet make her look like she's just walked out of a Wes Anderson movie. She was so laid-back when I worked with her two years ago that I figured she was permanently stoned. I was quite jealous, actually. She's not some out-of-it hippy though – she'd call bullshit from two miles – but she's pretty chill with her lot.

So when she told me, over what I mistakenly thought was an after-work pint (Becks Blue: all the beer reek, zero the alcoholic enjoyment), that she'd been 'frantically attempting to pop a sprog for three whole years', I was pretty shocked that she was the type of person to 'try' at anything. She just looked like she was having fun and that all the incidentally cool stuff surrounding her – the hot scruffy boyfriend, the flat bought just before the cheapo area became the most sought-after spot in London – just happened by some hazy chance.

So now we know. Even the extreme relaxers of us can't be relaxed all the time. This is the insidious truth: people make it look so easy. That is, until you realise they're living on a knife-edge, denying themselves every pleasure, keeping a laissez faire look plastered on their faces, just waiting for that one ~~little~~ massive thing to change.

You can't choose your family, but you can choose the egg and sperm that create it.

**Olivia:** Lyds, you managed it! You got your wish!

**Lydia:** Yup. It only took four years and some exploding ovaries, but he's pretty sweet, right?

**Olivia:** He is . . . Hello Sonny [I pan the camera to look at his cherubic face and his adorable star-print onesie]. Glad to make your acquaintance, finally. So, Lydia, take me back to the start. Did it really take four years?

**Lydia:** I think we started trying about thirty-three. I'm thirty-seven now. I'm thinking about a year after we'd been trying we went to the doctor and they sent me for a whole bunch of tests. I remember that dye one hurting a bit.

**Oliva:** I haven't had that yet!

**Lydia:** Don't worry, it's nothing once you get to childbirth—

**Olivia:** If I ever get that far.

**Lydia:** You will. I thought I wasn't going to either. They've got some pretty mean tricks they can do to get you there. Once I'd had the tests, the man went through this book – it's like some IVF burn book, so you'd better be nice to him, and if not, move house – and he said, 'Right, I need to know your exact postcode' and he ran his finger across an actual page – wasn't even a computer or anything – and said 'You're lucky you've got three rounds, because the postcode next to you gets nothing.' That's the NHS for you: dreamy, but also sometimes your worst nightmare. Then he told us we'd be seen in the May. Which by that point would have been about two full years after all the to-ing and fro-ing with appointments. I think we were lucky, because there was a six-to-eight-month waiting list and we managed to skid in around six months to see the actual fertility consultants.

**Olivia:** So you were trying in the meantime anyway? Were you doing loads of stuff to try and help yourselves get pregnant?

**Lydia:** Yeah, we'd both already knocked drinking on the head, and everything that comes *with* drinking, about a year before that. It was fairly boring even though we were a bit half-hearted, really. It felt like a bloody long time when they told us it would be another six months, but then it actually came round quite fast. In that time, we decided to enjoy ourselves, so we had a holiday and went back to drinking for a bit. We thought we might as well if we were taking it in hand.

**Olivia:** Had it been getting you down then?

**Lydia:** I was so depressed, yeah. Because you don't have the end result, everything is on hold and you don't 100 per cent know that this option is even going to work. It got me down.

**Olivia:** So by the time you got to the IVF you were super serious about it all then . . .

**Lydia:** I was zero on everything. I didn't want to look back and wonder. And I clamped down on Jez too, which isn't like me at all – you've seen how chilled I am – but I was like 'You are *not* drinking, and you will also take ten vitamins a day.' If I was going to be shooting up hormones, he was going to be at least eating some broccoli and giving up the burgers and IPA for a couple of months. To be honest, I got quite addicted to all the fertility hormones – they're so good for your bloody hair. I'm still taking them now, and I've got a baby! My body was a temple . . . I was having homeopathy and acupuncture too.

Olivia: So after all those needles, you were ready for the injections when you came to that?

Lydia: Erm, I was really nervous about doing them to be honest . . . [pauses and looks a bit embarrassed] I've got a very low pain threshold so I thought I wouldn't be able to bear it. But actually it was absolutely fine. When you're injected by a nurse, they do it dead fast. I found, if you inject yourself the rate I was going – *so slowly* – you don't even feel it going in. It's when you push that button and the stuff goes in that it hurts. Oh, it's disgusting. Some people are like 'Oh I got my partner to do it.' I just couldn't let Jez near me with a needle because I would hate him too much. So I had to do it myself. I was bruised, bruised, bruised. I had to keep doing it up until I was three months pregnant. So you feel like utter shit in the early days of being pregnant, and you're scared that it could change at any minute, and then you have to do these fucking injections on top of it. Oh my god, it's the worst.

Olivia: I heard that you can do pessaries or even supposi-tories instead of injections – is that right? Or did you choose to do the injections instead?

Lydia: Oh yeah, I had those too! My god, those are hideous! That was worse than any injection. They say don't put them up your vag, because they'll just fall back out unless you go *deep*. So they said, 'Put it up your bum, it'll suck it up.' What they don't tell you is how much those motherfuckers burn!

Olivia: Yep, we'll edit that bit out!

Lydia: I wish I could edit it out of my mind . . . And that's not even the worst of it! Then I overstimulated.

Olivia: What's that?

Lydia: The whole point of IVF is that they give you injections to stimulate your ovaries to create as many eggs as possible, so they can make them into embryos. When I got to my check-up they were like: 'Oooh, your stomach is really distended! We'd better get these out quick.' Apparently you can have too many eggs. I had like thirty-one sacs or something. That's *a lot*.

Olivia: So are there eggs in all the sacs? Were they all usable? Soz, tell me if it's TMI.

Lydia: It's fine! Some of the sacs can be empty, some will have little eggs that won't amount to much. We had eleven good ones in the end, and they managed to make those into embryos and then every day they ring you to tell you how many have died, which is nice!

Olivia: Did you feel frightened that it wouldn't work?

Lydia: Hmmm . . . nervous, I would say. They had already told me the ones we had were good quality. When I was having my results after the egg collection – where they suck all of the eggs out of you – you're all on a ward together. So there's about six girls sitting behind curtains and you can hear everyone else's results. I could hear the girl next to me saying it was her fifth round of IVF and the consultant told her, 'Right, well, you've got two eggs.' So when they came to me and told me I had eleven, already I knew that I was in a good place. Over the course of five days we got it down to five really strong whatsits – blastocysts – and then they were like 'We can't put them back into you because your body needs to recover.'

Olivia: You must have been so frustrated?

Lydia: Yeah! After all that hyping myself up that I was potentially going to be pregnant the next week, I was absolutely distraught at having to wait another three months. But it went past really quickly. Our little five-day-old embryos were frozen and we booked another holiday to the deep south of America and *really* enjoyed ourselves on that one. When we came back, they put the strongest embryo into me and that was Sonny. Two weeks later, too early to do a home test, you have to go for a blood test and then phone them to get your results, and they told us we were pregnant.

Olivia: How emotional was that day when you found out?

Lydia: Very emotional. That day was amazing. Jez came and met me at work, everybody knew what was happening that afternoon, so we thought we'd go to the pub and ring, but the pub was packed so we just had to do it on a roundabout near my office. And the first thing the woman at the hospital said when I said who I was, was, 'Can I ask if you've had any bleeding?' I was like 'no' but I thought, that means it was a no. So I mouthed to Jez, 'It's a no.' Then she went, 'Well, that's great, congratulations!' I was like 'What?!' We both cried, it was just so exciting telling everyone – sending the text out to the friends, ringing the parents: it was such a special moment. We were supposed to wait until we had a viability scan at seven weeks, but we couldn't contain ourselves. I'm not one of those shy-IVF-ers. I don't care if people know Sonny came out of a petri dish as long as he's here.

Olivia: Looking back, were there any crazy things you did to try to get pregnant?

Lydia: Ha, well one thing I heard was that you have to dice the core of a pineapple and eat one cube a day for five days once the embryo has been implanted because it makes your mucus all sticky and it helps it to stick. Then after that you need to stay away from the pineapple!

It's not an exact science. And then someone also told me that when you've had the embryo put back in you should just spend as much time laughing as you could. They recommend you take a week off work, so we took some holiday and just watched comedies. I also visited a friend who's a really happy person who'd just had a baby. I thought maybe my baby might hear her baby and think 'I wanna be alive.' You never know – that might have worked!

Also, one other crazy thing I did was that on our trip to the deep south, we went to New Orleans so I could visit a voodoo shop and buy a fertility gris-gris bag which was blessed by a voodoo priest. I carried it with me at all times in my knickers (in the top section not in the undercarriage) so that it was touching my womb at all times. It's about the size of a ping-pong ball so it would stick out of my jeans. I also bought a voodoo doll called Azuli. She's a bit of a tie, to be honest. We have to top her up with rum and rice and black coffee every week on a Tuesday. She's like the voodoo patron saint of single mothers, so she cares for children. She really goes through the rum, oh my god, she absorbs it all right! So I went properly mental about it all you see.

**Olivia:** And was it a straightforward birth, given the less-than-straightforward beginning?

**Lydia:** God no, it was a hideous birth, he was three weeks early, I had a blood transfusion, I was in for eight days and Sonny was in special care. It was really hard – you go back on to a ward and everyone else has got babies. I got discharged a day before him and I was like, 'I'm not leaving without him.' So I had to stay in this hideous ward where all the premature babies were . . .

**Olivia:** But then you got him home and all was fine. Do you think because you tried so hard for a baby, it's made it better?

**Lydia:** Possibly, yeah. It made me want it even more. I did get lucky too, I realise – he's not a crier, so that helps. Being a mum is what I thought it would be, to be honest. People had given me loads of horror stories – I hate it when people do that – but it really isn't that bad. The thing is, your entire job is to keep this one little person happy and that's a lot easier than work a lot of the time. And it's just getting more fun as time goes on. Thinking about going back to work makes me feel sick. I mean, I'm desperate to get back to life in one respect, but in another I would really like to bring Sonny with me.

I'm filled with fear. Will we have to go to those lengths to get our child? Or be like the girl on her fifth round hearing she's got only two eggs left? HYGGE aren't going to want to hear about pineapple, but maybe they'll start manufacturing voodoo dolls if they think they can make a quick buck out of broody couples desperately in need of a magical intervention who also want it to tie-in with their mid-century aesthetic. Actually, maybe I can pitch that in the next design meeting.

*What have I become?*

# Cycle 22

*AN ODE TO MY PERIOD. Hello again, old friend. I hate you. I hate it when you call. I hate the time, two days out, when I can feel that I am counting down to seeing you again, and it makes me cry. Cry at the loneliness of an elderly lady packing her meal for one with arthritic hands. Cry at the news. Cry at rousing strings, wherever I am, and however badly they're played. I'll drop everything and cry, and know that it's for you. Then, when you're done with my heart, you get into my head. My head throbs for you like a deep longing. It feels heavy and thick, like the fog of remembrance of all the other times you called on me. And, when I think I've had enough, you hit me where it pains the most. My womb. You hurt the most vital part of me. You contort me and stab me, like I've done something terrible to you. When for all those years, I was glad to see you, period. You were a shiny red example of being a woman. You were a sign that all the fun hadn't ended in consequence. You showed me I was still young. But now, I feel you catching up with me. You run me round in circles and make me work to your rhythm. You have me looking over my shoulder, because I know I can't beat you. I hate you, period. I never want to see you again. ---- Or at least not for nine months, anyway.*

149

'WHAT'S ALL THIS?' Felix says. We're sat on the sofa, with the cats on our laps. He shows me his phone – it's a message from Jack. I forgot to tell him he was about to become a fertility surrogate, even though we might need one ourselves.

> **JACK**
> Mate! I hear the girls have been conspiring to get us together 'to talk'. I feel like this fertility bullshit deserves a drink and I've not been out of the house much because I'm extending the map on the game. Fancy a Dalston crawl on Friday?
> 10:15

'Just say yes, all right? Ada needs him to see sense about their baby situation,' I say. 'I know we call him "Jack on smack", but how bad can it be? You two used to be best friends . . .'

'We are!' he says. 'But he's such a caner, I can't keep up any more.' Felix looks genuinely worried for his liver. I'm secretly glad he can't keep up.

'Well, just say you'll go for dinner and then you can talk properly.'

'I'm not going to be able talk any sense into him.'

'No pressure, darling, just plant a seed in his mind.'

'I'll be too out of my mind.'

'Just say you'll go.'

Ada's in even more trouble than me.

Peak Fertility    Happy

'I'M REALLY SORRY TO TELL YOU THIS, but it's that time again.'

'Bedtime?' Felix is acting the wise guy but I can tell already he's not into it tonight. After the day I've had, neither am I, but we need to keep the momentum up.

'Special bedtime,' I say, with a cheeky wink.

'*Already*?' he says, his face crestfallen as if Spurs have just missed a penalty. I know full well that my very sultry scheduled sex reminder would have appeared in his iCal this morning.

'Yes, *already*,' I say, trying to hold back the passive-aggression. 'It happens every month. I don't know how you can't keep track by now . . .' I'm going with *sexy nag*.

'Sorry, they don't do apps for forced fun,' he says.

'You should write that down, it's the best idea you've had in ages.'

'Better than marrying you, that's for sure.' At least he's laughing now.

'Right, I'm getting naked,' I say, unsheathing myself of the stained baggy T-shirt and *slightly* too-tight flannel bottoms. I'm feeling *sexy*.

'Yep, me too.' Felix rocks back and forth like an upside-down tortoise as he removes his pyjamas, then we both throw our discarded items at the foot of the bed, narrowly missing Bret, who hisses before slinking away. This is not for your eyes, cat.

We're getting off to a strong start: he's *almost* standing to attention *almost* immediately.

Skipping the foreplay – because it's 11.45 and I'd rather get seven full hours of sleep than have a good time – we get straight down to it.

'Do you want me to go on top maybe?' I haven't been allowed to go on top since Cornwall, but I always try my hand.

'No, you're fine where you are.' He's enjoying his view of the pillow too much. It's more laboured than usual tonight. He's screwing up his whole face as he chugs away.

'Are you OK, lover?' I say, in my best seductive-but-caring voice, running my hands across his chest.

'Absolutely fine.' He keeps going on his see-saw contrition. I feel him slip a bit.

'Are you sure you're all right?' *Sexy nag.*

'I'm . . . Oh, fuck this.' He slides out of me like a worm, and throws himself back up on his haunches.

'It's fine. Please, don't worry,' I soothe appealingly, placing my hands on his thighs as he jerks away, attempting to restart the ignition, grabbing a boob as if it's a battery.

'Stop it. Just shush.' He's fuming now.

'OK, well you're not having access to these if you can't be cordial . . .' I say, crossing my arms across my chest.

'Liv, stop ruining it,' he says exasperated, still tugging away at the shrinking slug. 'Just be normal.'

*None of this is normal . . .*

'Look,' I say, formally (completely normal then). 'Let's just leave it, shall we? We can start from tomorrow. It won't matter. I mean, it's not like we'll ever have a baby anyway.'

'No!' he says, wounded. 'I'm not giving up! We have to do this! Look, I'm ready.' He folds himself in and begins a half-hearted hump.

'OK, whatever you want . . .' I clasp his shoulders again

to help him stay in place. I'm not going to slow his roll if this is how he wants it to go. We need to get the job done.

He slides out again.

'Fuck.' He shouts, throwing himself down on the pillow next to me.

'It's absolutely fine, baby,' I say, gently kissing his forehead. 'I wasn't feeling it either. And there's always tomorrow.'

As I caress his face, I feel that he's crying.

'Baby, what's wrong? It's really OK.' I say. It's not OK. None of this is OK.

'I can't handle this pressure,' he says, angry now in the darkness. 'It's too much. You need to tell me out loud – I don't look at anything but my work calendar. Seduce me. Do it earlier in the day.'

'How is it always my problem? Why do I have to be the gatekeeper of *our* fertility?'

'Because it's *your* bloody moon cycles or whatever they are . . . and springing it on me can turn me to jelly.'

'It's not jelly, darling, it's more like an uncooked sausage,' I reply, laughing. But he's not laughing with me this time.

---

*To my woman,*

*I wanted to remember how much you turn me on in this very moment, so I'm writing you this note on the flap I've just pulled out of the A to Z. I know that the way I feel about you right now will go on for ever, but if I'm ever selfish in bed, get this note out to remind me that I owe you always for what we just did in the back of our new car. You're the sexiest person in the world and that's why I'm the luckiest man alive. XXX*

---

ORLA IS CALLING ME. It's 10.30 a.m. on a Tuesday and I'm completely surrounded by print-outs of potential store posters. It's like a typo-ridden game of spot the difference and I'm in the zone. Her job might be warding a faintly ridiculous large rich lady round council estate youth clubs, but she's usually pretty respectful of the fact that I have an insurmountable cosy cushion mountain of work on at all times. It could be a pocket-dial, but I should pick it up just in case.

'Liv, I'm at the hospital.' She heaves. I can feel the intensity of her tears down the line.

'Oh god, what's happened? Are you OK? Is it your parents? Where are you? I can come to you?' I get up from my desk, and Rachel shoots me a worried face as I mouth 'got to take this' and move into the meeting room, pulling the glass door closed.

'I think I'm going to have a miscarriage.'

I'm struck dumb as I scroll through the options in my head. How can she be having a miscarriage? She wasn't even pregnant . . .

'Oh Orla, I'm sorry. I didn't know . . . Are you sure?'

I'm reeling, speaking slowly, carefully. *Got to be sensitive.* My scalp is on fire, my breath speeding.

'I only found out four weeks ago, I'm sorry I hadn't told you yet.'

I thought she'd been quiet. I just thought she and Rich were spending some time together.

'That doesn't matter. What matters is whether you're OK?'

I'm bent double by this gut-punch of emotions. I lean my head between my knees. The recovery position for a nosebleed: not the revelation that your confidante no longer confides in you. Well, not until it's too late. The office is gathering in small huddles, wondering in at me.

'I'm at the hospital now, they've not said much but you can see it in their body language that it's bad,' she gasps. 'I'm just waiting for another doctor to give their opinion.'

I feel her fear, but I'm not equipped for the normal soothing. It's her body, but it's unchartered territory for us both. *Selfish Liv. Making it all about you.*

'Take me back to the start . . .' I say, so I can get my footing again. 'When did you find out? I thought you were going for those private tests, and then to the GP to be referred for IVF?' I need to feel my way through.

'I was. They referred me on within the week to have my AMH levels checked and to see if I was ovulating, but when the results came back, something was off, and they called me in and told me I was pregnant. But they said they couldn't tell quite how far along, so they wanted me to come in for a dating scan. I didn't even get to see two lines on a pregnancy test. I'd been waiting for that moment all along, and I didn't even get that.'

That knot in my stomach is twisting and distorting into a tangled web.

'So what happened then? Are you at the hospital on your own? I can come if you want me to, just tell me where?'

I reel through the list of excuses I could call up to escape for the remains of the day.

'It's OK, Liv. Rich is on his way from work, and Mum is just parking her car.' *That was my chance to be there: to act the good friend.* 'The dating scan was about three weeks ago, and that was all fine. So today was the private harmony test. I came in expecting nothing really. I was kind of taken aback that I could actually be pregnant after all that time. But it didn't look good from the beginning. I'd had some spotting. I don't know really – I've never done this before . . .' she breaks off into a wail. 'My boobs were a bit sore, I felt really bloated, but apart from that, it just didn't feel that different.'

'So what happened today?'

I'm fresh out of questions after this. My best friend has spent three bountiful weeks listening to me continuing to fail miserably. I need to listen more. *You're such a bad friend.*

'So they were scanning me, there was a little pulsing, and they said it looked as if I might be about seven weeks along, which didn't make sense, and then the technician got this concerned look on his face. I hadn't even had a second to get excited when he called the consultant in to have a look. And she looked just as worried. But they didn't talk in front of me. So then a nurse comes in and starts to make small talk, probably a distraction thing, while the two of them go out of the room. And then they returned with another doctor, much older, a man with a big grey beard, and he took a look and then he turned to me and said, "I'm so sorry. You are pregnant, but it's not developing as it should"—' She draws breath sharply again, and I wish I could be there to steady her, '— "which might have been the reason for the confusing hormone test and the spotting. And it may well not make it past the next few weeks."

'So now I have to just wait a week to see if it develops, but they're quite certain it's not viable.' The tears begin to trickle down my face as I hear her now in floods. I'm thankful I can hear the clacking of her mum's hurried footsteps along the corridor: help is on the way.

'I'm so sorry, my love, I can't even imagine what you must be going through.' I pause, groping for something positive to offer up. 'But maybe it will be all right? There's still a chance that it'll be fine, right? Are you sure you don't want me to come to you? I could leave work?'

I don't know what I'm talking about, but I can be there in body.

'No, it's OK, thank you though. I'm just going to go home and try to not think about it, not get any hopes up. I've just got a feeling that this is it. This is the way things have worked out after all this trying.'

She sobs, and I sob, although I keep mine silent. Because I know my tears aren't just for her. They're for the fact that I can't even manage to experience this sadness. This could be the moment when I get left behind for good. The only one who can't even fall pregnant at all. The juxtaposition is unbearable. Before, it was always Orla and me in it together. Now it would be me on my own, looking on. I put my iPhone down on the conference table and rest my warm tear-stained face in my palms.

'Liv, are you OK, love?' For once I'm glad to see Rachel.

'It's Orla. She's pregnant, but they think she's going to have a miscarriage.'

I start to cry again, playing the empathetic friend: the person who isn't jealous of suffering.

'I'm sorry to hear that, it's so shit,' she says, putting her arm around me and nestling her six-month bump into my side. It's so comforting. I want to place my hands on it, to warm myself on its two-thirds cooked roundness. Instead, I wring my fingers.

'My cousin had a miscarriage a couple of months ago. It happens so often that's why they tell you not to tell anyone before twelve weeks. But they should. Women need to be together in this.'

Say what you want about Rachel – and plenty do – but you'd always text her in a crisis.

'But what should I say to her, Rachel? What can you say?

157

I feel so off-guard . . . I didn't even . . . She hadn't even told me yet.'

The feelings seep to the surface as I stutter. I wonder if she can read me. I hope Orla can't.

'Well . . .' Rachel's stalling for time: she's ill-prepared for this too. 'All you can do is be there for her. She'll understand that you've not been through it before and don't know what to say. I'm sure she doesn't know what to say.'

'I just, I just can't believe she's pregnant and now it's all going to be taken away after she's tried so hard.'

After I've tried so hard. Life's most hideous leveller.

'Liv, you have to be strong for her. She'll be crumbling, but it's early days and it happens to so many women. Do you want me to go and get you a cup of tea? Or do you want to go for a walk and I'll cover for you?'

Saint Rachel. What is my problem with you?

'Thank you, Rach, you're the best. I really appreciate you being here with me. I don't know why I'm getting upset like this.'

'I think it's completely understandable,' she says slowly. She's been on to me the whole time. 'Orla's your oldest friend. She's like your sister. And it's a shock. Just allow yourself some time to absorb it all.'

And with that, she rises, pats me on the shoulder, and goes back outside, pushing back the masses and taking questions like my hardy pregnant press secretary. I'd promote her if I were Trish.

**I OFFLOAD MY TOTES OF NOTES** on the sofa, and flop beside Felix in a sweaty, tear-marked heap.

'I'm sorry I couldn't talk earlier, Liv, I was in back-to-back meetings, and I knew you needed to offload properly.'

He shouldn't have to drop everything for my best friend's gynaecological issues, or even my stupid insecurities.

'These are for you, to tell you I love you.' He produces a bunch of sunflowers from under the footstool, and kneels down in front of me, kissing my bare knees. My tears flow hot and heavy on to the back of his bowed neck.

'I just adore you, Liv. And I promise that everything will be OK with Orla, no matter what is happening now.'

'But will it be OK with us?' I ask, exhaling deeply. 'This is a sign that she can have a baby. We've had no sign at all . . .' I trail off. I know how bad it sounds. I don't want the love of my life to know how bad a person I really am.

'We'll get a sign too, love. We will, we just have to hold on. And I know this has all been a shock, for Orla, and for what it means for us, but we'll all get through it. Me and the boys are going to look after you,' he says, cuddling my knees as Bret and Jemaine join us on the sofa. Because they're my babies, and they're not going anywhere.

POST-NETFLIX, THE APPLE TV throws up a haunting beam at the foot of the bed, but the room is as black as space. I can't see Felix's face, or hear his breathing.

'Are you still awake?' I whisper.

Nothing. The silence is as empty as the darkness.

'Are you still alive?' I'm louder now.

Nothing. My hand slithers beneath the covers and up inside his scrappy, tea-stained bed T-shirt. Must check for signs of life.

'Gaauuuhhh!' he gasps. He's laid that on thick. He couldn't be that deeply asleep fifteen minutes after we switched off on such a cliff-hanger.

'Do you want to have sex?' I whisper seductively, my face in his like a hot breath-seeking missile.

'Uhhhhggghhhh . . .' A grunt of indecision, or a snore? I snake my hand down into his shorts.

'We *need* to have *sex*. If Orla's pregnant, we need to catch up. And my app says this is the penultimate day and we've only done it once this cycle.' I am entitled, whiny. I know I didn't express the time-sensitivity of the matter directly after *House of Cards* because I couldn't be bothered, but now I have worked up just enough depressed energy to do the deed. He needs to get involved.

'Leave me alone, please. I'm asleep.'

'You're not asleep, you're answering me.'

'I *was* asleep, but you keep making demands.'

'OK, well, now you're awake. And it'll only take five minutes.'

'It never takes five minutes.'

'Oh, it does.' I gently begin to turn my hand in circles, I know this verbal exchange counts as minus pillow talk so I need to counteract it manually.

'All right, but I'm not making any promises as to my performance,' he says, pulling me towards him with a sigh, unbuttoning the unseasonal tartan pyjama shirt that flannels my modesty. I'm making this real easy for him. 'In the meantime, you could at least pretend like you're into it.'

'I *am* into it,' I say, edging into his bulge with my hip to feign participation. And as he clambers sleepily on top of me to perform his sedentary grind to completion, I think: *It's you who's not into it.*

Just been to the doctor . . . It's not good. The scan still showed inconsistencies. They told me it's definitely not viable, so it's not a matter of if but when I'm going to miscarry. Why did this have to happen to me? xxxxxx

Oh darling, I'm so sorry to hear that, you don't deserve this. But you will be fine. This happens to so many women and they get pregnant really soon again afterwards. Don't let it deter you. But I don't want to take away from the pain you must be in. And I hate that you've had so much waiting. Shall I come round at the weekend and we can just hang out in the garden together? Just tell me whatever you need. I can do anything. All my love. xxxxxxxxx

Delivered

**WHERE DO YOU GO** when you most need solace? Who can you run to? As you grow older and people develop lives – proper responsible lives, not just flaky flatshares and weekends lying in Victoria Park – most of your friends don't want to know when you're sad. You'll be lucky if they'll still meet up with you on a Saturday like they used to, let alone go on a weekend break. But your mum: your mum will always make it all right, right? And as I pull into the drive in our old Volvo, and open the door with my old key, the warm familiarity of relief floods over me. I shout up to whoever is pottering about upstairs, my dejected tone warning them of how to receive me.

'I wasn't expecting to see *you* this weekend,' shouts my mother brightly, her legs hurrying to catch up with that loud voice down the stairs.

161

'I felt like I needed a bit of Mum time,' I say, watching the worry cast over her face immediately. She swaddles me in her arms and draws me into the living room.

'What is it that's happened then? Is it Felix? Or work? Are *you* OK?' She's looking at the wrong womb for answers.

'Orla's going to have a miscarriage . . .' I say, quietly, as if to shield my own ears.

'Oh, so she managed to get herself pregnant then?' she says sharply – brazen with bitterness on my behalf. 'I'm sure she's not having a miscarriage. She'll be fine! That one always is.'

She begins to gently plait my hair on the couch, but I pull away and stand up to pace the rug.

'No, Mum, she's been for two scans, and they've said that it's early days but it's not viable.'

'Sure, Liv, I can't help but feel that people know too much too early these days. I mean how pregnant is she? Had you known about it for a while? How come you didn't tell me?'

'She hadn't told me,' I say through gritted teeth. 'The first I heard, she was at the early pregnancy unit getting bad news.'

'Well, there she is, keeping news from you. What about you, eh? Has anyone stopped to think about you in this?'

'It's not about me though, is it, Mum?' I say. 'I'm fine. Nothing's happening to me—'

'Well, *exactly*. That nothing is something. I see you, avoiding it. You're not owning up to it. I can see it in your eyes. You know I know you better than anyone else.'

'I'm sure Felix would beg to differ,' I say raising a tired smile.

'Did you pop out of Felix's stomach like an eight-pound beach ball? No! I get to know you the best. You're my baby. You're part of me. And I have to think about you in this. Just you and your happiness. And I can see that you're not . . .'

Here come the floods.

She wraps me up in her arms again, and bundles me on to the sofa. I'm like a distressed sea lion lately, flopping and crying, flopping and crying. Never clapping, only able to drench my flabby face and body by turning the sprinklers on again. Not fit for my usual performance of *everything is fine.*

'Do you think it's time to speak to someone, Liv? Have you not thought about it? I know IVF is harsh, but maybe it's time?'

Always time. Time is ticking. Time you got a move on, Liv. Time you stopped drinking. Time you thought about yourself instead of your best friend who needs your attention. Time to be selfish. Time to not be selfish. Time to be a mother.

'I've been doing the research,' I say, because all this has made me laser-focused on what I need to do. 'I've got to go to the GP first and then they'll run some tests and refer us. We're still young in the scheme of things though. They give IVF to you on the NHS until you're forty-two. We've still got time.'

'Well I think there's no time like the present,' Mum says. 'I've got a doctor's details from one of the regulars whose daughter has just had a baby.' They must keep little tallies behind the bar, no wonder she's keen for me to get a move on, I'm letting the side down.

'This guy is *the* man to see in London. Their whole family are doctors so they *must* know. Make sure you get an appointment. I'll give you the number.' She goes through her phone decisively. 'Make sure you write it down and call him immediately.'

'But I can't do that on the NHS,' I say with certainty

'He takes a certain number of NHS patients. Let's make sure you're one of them.'

'Mum, I came here to talk about Orla,' I say. 'And all we're speaking about is me. What should I say to her?'

'Tell her it happens,' she says seriously, commiserating now. 'And that she'll be fine. She'll be pregnant within a month again once she's back on her feet, you mark my words. She's got the money, so she'll just make it happen.'

'But you always say your health is your wealth,' I say sorrowfully. 'And she doesn't have that right now.'

'But you can always buy a bit of health with your wealth in the end.'

'HULLO, SILVER HORSE MEDICAL PRACTICE, how can I help you?'

'Hi, I'd like to make an appointment with the GP . . .'

'Is it urgent?'

'Well, it's been two years, so I guess it could wait? It's for a fertility referral?'

'So non-urgent then . . .'

*It feels pretty urgent now.*

'OK, so how long is the wait for a non-urgent appointment?'

'If you could just give me your date of birth first . . . And then I can check.'

'Twenty-first of November 1983.'

'Oh, well it might be more urgent than we thought.' [laughs]

'Right . . .' [seethes]

'We've actually got something with Dr Manjeet on Thursday at 3 p.m.?'

'I work in central London, actually, so do you have an early or a late appointment?'

'How about 11 a.m. on the tenth?'

'That's not really *early* though, is it?'

'Four forty-five on the thirteenth?'

'Again, I'd need to take a half day. When's the first spot before nine o'clock?'

'That'll be the twenty-second of August. So three weeks from now.'

'I guess I'll take that then.'

'OK, all booked for you Mrs Gy—, Mrs G—, that's all booked for you, Olivia.'

'Thank you. Bye.'

*Another month gone.*

Exhausted

Sad

**THE SHEETS ARE DRENCHED WITH SWEAT** when I wake and yet I don't want to untangle myself. I look over at my phone and see a message from Orla confirming the worst.

Orla
Today 08:15

Well, it's definitely happening. I started bleeding heavily this morning. So that's the end of it. xxxx

That's the end of it. Anguished, I extricate myself from the safety of bed, and throw myself up into the bedroom's dead

165

air, moving slowly through it like hot water. I open the windows and suck in what I can of the outside freshness. It's so still, so calm. The clatter of a child on its bike echoes up the street, amplified by the haze. I pick out a simple dark sundress, a kind of mourning garb, so Orla won't feel mocked by pristine white. I pull my hair back into a hair band and wash my face free of the remnants of smudged mascara from yesterday's tears. Today, I am strong for her. *Today you stop thinking about yourself for once.*

I've got a basket of everything I could think of to help: a pretty jewel-coloured box of chocolates, prosecco, a plastic ice-cube tray shaped like fat owls, a tub of pralines and cream Haagen Dazs (quickly melting), a grab bag of Wispa bites in case the Prestats seem a bit ostentatious for a Saturday afternoon, a fluffy bunny toy I saw all on his own, clearly left over from Easter, who seemed to sum up the mood with his floppy ears, a pair of comedy sunglasses in the shape of pineapples, and a pair of thick socks, because they seem like a care necessity despite the summer heat. I've also made ten playlists for every conceivable mood we might be in and scoured multiple streaming services to pick out laugh/cry movies and shows we could watch (*Beaches, Steel Magnolias, Gilmore Girls, The OC, Parks and Rec, Four Weddings and a Funeral* plus our favourite, *Love Story*). I've essentially packed for the oddest girls' holiday of all time.

I arrive to see Rich pulling out of the drive absent-mindedly ignoring my hello from the hand-wound window of the Volvo, his golf clubs tucked in the back of their posh Audi. He speeds off before I can tell him how sorry I am. *How sorry are you?*

My knocks grow progressively harder until I have no

choice but to buzz. Will its shrillness perforate a bittersweet moment and become a trigger? I'm second-guessing every decision. Should I sweep her into a hug and hold her so she can soak my bare shoulder with angry grief? Or should I be light for her, provide a distraction? I finally see a figure speckled behind the grand door's ornate glasswork and I take a deep breath as it's pulled open to find her greeting me as normally as she would any other day. She's wearing a slouchy white T-shirt and indigo denim cut-offs, and her blonde hair is in a messy bun on top of her head. She looks perfect, calm. My eye is drawn to the dainty platinum chain with precious stones along its length that sits loosely on her tanned chest, then I look down at my frumpy seventies pinafore and feel foolish in my austerity.

'Have you been here long, Liv? People will think you're a Jehovah's Witness I'm trying to ignore.'

She smiles, taking off her mirrored aviators and pulling me into a hug. I search her eyes for a tip on how to react, but her face is so calm it melts me like the hot tarmac, sticking me to the spot. 'I was out in the garden with the music on so I couldn't hear . . .'

As we pass through the large expensive cream kitchen and out of the big French doors into their wild garden, she's set out two loungers with dark green cushions under the linen parasol for us. Magic FM is playing softly in the background. Pop from when we were kids is for mums now. The smell of barbecue wafts over from the next garden.

'Let me get you a drink,' she offers, the hostess on auto-pilot. 'I've got some rosé open. Or maybe you'd like a lolly? It seems like lolly weather . . .' It's then that I catch sight of what it is that's happening. The motions she's going through. The making it comfortable for me. The numbness.

I drop the basket on the grass and move towards her, to hold her, to be with her in the blunted pain, but she senses me and steps back. The distance between us as I drop my arms by my sides is the length of a school ruler, but it feels like miles.

'I'll take a lolly,' I say, checking my emotions to neutral and taking my place on the fresh lounger. I scrabble to retrieve the embarrassment of shitness that has fallen out of my basket and all over her lawn.

'I've brought you some things. Just silly stuff, but it felt like a day for presents,' I begin passing some of it up to her. 'Some of it needs to go in the fridge, shall I come and help you?'

'Oh, it's OK, I'll take it,' she says, prising the basket handle from between my insistent fingers. 'Do you want to wear these, if you haven't brought any others?' She hands me the pineapple glasses blankly, and then retreats back into the kitchen with everything else.

I put them on, and it is all yellow.

I won't follow. I know that's not what she wants. She doesn't see the distance and the separation. She doesn't need to care. I just have to linger here on the periphery until I'm needed. And if I'm not needed, then I was here.

'I love your necklace,' I start, as she returns to me with a tray of rosé, glasses and Fabs laid out like a gourmet platter. 'Is it new?'

'Rich bought it for me yesterday,' she says. *You were supposed to stay on the periphery.* 'He said he would have bought me diamonds . . . A push present, or whatever they call it . . .' She's floating serenely above the pain. 'But he said I deserved something now. Something beautiful to remind me of this and of all the chances there will still be.'

She plays with one of the jewels, amethyst maybe, as she looks out calmly across the garden.

A tear starts its path from my left eye, and I blink hard to try and catch it. I'm thankful for the protection of the ridiculous pineapples. Better to be a clown now than a snivelling wreck in the face of such strength.

Orla brings up her lithe legs and reclines on her lounger, taking a deep breath, and bringing her sunglasses back down over her face. I lie down next to her and think about taking my lolly, which is now becoming a package of multi-coloured mush, but instead I reach for her hand across the mini table. She takes it. At the same time, her other hand reaches to clutch her stomach. I squeeze her hand softly, and she squeezes it back harder. I can't tell if she's feeling something, or remembering it.

And so we just lie here. Holding hands. Not communicating apart from the intermittent squeeze of fingers. The radio continues to waft our childhood over us like a distant dream. She searches the sky, I stay still and shut my eyes under the pineapples and think about what I could say, and whether I'm going to have oddly shaped sunburn because I haven't put on any suntan lotion.

*Always about you, Liv.*

# Cycle 23

'AND YOU'VE BEEN TRYING FOR *HOW LONG?*' Dr Manjeet couldn't put more emphasis on that '*how long*' if she'd cleared the chairs in her frugal office to perform an interpretative dance of just how empty my womb is. She's basically massaging Felix, purring that he's 'so strong and healthy' and playfully prodding him with a tongue compressor. *I'll compress your tongue.* With me though, she's as austere as the surgery's peeling Georgian walls (budget for redecoration well and truly Brexited). She's only about three years older than us – and wearing a tight dress, I noted with a 'right on, doctor' upon entry – but she might as well be a pensioner with her tiny glasses balanced on her pointy nose. *I hope I don't look that geriatric when I flirt.*

'So, Mr and Mrs Gyamfi, just to give you an overview: by a year, 85 per cent of couples will be pregnant. At the two-year point – where you are now and at your age – most people have been successful.' That positive reinforcement works a charm. 'So, we need to do some examinations into what's going on.'

Felix and I nod in the right places as she reels through details of blood tests and scans. All but one is for me. My palm is clammy as he leans to squeeze it.

'We're doing the right thing, we just can't ignore it any

more,' Felix reassured me, *himself*, into the mirror as we brushed our teeth last night. But now, hearing the numbers – 59 per cent conceive in three cycles, one third get pregnant in the first month they try, I want to scream 'why did we have to be the 10 per centers?' at her pointy face. I preferred our pre-facts world.

'So,' she smiles at Felix, thinning her lips as she glances to me, 'are you having enough sex?'

We look to each other in mock horror. How much is enough?

There were months after the wedding – both of us changing jobs, coming to terms with the suburban future stretched out ahead of us, the expectation of coming off the Pill – when the sex elephant loomed large in every room. But we got it back. We're back. Right?

'Yes, absolutely enough sex . . .' Felix jumps in. He's convincing. *Does he think this is enough?*

'So, that's every second day, for the whole month? Dr Manjeet probes.

'That's *a lot of sex* you must be having, Dr Manjeet . . .' I laugh, my eyebrows reaching for the sky. I'm becoming my mum, even if I can't become one. 'At least twice a week, yes . . .' I add, to bring it back to serious medical endeavours. Must try harder.

'Listen, that's one thing that *you're* going to need to look at,' she's looking directly at me. 'It might sound unrealistic, but you need to do it a lot to make a baby.' *Blame.* 'It should be fun, anyway, right?' she jokes, tapping Felix playfully on the knee with the tongue prodder as he laughs, not even looking near me.

'Also, how are your *stress* levels?' Dr Mindfulness, back with that killer emphasis again.

'I think it's fair to say we're both pretty stressed,' I answer for both of us.

'I reckon I'm all right, really.' *Felix, you traitor.* 'But Olivia has always got a lot on.'

She's gone from GP to divorce counsellor in one question.

'I worry my stress may be affecting things.' I say. 'I stress about stress!'

*What a cliché you are.*

'Well it's something you need to look at, Mrs Gyamfi. If you want a child, you have to look at your priorities.' *Blame.* 'Do you smoke?'

'Nope,' both of us chirp smugly.

'And how much do you drink?'

'Not too much, maybe once a week,' I say, keeping back the *amount* I put away.

'Well, you need to stop drinking, now,' she replies, typing on to her screen.

Mum's in my ear: *vindication, at last.*

'I'm writing it in your notes. You are no longer drinkers.'

Should I explain my teehalfism? Dr Manjeet probably doesn't do much social drinking (too busy seducing patients' husbands), but she might enjoy it as a new medical method?

'So what's next?' I'm keen to move it along now. We had a single 8.30 a.m. appointment between the two of us, but there are no windows so I've lost track of time. It feels like we've been in here as long as we've been trying.

'So, we'll refer you for the bloods and the scan to see if your hormones are working and your womb and ovaries are in decent shape. And for Felix, we'll have to do that swimmers' test sometime before you get your results back. Then you can come in and see me again.' Felix looks concerned that his junior ten-lengths badge might not hold up to inspection in 2017.

'She wants your sperm in a cup, darling . . .' I say, squeezing his now-clammy hand.

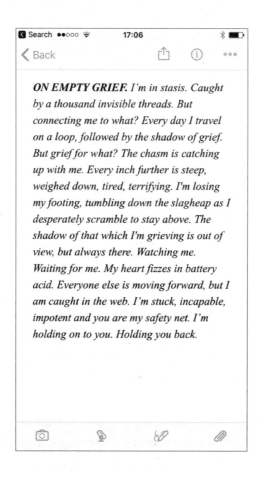

*ON EMPTY GRIEF. I'm in stasis. Caught by a thousand invisible threads. But connecting me to what? Every day I travel on a loop, followed by the shadow of grief. But grief for what? The chasm is catching up with me. Every inch further is steep, weighed down, tired, terrifying. I'm losing my footing, tumbling down the slagheap as I desperately scramble to stay above. The shadow of that which I'm grieving is out of view, but always there. Watching me. Waiting for me. My heart fizzes in battery acid. Everyone else is moving forward, but I am caught in the web. I'm stuck, incapable, impotent and you are my safety net. I'm holding on to you. Holding you back.*

Hey, how are you? Feels like we haven't spoken in ages. What's going on at work? Jemima still being an irritant? How are you feeling? I've just been to the doctor, and we've got a referral to see what's going on. One of the scans is next week. It's scary, but it's good to face up to it I guess? Miss you. Lots of love xxx

Orla doesn't need to hear my shit, does she? DELETE.

**I AM NOW IN DENIAL.** Not about my life, just in denial of its simple pleasures. I have not drunk for a month. I'm buoyed about making positive strides for myself. I can make this baby happen with chia pots, steaming pho and YouTube yoga. 'Your health is your wealth,' repeats Mum in my head.

Lean and serene, and with a seven-quid cold pressed kale juice, I'm ready to take on the day – until I get to my desk to find what looks to be Mads's battered leather jacket lobbed over the back of my chair.

I consider taking my normal place and then nestling back to let it imprint me with his musky scent (before he wrenched it from beneath me to march me to HR). Instead, I prod it with one finger so it's left hanging precariously off the furthest left corner of the chair and flip my hair across the shoulder of my chair to reclaim my territory.

'Oh, *apologies*, Ms Galvin, am I in your way?' I hear as he saunters leonine from the conference room. *Don't move to him, Liv.* I swivel just a semi-circle, leaving my straw purposefully hanging from my lips. Green slime is always such a turn on.

'Mr Rasmussen. Did you not see enough of me in Paris?'

I smile, my best *imagine what else you could have seen* smile. *Imagine what else I could have seen.*

'Ha. You were too good for us, eh?' he says haughtily, flipping that strand of hair off his forehead to reveal that pale bit of under-bicep again. Then he pauses a beat – almost as imperceptible as a hummingbird's wings – before leaning across me to turn my chair towards him with one tanned, perfectly roughed-up hand. I put down the green juice in shock, steadying my elbows on the cold arms of my chair. Slowly – time is elastic again – he bends forward until I can feel his hot breath on my face, then runs his fingers back through the sides of my long hair. 'You were too good for me?' he says quietly, taking me by the sides of the head and kissing my open, disbelieving mouth deeply, one knee between my legs so the whole chair rocks back.

'Olivia?'

I come to and he's standing just where he was, holding his jacket (not my pathetic head), having grabbed it off the corner of my chair.

'You glazed over there.'

Is that a *concerned* look on his face?

' . . . drink some more of whatever that concoction is,' he laughs (at me). 'I don't want you fainting when I'm the only one here to witness it.'

'I had a family emergency, which is why I had to make a run for it,' I reply hastily, taking a big slurp to compose myself, knowing full well *he knows*. And it's then, just as I smile a broad, patently lustful smile as he retreats back to his glass enclosure with his leather jacket slung over that faultless muscular shoulder, that I realise I have kale between my two front teeth.

Peak Fertility   High Sex Drive

FELIX HAS JUST LEFT FOR A LADS' DAY, so I'm starting off the morning with restorative Pilates. As I lay the mat out on the living-room floor, drawing the curtains so the neighbours don't catch sight of my Lycra-clad arse lolling around, and flip through YouTube on my phone, I catch sight of my yoga roller in the corner. Pink and thick and solid. Proud even. *Mads.*

I'm on my back, and draw the foam sausage towards me, under my knees. *You're ridiculous, Liv.* I knew this move would open my skeleton up, but as I roll its dense heft beneath my calves, and feel the solidness pressing into the back of my thighs, I can feel the tenseness build. My mind's telling me no, but I flip my phone to Private and 'Pilates sessions' becomes 'sexy Scandis fucking'. Yesterday's chair incident plays over and over and I'm dizzy as I spin in my chair and squirm against the knee wedged between my legs. Just the sight of one bare Danish arm and I'm gone, so when I find a guy on Tumblr who looks just like him – he may have an additional moustache, which I enjoy, hair slicked back with just that single tendril falling into his eyes, biceps bulging as he does a girl from behind – I'm almost too afraid to watch it dipping in and out for fear that pseudo-Mads's cock might not live up to my expectations. Mesmerised by the motion, looped on a never-ending filthy GIF, it's largely irrelevant what it looks like (could be a troll's toadstool, I'd still have a go) and I'm done in two minutes, legs frogged on the living-room floor.

It's only when a WhatsApp from Felix takes moustachio-Mads's head off, leaving him jabbing unstoppably underneath, that the guilt really sets in.

> **Felix**
> Just got here. Everyone's brought their
> babies.                                          11:16

His worst nightmare made real: everyone's babies but ours.

> Oh, the twats! Where are you?   11:16

> I thought it was a festival . . . It's a bloody baby
> rave. The only gurners are toddlers teething. I
> could see that a lot of the people heading in my
> direction had buggies and whatnot, but I just
> thought at some point we'd diverge and I'd see a
> queue of wankers in wellies (and breathe a sigh
> of relief). People are dismounting buggies at
> the bit where you used to have your alcohol
> confiscated. How is *everyone* in the world so
> fertile? I'm so sick of feeling inferior to even the
> lamest twats.                                    11:18

WhatsApp is now WhatsWrong.

> Bloody Liam can't be trusted . . . Maybe
> the baby ravers will go in a bit?     11:18

177

These buggers are in for the long haul. They've got picnics and ear shields and they're changing nappies in the middle of the dance floor. The DJ just mixed Diplo with 'Wheels on the Bus'. It's like a war zone. I'm going to go live in a treehouse for a while, I can't do this any more. My friends are no longer human, they're just walking, talking dad machines and I literally want to cry. They said this was a lads' day, and there are five adults and six children between us. I've been handed Huck as my personal ward. He's pretty cute and is keeping my chest warm, but it's lucky I didn't take anything on the train in anticipation . . .                    11:20

Shall I call round all your players to see if they'll come down and party with you? Or I could hire a DJ to play EDM at a volume unsuitable for children on a mini stage in the next field? I have to go and pick curtains with Mum, otherwise I'd be straight round the M25 with the banging techno to whip you off to an illegal rave. Except twenty-somethings don't do raves now, do they? So you're actually probably in the most sociable place anyway. What about if you just tried to enjoy yourself with your friends? You need to practise your dad dancing. Maybe it will free up your sperm if you lose all sight of rhythm and co-ordination. Did you buy some beers even though I asked you not to drink?                    11:21

Yes. Sorry . . .  11:22

Just drink them, have a little dance with Huck, put some pictures up on Instagram, get lots of likes because you're hot and he's cute, and then come home and impregnate me so we can join in. And make sure to get some incriminating video of Liam so he can go viral as payback for what he did to me. xxx
11:23

'NO NO, NO NO NO NO, No No No No, No No, THERE'S NO LIMITS!' Felix and I have rolled the shagpile up to have a living-room dance party, because there was nothing in our diaries, there's nothing on the Sky Q planner, and neither of us is in the mood to watch a documentary on Netflix, even though we know we should really. And because yesterday's 'rave' was such a baby bore out. So we shall dance and dance, until a parent calls and interrupts.

'You know,' I say breathlessly between arm flails, 'I never noticed 2Unlimited was grammatically incorrect . . .'

'What do you mean, with all the noes?' Felix is getting low with some lunges – this is actually the most decent workout I've had in about six months.

'It should be "THERE ARE NO LIMITS!"' I say, proud of myself for dissecting the poor Dutch translation.

'I think it's "no limit" singular, love,' says Felix.

'No, it's multiple limits. Like the limits on us: work, parents, baby nonsense, money . . .'

'I don't want to think about that,' he says, changing the channel. 'We're dancing!'

Kate Bush comes on, and I instantly burst into an interpretive play on 'Babushka', wind-milling my arms wildly and fanning my hands in front of my face.

'You're never sexier than when you're doing a bit of Bush,' Felix laughs, kissing me then plonking himself back on the sofa to make this the most unconventionally over the top, over-clothed lap-dance. *Maybe I'll buy that chain-mail bikini, give him a real surprise one day.*

Tonight though, the body underneath this tracksuit will have to suffice and I straddle Felix on the sofa, out of breath from the exertion of the eighties swaying in my grey marl; this beautiful seduction. I kiss him, pulling his hands on to my body by way of invitation. I peel away my white vest, pushing his face down into my Calvin Klein crop top cleavage. He comes up for air and in his eyes I see a haze of 'do we have to?' as I plunge him back again. *Get turned on. Do what you need to do. Don't waste this chance.* When we bought it five years ago, I worried this sofa would splinter like matchwood, we'd ridden it in so many different ways. Now I'm willing him to give me permission to relive the memory, one last time.

'Shall we take this upstairs?' he says, patting my joggered-bottom to jump off.

'I thought we could show the sofa a good time,' I say, coquettishly hopeful.

'It'll put me off my stride,' he says. 'And isn't it better for biology if we're horizontal?

I sit back on my haunches, offended then resigned, and swing my leg so he can turnstyle out of the awkwardness. He leads me up to bed, and I lie back in my sports bra and let him do what he needs to do.

**The Baby**
*Nightmare*

MY RECURRING DREAM. There's a baby. It's so small, and far out of reach. I am trying to look after it, but over and over again, people – Mum, Orla, Dr Manjeet, Trish, Rachel – keep taking it out of my hands. When I do finally grab my baby (I think it is mine, judging from the primal urge I have in trying to protect it) I peel back layers and layers of swaddling, until the baby fits neatly in the palm of my hand. And when I see its face cooing up at me, it is Mads.

**THE WALLS ARE PAPERED** with pamphlets. Baby pamphlets.

I get it, most people walk out of this ward with one eventually – a baby, not a pamphlet – but as I sit here, swinging my feet unable to speak to Felix beside me, I wonder if we'll get that walk. A breast-feeding instructional video loops loudly on a flat-screen in the corner. Latching looks tricky. Even trickier without a baby. Or with the tiny one from my dream.

'Are you OK, baby?' That word again. Felix puts his hand to the side of my face to angle me towards him, his face clouded with concern. I pull away. This is not the bit where I cry.

'Oh yep, nothing to worry about. Not nervous at all. Dr Google has given me extensive reassurance that the trah-hans-vagi-hinal ultrasound doesn't hurt a bit.' I hope my falsetto reassures him, even if it hasn't reassured me. A heavily expectant woman pacing the waiting room looks at me like I'm an imbecilic child. My stomach is as rounded as hers as I attempt to keep my bladder intact. I should have read the instructions ahead of the appointment, rather than realising it needed to be full when I arrived, then mainlining two large Capri Suns in fear. I can't be held accountable if I lose control on the table.

'Olivia Gyamfi?' The tired nurse in tired shoes lingers impatiently as I give Felix one last peck before meeting my destiny at the hands of the probe.

'Now the point of the transvaginal ultrasound' (I'm sing-song-ing 'trah-hans-vagi-hinal' with the sonographer in my head to distract myself) 'is to check that everything is looking as it should be in your ovaries, your tubes and your uterus. But first we'll do a normal external ultrasound to see how your womb looks.'

He's not much older than me; one of those hairy men who look embarrassed at their own existence (and body odour). But it's a dark room, I'm shrouded in paper and he must do this at least ten times a day, so he needn't be coy. I point my nose towards the ultrasound monitor. As I feel him squeeze the gel on to my stomach, and start rolling the thing – the transducer, he explains – around to find the spot, I realise I've seen this image before. The glee at the spread of the gelee. The first pick-up of that magical light on the screen above the bed. The pulsating sound. In the movies, there's always a flicker of life.

I baulk at how black and empty it looks. The screen stays

blank. My unfilled womb. The nurse is acting as notary for the occasion, jotting down just how vacant it is.

'This all looks fine and normal. No scar tissue, all seems to be the right shape. Now, we need to see inside at your ovaries. So I am going to insert this sheathed probe' – he raises a white stick attached to a lead, covered by a flaccid condom – 'inside your vagina.' *Vah-gih-na-ha*.

'Would you like to place the probe?' he asks considerately, as if he's asking if I'd like to order my lunch first. I'm sat with a paper skirt around my bottomless body, knees up, womb empty, so what fresh embarrassment could shoving a shrivelled dildo inside myself in front of two medical practitioners cause me?

'Sure, give it here.' I say, angling it in with one sexy slide; then he takes control of its road. The picture slithers through my insides, even though it's gone no further than two or three inches deep. Just the tip.

'You're doing very well, Mrs Gyamfi. We've got the cervix there, and the uterus, which we just saw looking healthy and spacious' – *blank space* – 'and now we're heading up to see the fallopian tubes. Those are your eggs there on the screen.'

And then: 'Left ovary looking a little polycystic', he circles the probe, clicking buttons to zoom in and snapshot measurements. 'One point five by three,' he calls to the nurse. 'Right looks nice and healthy though.' *One looks nice and healthy though.* Which means one does not. I zone out as he continues his topography of my barren landscape. 'We'll share the results with your doctor and that's you done.'

'I'm just pleased I didn't wet myself,' I joke to the room, now sterile and cold. The notary nurse looks at me like the heavily pregnant woman did: no self-control. *They shouldn't swaddle you in toilet roll if they don't want you to immediately relieve yourself.*

I pull on my jeans behind the blue curtain, and leave the crumpled paper mass, sticky with gel on the bed. Why is bottomless nudity always the most conspicuous kind? Felix is waiting, glued to Twitter, modesty intact, as it will always be. The only time he has to vaguely debase himself is when he's forced to take a perfunctory wank in a weird room and make sure he successfully aims at the cup— and even if he does miss, there won't be two people in scrubs in the corner examining his methods.

'All OK, darling?' he asks, barely even looking up from the football chat.

'I think so . . .' I say.

*Left ovary, you scoundrel. So it's all your fault?*

Sad

Felix
Today 9.23

Sperm safely deposited! I 'did my sample' (sexy) twenty minutes before the appointment, then jumped in a cab up to the hospital. I kept it in my pocket for warmth like you told me to, although it's boiling today, so they probably got a bit baked. At least I didn't have to have a danger wank in the hospital toilet! I thought of you while I was producing them! Xxxx

I'm sure Emily Ratajkowski lent a hand. *At least they weren't real hands on his face.*

'DO YOU WANT TO HAVE SEX TONIGHT?' Felix rarely does the initiating, but we've enjoyed a rare posh dinner out and we're spending tomorrow together – at a christening, but never mind – so perhaps he's feeling amorous.

'I mean, we don't *have* to, it's day eighteen, but I mean, we *could . . .?*'

Everyone remembers the first time they had sex with the person they love. It might be jumbled with all the other make-ups and slow-steadies, and risky bits as the months turn to years, and lust turns to love, and the security turns to boredom. But you can usually picture the first time vividly.

We were both living with our parents then. I'd been made redundant, which was not the making of me (as a lot of people who have never been *redundant* are so keen to tell you), it just meant I had to bail on my Shoreditch flatshare, while Ada and Margot swapped me for a stand-in who smelled of mildew. But then came Felix.

After the hospitalisation, there were drinks, and after that night, I figured I should keep him waiting, (although I nearly wept with frustration). After the next date I rang him as soon as I got back and we had phone sex – very quietly so we didn't wake our parents – which I had never done before, or indeed since. By the third meeting, at a pub in Soho, we were virtually undressing each other in the darkest corner we could find. I wasn't even halfway through my gin and tonic when I stood up and took his hand, a wicked look in my eye (which may have just looked like a squint).

'Do you want to have sex tonight?' I said, because I was subtle like that. Felix's eyes were a bit loopy with lust. He'd clearly wanted it ever since he saw my chicken costume.

'I mean we *could*?' He was still cautious. I'd lost the neck brace, but to him I was now some rare species to be handled with care. But he'd have to sully me eventually. 'It's not like it's private?' he said, looking around at the packed tables.

'I'm not going to ride you like a pony in front of the diners,' I snorted, smiling at a table of fifty-year-olds enjoying their gambas pil pil. Standing up and wriggling my skirt down – from where he'd rucked it up trying to get into my knickers covertly on the couch – I pulled him down to the only place I knew would be dark, private and would only smell *slightly* of sick. We did it up against the door, perched on the sink, even on the toilet. By the time we emerged, we'd agreed on him getting a flatshare immediately so we could reprise such activities in the comfort of somewhere not splattered with piss, or with a queue of angry-bladdered punters tutting at us.

Now, the only people wishing we'd '*get it over with already*' are us.

## Christening Gift Registry

| | | Add to basket |
|---|---|---|
| Bunnygirl medium hamper | £150 | |
| MAMA'S LITTLE #GIRLBOSS slinky sleep suit | £45 | |
| Rose gold-plated baby cup | £60 | |
| Gold lurex sleep cocoon | £100 | |
| Armani baby bottle | £30 | |
| Astrology playmat (in mystic moondust colourway) | £100 | |
| Hand-sewn cashmere baby blanket | £125 | |

'THEY REALLY DO HAVE SOME NERVE,' I say, as we enter the baby department of Selfridges. 'Having a registry for a christening takes the piss, but having it here . . .' I run my fingers through a stack of cashmere blankets to swaddle newborns. 'They're just laughing at us. In our faces. Our poor penniless faces.'

'They are not laughing at us,' says Felix. 'They're laughing *with* us. They've just got a lot of rich workmates who look down their noses at M&S. Luke told me they're only having it here to get as much as he can out of his bosses. He said we don't need to buy Esteri anything because we're the godparents. If they die, we're going to have to put her through university.'

'We're only godparents because we don't have one of our own.'

'It's *because* Luke is one of my best friends,' he says, trying his hand at rolling a white brocade Versace pushchair, the assistant eyeing him like he's hotwiring her car in his best suit.

'Well, we are not *not* giving our godchild a gift,' I say.

'Make up your mind, woman. It's either too much and an imposition, or it's not.' He unhands the buggy when he spots the £2,700 price tag hanging like a golden albatross on its handle.

'Oh, don't get me twisted: it is an imposition, and it is too much,' I say, guiding him back round to the gifts via my saucy demonstration of two breast pumps against my emerald vintage midi dress. 'But there is no way we're going empty-handed to a party full of bankers and brokers. It doesn't matter how empty our current accounts are.'

'And empty they are. We're going to have to put this across two cards and possibly the dregs of my Paypal,' says Felix. 'Trust them to do it the weekend before payday.'

He's unfolding the most darling 0–3 months Kenzo sweat-shirt next to the pregnant twenty-five-year-old wife of a paunchy, Rolex-ed fifty-something. *Do I wish I was her?*

'Trust us to leave buying the present until the morning of the christening . . .' I say. 'Now what's the cheapest thing in here?'

**I STAND AT THE END OF THE GARDEN,** hiding from the sun and waiting for Orla to pick up. I need to be out of earshot in case I say something I might regret in front of Felix after the christening yesterday.

'Hello?' she answers, crackling like she's in the Bermuda Triangle.

'Hey! How are you?' We've hardly talked since it happened. I've missed her.

'I'm just on my way back from bloody Beth's. It's going to take me like seven hours on the train.'

'Where is it she's moved to again?'

'Deepest Surrey . . . I mean, I know I basically live in the country, but I work in London and at least I can see some wildlife from my windows. Also, if you're going to move to the sticks, pick somewhere with some character! She's got this hideous eighties build on a main road. And yet the Facebook posts are all gloats about the gravel drive and the leafy view . . .'

'Maybe she Airbnb-ed a house for the pictures . . .'

'There was a definite heritage bullshit feel to what she put up there.' Orla laughs uproariously. 'The only heritage is hand-me-down Argos.'

'Could be worse, could have been HYGGE.' I laugh. 'How was the baby?'

'The "Darling Daughter"? Oh, Sophia's exceptionally cute

with her little chubby cheeks. I usually love them when they're that age. But now it just makes me want to cry.'

'Oh love, I'm sorry.'

*You never think before you speak . . .*

'It's fine, I was too incensed by Beth's behaviour anyway. As soon as I walked in the door, I hadn't even handed over the presents – I never got a thank you by the way – before she'd dumped a load of shit on me about how hard it's been the last few months. The sleepless nights. The NCT mothers. But it's all just one long humblebrag. "I'm so tired, but Sophia is such a dream baby, she feeds then goes straight back down." "The NCT mothers are such a drag, but it's so nice to get away from Londoners and their constant pushiness." "Doing the house renovation has been so draining, but we've made a hundred and fifty K already." Unbearable! Know your audience, woman.'

'Speaking of knowing your audiences *and* baby presents – we had to smash and grab our way round Selfridges yesterday for Luke and Azi's baby's christening. I know we're godparents, but it cost us two hundred pounds!'

'Ugh.' Orla *sounds* disgusted, but she'd freely admit that her taste is more Selfridges than Mothercare.

'And when we got there, all the rich gits from their work had just bought them stuff from John Lewis. We're fools for ourselves.'

'You're good friends and they know that too, or else you wouldn't be godparents,' Orla chips in, still cracking up.

'So what did Beth do then?'

'She got "the DD" out of her bouncer – and she's all cooing and lovely – but then suddenly Beth kind of zones out. She handed her to me and basically went into a cata-tonic slump. I wonder if she's handling it all as well as she

189

makes out. Or even at all. I mean, I know she's five months along now, but have some sugar or something.'

'Oooh . . .' I am listening.

'So I take the baby – well, she's quite a big girl now, more like a five-year-old in weight – out to the garden, and leave Beth there having a nap. I mean, it's taking the piss to invite me up and then fall asleep when I'd only been there for an hour. I even had to make my own cup of tea.'

'So did she get back up?'

'Well, no . . . Then about an hour later, Pete came back from work – he was going on about his stupid sit-on lawn-mower, the tiresome bore – and she suddenly perked up and went back to normal. It's like she reserves her shittest self just for me. I'm not going up there any more. She doesn't ask anything about me. And then when I *volunteered* about the miscarriage, she was just like "Aww, that's a shame. But it'll happen again soon, just keep trying." It's a mix of pity and giving zero shits.'

'The magic combination. *Shity.*'

'Sophia is lovely though – bit inactive, lucky they're cute when they've got little chub rolls on their legs. I guess you can't run around after them when you get pregnant immediately after having a baby.'

The bitter weight of Orla's words hang around us.

'Imagine double babying.'

'We'll be lucky if we get one between the two of us.'

'I'm happy to share if you are. Maybe me and Felix can just move in below stairs at yours and we can start a commune.'

'Rich's at work all hours and Felix is away so much that it would just be like we were the couple . . .'

'Double O babying,' I laugh.

'Sounds good – your womb or mine?'

'Well mine is like an empty warehouse according to the scan: I've got the space, but seemingly no way of getting it in there.'

'And to think that Beth had the cheek to get pregnant in an instant, just as she was getting so bored to death by Pete that she was going to have an affair with her PT. Oh god – maybe it's not his!'

'Yeah, about that . . .' I say, not sure how to segue into what it is I need to say after weeks of silence. 'I wanted to tell you about what happened in Paris, but then I didn't want to come off insensitive after all your stuff last month.'

'Oh shushy. What happened?!' I can hear Orla jump to her feet and move to a quiet bit of the carriage.

'I had a weird moment with Mads.'

'Weird how? Angry weird?'

'Remember I came back early when I was supposed to be there two days? It was because of him. We went for a walk.'

'A *walk*?!' She coos sarcastically, Pink Ladies style.

'It was a bit more than a walk, it was a whole evening . . .' I hear a sharp intake of breath. 'And at the end, he did the lean.'

# INTERVIEW 3: SAMIRA

I figured that Samira was just one of those baby bore-offs. When I didn't hear from her post the compulsory initial 'I've had a baby!' message, despite my WhatsApp tickles here and there, I assumed that – like a few of the other people I used to party with – she had just ghosted me for her contented new life nuzzling into mummyhood. She'd moved away to Margate, so she was splashing by the seaside with her baby and a bucket and spade, while I continued the London toil. I wasn't satisfied, of course. I missed her. One Saturday, I went scouting through her social media for clues. Usually it's just a slew of babies holding those heinous 'I'm blah month old' cards and extreme close ups of their dribbly faces. Samira's was empty.

I ditched the WhatsApps and picked up the phone. We hadn't been the kind of mates that call each other before, but I sensed this might be the only way. Bella was about six months, so I was long overdue a first visit. She sounded different, distant. I asked if I could come see her, said that I'd bring wine. She agreed, but I could tell she desperately wanted to tell me to leave her alone.

When she opened the door, the distant voice matched this new shrunken version of her. Her miniature frame always belied a big party persona, but at this point, she was like a waif. Her hollow eyes immediately welled up as

I swooped in and hugged her. I felt like such a bad friend that I hadn't called sooner, or done more.

Olivia: I'm so glad that you're here. How are you feeling now?

Samira: I literally can't even explain how much better I am. I was like a husk that first day you came to see me. I'm actually pretty good now.

Olivia: So – for the purposes of the interview – when were you diagnosed with post-natal depression?

Samira: It was probably around the time that I saw you. I went to the doctors not long after that. So about six months after having Bella. I just couldn't stop crying. I can't remember exactly what they said to me, it was a bit of a blur, but they asked me if I wanted to go on antidepressants.

Olivia: And did they help?

Samira: Completely. Before them, I was in such a black hole. All through the pregnancy, I thought I was going to be overwhelmed with love and joy and peace and tranquillity, because the baby was out and I could stop worrying. But the worrying just escalated and everything got worse. I'd be walking round so anxious about her, like I was going to kill her or something. You can't take your eyes off them even for a minute. I kept worrying 'is she breathing? Is she eating enough?' I wouldn't leave her in a room on her own for the first couple of months. I wasn't thinking straight. Everything was very dark and I lost myself for a bit. I really loved her, but there was no joy in it. When you're depressed, you can't laugh and see things for what they are. The tablets probably kicked in after about a month and I felt a lot less anxious. I wasn't quite the walking wreck that I had become.

**Olivia:** How did your family react to the news that you were suffering with post-natal depression?

**Samira:** I think they thought because of the lack of sleep, and because I was anxious anyway that it was quite a normal thing to happen. But I don't think I really expressed how bad I was feeling. Because I was thinking: time and sleep will help it, so let's just brush it under the carpet. But I do remember, I was breast-feeding once, and it was so painful, I felt like I'd been hit by a bus. And my mother-in-law came to check in on how I was doing, because I was holed up in a room upstairs, and she just saw me and started crying because she felt so sorry for me. I was dead behind the eyes. I guess people are wrapped up in the new baby and because people expect a new mum to be super tired and anxious and emotional, it's just normal to be like that. So it wasn't like a 'Is she OK?' It was more like 'she's having a wobble but she'll get through it.' I wasn't suicidal or anything – I was just really low.

**Olivia:** Were you spending time with other new mums at the time?

**Samira:** I had quite good connections with the NCT group. And a lot of them were like 'this is shit, this is bad,' but I know none of them were feeling quite like I was. I think I compared myself to them, but it was more the stuff that I'd read before in the media. That I should be so in love and seeing stars, when all I was feeling was shit and in a black hole. I was not really connecting with anything, and I don't think I really connected with Bella at the beginning because I was in such a lot of physical pain that took ages to heal, but also emotional pain, which was very difficult. And that made me feel even guiltier.

I always imagined that the love I have for my niece and nephew, which I had immediately, would just hit me, whereas I felt that this child had absolutely wrecked my body and my brain and I felt guilty for not absolutely idolising her. That's totally changed now, but at the time I was expecting these waves and gushes of eternal undying love. And I didn't get them. I was just screwed.

Olivia: So was there part of you that saw her as the enemy?

Samira: Yeah, especially as she wasn't planned. I remember in labour, thinking 'this is so painful I want to die, I don't even want this baby that much'. And as the woman because you're the only one who can provide for the kid, I felt very alone. The only one who felt the pain I was going through. And even though Joe was amazing, I felt that it was all on my shoulders. I still think it would have been really bloody hard if I'd have stayed in the same environment, but I felt so isolated and miserable. Even the time of year – January – I would dread the afternoons because it would be pitch black by four o'clock. And it was so bleak. It was like hibernating, but not in a good way. I didn't want to see people or speak to them. I didn't want to go out. It was not good.

Olivia: So obviously, you said you found it difficult to make the connection at the beginning, but the two of you are thick as thieves now. When do you think that happened?

Samira: I don't think it was for a long time. I obviously loved her really deeply and I was fiercely protective of her, it's not like I didn't care about her. I just wasn't in love with her. That only came, probably about a year later. Literally that long, that's when I fell in love with her. To be absolutely besotted only came a long way down the line. I hold new babies now and it's just all a blur. I can't remember her being that small and delicate. And I wish that I could have appreciated it more, but I just wasn't capable of doing it.

Olivia: Would you have any words of advice for anyone who might be suffering with post-natal depression?

Samira: I'd just say go and speak to someone immediately, speak to everybody. And just don't listen to other mums who are fine, that's the worst thing you can do, because you feel like you're a bad mum or a bad person and you pit yourself against them. Nobody needs that.

Olivia: So would you ever consider another one?

Samira: I'd like to think I'd be prepared now, and I would love to experience a new baby without feeling that over-bearing darkness. But the reality is, would that be possible for me? Maybe one day, but I think I need to concentrate on Bella and looking after myself for now.

I'm shell-shocked. I've been obsessing over just getting one out of me, but if you didn't bond with your baby? How do you form a family if you can't even come to terms with yourself?

# Cycle 24

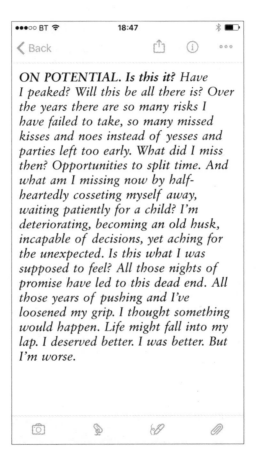

**ON POTENTIAL. Is this it?** *Have I peaked? Will this be all there is? Over the years there are so many risks I have failed to take, so many missed kisses and noes instead of yesses and parties left too early. What did I miss then? Opportunities to split time. And what am I missing now by half-heartedly cosseting myself away, waiting patiently for a child? I'm deteriorating, becoming an old husk, incapable of decisions, yet aching for the unexpected. Is this what I was supposed to feel? All those nights of promise have led to this dead end. All those years of pushing and I've loosened my grip. I thought something would happen. Life might fall into my lap. I deserved better. I was better. But I'm worse.*

**BRET AND JEMAINE ARE NOT HAPPY.** Sitting on the 19.58 home from another late one helping Rachel with her handover – only two weeks left – I flick through Instagram to decompress my brain.

There, at the top of the screen, like a flashing cry for help, is a post from Felix. The cats are posed louchely on our plush multi-coloured footstool, jauntily modelling miniature red and yellow scarves. I turn up the volume. You can just about hear Serge Gainsbourg crooning and crackling on the record player in the background over their bemused miaows. They're supposed to look nonchalant, but Bret is biting Jemaine's scarf, and Jemaine has his paw primed for retaliation.

So this is what Felix has been doing with his day off.

As I walk through the door, he's is still on the floor, trying to get the yellow scarf back from Bret's dainty brown jaws. Did he knit those himself? I'm starting to worry I might not have looked at him in weeks. It was easier when all he did was play FIFA.

'Hey, baby,' I say, as I pass the living room. 'What are we doing about dinner?'

He doesn't get up, doesn't even look. In the kitchen, the washing up is precariously piled and there's certainly no sign of food.

'Shall I go back out to the Co-Op then?' I say, returning to the living room passive-aggressively. 'Or is it takeaway time again?'

'Whatever you want, I'm not hungry,' he shrugs. I look at him now. He's like a sullen, shadow of himself, still in his dressing gown, his hair on end. Today wasn't a sick day: he booked it off to be alone. Doesn't he realise that I reserve my annual leave to be with him? That sometimes I need a day on my own but I won't ever get it because Mum needs me, or a friend's child has a birthday party or there's a work thing to eat into my very core? When we first bought this house we would run down the hill from the station just so we could get a kiss fresh on the threshold after work. Has someone told him about Paris? That I wasn't running home to him, but running away from someone else? Because something's happening here and I don't think a chicken tikka masala is going to solve it.

Peak Fertility   Sensitive

'HANG ON A MINUTE, WILL YOU, LIVVIE?' I can hear I'm on speakerphone as my mother rustles in the background, obviously concentrating on doing seven other things at once, which is very unlike her. She's a mono-tasker by trade.

'Mum, are you still there?' She's still struggling with the fundamentals of using a mobile phone: speak while mobile.

'Sorry, my lovely daughter, I'm just cleaning up,' she says, jubilant. 'I've just baked a cake!' Mum has never baked a cake in her life, not even those packet ones with the rice paper cartoons that everyone else did with their mums when we were little. I feel cheated. 'I've got all the ladies coming round – we're having a grandbaby shower for Sandra tomorrow.'

'A *what* now?' I say. Surely this hasn't filtered up to the generation above me? The mother I know does not go in for forced fun. Last time she was this excited, Grace was paying her surprise visit. At least now she's not joy-crying.

'You know, darling, a *grandbaby* shower. To celebrate the wee'un. Jenny's due in two weeks, so we've left it a bit late.'

*Like thirty-four years too late.*

'But isn't it usually just the impending mum who gets to celebrate?'

'Oh no, I saw it on the *Pinterest* . . .'

Why is my mother scouting for Internet parenting tips when her children are in their mid-thirties?

'Oh yeah, they're all the rage!' she says. 'Plus, why should you young ones get to do all the celebrating? No doubt Sandra will be doing plenty of the hard work when Jenny goes back to work in three months. She's got her own business . . .'

'Yes, Mum, you tell me every time,' I say, as exasperated as I am every time. 'Jenny's so rich, she's not got a single bit of debt (*because she didn't go to university*) and *two* houses in Hertfordshire (*where I don't want to live*). I get it. You wish you had a Jenny. And a Jenny Jr.'

'Oh, stop it, love. It'll be you soon enough – I'm just *practising*. The cake is chocolate with white icing – like a dirty nappy! I got the idea on-the-*line!* Have you heard of that Pinterest then? It's just got all these *lovely* ideas on there!'

That's it, she's gone rogue. I don't know anyone around me any more. I rang her to talk through what's going on with Felix and potentially spill my guts about our baby issues, and instead I'm going to have to stage a full family intervention.

'Can I speak to Dad, actually?' I say. 'I've got a question for him.' I don't have a question; I just want to hear one sensible person's voice before I implode. Even just a familiarly unfunny dad joke.

'Oh darling, he can't come to the phone – he's building us a swing. I saw that on Pinterest too!'

I'm calling social services.

'FELIX, COULD YOU COME up here a minute?' I arrange myself hurriedly on the pillows, my arms stretched up above my head, breasts lolling to my sides with the heavy 'diamond' necklace between them as I perch on one hip facing the door, legs loosely laid on the bed.

'What is it, darling? I'm just preparing for that conference call at eight.' Felix stops dead when he realises how naked I am at just 7.45 on a Wednesday evening.

'I want you to transfer me like one of your French players.' The remixed line sounded funnier in my head.

'I'm not sure I have time . . .' I can see from the bulge in his gym shorts that he definitely has time, so I raise myself on to my elbow and pull him closer to me by the bottom and start to pull them down.

'I just thought we could get this over with early so we could get on with our evening . . .' I say in a husky voice. His face falls. So does the bulge.

'Oh, so that's all it is then? Getting it over with?'

'No, that was not how it was supposed to sound. I just mean: I wanted to catch you while you've still got the energy . . .'

'I've always got the energy!'

'OK, well, good! I thought you might fancy some early evening delight.'

'Better . . .' he says, throwing himself down on the bed next to me and grabbing a handful of flesh. 'But I am going to have to jump on that call at eight, whether we're done or not.' He smiles that beautiful, sexy smile. 'So I don't know how you feel about two players and three lawyers joining us via FaceTime?'

'That's the sexiest thing you've said all year,' I say pulling him on top of me.

| <14 October | Event Details |
| --- | --- |
| **Dinner at Rachel & Chris's** | |
| **Walthamstow** | |
| Saturday, 14 October | |
| 7pm | |
| Calendar | Felivia shared |
| Invitation from   Olivia | |
| Invitees | |
| Alert | None |
| Notes | |
| Expect smuggery | |

Shit. Must start drinking immediately in preparation.

**'I CAN'T BELIEVE IT'S TAKEN** us this long to get together!' Rachel is positively rotund in her excitement for tonight's double date. I feel bad, because they're having to cook for us, but then, what do you do when you have toddler twins and are on the hospital's most wanted list in case you burst with your third?

As I look across the table at her discomfort, six months of resentment boil down into a serene feeling of acceptance. Neither of us got that promotion.

'Here's to getting out of that place for a while! You deserve the rest!' I toast.

I sometimes worry that my constant urge to raise a glass to everything is not the feminist power play for airtime that

I think it is, but just papering over my social insecurities with a loud clink. *And the fact that I can't stay away from alcohol for too long.*

My eyes flit around their beautiful pared-back kitchen – open units with Lego-coloured eclectic vintage earthenware all neatly styled in 'these get used all the time' stacks. A sublime mid-century pendant lamp interrogates the Châteauneuf-du-Crap I'm responsible for (Felix laid into me about my obvious, uncool wine taste on the tube to Walthamstow as if he's some sommelier) that now stands in the centre of their reclaimed wood dining table. The pair of highchairs in the corner, still encrusted with organic gunk despite obvious scouring, stand in judgement.

Chris, sweaty from toiling behind 'the Wolf' (their wanky new range cooker), hands round some beautifully presented mushroom polenta tartlets and snorts at my sentiment. *Of course, you – unenlightened childless one – think that maternity leave must be some walk in the park,* I feel him mentally tallying. Except, all Rachel did on her last one was post pictures of her walks in the park. *Validation is mine.*

'So, Chris, feeling primed for the third?' Felix asks rather cheerfully, considering the gruffness he volleyed my way as we wound our way through the Village. He always boils into peak resentment in Walthamstow's rabbit warren roads: I can sense his blood pressure rising with every renovated Victorian pub and Baby Bjorn carrier we pass. And in Walthamstow, that's one of each, every seven steps.

'You know what?' Chris laughs, uncharacteristically, 'No!'

Bitter as shit as always then, despite the perfect life.

'It's going to be more than a handful. Beckett and Freja are at that point where they're sleeping nicely and they're in a routine, and this,' he gesticulates at the bump, 'this is going to capsize the whole thing.'

Someone wanted this child more than the other.

'But nothing beats that new baby smell!' pitches in Rachel, desperate to bring the situation back around. We all laugh, but I've only experienced that new baby smell second-hand off the heads of three-week-olds who belong to someone else. Maybe it's possible to win such a life-altering debate if you've snorted one in all its grisly newness.

'Plus all the NCT lot are on their seconds now,' she continues. 'A few of them cashed in and took their Walthamstow money to where they could afford bigger places – *south of the river*,' she whispers, as if heading south is desertion. 'Actually, there's also a few round by you now I come to think of it!' *I can't wait to avoid them like the plague at the Co-Op.* 'But the good ones who've stuck around have got big plans for Wednesday baby sound-bathing at God's Own Junkyard and mooching around the farmers' market. It'll make a nice change from folding the bump on to the Victoria line every night after being yelled at by Trish.'

I titter politely. Inside I'm folding myself into a tiny origami square to lock away my jealousy. *You can shove your Walthamstow money.*

'And what about you two?' Chris asks, casually forking his chanterelles. 'Any plans? No pressure, *obviously* . . .' He basks in the rising emotional temperature of the room.

My face – mouth open, eyes wide, cheeks more gaunt with every passing month – has morphed into *The Scream*.

*Well, Chris, we've got all sorts of plans and pressure. Plans to have a house like this. Except our families couldn't help us with a £100,000 deposit. Pressure from our families to be present, all the time. Plans to have a kid. Except my womb, or his sperm, or just us trying to have sex, doesn't work. Pressure to get on with my career, while knowing that a baby will hold me back. Plans to get promoted, but your wife got in the way. Pressure from people like you, being so perfect. Plans to actually love each other. But even that doesn't seem like it's viable any more.*

I stuff a loaded forkful of crunchy polenta into my open gob to stop myself spurting it all out. I've managed to unravel silently. I'm quite impressed with myself. It might be bubbling visibly beneath the skin. Pulsating like a blue vein, waiting to be drained. But we can't actually let it bleed.

'We're working on it, mate, we're working on it . . .' Felix laughs lightly, taking the bullet with a smile. His intonation even suggests that in the process we're having loads of sex and the time of our lives. I adore him for it, and write off the wine outburst. We express ourselves differently in the face of these trials. I reach to squeeze his hand under the table, but he pulls it away.

*I miss you even though you're here with me.*

'And in the meantime,' Rachel says, sensing the change in mood again and determined to make this a 'good night' before things get sleepless again, 'you get to build the HYGGExperience.'

'THE LADS SETTLE in for high-level football criticism (no one could accuse this pair of 'banter' – they're basically composing a tactical theory tome out loud) and a couple of whiskies (Felix hates whisky). Rachel pulls me upstairs to show us the Scandi shadows of their new loft conversion. It's all white wood and layered rugs and reading nooks, of course. Only they could manage a major house renovation with two toddlers and another brewing. As we pass back down the stately landing, she motions for me to join her to check in on the twins. Maybe I should be allergic to this by now – I know Orla is – but as we quietly push the glossy white door to their little room, I'm filled with the usual longing. That one day it'll be *my* miniature person snuggled under the ceiling stars, soothed by the night light and dreaming peacefully of a day spent splashing in puddles.

Beckett and Freja make picturesque surrogates. They've somehow found their way into the same little bed, and are gripping each other's hands like they're locked in the world's cutest arm wrestle.

'This is all coming your way so soon, Liv,' Rachel says, sensing my solemnity and rubbing her bump gently. 'Don't let it eat you up. Remember what a good life you've got now. When it happens, you'll be ready. Just try to enjoy the journey.'

And I know she means every word. And I know she's right. But I also know I can't keep the tears from tumbling out in the half-light. And there are only wet wipes to dry them.

## 04:04

**MY EYES OPEN JUST A CRACK.** The bedroom is dark and still, the cold hitting my bare shoulder, which means the heating hasn't yet kicked into life. I look at the clock: 04:04. Under the covers though, is a melee of heat and movement. Waking up from a deliciously sordid dream – I drift in and out of the memory of some tall faceless younger man who I just couldn't get space to be alone with – to realise you're already halfway through re-enacting it is a mild shock. At first I'm frozen: whose hands are these devouring my body so furiously? Then I rouse more and realise I'm arching back into him: I'm safe, it's Felix. He fondles wildly but aimlessly: I'm his virtual reality substitute for whichever dream he's in. I take him by the shoulders and kiss him like a prince reviving his sleeping (but horny) princess. I can sense some sentience now. What are the ethics here? I initially thought I was having sex with someone else, he obviously still does. Should I continue? We've got to take our chances where we can, especially when we've hardly been talking lately. But do either of us really want to do this? I take the decision for both of us. I turn him away as if I'm diverting his snoring, stroke his head until he settles, then go back to my dream.

---

Olivia Gyamfi

Appointment
With: Dr Manjeet
Day: Friday
Time: 10am

If you are unable to keep your appointment, please contact within 24 hours.

---

'SO THE RESULTS WILL BE IN WHEN?' Felix can hardly contain his contempt for me this morning as he straps his trainers on to go for a run to 'clear his head', just as he has done for the past eight days. Usually, I'd be plotting ways to make him smile, but now I'm just easing off to give him the space he needs. And so he runs the distance between us, an ever-expanding marathon. At least he's still vaguely interested in our progress.

'They said wait three weeks after the last test, so I've booked us an appointment with Dr Manjeet for next Friday morning . . .'

'Why do you never fucking check anything with me first? I've got a meeting first thing that day!' He's exasperated. I should have checked. He doesn't need to swear.

'Sorry for trying to get us sorted' – fight petulance with petulance – 'I can just go on my own . . .'

'Well, *obviously* you're *not* going to do that,' he says slamming the wardrobe door shut. 'What time is it? I'll push my meeting back. It's fine.' He's seething. Every day is a new version of Felix. But never *my* Felix. I prod to explore his new boundaries, to uncover what's beneath it all.

'Look, I know this is more my thing,' I say, simpering now. 'Just don't worry about it.'

'You think you care more about having a baby than I do?' His volume is rising as he paces the bedroom, making a concerted effort to untangle a pair of white headphones. 'You think you get to be proactive and leave me behind? What kind of husband would I look like if you went on your own. Don't make me out to be a dick!'

The bandage is off. Let the blood flow.

'You always make everything about you!' he continues, a vein I'd never noticed pulsing loudly across his forehead. 'I'm in this too. I *know* it's my fault. I *know* I'm away too much. And Christ knows if there are any problems the doctor is going to tell us about. It hurts my heart and my head and my fucking . . . dick that I can't give you a baby.

Give US a baby. It's all I want. How can you not see that? I sometimes think you don't know me at all any more.'

His eyes are filled with a sad rage as he turns from me to pelt down the stairs and out the front door.

As I sit there on the edge of the bed, fierce tears marring my cheeks, I wonder how I'd even feel to let my easy life go? Would I wish we'd never had these rows or pushed to have a child? Will my life just slip through my fingers like it was never there, or will I clench my fists as I try to time my baby around my life, not my life around my baby? But that's not how babies work. And there is no baby. At what point did I need it so much anyway? Why do I feel like the entire world told me I needed one? Will I feel less human if I don't manufacture a person from my own flesh, like I'd never feel whole without love? And isn't that all just bullshit fed to us by songwriters and memes anyway? I know the urge is real, like a hunger that I might never sate – even if it is just a ball of hormones pulsing inside of me. Why do I burn with resentment that everyone can do it but I can't? And why am I allowing it to build a gulf between Felix and me? Is my jealousy because I'm denied entry to a special club? And do I really want to be a member of it anyway? There are plenty around me without children – decisive, content – so what leaves me hating the way it is? If I could just let it go, I could have it all. Love, excitement, experiences. I don't need a child – I want one. But I've lost sight of the reason for trying, lost sight of the potential completeness, or the joy of seeing myself in a child, the unconditional bonds, the family. Now there are only patterns. Crossing off cycle after cycle of my life, counting me down to doom: to childlessness, to menopause, to death. And that is what a baby is about: extending your life. Creating a legacy. Maybe the world doesn't need me to leave a piece of myself behind.

Low Energy     Sticky

**IF ONLY YOU COULD SPLIT A MOMENT IN TWO.** The moment where you could stop or go: the moment where you don't look, or the moment you see. You should know better. You'll always find something you don't want to.

The urge attacked me like a sciatic itch. All in my mind, but couldn't help but scratch: the long desperate reach to claw at your flesh. The revelation that in this one move you can't stop, that you're only hurting yourself.

My scalp prickles as I pick up Felix's iPad. It was just sat there staring at me in the kitchen, its open flap beckoning me. Goading me. *I know something you don't.* Felix won't be home for hours. I think I know his password. I'll put it down if I'm wrong. Wasn't meant to be. Wasn't meant to see.

I try his normal one – his favourite childhood wrestler that we used to laugh about back when he still loved me – and nothing. Access denied. I roll the cover closed with a diffusing snap. Take myself to another room. Swerve the temptation.

But I need a cup of tea. The iPad is just there by the kettle. Just one more hit, one more password to see if I know Felix as well as I thought I used to. The lock screen bumps incredulously. *Leave it, Olivia. This is not you.*

Whatever it is, you don't need to find it. It continues to creep. He's been distant for weeks. There's something I'm missing. It's not just the pressure. I try again.

My final combination – the cats' names in tandem, his best friends through all of this – makes the screen give way. I'm faced with blankness. Other women? Messages? His browsing history? What am I looking for?

I don't care about porn. What he looks at before we get to it is his business, as long as we get it done. But if there's a person at the heart of him drifting away from me, if there's a real emotional tie, I don't think I can bear it. *Hypocrite.*

I pick my way through his emails, my chest tightening with every female lawyer or physician in his inbox. He's so professional, there's not a single 'x' in his working day. I shut the flap tight. I can't do this to him. What am I hoping to dredge up? Some sordid affair? Some great love to come between us?

But here's that itch again. I need to pick the scab. I open it again, and hit on the Facebook icon. My heart takes one single deep beat as the air escapes from my lungs: the most recent message, read, but unanswered from his waif of a university girlfriend.

Felix, I've been thinking about you this week . . .

Did you remember it's been fifteen years today? Doesn't that feel like a lifetime? Fifteen years of life that we bought back for ourselves: a teenage life that would have come between two teenage lovers.

It's only recently that the moment has come back into my mind. After that day, when we walked heavy-heartedly down Old Shoreham Road hand-in-hand like nothing could prise our fingers apart, I had to let you go like I let it go. But the loss of both throbbed in me long after. The right decision isn't always the easiest. I took a pill and left it all behind. I buried that memory so deep. And even though I smiled and we talked after, I never let it be said again. I wonder if you knew what I was doing and played along. If so, I'm thankful. You made it easy on me when I know it probably wasn't easy on you.

But, you see, Felix, today I found out I'm pregnant again. And that fifteen-year expanse closed in a flood. I felt the warmth of your hand squeezing mine so tight as we said goodbye, as I welcomed something new in me for the second time. This is the right time – the right life – and I wanted to make sure you had that also. That if you thought of it this time every year; that you knew I was thinking of it too.

I hope all is well. Love to you and Liv. You deserve it. X

My vision clouds and the words jumble on the screen.

Felix was a father, even just for a few days. How could he not tell me after all these years together? How could he hide such an important piece of information from me? Trying and failing, trying and failing, the tests are in and it's all my fault. Just me all alone. I imagine the disdain he must feel for me now, with that fresh reminder in his head. The knowledge of what he's capable of if I weren't here letting him down. The loss that he's suffered repeated on a loop every month.

*You have no loss, just emptiness.*

I chuck the iPad across the work surface and crouch down on the kitchen step. Staring at the crumbs on the floor between my fingers, my aching head cradled in my stupid wandering hands, I try to still my breathing. *We're still alive. We're still alive. We're still alive.* But can Felix still love me even after this?

Sad    Exhausted

**IT'S TAKEN ME ALL WEEK** to regain control. Felix had to go away again. This time, I welcomed it. I can't control my tongue for long and the divide has helped silence me. I can't speak much now anyway. When he calls, I'm busy. When he texts, I'm perfunctory. And in between, Mads keeps calling and I can't answer those either. I can't tell Orla. I can't tell Mum. I just keep it all brewing and mixing in my head as I lie here flanked by cats, wishing I was anyone else but me.

Then tonight, I felt a pang of myself return. I was staring into the abyss (well, *Celebs Go Dating*) when Mads started calling again. Ten o'clock on a Wednesday night. The cheek. No care that my husband might be beside me. Or maybe he's heard Felix's away and had to seize his chance.

The heat from Paris returns to me, here in my fleecy dressing gown and woolly socks in late-October Borehamwood. The way my face flushed as his hand rested against my cheek. How his mouth parted just enough to let me know everything he wanted to say without a word. How new I was to him. How I ran in the opposite direction when every shred of me wanted to jump on him. I need to look at him, to examine that face again. The fog of the Facebook revelation subsides enough for me to open Instagram and type in *Mads Rasmussen*.

Every picture is unfeasibly hot. His feed is a slew of fuck-me-now images of him holding cameras in front of vintage mirrors, hair artfully ruffled, every T-shirt bed-sheet rumpled, every jumper hold-me warm, every backdrop take-me-now sexy. I fumble as I scroll through each one, wanting to strip naked and FaceTime him instead. I'm far down his feed now, and can feel how wet it's making me. Oh, and there it is. A beach shot. His unclothed body bathed in sunset. His hand running through his hair as he squints and smiles at whoever is taking the picture. The twenty-three-year-old heartbreaker? I prod at the screen to zoom in, take in every inch of his body. Sear it into my mind. And as I poke and tap with one hand, the other doing the same elsewhere, I realise I've liked it. I've liked the bloody photo. I undo it in one millisecond, but it's done. I've shown my hand. Oh, but his hands. I can't help myself, I come thinking about him seeing this Vag-Signal, and flying through my window to fuck me here and now, socks and all. And now Felix is calling. But he can't have me tonight.

**Mads Rasmussen**
Re:
To: Olivia Galvin

Olivia, I understand why you didn't want to take my calls, but we have to talk at some point. We can't continue to work like this, especially once Rachel leaves. I don't think she realises she is playing go-between. At least reply to my emails.

I'm so sorry that I so obviously offended you that day, but it's been months. Let me make it up to you? Or I can never speak of it again? Do you want to report me? Just tell me what you want and I will take the lead from you. But we do have to start talking again, or people will start to talk about us.

M x

PS. I saw the like. And I like you looking at me.

Mads Rasmussen
Creative Director
HYGGE
+45 (0) 7925 074 053

**Olivia Galvin**
Re:
To: Mads Rasmussen

There's nothing to talk about. Nothing happened. We just need to get on and do what we need to do. No apologies needed, no dwelling, let's just get back to work.

Olivia.

PS. I like nothing.

Olivia Galvin
Marketing Manager
HYGGE (UK)
+44 (0) 7757406596

**Mads Rasmussen**

Re:

To: Olivia Galvin

Done. Nothing to see here. x
PS. I like you.

Mads Rasmussen
Creative Director
HYGGE
+45 (0) 7925 074 053

FUCK.

As I consider the disintegration of my marriage over a simple mis-like, I look up from the email and see Rachel roll herself to her feet faster than she's done in the whole last six months. She's started a kind of slow run towards reception with a broad grin on her face.

I see the giant bouquet first. Then the arm. And then his face. He turns out of the lift and walks efficiently along the office, towards the pregnant steamroller coming for him shrieking.

Why is he here? Why did I have to reply so eagerly? Why do I never notice when it says 'sent from iPhone'?

'Happy last day, Rachel!' he yells, throwing his arms around her as she beams, unaware that his gaze rests only on me. 'You've been such a help over the last few months, I couldn't resist coming over to see you off.'

*Couldn't resist coming over to get me off.*

He looks at me, and I look at him, and I run my hands under the desk as he watches them intently.

'In that case, it's time we threw you a party!' I say, as I

take my sweet time dragging the bags of food and decorations from under my desk, lingering out of sight until he can hardly stand to not know what I'm doing with them. Mads laughs, but his eyes are hawkish, the same look I was searching for last night. I take my bags and head for the kitchen – an open invitation. He trails me, just two steps behind. Luckily I wore my good arse jeans today.

I lift the bags on to the corner of the work surface as I sense him come in behind me and close the door.

'Need some help?' His body is so close, I can feel the molecules of heat emanating from his grey cashmere sweater and yet we're not touching. The negative space aches and I move back, ever so slightly, to close the gap. I arch my back and push the perfectly engineered rump of my Levi's into him and he doesn't move an inch. I feel his hair graze the side of my face as he kisses the nape of my neck *almost* imperceptibly. I shiver. I can feel him getting hard through his soft navy trousers and his hands run down the sides of my body greedily. No one can rob us of this moment. HR could rob us of this moment. *I don't think they have cameras in the kitchen.*

I turn to face him. I'm not letting a second pass this time. I take his face in my hands, and run them up along his beautifully sculpted jawline into his hair, and clench fistfuls of it as our faces crash with crazed inevitability into the deepest kiss. He continues his grabbiness, hands covering every inch he can reach of my body while still attached to my face.

I hear a noise, and come to from this frenzied intensity. I pull back: his face is momentarily satiated, mine probably startled, and I separate my body from his hands and back to good graces. Unable to say anything, I motion for him

217

to open the door so people don't suspect, and hurriedly begin unloading Percy Pigs and grab bags of crisps on to the worktop. I look like I've been doing this all along. I can hear music coming from the meeting room, so know no one is coming through to disturb us and I take one last glance back to him, loaded with longing, to see that he's still hard and is staring at me performing this mundane task. *Unwrapping Rachel's cake when I just want to be unwrapping him.*

'**THANK YOU FOR SUCH** an amazing send-off, Liv,' Rachel hiccups from the hibiscus mocktails I've been plying her with all night so I could continue to stay out. 'You're such a good friend.'

*Hmmm.*

As I pack her into the Uber, planting Mads's ostentatious flowers and the giant bags of presents on the seat next to her, I peep back into the pub behind us at the thinned-out crowd. Just Mads pretending to have a conversation with the hardier programmers and not looking voraciously at me through the window. YPNO moved on half an hour ago to a karaoke bar in Soho with an open invite for us to join them. The only invite I want is in there.

'Get home safe!' I wave, pretending to order an Uber for myself as I promised her I would. But instead . . .

> You've had enough for one evening . . .
> Time for a walk?

I see Mads glance at his phone then make his hasty good-byes, gathering his jacket and heading towards the door as I move around the corner out of sight. I begin walking in the direction of the churchyard, my heart keeping time with the sound of my red stilettos on the paving stones. I listen carefully for his hurried steps as he keeps pace without actually joining me in case his new friends spill out of the pub behind him. The pulse of anticipation has never been this thrilling as I turn into the alley between the Georgian terraces. I feel his hand grab for mine from behind, as he turns me towards him like he did that night. This time though, when he puts his hand to my face, my eyes just as wide, I nuzzle into it and bite it lightly. And then I pull him towards me with every last ounce of my energy and kiss him hard.

# Cycle 25

**TEARS SLICK MY FACE AS I WAKE.** The room is so cold I can see my breath. When did I crack a window? Drunk me attempting to air out the foul stench of deception. I didn't know it was possible to cry in your sleep.

The light from my phone appears on the ceiling like an apparition. Ten missed calls. Felix on his way back to me, to this: the dissolution of our union. My best friend, my man, the love that I thought would remain unbroken smashed into a million irreconcilable pieces.

I lie spread-eagled under the duvet, my fingers and toes finding their way into the coldest reaches of the mattress. How would the bed feel without Felix in it? Dead. Frozen. I concentrate on the clouds of breath above my face, while I map out how to proceed.

Felix already knows. Ten calls means he knows. Someone tipped him off. Caught a glimpse of what happened in that alley. Felix has the CCTV footage. I'm on the Internet. Mads posted revenge porn. Thoughts spider from my mind, each seed worse than the last. Mads has impregnated me, via his fingers, in one encounter and Felix won't know until I birth a suspiciously pale baby. Felix is coming home to tell me he's impregnated some California girl in one night. His university ex arrives to introduce me to their teenage progeny. All this passion has inflamed my brain.

I try to concentrate. What are the facts? The real ones. Not the alternative facts, not fake news. So what is really real? I have strayed. Both emotionally and physically, that is now true. We did not have sex. Therefore I am not a full adulterer. Am I? I did desperately want it, right there on the steps of the college opposite the church. We were barely shaded from the streetlight, let alone the view. We were interrupted: this is a fact. The delivery guy didn't see where our hands were, but he saw something worse: animal attraction that we couldn't contain. Is that a fact, or an opinion? We could have stopped ourselves. He was barely past us when the rubbing and the riding and the touching started again like he'd fired the starting gun. I'm the worst kind of human. Opinion. The worst wife. Opinion? I need to close the window. Fact. Mads and I can never see each other again, that is another fact. Felix will be home in half an hour and I smell of another man. I am both psychotically turned on and emotionally repulsed by this fact. *I want to lick you off me.*

**FELIX TUMBLES THROUGH** the door. 'Hello, sweet-heart!' he calls up the stairs. 'Where are you? I've missed you!'

He's brighter, the Felix I'd been trying to find: the one who had never been a father even just for a few days; the one who would have halted last night with just a wink; the one I felt this same raw passion for about five years ago. I'm compelled to run down the stairs to him. Maybe last night was a dream. Maybe it was meant to happen to reignite this?

'Don't ever leave me again!' I rush, covering his face in tiny kisses, each one a star-sized apology in a galaxy of regret. As our lips touch, I'm gripped by how different it feels. How I'm able to juxtapose in such vivid detail. Every flick of the tongue. The map of their teeth. The warmth of their lips. The intensity of my desire.

Felix lifts his battered leather weekend bag and heads up the stairs, and I follow like a bodyguard on close detail. There's nothing to see. I've showered, stripped the bed and compressed last night's filth into one single white wash. I worry the invisible stains of my sin will never come clean, so I'll wait until he's asleep to hang them out. My phone is on silent in my pocket, and Mads has been renamed 'Maddy' in case of emergency.

When we reach the bedroom, Felix scouts around as if something's different. 'Why's it so cold in here? You know it's thirty degrees in LA? Do you want to freeze me back out of the house?' He's satisfied nothing's changed and lies on the bed, trainers and all. I cranked up the heating, but it's still like ice in here. 'Did the heating break, baby? Come here and warm me up.'

I linger over him perhaps a fraction too long. Returning to Felix's arms feels suddenly too intimate. I feel obvious, so I slink quietly to my side of the bed and settle beside him with my arms at my sides.

'Are you all right?' he says, his face concerned, his breath stale and sleepy. 'I'm so sorry about how grizzly I've been. I know you probably don't love me any more.' He smiles tenderly and touches my hair. Am I grimacing? 'Can I make it up to you?' He dips his head to kiss me but I pull away ever so slightly. It feels forced. *Who are you cheating on?*

'Shall I make us a cup of tea?' I say cheerily, propping myself on my left elbow and brushing his shoulder with my fingertips to force myself to be used to his touch. 'You must be knackered after eleven straight hours in *economy* . . .' *Let's change the subject.* 'Did they give you breakfast on the plane?' He's pulling me back to him. Pulling me on top of him. I'm flying. *Is this economy or first class?* Usually I'd laugh, but instead I'm planning my dismount. Looking for the exit signs like I'm bracing for a crash.

'DO YOU EVER THINK ABOUT what it would be like if we just didn't have children? Like, would that even be more selfish?' Orla says, snuggled up on her dove-grey velvet chaise in an equally kitten-soft cream mohair sweater. I look like I've been electrocuted. As soon as Felix laid his beautiful head down for a nap I ran out the door with my hair still wet and drove to Orla's house at top speed. I didn't trust myself to impart this information over the phone. What would I have done if Orla had been out? Freaked out in her drive for an hour? We're drinking again. Since that weekend – I'm in consternations that three months have already trickled by, though it feels like a lifetime ago – we've done this a lot. I'll visit, and we'll drain two bottles of Pinot, but I'll only have two glasses. She'll ring me and as we finish the conversation after an hour, I can hear her emptying a bottle of rosé. Three months is a long time to drink more than a bottle a night.

'Shall I crack open another?' She's dancing into the kitchen, her grey fluffy slippers at odds with the grown-up sophistication of the rest of her cashmere leisurewear. Everything billows on her now. She's always been lean, her long tanned legs always the opposite number to mine, but now she's gaunt. She's also smiling, so I let go of this addition to my neuroses for now.

'Not for me,' I say, conscious that I need to get back to Felix soon and can't afford to leave my car stranded in Hertfordshire. I'm still safe: I've only had one glass out of the bottle of prosecco 'we' demolished in an hour.

223

'I'll just have one more then, if you're going to be boring,' she says, topping herself up and launching back on the dove-grey couch. She can't have a problem. I could just fall asleep here in this pillowy cosiness, away from the issues clawing away at my mind. *Maybe I don't have to have a problem either.*

'I guess I have in an abstract way,' I reply to her earlier question about not having children. 'All the holidays we could go on, the things I could buy for myself if we weren't spending money on baby Air Max and saving up for crippling university tuition fees. But never properly . . . I just figured if this doesn't work we'd end up adopting. Why, what have you been thinking?' When do I tell her there won't be a baby coming out of this mess?

'I mean, the need to perpetuate your own image – if it even is a real need? – it's a bit selfish, isn't it?' Orla continues. Why is she throwing up the big philosophy now? The drink has made her examine all of her deepest fears. Mine is about to carve its way out of my chest.

'I've been really selfish,' I blurt out. Blame the selfishness.

'What do you mean?' She looks at me bemused, putting her prosecco on the floor next to her feet and settling in a straightened concerned adult pose. 'Selfish how? Liv, are you OK?'

'I did something last night . . .' My eyes well up, but my lips curl in excitement. Hateful but horny: how teenage that I can't even decide what my face is doing.

'What, Liv? You're scaring me!'

'Mads. Something happened . . .'

'Fuck, what?' she says. 'Where was Felix?' She stands up and closes the door, even though Rich is at golf. Our makeshift panic room.

'He was still in LA. Away, as usual.' I'm not even bitter. I don't know why I'm setting it up like he was even an ingredient in this shit pie. 'I was glad he was away – I've been wanting it for months.'

Sharp intake of breath from Orla.

'But what do I do now?' I *need* an answer.

'Tell me what happened first. Don't think I can make that kind of judgement call on "something happened".' She picks up her glass with two hands, as if gripped by a scene on TV. I'm her tawdry drama.

'Well, you remember I mentioned it in the summer – we went for *that walk* in Paris. But I didn't let it happen. I left it at that and ignored him for what seemed like an eternity.'

'I still don't know how you managed to ignore your boss for months on end . . .'

'I just let Rachel speak to him. They became good friends, sickeningly so. It was unbearable to watch, but safer for me. But then she *had* to go on her maternity leave. So he took it upon himself to come to London again. And this time . . . I just couldn't help myself . . .'

'You could have . . .' she says. She's serious now.

'Do you want me to show you a picture of him?' I unlock my phone and scroll through his Instagram feed to *that* photo again. I hand it to her, not even needing to warn her not to accidentally like it.

'OK, so you *couldn't* help yourself,' she says, lightening her tone but still judging. 'No one could. Just show Felix that picture and he'll probably ask if he can watch next time.'

I burst into tears.

'Sorry, Liv, too soon,' she says, climbing across on to my sofa to gather me into her mohair. 'Can you bear to give me more details? Or do you maybe just have more pictures I can see?'

'Yes. No!' I say with a dark laugh between the sobs, burying my face in a gold embroidered cushion. 'It was probably the hottest experience of my life. And therefore the most ruinous.'

'This is not your ruin. Remember when I snogged that awful house DJ in a members' club in Soho just after Rich proposed? He kept his headphones on the whole way through.

I was just freaked out by the commitment – and you are too. It happens. You don't have to tell Felix. Just tell me, so you can get it off your chest, and I can record it in my mind as if it was I who was seduced.'

She puts her hand to her brow and flops over me and the cushion. *This is why I love you, Orla.*

'Well, it all started in the kitchen . . .' I laugh-cry. I'm not sure I'm going to be able to stop the eyes leaking, but I'm weeping my share before I have to go home to Felix.

'The kitchen? At work?' she snorts. 'A real steamy scene. I'm sure you have literally zero to apologise for, Liv.'

'Well, it was a bit. We sort of had a bit of a groping session while I was supposed to be dishing out the beige party food for Rachel.'

'Were there Percy Pigs?'

'Yes. He touched my boobs over several packets of Percy Pigs, Orla.'

'*Gelatinous*!' She laughs. 'So then what? That can't have gone on long if everyone was still at work?' she says. 'Oh my god, you didn't have sex in the office did you?'

'No!' I say, proclaiming my innocence. 'We didn't have sex at all – sorry, spoiler – but we all went for drinks after to give Rachel a proper send-off, and we didn't talk to each other in case anyone spotted us. Then, at the end of the night, we left together and did some probably quite arrestable stuff on a step down the back of that church by my work.'

'Lord bless us and save us!' she says in her Irish nun voice. 'I should be judging you right now on Felix's behalf. I really should. But I really want to know how it was. It's fine: you're bad, I'm bad, Mads is worse. Let's call the whole thing off.'

'Poor Felix!' I snot, narrowly missing the precious scatter cushions. 'It's not his fault! I'm the worst wife!'

'You are not the worst wife. You've just had it up to here with baby-making and career-pushing and mundanity. Something had to give. And it just had to be your knicks.'

'Oh Or, he was so filthy.' I feel the heat rising, I'm deranged with lust. Orla squeals with delight. I need to repent. 'I think I need to pay some sort of penance for what I've done. I'm not going to be able to keep it together now Felix is back. I'm fully expecting that Mads will start texting me any minute. How can I explain that?'

'Just change his name.'

'I think I need to tell Felix. He tried to kiss me when he got back and I pulled away as if I was cheating on Mads. What's wrong in my brain?'

'You're infatuated,' she says.

'I know that! How do I make it stop?'

'You need to have sex.'


I'M INCREDULOUS. Orla's best advice was 'have sex with Mads'? And yet . . . now the seed is sown, it's dulled the edge of my everything-but impasse. I return to Felix levelled out. It's all about context.

Felix is just awake in the dark – dark like my blackened

227

heart – when I return. 'Where did you go?' he whispers, confused through his jetlagged haze. He takes a shower while I make beans on toast and cups of tea, and I put his pyjamas and dressing gown on the radiator so he's extra warm.

I used to ache for Felix. When he was away from me for more than an hour I would yearn. As the years unfolded, so did the missing him. I knew I would see him soon, so I relaxed. When we moved in together, it intensified again. I wanted to be with him every minute of the day. I was excited by his presence, I wanted to be attached to him. We'd ride the train together, picking apart Twitter, working out the plan of attack for the day, fingers woven like vines. Then when we parted on the tube, our messages about how much we loved one another would transect from opposite platforms. I'd count the minutes until I could see him back in *our* house. I was abundant with love. And then we got married and I *was* attached to him and that love was anchored and we *knew* it was safe. We took different trains because one of us would go too slow to match the other's pace. At first we'd be upset, then it became expected, until we realised that riding different trains gave us an extra two hours of reading, of music, of solitude. And then came Felix's job. The tiny perforations of our daily life: me still here, him in Manchester, Spain or eight hours askew in LA. I missed him when I'd make another excuse for him at our friends' parties, or as I lugged cat litter back from the Co-Op on my own, or watched forty-seven hours of *Gilmore Girls* because I couldn't Netflix cheat on him with anything else. But we were feigning that craze now, only calling to check in. Surely a baby would change all of that, wouldn't it? Except, trying to have one just made it all so much more distant.

So what would happen if he weren't here? If he'd never

come back from this trip, or if he stayed in California and our lives parted like that old commute? Would my life go on like those times when he's away now, missing him vaguely, intangibly, but having a perfectly full life? Knowing it would all be OK because I am my own person? Or would I languish over my lost love? His deep brown eyes melting warmly as he cracks a goofy smile. The way he dances to make me smile every single day, even when he's feeling blue himself. That feeling of being safely tucked under his arm and away from the world. How he looks at the cats like they came from him and how I want to be the one to give him a child so he can look at it just once in that profound way. How I can tell him anything in the world, however shocking or ridiculous, apart from what I've done. Losing him would be like losing my soul.

After our conciliatory tea, I tenderly massage Felix's brow while he lies in my lap and we re-watch his plane movie. He says he wants to experience it with me.

'Would you come to California with me, baby?' he says, drowsily.

'What are you on about now?'

'I got approached about the communications director role at LAFC,' he says, his eyes flickering in and out of range. 'Would you come with me?'

'What? When?' I say, suddenly confronted. 'But we can't really . . . what about having a baby?'

'I know, but it's not like anything's happening here. And they really want me.'

'But obviously you said no, right?' my heart is beating fast now. This is too much to process. 'We can't move to LA when we're going to need to have IVF . . .'

'And then be near to your family once we've had the

baby,' he says, more awake now. 'Yeah, I know. I know my fate. Destined only to dream of these once-in-a-lifetime opportunities.'

'Why don't you just go on your own then?' I snap. 'It can be your own little Christmas miracle.'

'Fine. I will. See if you and your mum, and my mum and everyone else's bloody mums can bloody stop me.'

'Fine. I'm not going to stop you, but they'll be at the airport waiting like Trump's rogue passport controllers.'

And with that he falls asleep again and my heart drops into the sofa. As I circle Felix's temples with my fingertips, his breathing slow and steady, I shudder at the stabs of my memory – *his* head in my lap, *his* fingers circling, *his* urgent breath as he tried to stop himself. *You need to have sex. Come with me to California.*

'Come on, my love, time for bed . . .' I gently part Felix's head from the cushion and lean him so I can slip out from underneath. He moans, but hardly rouses, so I double tuck him into our two sofa blankets and turn off Netflix to slip up to bed.

As I lay in the pitch black staring up at the ceiling, the thoughts creep in again. The ones I burned my sheets over last night. I look at my phone. Nothing. Better that way.

High Sex Drive    Sad

**DR MANJEET HAS DRESSED FOR THE OCCASION.** This week, she's gone short *and* low. I feel self-conscious in my battered Nikes and frayed jeans. I'm sure she noticed

Felix's name on the register before she got dressed this morning. I know he's as nervous as I am about these results, but he's still managed to get some good suck-up time in with her before she reveals our fate. But then he knows he's not going to get bad news – he works, even if I don't.

'Well, the good news is, there is no news!' she has taken off her little pernicious spectacles and is smiling heartily to Felix. 'All of the results came back fine. Olivia, your hormones appear normal from the bloods, and I hope the sonographer set your mind at ease at the ultrasound – that was all fine.' (*Apart from that bastard left ovary.*) 'And Felix, your sperm count and quality are very good indeed. Do you run?'

'What does running have to do with this, Dr Manjeet?' I ask, bemused at her flirtation even with this bounty of good news. *Hypocrite.*

'Well, running is supposed to be especially good for men in this situation, and it has a very enhancing effect on the *swimmers.*'

She grins again at Felix, as if she was weighing him up to be her own sperm donor. Probably will be at this rate.

'So what does that mean for us, though?' I ask. 'Why is it not happening?'

*Because of you. Because you're sleeping with someone else.*

'It's what we call unexplained infertility. There's no reason why, it just hasn't happened yet. But that is good news. You just need to keep on going with the sex every second day' – I'm sure she just winked at him – 'and in the meantime, I'm going to refer you on to the next stage of the process.'

Through to the next round. We're on to Judges' Houses, blameless. But what if we are both to blame?

**MY FINGER HOVERS** over the delete button.

---

| NOV | **SUBURBIA WE SALUTE YOU!** |
|-----|------------------------------|
| **21** | Private • Hosted by Olivia Galvin-Gyamfi |

---

In celebration of our mid-thirties' unstoppable approach and our continued descent into suburbanity, join me for my big 3-4 at Boringwood's hippest local, The Jolly Hay Baler.
**Expect:** Warm gin and tonics! | Frazzles! | Slot machines! | Garage music!
**Dress code:** No Burberry, no caps, no Classics (just like when we wore them the first time). Warning: jeans and sheux = no service.

---

I can't do this. Not even ironically. I'm going to be thirty-four. It's not a sexy age, is it? Thirty-three sounds rounded, but thirty-four is perfunctory, frumpy. Closer to forty. Well past becoming a grown up. And yet, is it? Do I feel grown up? What does that even mean? That I stop wearing hoodies and hoops? Or that I purchase a waterfall cardigan to sensibly conceal my hideous lumpen form? That sexy will be only a leg-lengthening nude court? What if I want to wear Nikes that make my legs look short? Isn't this the year I fade into invisibility anyway? It doesn't matter if no one sees you by thirty-four, you've accomplished *things* by now. Haven't you? What do you mean *things* are not locked down? That you're just a sensitive millennial like all the anxious twenty-four-year-olds at the end of the spectrum and a decade your junior. *We're all the same*: Soon to become obsolete and overruled like the generations before us. But before we pick our brown cars and our pension and our polo necks to hide the jowls and we get comfy and secure and complacent, shouldn't we grasp the uncertainty with both hands while we still have it? Embrace the anxiety. Everybody's got it, nothing to fear. Take it on the chin, thirty-four is nothing, mate. But time is ticking, the clock hand oars are splashing faster and faster – Olympic speed. And what if we've not done enough? What if we run out of time?

DELETE POST.

**WHAT TO DO WHEN** you've cancelled your own birthday party? Go see your mum, of course. Since denying Boringwood the only chance it'll ever have of 'becoming a thing' last night, I've become convinced that it will be the place untouched by taste until the end of time. In a way, I almost admire its refusal to deny its authentic dullness. We're post-hipster now anyway, I read it on a HYGGE press release where they outed exposed brickwork and twiddled beards. Now, we're in a phase of moderate normcore that Swedes call '*Lagom*'. This translates to 'just the right amount', but I prefer to see it as a greige rendering of 'neither here nor there'. So maybe Boringwood is suddenly on trend. And it's exactly why East Barnet has just arrived at hipster town with a café sporting bare walls, distressed vintage furniture, a suspicious beard-oil stand and an untouched record player. But it does do good coffee. I'm already twenty minutes overdue at the pub to help with some sort of garden-planting endeavours, but the coffee smell is taunting me as I walk up from the bus stop, so I poke my nose round the door.

What a mistake to make. There in my path to caffeinated enlightenment, is not one, but four pushchair-wielding old school mates, perfectly coiffed, bestrewn with modesty pashminas and cooing over cappuccinos. They're basic perfection. This is why Orla and I don't have any school friends remaining.

'Oh my god, is it Liv?!' Their leader – Giuliana – is standing now, waving at me with the same long French polished fingers she had back when we were fifteen, her enormous rock visible from my side of the café (and from space).

'Liv! Come and join us! How are you, gurrl?!' She air kisses me, flicking her artfully curled bronde extensions in my face as I arrive beside their table, drawn like a moth to the flame. 'You remember Claire, Claudia and Aisha.' They all nod up at me, their babies asleep variously on shoulder, under boob-tent and in a pushchair. How could I forget their relentless Britney routines and how they used to get picked up from school in their boyfriends' Ford Fiestas while Orla and I did our homework in the square and got the bus home?

'So how are you all?' I'm polite if nothing else. They can't harm me now.

'Sooo great,' effuses Claire, sub-team leader, still maintaining those thick stripy highlights. 'We've all moved back here since we started families. It's just so nice having the gang back together.'

'Lovely, well, it's been great seeing you all . . .' I make a move towards the counter to get my order and escape, but Giuliana is blocking my path again.

'Oh Liv, we haven't heard about you? Where are you based now? Any little ones?' Always the same question.

'Well, we were in Hackney, but we've moved out to Borehamwood to get a bit more space. No babies just yet.'

'NNOOOORRR. Poooor you, has it been tricky? Sure it'll happen for you soon,' pipes in dull as shitwater Claudia. How she's managed to trick someone into impregnating her I'm unsure. Her voice is as flat as the palm of the hand that I want to slap her with. 'It took me three months and I was sooo frustraaated.' *If I still had my hockey stick I'd take you smug bitches down.*

'Borehamwood is so up-and-coming,' says Aisha. 'It's getting so gentrified round here now it's almost too expensive to invest. Lucky we got in when it was still affordable to get a four-bed Edwardian villa. And it's great, because we all live right round the corner from our mums.'

'Oh perfect!' My smile is plastered on, but slipping like unbaked clay. 'Well, honestly, I must go, my parents are waiting on me. They run Molly's on the corner there, you should pop in some time, it's still the same old place . . .' Might as well drum up some trade, although they collectively crinkle their noses in just the way I wanted them to. 'See you all soon, I'm sure.' *Not if I see them first.*

I'll gladly make do with Mum's instant coffee now.

## 05:30

BEING RACHEL (AND MYSELF) is harder than it looks. I've always been first in line to fight for women's rights – maternity leave and flexible working to keep women with kids in the workforce – but, on those days where they're running out the door at 4.45 'to make it to nursery for pick-up', you can't pretend that there's not part of you that's thinks 'What about the poor childless gits who get left behind?' I know, I know, totally not the point. We've got nothing on our plates. We should just get on and pick up the slack. But covering for someone is just that: you're not just papering over the cracks, you're also spreading yourself thin.

In the fortnight since Rachel left me, I've created myself

a whole new working style that I like to call the 'Guilt Edge'. I'm going to write a book about it when I eventually get to go on my own long awaited maternity leave. Meanwhile, Rachel's at home relaxing because the baby hasn't even come.

It starts with a cold sweat around 5.30 a.m., where I wake in a panic with a griping pain deep in my soul. I wriggle out of bed, so I don't wake Felix, put on some Lycra and hurl myself out into the cold for a deranged 5km. The asthma-attacks keep the hyperventilating at bay. Then, after showering my despair from my shrinking body (hip-bones are an upside to stress), I kiss my unsuspecting husband goodbye as he wakes at 7 a.m., and catch the early train to work with all the bedraggled bankers who get paid ten times my salary to look this shit. On board I write a list for the day ahead, while drinking the first of three shockingly strong but almost impressively tasteless coffees. By the second espresso at 9.30 a.m., my hands are whirring like vibrators, but I chalk this up to my vigour for the day, as I go into my first team meeting with the designers for the new Purley Way store. I save time for more work by ignoring food – it tastes like cardboard now anyway – and pin a couple of extra hours of HYGGExperience admin time on to the end of the day to avoid dinner too. Trish has never been more impressed with my ethic, and has let me off management meetings to free me up for the tasks in hand. *Or is she side-lining me.*

Tonight, I'm having a Guilt Edge all-nighter as we go home to my parents' for a pre-birthday 'surprise'. Plus, the ovulation test is telling me that we need to follow that with some 'special time'. Might need more coffee (or harder) for that.

I've had no emails, nor texts, nor indeed dick pics, from Maddy. Orla's advice has been buried deep beneath a layer of self-hatred and denial.

I must say, she's only been gone for two weeks, and the baby's still not been born, but I can't help but feel it's all a bit dull now without Rachel to compete with. Having all of the jobs (and only the most laughable bump in salary) is a distinct anti-climax. Don't they realise how un-Hygge my bank account is looking?

> **Chris**
> Keith has landed! The family band was completed at 7.15am this morning by a 9lb 2oz wonder who will no doubt grow up to be the drummer. Mother and child are resting and already in love. xx    12:15

Of course. They'll spark a resurgence of Keiths now too.

High Fertility    Sensitive

IT'S MY BIRTHDAY. It's my birthday. I can't take the regime any more. It's 8.30, my legs are like dead weights and Bret and Jemaine are flanking me so as to secure my non-release. Work can wait. I deserve this time in bed.

'Happy birthday, my beautiful queen. Please accept this croissant as a symbol of my unending service.' Felix has a tray. There's even a rose. I shield my eyes under a dead arm as the tears start pouring down my face.

'Hey! What's all this for!' he says. 'You're only thirty-four! I know I'm a younger man, but you make a very sexy cougar.' He's doing a little bedroom dance with the rose between tucked down the back of his pants, like Morrissey doing a Morris dance.

'I just . . . I just don't deserve you!' I wail. 'All this. It's too kind. You shouldn't do this for me.'

*He wouldn't do this for me if he knew.*

'But I want to. And you do deserve it. You've been working so hard lately, I've hardly seen you since I got back from LA. So I took a bit of a liberty . . .'

*Oh god.*

' . . . and booked you the day off. Trish was away, so I emailed that Mads fella in your head office and he said it was fine that I take my wonderful wife out for the day for her birthday.'

My cold sweat is back. *They've been talking about you.*

'You emailed work? You shouldn't have done that . . .' I bite, suddenly upright. 'You shouldn't be speaking to them and booking my annual leave.'

'But I thought it would be a nice surprise. And he said you've been so hard at it that you could take it off as a day in lieu . . . Happy Birthday!'

I flop back, imagining Mads — dressed like some Bond villain in his royal blue double-breasted suit — taking immense pleasure at the soppy husband pleading for my freedom from his immensely pleasurable grasp.

'I did think you'd be a bit more pleased than this,' Felix says, deflatedly plopping the tray by my feet, removing the rose from his Calvins and standing hands on hips beside me. 'Can you be cheerful now, please?'

I have reached the precipice of the Guilt Edge.

'FIRST OFF ON THE BIRTHDAY schedule, is . . . There is no schedule.' Felix is forcing the Volvo to consider 80mph up a country lane, so I have a feeling he might be giving himself some positive reinforcement about a schedule that we're not quite keeping to. We've been on the road for about forty minutes already, but I moped my way around the house before Felix eventually presented me with a ready-packed overnight bag, and tied my hair up with the rose in it, and then forced me to get in the car. I smell a Secret Escape.

'Are we nearly there yet?' I'm regressing fast – which, on one's thirty-fourth birthday, is a right and a privilege. I intend to get all the way back to an impetuous nineteen-year-old today: just old enough to enjoy a sexy spa break, but young enough to be a complete cow without recrimination. Not that I'd do that to Felix when he's trying so hard.

As we pull up the gravel path, I'm loaded with remorse again, but pretend the tears are of joy, not drips of salty sin. I hope there's somewhere I can get a wax before my treatments, because I haven't done anything about this situation since the night before Rachel's leaving do. I've been leaving it fallow by way of protection, hoping it would thatch over all together. But with an unadulterated thumbs-up on the piss stick, I am going to have to get under it to get over it tonight, or Felix really will start to realise something's up.

As he checks us in, I lurk by the fire, inspecting the fashion types on their laptops in the bar. Soho Farmhouse is an expensive choice. He knows something's up. He's thrown money at the problem. He returns to me, grinning and carrying our tatty weekend bags with ease (we need to replace those), handing me the chunky block of wood with one key attached and patting my bottom to direct me to the door out to the best cabin (available at reasonably short notice).

If this had been any other time – even just three weeks ago – I would have been on Felix before we'd even closed the door.

The room is insane. The luxurious bed dominates the room like a giant mid-century marshmallow against the stripped wood walls; the freestanding bath overlooks perfectly manicured gardens. The champagne chills elegantly in a bucket by the foot of the bed: carefree sex hanging in the air. Or is it just the sex elephant in the room breathing down my neck?

It's actually Felix breathing on my neck. As he tenderly kisses me across my shoulder, a chill sparks through me. It's electric, but more of a tightening, an impulse: a revulsion. I try to soften my body, to relax into it. *Why can't you just be grateful?*

'Sooo . . . what's the plan, Stan?' I half-laugh. My 'humour' turgid, needless. I'm spoiling it for him. I'm spoiling it for myself.

'I've booked us a couples' massage in an hour . . .' he says, fiddling with the wireless speaker. 'But there's no rush. Let's just take our time.' His choice of soundtrack pierces my silence with a smooth groove. 'This is a day for you. Just us, at last . . .' He has his arms around me from behind, his hands gently grazing the places that Mads was groping lasciviously just a fortnight ago. Felix's touch is so subtle, loving, but right now it feels like the creep of a boa constrictor primed to suffocate. The irony is lost on him that he's playing our favourite Thundercat song, 'Heartbreaks + Setbacks'.

'How about some champagne then?' I release myself, the song bringing tears of frustration that I'm unable to break my brain free from this sensation. 'A little toast?' I congratulate myself in an unhappy reprieve – how long can I delay the inevitable? For ever? 'To being old!'

**HE'S RUN ME A BATH.** Because my husband is the best man in the world, while here I lie, a heinous prune stewing in her own juices, half-cut from drinking *all* the wines with the tasting menu and delirious from the massage. I'm more amenable than when we got here, I just needed to be gently unwound like a mangled Slinky. Felix is attempting to hook his Netflix account up to the space-age TV in front of the bed. At least that will give us an excuse if I'm still incapable of mood maintaining.

I'm trying to avoid my phone, but then a WhatsApp flashes up on the Victorian sidetable. *My sister?*

**Gracie**
So . . .
I haven't heard from you in a while
little sister How are you?          21:22

Well, it's my birthday          21:23

**Gracie**
Yes, I was getting to that
Many happy returns          21:24

Very formal          21:25

**Gracie**
You know me
What are you doing to celebrate?          21:26

Felix looks up from the tangle of wires under the bureau, his thick left eyebrow raised as if to say, '*Who are you talking to?*'

> Taking an interest now? I thought you'd forgotten about me
> I'm at a spa – Felix whipped me off as a surprise    21:28

**Gracie**
He's good
I thought you'd forgotten about me
I'm not the one surrounded by all the home comforts    21:30

> But you are off doing as you please
> Surrounded by shrapnel
> And isn't that exciting?    21:31

TYPING . . .

Felix has stopped what he's doing to stare at me, but I continue to stare at my screen for Gracie's revelation.

**Gracie**
I would fancy being home now though    21:33

She's homesick! Sick for this. I look at my pale body submerged in bubbles in the bronze bathtub, the candle flickering against my champagne glass. Maybe I'd be sick for this too.

'It's just Grace, darling. WhatsApping me a happy birthday. She's HOMESICK!'

'OH!' He's trying to hide the sigh of relief by burying himself in the tangle of wires again. 'Poor thing. Send her my love . . .'

Has Mr War Reporter's sexy helmet lost its gleam? 21:34

**Gracie**
You're so funny.
No, Henry is all right, he got over the kid thing. I'm just tired, you know? 21:36

Tired with work? But you love war 21:37

**Gracie**
I don't love war!
I'm tired of the sneaking around so the neighbours think we're married, but that work thinks we're not shagging. All the keeping a low-profile so we can keep doing our jobs undisturbed – it's knackering 21:38

Sounds a bit shit, sister dearest
What's a girl to do? 21:38

**Gracie**
I'm thinking of transferring somewhere safe 21:38

Such as . . . 21:39

**Gracie**
Washington – I've been offered a job with an agency.
I've met Assad and been shot at by ISIS, Trump isn't going to grab my pussy
What's he going to do, tweet me to death? 21:39

> Err, nuke you? Block you at the airport? Won't that visa be less than forthcoming after holing up in Syria for a year? 21:40

**Gracie**
Which leads me neatly to my next point: I'm coming home!
It's my birthday gift to you –
parental peace at last 21:40

> Oh my god, they might leave me alone and you can deal with it. Can I tell them? I never get to break good news . . . 21:41

**Gracie**
Just to let the dust settle
between jobs, of course 21:42

> Well, I shall look forward to having my sis back
> You can help me edit that film I'm making 21:42

**Gracie**
As shall I, even if you're a little cow 21:43

> That's BIRTHDAY cow to you xx 21:43

I raise myself out of the tepid suds, conscious of whether Felix is looking at me (he isn't now) and wrap my body in the fluffy white robe that he'd draped over the radiator to warm for me. I slick my hair back in the mirror and take a deep breath. *This is not your first rodeo, there's no need for nerves.* I walk slowly across the room, ten steps from bath to bed, eyeing my husband stretched out on the expansive king size, bundled in an even bigger robe and concentrating on a basketball game. His lips are parted slightly in anticipation of a point and I'm struck by the sudden urge to kiss them. *You can make it right.* I climb steadily and quietly across the bed towards him, prowling like a lioness, until I snake my arms into his robe and straddle him, burying my head into his warm chest.

'That's nice, my love. What's that for?' he says.

'Just for you being you,' I say, as I kiss his mouth, and taste his taste and pull both of our robes apart to see if we can be as we used to be again.

'. . . SO HE SURPRISED ME WITH A SPA . . .' The hangover is making me sound even more feeble than before. Orla, understanding my lulled tone as sadness, pauses to gather her new tact. Sending me off to the penis of another man wasn't really going to prepare me for my actual husband trying it on with his.

'Oh, Felix. He's so good.'

I roll my eyes, as I trail the mini wheelie basket round the Co-Op. I'm making all sensitive phone calls outside of the house now. The walls have ears. Or at least, we have an Amazon Alexa now, and she records everything.

'I wish everyone would stop calling him that. He's not a dog. And I'm sure he's done bad stuff too.'

'Has he though?' she asks, suddenly exasperated. 'Apart from travelling a bit and trying to kick on – like you do – what's he done wrong?'

'OK, Professor Judgy . . . I didn't come here for a lecture.'

'No, I know. You rang me to tell me all about exactly how fancy Soho Farmhouse is.' She's waiting, there's more . . . 'Or did you call to say something about Mads?'

'Ssh! No! No mention of the boss that dare not speak its name.'

'Well then, how flouncy was it?'

'OK, I've got one thing. He knew it was my birthday, but I noticed on Instagram – and no, I wasn't stalking – that he'd posted a picture of himself in a very family-ish house in Copenhagen. There were toys in the background. It was like he was trying to make a point.'

'Or was he just at home for the weekend, and he happens to be creative director for the cosiest company in the world?'

'Yeah, OK. Well, on that note – Soho Farmhouse is more than cosy. I got kind of wasted though, think it was nerves. I fainted off the toilet . . .'

'You what?'

'I was on the loo in the middle of the night, and the room was really warm. And we'd had about four bottles of wine with the tasting menu and then another two champagnes in the room, and when I went to the loo, I just remember waking up with a thump, face down on the floor.'

'Bum up?'

'Completely bum up.' I'm lurking by the canned goods, but I look around conspiratorially to check no one is in earshot. 'Bare bottom. Up to the impressively corniced ceiling.'

'And did Felix find you?' She's laughing, but also mortified on my behalf.

'Well obviously, he'd done that *slightly* annoying thing that he always does where he takes the side of the bed nearest the door "to protect me" and so he comes running round the bed, but it takes an extra long time, because it's a mega king. I'd just about wiped once he'd arrived.' I've seemingly lost my sense of self, because I only found it warming to be rescued from the tiled floor by my heroic husband, not embarrassing in the slightest. 'It just makes me realise that this was all just a momentary distraction.' I say, almost trusting myself.

'OK, OK, I believe you . . .' She's pausing – there's something else to say, I can tell by how quiet she's gone on the line.

'Are you still there?' I'm inspecting the tubs of Ben & Jerry's on special offer. Always just the Phish Food – bloody ice-cream overkill. I put it in the basket regardless, with the block of cheddar and four pints of semi-skimmed. This dairy-only diet should be a hot new trend.

'So, I've got something I need to tell you . . .'

'You're pregnant!' I try to sound as excited as you can on the back of a hangover induced by tearing your life apart, but I'm not doing a good job. I nearly trip headlong into the rack of McCoy's as I wipe the fearful tear out of my eye.

'No, I'm not. It's just – we're going to be having IVF.'

Oh, it's fine. I've got time to ready myself. I'll need to sort my head out properly before solid baby news.

'That's good news! I know you'd said you might look into it.' I'm at the till now, knowing I'm going to have to buy another bag for life because I'm wearing a tracksuit, and an H&M bucket bag containing my cloth shopping totes didn't really match.

'Well, the NHS couldn't refer us for another year since the miscarriage, so I said to Rich, "I think it's time we took matters into our own hands." So we're putting our St Bart's money towards it. I can survive without a holiday for a few months.'

'Sorry, madam,' the eighteen-year-old checkout assistant is surveying my greasy hair and ropey grey two-piece with bed socks and trainers with true, tragic pity. 'Your card is saying DECLINED.'

**08:22  TO  LONDON  KINGS  CROSS  CANCELLED**
**08:37  TO  LONDON  KINGS  CROSS  EXPECTED  08:42**

THE 8.37 IS RAMMED. Not one, but two preceding trains were cancelled due to 'inclement weather': that rain that soaks you sideways as you wait and wait and wait. So now the whole of London's northerly commuter belt is squashed on to one boil-in-the-bag parcel of wet dog. I try to peel my coat off as I enter the steam, but I only get one arm out before I'm rammed on board by the crowd. Umbrellas are shaken on my shoes, droplet-covered macs are rubbed collectively on my half-revealed (and now sheer with sweat) white silk blouse, the sweat is collecting in the high waist-band of my vintage Levi's. My coat hangs precariously off one arm, and my hand is puce with the pressure of holding three bags and a faux fur on its extremity.

My usual seat is taken up by a large older lady (she's probably only five years my senior, see: Dr Manjeet) and around her, four man-spreaders gad their legs across the remaining space and into their aisle.

Being the passive-aggressive person who huffs 'I can see there's space down there!' loudly on a day like today is not a good look, so instead I mutter 'excuse you,' under my breath as I bash my bags into their knees, dragging the wet fur across their laps and squeezing through into the cracks beyond them.

Making it to the third bank of seats – where the men are less obvious in their space-taking and less ignorant in their

'I can't see you' Facebook scrolling – I decide that here is as good a place as any to linger. I plonk my bags, only partially spilling my Tupperware across the floor, and finally release myself from the soggy coat, folding it like a layer of insulation across my now dead forearm. As the train pulls falteringly out of the platform, I miss the handrail and nearly end up in someone's lap. He looks up – an unassuming guy in bad shoes around twenty-five – and says, 'Oh god, do you want to sit down?' These are dream words on a day like today, but I'm a feminist and I have no more right to sit there than he does. So I poo poo it with a puff of the lips and a fly of the hand, the universal symbol of 'No, honestly, don't worry, I love being packed like a sardine trying to stand on its tail.' But he's insistent: he looks at me, then points at his tummy and to mine, and says 'But you should, come on, it's yours, take it.' So now I'm forced into the awkward shuffle to switch places with him, lap-dancing across another man's knees as everyone watches on admiringly. He's smiling now, as I settle in with my coat piled up under my chin and every soggy bag on my lap.

'So when's it due?' he says.

I am never wearing these fucking mom jeans again.

**I'M A PAYDAY MILLIONAIRE.** Today, my card will definitely not be declined as I pay £15 for chicken in a box that has to be eaten covertly out of a brown paper bag on a park bench. I might even cautiously reveal my bank balance to myself and not cry. Which will be nice, because for the rest of the day, I'll be bathed in anxiety.

I'm knee-deep in Rachel's work as well as my own, and yet as I log on to my online banking to bask in the glow of the tiny bump Trish Chippenham agreed me for my covering both jobs while Rachel goes off for six months, my pay has gone *down*. I'm not even a hundred pounds clear of my overdraft. I usually have at least two days beyond payday before I remember that I can't afford my life.

'Have any of you had any issues with your pay this month?' I ask the skeleton of people still at their desks at payday pub time. Ryan has swerved the invite once again in favour of skulking at the end of the desk, surreptitiously stuffing his personal post into Hygge envelopes to go in the internal mail. I walk down to enquire more closely.

'Ry, is your pay all right this month?' I say. 'Mine seems to have gone down . . . As if it could be any less.'

'Nah, I think it's normal. One thousand eight hundred and five quid, every month. Never changes.' *That's what I earn.* 'Barely covers my rent in Haggerston. And I live above an abattoir.' *Try living in Borehamwood.*

So what he's saying here is that I'm on the same money – and now less – than a man who is five years my junior and spends most of his day on Depop selling his handmade shorts (he's his own best model).

'So Ry, are you telling me you're on twenty-eight K?' I'm going to be brazen, I deserve more.

'Yeah. Why?' he says, still stuffing his sideline (they are nice shorts, I should get some for Felix). 'Also, isn't it illegal for you to be such a busybody?'

'Nope, I can busybody my way into anyone's earnings if they're willing to tell me. Equal pay transparency.'

'Well, what about you, then? How much are you on?'

'The same as you,' I say flatly. His east London ghost face blanches. 'Except now, my additional work cash for covering Rach must mean I'm getting taxed more and my student loan payment's gone up too.'

'Equal pay, eh?' he says, as if he's the hard done-by one. 'Well, ain't this place just the shit.'

**Olivia Galvin**
Re: Equal Pay act
To: Trish Chippenham

Dear Trish,
It has just come to my attention that I am on the same basic salary as a lower member of staff – who is male – and I would like to ask for a meeting about my earnings. With the additional work money I am getting for covering Rachel, I am now over the next tax threshold and actually earning less after deductions. Is there anything that can be done to reflect my seniority and also five extra years of experience? Women have battled for decades for equal pay and I am incredibly disheartened to see that this is not happening here at HYGGE, especially as it is a Scandinavian firm, and it was my understanding that parity of pay is the norm there. I do not think that women should bow down and work for less.

I look forward to speaking more about this with you.

Thanks
Olivia

Olivia Galvin
Marketing Manager
HYGGE (UK)
+44 (0) 7757406596

**Trish Chippenham**
Re: Equal Pay act
To: Olivia Galvin

Olivia,
I have just looked at your HR file, and you do have equal pay.
Trish

Trish Chippenham
Head of UK Operations
HYGGE
+44 (0) 77235556475

**Olivia Galvin**
Re: Equal Pay act
To: Trish Chippenham

Dear Trish,
I shouldn't have equal pay, I should have more pay because I do much more work than said man.
Olivia

Olivia Galvin
Marketing Manager
HYGGE (UK)
+44 (0) 7757406596

**Trish Chippenham**
Re: Equal Pay act
To: Olivia Galvin

Olivia,
Your job is on the same pay grade as Ryan's, so you get the same salary. And I can't do anything about the tax on the additional work. I can take it back again, if you'd prefer to go back to your original earnings?
Trish

Trish Chippenham
Head of UK Operations
HYGGE
+44 (0) 77235556475


**Olivia Galvin**
Re: Equal Pay act
To: Trish Chippenham

Dear Trish,
Please put it in my notes that I am very unhappy with this situation and will be looking into legal counsel. Please do adjust my pay back to normal if it will keep my deductions down in the meantime.
Olivia

Olivia Galvin
Marketing Manager
HYGGE (UK)
+44 (0) 7757406596


*Screwed again.*

# INTERVIEW 4: ANNIE

I'm feeling nervous about this one. Facebook has facilitated this false sense of intimacy with the people you've collected over the years. And I know my life is someone else's background noise. Annie feels like she's been around throughout the years, despite the fact that we've seen each other only once since university. I'd liked the gorgeous pictures of Milo as a newborn, hoping that one day I'd get to be as happy as she was. But the real story didn't filter through social media. The pretty family images still landed, but her posts were fewer and further between. I checked in on her from time to time, but she'd just say she was fine, just getting on with life. I heard the truth from the friends we still had floating between us. And now I'm going to ask her about it all, and I wish I'd never started this film in the first place.

**Olivia:** Thanks for doing this, Annie, it's just so good to see you. So, in terms of the filming, just talk to me, not directly into the camera. Don't feel like you need to repeat my questions back or anything, but be as full with the details as you can. Are you comfortable?

**Annie:** Yep, sure, I'm ready. Thanks love.

**Olivia:** OK. What does family mean to you, Annie?

**Annie:** First off, I just don't want you to think I don't realise how lucky I am.

Olivia: What do you mean by that?

Annie: Well, it's not like I'll never hear a little one call me 'Mummy'. I've endured the extravagant pains of labour. And I've experienced that rush of childbirth. I can't even begin to describe it.

Olivia: So why is family so difficult to talk about then?

Annie: There's a moment, that one moment, where the sonographer is probing that little bit too hard, and doesn't meet your eye when you look up to ask what's wrong, when you realise there's no sign of hope. A little part of you gets extinguished. That a 'family' might be out of your grasp. Yes, I might have Milo, my healthy, beautiful four-year-old son. But after two miscarriages, and three years trying to add to him, it feels curiously incomplete. You feel empty.

Olivia: So maybe you could tell me why three of you doesn't feel like a family?

Annie: I don't want to sound greedy, I'm not. I love what I have. I know I have a family right now. But I just always had a picture in my mind. You must have it too? It's like a child would draw: a proud couple holding hands, with a dog loyally beside them, in front of a house with a pitched roof. They're guarding two healthy children. You can tell they're healthy by their cherubic rosy cheeks. Sometimes I dream there are three kids in the picture.

Maybe I was just from one of those 2.4 children families in the eighties – although I'm one of four. We didn't have a lot but we had enough. Family meant there being more of you. The parents didn't outnumber the kids.

Olivia: Can you tell me how it all started out? Trying for a family, that is? Was it hard from the start?

Annie: No, not really. The first month I was off the Pill:

255

bang, I was pregnant. Adam boasted about his 'efficient swimmers' until his friends pleaded with him to stop. It was sweet oblivion I guess.

My first pregnancy was touch and go though – I bled every month for the first half and was at the hospital every other week to check his heartbeat was still there. But then somehow the birth wasn't nearly as hard. You can't recreate the elation you feel after your child is born, it bloody hurts, but it's addictive. I knew immediately that I was not done with having that sensation.

**Olivia:** So it got tricky after Milo was born?

**Annie:** I just had it in my head that we'd pick up where we left off on that straightforward path. Try for baby number one, fall pregnant, and then as my maternity leave was ending, I'd magically conceive again and return to work pregnant. My boss told me his wife did it three times. I told my mum, my sisters, my friends: this is the plan. I put a lot of pressure on it. It consumed me. When I sat at my desk on that first day back, I realised that not only was I not pregnant, but that three of my friends were. And after a year of caring for your baby, being away from them five days a week makes you an emotional wreck. I was desperately clinging to having another reason to be at home again. It became my sole purpose.

I berated Adam for his cockiness. It must be karma. We've shown we're a fertile couple. We'd done it before. So what's changed? I feel like there's so much more pressure on baby number two. It's as if as soon as you have one, people feel like they have licence to keep tabs on why you haven't made the sequel.

Before all this, I didn't fully appreciate how insensitive people can be. I remember, I was just recovering from the first operation, and I'd set myself a project in the house to keep my mind busy. I was in the hardware store buying paint and Milo was in the trolley and I remember a woman coming up to me asking how old he was. I told her, two and a bit, and she said, 'Time for another one!' I was clinging on, keeping the tears back. My body wasn't even properly healed. But she just blundered in, no idea. You never know what other people's stories are. It's so personal, it's just best not to ask.

**Olivia:** Do you think that's part of the reason you felt under pressure to keep going?

**Annie:** I just felt like it was selfish to stop at one. That teenager who's sulking with its headphones in on the 'family' holiday with just their parents. There's a reason they're call them 'only' children. I worried Milo would get lonely and spoilt, or he'd become that little old man only used to talking to adults. Who wants to hang out with that kid? We wanted him to feel that closeness that we had with our siblings.

**Olivia:** And then you actually managed to fall pregnant?

**Annie:** Yeah, in the end my periods were so screwed up from breastfeeding Milo for ages (*don't ask*), that I didn't even realise when we actually did fall the second time. I was beside myself with happiness. It felt like we'd conquered something. I could move on with my life. But then, after feeling wretchedly tired for about a month, I started to have little shows of blood, and then I miraculously started to have a lift in energy again. I could read their faces as they explained that I needed an internal scan. I'd have to wait a couple of days to know the final score: that I'd lost the baby. We were at a wedding when we got the call. I felt like I was floating as I fixed this grin on my face to throw confetti, knowing I'd have to dash off as everyone sat down for the speeches. That I'd be staying in the hospital because they suspected it might be ectopic. I didn't even know how far along I was, so Adam was my only support.

**Olivia:** I'm so sorry, Annie, I wish I'd known. And I'm sorry to have to keep on asking you questions, are you OK?

**Annie:** It's OK, Liv, I can talk about it now.

**Olivia:** So how long was it until you felt ready to try again?

**Annie:** I was desperate to try straight away. The specialist advised to wait three cycles, but I ignored them and began again after the first month. It took us six more months of stress and tears – and I even tried acupuncture, I was feeling so vulnerable – until we were there again. Pregnant.

This time, I had horrendous morning sickness. I was worried I was neglecting Milo, because all my focus was on getting and staying pregnant, and I was so nauseous that I would just have to lie in bed while Adam took care of everything. I got to about nine weeks and then again, I had the bleeding. The doctor told me that the sickness was because I'd miscarried earlier, but the hormones continued to ricochet round my body with nothing to do. They told me I couldn't have the procedure for another week. This time, while I felt a deep sense of loss, my instant and enduring reaction was that I felt grossed out. I couldn't get over how repulsed I felt. Like my body wasn't my own. I was in a state of limbo and it certainly wasn't fair on Milo. So when it got to the operation, I just needed it out of me and to move on. I was quite clinical – I think Adam was quite shocked after I was such an emotional wreck the first time – and I worried it made me a horrible person. But it's a coping mechanism.

I still hate myself for feeling that way though. Please don't judge me.

Actually, maybe don't include that bit.

**Olivia:** Whatever you want. You'll see the final cut of this. I'm not going to include anything you're not comfortable with. And there's no judgement, I promise.

**Annie:** To be honest, I felt grateful that that was my sensation. That second knock was a traumatic realisation – maybe we wouldn't be able to make the family I'd planned in my head, but it took all of the emotion out of the equation. It brought me back to the here and now. I don't want to feel like this again. The worst thing people can say to you when you're trying for a baby is 'don't think about it, it'll happen when you least expect it.' Because unless you're really busy, you can't do anything *apart* from think about it. But that moment sort of switched that off.

I've got one child I need to focus on. He and Adam are my family. And three's a nice little crowd in our house.

**Olivia:** Right, I think I've got enough there. Thanks so much for talking to me, Annie, I know that took a lot to do.

**Annie:** Anything for you, darl. This should be a beautiful project. It's kind of like your baby.

I wonder if I can show this to Orla one day. Would she want to know that others feel the same? Or would it make it smaller somehow? Making a family is brutal. And it still doesn't make you sensitive.

259

# Cycle 26

'WHERE DID YOU SAY YOU WERE IN YOUR CYCLE AGAIN?'

'Erm, I *didn't*, Mum, because it's none of your business!'

She scowls, hurt, folding her arms disapprovingly, her shopping bags sandwiched like a fan against her furry gilet, making sure that every hassled Christmas shopper in Watford Harlequin sides with her. I should know better than to cross Mother.

'About two-thirds, if you must know.'

I've never been any good at keeping secrets from her about my love life. It all stems back to that time when I arrived home aged fifteen with a neck full of love bites and attempted to conceal them by getting into bed slathered in orange Rimmel foundation, my dirty polo neck and the duvet pulled tight to my head. My mum thought I was 'doing a Leah Betts' and started screaming 'what drugs have you taken?!' So, accepting the shame I knew she'd heap upon my teenage harlot self, I pulled down the covers and my sexy chenille cowl to wipe away the grime on my neck. She grounded me for a month and forced me to wear an even sexier roll neck to school until they'd healed, but you could tell she was relieved. Since then I've told her pretty much everything. Her knowing is better than her catastrophising about *not* knowing.

What I *won't* be sharing, however, is how little in that all-important two-thirds of a cycle we've actually done about it. I can't deal with their grand designs on my womb as well as how I've been feeling.

'Sure, well, we'll know the results in a week or so then . . .' she says, uncrossing her arms, and looping one into mine as we continue our walk towards Marks & Spencer. If anything ever does happen, I'll have to FaceTime Mum in the bathroom so she can see the test for herself.

'You'll be the first to know, Mother . . . After Felix, I suppose.' I know she'd prefer to go ahead of him really. 'Right, what are we here to get then, *mi madre*?'

I scope out the snazzy socks and comfy slippers all mounted neatly around the Christmas tree by the cash desk and wish I had an uncomplicated family that could be happy with such uncomplicated things.

'Well, lucky for you, I've made a list.' This is very unlike Mum. And then she produces a scrappy receipt from her purse. On it, in the tiniest handwriting that can only be visible to ants, is a list as long as my arm. At least twenty relatives feature, and each has a different shop preference, wanted item or dislike. Aunty Sharon would like a silk scarf in blue, but only a cool grey blue, and only a long one, not square. Grace has specifically banned all present buying, which means Mum will spend the most on her, overcompensating. Next to her name, it simply says 'CAMERA' which means she's about to purchase something extortionate and completely wrong. For my cousins Lou, Louise, Oscar, Paddy, Big Patrick and Una, there are various 'vouchers'. Mum still expects to gift those old paper monies issued by stores. She hates the new-fangled cards, and makes sure to always purchase vouchers from somewhere completely ill-advised for whoever the giftee might be. The woman is not yet sixty, but is set so formidably in her ways.

So, starting with the youngest of the bunch, fourteen-year-old Una's a big-eyed baby goth, so Mum will get her an irredeemable River Island lump sum which she will then hock at school to buy herself some piercings. Both the Patricks, large and small, will receive an HMV gift card, even though neither has owned a physical disc, filmic or musical, in the decade that stands between their ages. Neither of them play video games. Then for Oscar, a twenty-five-year-old *GQ* obsessive, who wouldn't be seen in anything less than Savile Row (no one's sure how he pays for it), she'll go to Topman. Every year. 'He can just buy some boxers if he's that ungrateful that he can't even have a look around,' she says.

She won't stop spending, but she knows she never gets it right. I've tried to just be thankful, but I've got to put a stop to this if only for her purse's sake. But that would all be a whole lot easier if we weren't at The Harlequin centre and this wasn't our only Christmas shopportunity.

'Let's try John Lewis, Mum. Maybe we could get everyone some new-year workout gear?' All the cousins are unified by their love of looking toned – even Una has all black Lycra for her dead-of-night runs – and I'm the only one who's let myself go to seed. Easter sports day has never been so difficult for me. Maybe Mum will get Felix and me some too if I do enough heavy hinting (i.e., taking selected gift to counter and making her pay for it), then we can pump our way back to being sexually attracted to each other. I won't tell her that bit for now.

As we ride the escalator to the top floor, I realise we're going to have to run the gauntlet of the baby section in order to get to their sports department. Mum has noticed it too, her eyes glazing over with a grand-broody glow.

'Come on, Mum, nothing to see here,' I say, breathlessly pacing my way past the racks of cutesy organza fairy frocks, miniature boating outfits and sterling silver christening spoons. Have we gone back to the Victorian age? I turn and Mum has already stopped, leafing through tiny baby-gros, a little tear trickling down her pale face.

'Do you think we'll ever have a wee one to complete the family?' she asks, looking up at me blankly, not registering that it's me who should be crying. 'I mean, it's weird that you've not even been pregnant once in this whole time.'

'You think it's weird? Do you? But, of course, Mum, it will happen.' Why am I reassuring her? 'When the time is right, something will come good. We just need a bit of time. It'll happen.' Now I'm reassuring myself.

'But I can't wait much longer! I'm getting old, your father's worn out from all that work he's doing on the pub, he can't stop. He just needs a diversion. We need something to look forward to. I know you don't understand, but it's hard for us being the only ones of our friends without a grandchild. I mean, I've never put pressure on you, have I?'

I turn so my back is to her momentarily, so she doesn't see my nostrils flare fire, and when I turn around, breathing deep and slow, she's smiling again and holding out a tiny little Santa baby costume to me with a manic look on her face. 'I mean, wouldn't this just be the most dear little thing? We just need to get the next generation underway. When I was your age, you were practically in secondary school.'

*Blame. Blame. Blame.*

'Step away from the baby clothes, Mother!' I'm angry now. 'You'll get a grandkid when it's time. And when it comes, there's no way you're putting it in a costume that crap.'

Hey, how are you today? I've just come out of the egg collection. It was gross. They use this vagina hoover thing to suck out the eggs. They said they got fifteen! So now they're mixing them with Rich's deposit (he was still boozing right up until last night, stupid idiot) and then tomorrow they'll give us an update on how many embryos we have. They've given me these pessaries, but I can stop the injections now, which is good. They said I didn't really have enough fat on me to have enough injection sites, so I look like a heroin addict. If it had gone on any longer I would have had to start doing it between my toes like Amy Winehouse. Xxxxx

That's good that it's all done for today, and that there are no more injections, bet you look like a pincushion. So glad to hear you're not in too much pain or anything. And think about it like this, you only need one to make a baby! Xxxxx

'ORLA HAD HER EGGS collected today,' I say loudly to Felix in the kitchen as I unpack the gifts I've bought for our various family members. I'm setting them out across the dining-room table to wrap; even though it's nearly 9 p.m. and I feel like I'm about to die, I'm going to be organised if it kills me. 'They're going to make them into embryos and then in less than a week, they'll put them back in.'

'Oh right,' he says sullenly. 'But I suppose there's something wrong, is there?'

'Yeah, she said there were fifteen, and I think they're supposed to get twenty or something.'

'I mean, this is Orla we're talking about . . .'

'And what does that mean?'

'Well, it's always worst-case scenario right? Just to keep you on your toes . . .'

'What are you trying to say?'

'Well, she's just always got something worse than you, hasn't she? Elevenerife.'

'Stop that right now, it's not like that. She's just had a lot of issues.'

'Yeah, a lot of issues: got pregnant once and is now going to get pregnant again.'

'I don't know why you're being such a bastard about this.'

'I'm not being a bastard! I feel really sad that she had a miscarriage, but we've had nothing at all. And yet we all have to go round feeling sorry for poor Orla. What about poor us?'

'Look, I think you need to piss off and cool off.'

'I will piss off – to LA!'

'Haven't you turned that stupid job down yet?'

'I'm getting round to it, let me live my dream a bit longer . . .'

'No! If you won't even give my best friend a modicum of respect, I'm not giving your "dreams" one little stupid thought.'

'You really are some kind of harridan, you know that? Why the Christ did I ever marry you?'

'At this point, I have literally no clue. Maybe you should just take that job. I'm sure you'll find yourself a fertile Barbie doll as soon as you land.'

'You shouldn't tempt me at this point, Olivia.'
There's nothing like wrapping in a huff.

---

**<17 December**          **Event Details**

**Jen, Al and Gordon invite you to ALTERNATIVITY!**
**Marylebone**
Sunday, 17 December
12pm

| Calendar | Felivia shared |
| --- | --- |

Invitation from   **Felix**

Invitees

| Alert | None |
| --- | --- |

Notes
Fancy dress wins prizes!

---

'FUCK! WE FORGOT THE FUCKING NATIVITY!' Felix has launched himself out of bed and is running around pulling on what looks like long, red-and-green-striped elf socks. 'We forgot the fucking nativity!' We didn't even make up last night, and now we're hurling ourselves out the door even more angry.

'So we're not only supposed to be at some fake news interpretation of the nativity in some *private theatre* – in Marylebone – in exactly an hour . . . but we're also supposed to be in *fancy dress*? Sorry, but could you pass me Santa's swag bag, he's left it at the bottom of the bed – surely he's deposited something in there for me.'

I start to huffily rifle through the bottom of my wardrobe, pulling out anything that could even vaguely be miscon-strued as festive-looking. I whip my red flannel pyjama bottoms around my head. 'How about these?'

Felix barely looks at me, flapping the back of his hand dismissively and scowling. He's now wearing a pair of

266

brown board shorts with his stripy socks, and is fastening large glitzy fandangles to his work shoes. We'd better be getting an Uber.

I keep rooting. *Jackpot:* one 'sexy bag' safely stowed at the back of the cupboard.

'I've found something,' I say emptying the contents of the plastic Ann Summers bag on to the floor and casting a once-used neon pink spanking paddle under the bed. How does one dispose of these unwanted spicy artefacts? And then, feeling the gloss of some wipe clean PVC and a whole lot of Lycra, I lay my hands on what I was searching for: my naughty nutcracker uniform. I knew it would come in handy again one day.

'Give me five minutes and then order the Uber.'

I *will not* be sexualised at a kids' party (even in an outfit purchased six years ago to make Felix want to have sex with me at a Halloween party), so I scout through my knicker drawer in the hallway, finally finding the white tights I knew I'd abandoned in there for being too damn disgusting. Weisswurst legs: sort of festive?

'Don't we just look a Christmas treat!' I laugh as we run out the door. Felix is still fuming in his Santa's little helper get-up.

**THE CACOPHONY OF CHILDREN** is audible even inside the Prius.

'They've started without us then . . .' I muse, even though I'd rather miss as much of this as possible. Felix is antsy, because we'd nearly forgotten all of the kids' presents, then he had to write the cards while I wrapped in the back of the Uber. I nudged, he smudged, and now we're definitely not talking.

'ALTERNATIVITY!' screams a poster pinned to the huge wooden door, which Al has designed using a 1994 version of Clip Art (and not in an ironic way). The Victorian theatre is unfathomably fancy, and should surely be in use just a week away from Christmas, but since having Gordon, Jen and Al have made a habit of creating lavish baby festivities, renting ever-more extravagant venues to rub their parenthood and pay packets in our faces. As we use our combined strength to push our way in, we're swarmed upon by ten toddlers. We only recognise one – bloody Gordon – who's throwing a hissy fit because he's not first in line to grasp on to our legs.

'Look, everyone, the strippers have arrived!' laughs Al in his trusty dad jeans, boat shoes and Gant rugger top, moving aside to let the Pied Pipers of Alternativity through, and swooping to pick up his screaming mini-accountant progeny.

*Just shut up, Gordon. No one wants to hear it.*

'Well, it's not a party unless we embarrass ourselves, is it?' I'm not letting him elf-shame us first. I grab Felix's hand and shimmy through the crowd as if we're the main event, and they've all won the golden ticket to check us out.

'Oh, darlings! You are good! You didn't have to dress up, I only meant could you help with the kids . . .' says Jen, bonneting a smug little red-faced girl for her stage debut. 'Stop struggling, Arabella, don't you think the children in Syria would be pleased to be having a party like this?'

I look up and around. All the little angels have dirty faces and slightly grubbied up Jojo Maman Bebe sweaters. They've formed a snake up on stage towards what appear to be armed guards at a check-point and some tents.

'Yep, you aren't tripping: the "Alternativity" is set in a refugee camp,' laughs Liam, as he wanders up beside us, handing Felix a Christmassy IPA, and me a tinsel-covered piñata bat with a wink. 'It's all looking decidedly ill-judged. Ten middle-class toddlers from Richmond pissing around on stage in their park-muddied Petit Bateaus so we can all feel smug that the proceeds are going to Help Refugees. I suggested that we just take the day to hire a van and drive supplies over to France to a camp that actually needs it, but Al told me to stop being such a leftie snowflake. God forbid we might rob poor Gordon and Arabella of their stage debut.' I let out a snort, and everyone turns to inspect the honking sexy nutcracker.

'Oh, he's changed since he moved to south-west London,' pipes in Felix, draining his bottle with one hand and scouting out a second with his other, sperm perishing with every gulp. 'It used to be us lot at a garage night, and now it's these dry lunches talking about how big their ga-rah-ges are.'

Liam clinks to that.

'Prepare yourselves – you think parenthood won't change you, until you realise one day that you've not slept, let alone had sex for six months and no one has even noticed.' *Surely it can't really get any worse than this? Have we had our last good shag and not even said farewell?*

'Sure it's not that bad mate, you managed to make number two . . .' says Felix, hiding his jealousy well.

'Well, after a while, you realise you've fallen off anyone's social A-list, so you have to make your own fun,' says Liam.

Felix grabs his friend into a one-armed hug, but he knows that we've all been relegated lately.

'I'm just glad that Jackson is too young to realise that

269

he's being made to play an angry border control officer because Al was insulted that I'd tried to stop the festivities.' Liam waves to Jackson, who is chewing his fingers and looking rumpled in his age two army uniform as the muddied Gordon and Arabella (even she has a bump) attempt to make safe passage into the tent with a manger flanked by three wise little Médecins Sans Frontières volunteers.

'Maybe if none of us puts it on Instagram,' I say – mainly so no one will be reminded of my fancy dressing – 'it'll be like it never happened?'

'Sweet,' says Liam, still rummaging for his phone. 'But maybe just one of you two? For posterity?' Felix scowls as Liam pushes us together so he can frame us full length. *Scuppered at every turn.*

Orla
Today 15:23

Hey, what are you up to today? I'm starting to feel quite sad. I don't think it's going to work. I went for the blastocyst transfer yesterday and since then I keep feeling this weird dragging sensation like it might fall out. Do you think it's going to fall out? I'm sitting still watching all the comedies you prescribed me (was it *Broad City* you said was good? I'm going to try that next . . .) but I just can't relax. Rich has had to go in to work, so I'm just here at home on my own, thinking about what happens when we find out it's a no. This is the last resort, Liv, what if we can't have a baby at all? Xxxx

Felix saw my phone. He's looking angry now in the corner, passive-aggressively wrapping and re-wrapping a pass-the-parcel gift like I was doing last night. Maybe Orla getting pregnant will send him mad before me.

270

Don't feel sad at all! How was the transfer procedure? You don't have a big cavernous vagina and there's no way it'll fall out even if you did. Glad you're taking my advice on the laughing. I hope you're eating the pineapple core that I told you about too. Five days to implant, and then no more pineapple – apparently organic is best, but then of course it is. At least you're there getting some rest – we're in the hellmouth of friends' children and Felix is about to start crying. And he's dressed as an elf. We've hit a new low, even for us. I hope the IVF works for you so we can timeshare that baby and stop being dragged in as entertainment. xxxxx

**FOLLOWING THE 'PLAY' COMES MORE PLAY.** This is the bit that Jen was enlisting us for. Everyone knows that parents go to kids' parties in order to offload their kids – not help with other people's. Thus, Jen and Al draft in the ringers – the old spare wombers – to pick up the slack. We're lower paid than the room's flock of unfortunately absent au pairs and more over-dressed than the staff at that medieval soft play place on the North Circular that I always mistake for an asylum.

Azi settles next to me with little Esteri, her beautiful green eyes staring up at me and piercing my soul as I try not to flash my sausage legs at any dads on crouching level. Felix finishes fiddling with the speakers and dumps himself to my other side on the theatre's cold parquet, hitting play on a Katy Perry song for pass the parcel.

'What's with all the galumphing?' I hiss, as we move the over-wrapped present past us and on to the other side of the room, before he hits pause.

'I'm just sick of your attitude, that's all. Always have a face on you when it's my friends.' He's trying to keep an eye out

271

for the kids that look like they need a turn on the present first. So that's none of Gordon's Montessori mates then.

'My attitude? I'm not the one who's been storming around. I dressed up like a fool only to get here and find all the Boden Bitches out in force, while I look like a Lego prostitute. Why don't you ever read your invites properly?'

'It's not just you who looks like they got lost on the way to Lapland, but it's me who's the failure again! I get it, Felix is a shit, Felix never gets anything right, let's all pile in on Felix.'

'Felix needs to stop speaking in third person and get over himself.' I say, as I grab a marauding party-goer dressed as a Syrian reindeer who's trying to toddle off with the parcel and settle her in my lap while trying to prise the present from her mouth.

'You're so good at that,' whispers Felix, sadly now. 'I'm just sorry it's always us who's the spare part.'

I pass the rogue toddler back to her mum. 'We're not the spare parts – we're the working parts. We're just always getting used and until we have a baby of our own, no one is going to leave us alone. So we either pull our elf socks up and start trying harder, or we just accept it.'

I see Azi tending to Esteri who's lying on her outstretched legs gurgling with joy. They're in their own little world.

He hits pause again and leans over and gives me a kiss, and I grip his face in return. We've just got to try harder. All the kids in the room shout 'awoooooo!'

Exhausted

'DEEP BREATH. Deep breath,' Orla whispers in my ear as we make our way in a line of three into the Christmas opening of the HYGGExperience. My cornflower-blue jewel-encrusted jumpsuit is starting to itch. I feel ridiculous, why did I make this much effort? Rachel couldn't bear to be parted from baby Keith for a moment, so this night is all for me – and the *other* giant sparkling monstrosity I've somehow built on the basement floor of the Tottenham Court Road store. I clutch both Orla and Felix's hands tight to steady myself in my four-inch black stilettos as we make our way down the wide staircase and I see Mads in a jet-black double-breasted suit and polo neck looking expectantly up at me, clapping my entrance. Eagerly accepting a flute of champagne and downing it in one gulp, I drop Orla's hand but not Felix's. This is my show of unity. He's my talisman to ward off evil advances.

The octagonal mirrored *thing* sits dead-centre on the shop floor, spotlit within an inch of its life. I worry that those school tales of mirrors causing fires might be true, especially in such an enclosed space, but it does look gloriously twinkly against the lowered lighting of the party around it. There's a queue to go inside and see the cosy home of the future – a kind of space grotto on acid. I imagine they're all expecting a glittering *Julemanden* inside, but they'll be sorely disappointed. HYGGE overruled Father Christmas for tonight. Instead, it's just new season short-haired sheepskins, iridescent cushions and more booze: it's basically just a massive marketing bauble. Out here, the DJ is playing synthy versions of festive classics. The overall mood is Luc Besson directing a Scandinavian detective drama: space age, but somehow bleakly cosy and festive too. There's an ice luge shaped like a large Christmas tree, lit purple and blue from which to drink Aquavit. Felix fills up a festive crystal glass, his face filled with joy as if I'd sculpted the ice myself. I try to ignore the repulsion at that smell coming from Felix's lips, instead focusing on Orla passing her full glass of champagne from hand to hand. I see Mads in the corner of the room raising an emphatic toast in my direction, his eyes lidded hawk-like, his lips creeping into a wicked smile.

'I'm so proud of you, darling,' whispers Felix into my ear, kissing my cheek lightly. 'I can't believe this is what you were up to with all those early starts. Makes it all worthwhile, right? To be building things again?'

'Thank you, darling,' I say, cradling his chin in my sweaty palm and drawing him up to a kiss, knowing Mads is watching me. Feeding his jealousy. 'I'm glad you appreciate it.'

He wanders off to watch the bloggers photograph the installation from every angle, his reflection in all of their pictures like a ghost. I see Mads making his way round to him, but can't intercept them both without sounding the alarm.

'Orla?' I say, my voice an urgent warning. 'Can you look after Felix, somewhere in this corner while I do the rounds quickly?'

'I see my mark,' she says, as she grabs Felix and pulls him back to look at some new lamps we finally had signed off by head office, *away* from where Mads is now loping slowly towards me trailed by five Klauses.

'The woman of the moment!' he says seductively, air-kissing me too close to be neutral. On the second peck I hear him breathe, 'I see you.'

'Can we have a picture?' calls a girl dressed in as much silver as the construction behind me, waving her camera in our faces, but dismissing the Klauses with a parting hand.

'We'd love to have a picture together, wouldn't we, Olivia?' he says, smiling down at me, drawing me in again. *You can't do this, not here.* And as her flash goes, I know that my smile is pure passion and our bodies are too close and that his hand is too low, and I wonder what the Klauses can see, and if Orla is still keeping Felix out of sight. As I withdraw myself from his grip, I catch Orla making big round warning eyes at me, so I leave Mads to charm the blogger and glide as unnoticeably as I can around a hall of mirrors in a glittering jumpsuit back to her side.

'All quiet on the Felix front?' I whisper.

'I kept his back turned that entire time, he either thinks I'm a nutter or that I'm coming on to him. Which at this moment,' she says, nodding in Mads's direction, which sparks a devilish smile to her, 'I see is safe to do . . .'

I go back to my husband and put my arm seductively around his waist. 'What do you think of it all?' I pull him in to dance as the slow strains of an electro 'Driving Home for Christmas' kick in.

'It's all wonderful, just like you,' he says, kissing me sweetly on the forehead. 'Orla's being a bit strange. Do you think she's back on the old drink?'

'She doesn't get out much,' I lie, not wanting to ruin his evening with the reason for her obvious abstinence, as well as my obvious attraction to another man.

I can see out of the corner of my eye that Mads is making moves in our direction as 'All I Want For Christmas Is You' jingles into life, so I push Orla forward to slow his roll, while I move Felix in the opposite direction. She's wearing a low-backed black dress split to the thigh – how could he ever resist?

I feel a pang of jealousy as I catch how she's charming

him. But he's laughing in my direction, which means she's admitted that I'm their person in common. She takes him in a slow-dance hold and begins tangoing him away from us, kicking her leg and her dress like a bullfighter waving his cape as a decoy, drawing as many stares as possible in the process. Felix is trying to see what all the fuss is about, but I keep spinning him. Divert him at every turn.

Just as the coast looks clear, I hear the opening bells of our teenage favourite. Orla's running footsteps behind me means she's heard it too. Felix nods in admission and heads to the bar to top up our drinks, and I turn to join her on the thinned-out dance floor as 'Christmas Wrapping' sparks into life.

'Bah humbug; now that's too strong! 'cause it's my favourite holiday . . .' we sing along, prancing like glittery reindeer and forgetting our sultry thirty-something ambitions. I note Felix has been accosted by Zara and Ryan (wearing silver foil shorts in homage to my work) which means he's safe, for now. Orla and I stand back-to-back and link ankles, pumping one leg in time with the music and lifting our arms above our heads, screaming into a running man then turning back to each other to reverse arm cross each other.

'Did he seduce you down the back of the sparkly bike shed too?' I ask her, out of breath from the moves I could do without breaking a sweat just a few years ago.

'No, but I wish he would. He is HOT. Fuck, Liv, what have you got yourself into there?'

'Nothing! I am not into *anything*.'

'*Sure*,' she laughs, looking over at him with a wink. 'But that's not what he's thinking. He was saying you should be the next creative director of this place. Maybe that's his indecent proposal. His job for your body.' We've drawn a

276

crowd now. The Klauses are lining the floor, clapping in time with our moves.

'He's hardly Robert Redford . . .' I pant, as we kick and clap. 'I mean, his hair's a bit similar. But I'd rather have the million than the job. Then I could go do my own thing instead of getting up at five stressed about whether the mirrors will fall off that ugly piece of junk.'

'A million wouldn't even get you a semi in Barnet now,' she says as we swing our hair from side to side.

'OK, well, maybe the offer could be in line with inflation twenty-five years on,' I say, spinning her round so I can check Felix is OK. Trish Chippenham is now boring his ear off, her blue hair braided into a Viking crown. Still safe.

'Or maybe you just don't take the offer and stay with Woody Harrelson, who you're supposed to be with all along?' We're dancing so close to the HYGGExperience now, I can see my whole outfit refracted on the ceiling.

'Must learn to be much firmer with my noes,' I laugh. And as I say this, I feel a hand around my wrist, and I'm yanked with dancer precision into Mads's arms, leaving Orla alone to style out the last chords of 'couldn't miss this one this year.'

'You can't just do that . . .' I say, trying to pull away subtly enough to not make a scene. He has me in a hold that is so professional that if I stormed off, all eyes would be on me immediately. Close enough that I can smell his cologne but far enough away that I am not able to thigh-graze an erection. I eye the exit routes. And see that Trish still has Felix cornered with his back to the action.

'Don't pretend you've not been flirting with me across the room all night,' he breathes. 'That you don't want people to see . . .'

I look back over to Felix's safe zone. He's not there. Where is he?

Mads pulls me closer.

Just then Felix taps me on the shoulder. His beautiful face is clouded with jealous questions, his jaw clenched at this man god touching his wife's bum.

'Oh my god, Mads, there you are!' flies in Orla clutching a bunch of silver mistletoe and prising me away from Mads's grip. 'I just wanted to give you this . . .' And right there in front of us all, she kisses Mads full on the lips and the whole room stops.

'Are you sure she's not drinking?' says Felix flatly.

'**SO YOU OBVIOUSLY WANT TO STAY HERE,**' says Felix, pulling on his smart navy J Crew coat. 'But I said I would go to *The Times* party to see everyone.' He's shaming me now. But how can I leave a party that is essentially built around my work? He's only partially convinced by my protestations that Mads was interrogating me about Orla, who I've left in his clutches while I see my husband out the door. 'Go and enjoy your party,' he says, not meaning a word. 'And I'll see you at home later.'

I kiss him goodbye, but it's steely, dispassionate. He might as well have patted me on the back goodbye. *You need to fix this.*

'**GET IN HERE NOW,**' I say, anger building as I stomp back into the party, dragging Mads away from Orla and into the HYGGExperience, my face set to neutral so as not to alert the Klauses.

'I just wasn't expecting it to look so . . . sexy . . . in here,' he whispers, grabbing at my waist greedily. 'It's like some sort of robo boudoir. Are there sex robots, Olivia?' He's pressing himself into my back now, devouring the sides of my face with wet kisses. I step away from his reach and sit down on one of the silver banquettes.

'I think this might have been Rachel's hormones getting the better of her,' I say, coldly. 'I've just executed her vision.'

'And quite the vision you are,' he says, sitting down next to me so we're leg-to-leg. With every inch of body contact I can feel the pressure building. He's drunk, lecherous, but I'm still physically restraining myself. *I hate how much I want you.*

'You've gone quiet on me again, Ms Galvin. But you noticed I didn't press you,' he says, pushing his muscular thigh against my much softer one a little bit harder than before.

'I thought it was for the best,' I say, against myself. 'It all got well out of hand . . .'

He raises his hand to run it through his hair. 'I never wanted it to be like this: me getting drunk watching you across the room with your handsome husband. Is he possessive? I would be. I like you, Olivia. A lot. I know you have your life, and I have mine. And I respect that. But it doesn't mean I don't want you.' He's bitter, mocking himself over how attracted he is to someone so beneath him. 'But I'll back off if that's what you need me to do.' He issues a slithering laugh, which makes his face crease up in a way I hadn't noticed before. The purple and lights show a hideous façade.

'Yes. This is what I need . . .' I say, but our faces are too close. I can almost taste the familiar Aquavit, sweet on his lips. He reaches up and cradles my face in his hands and our lips meet intensely, but I feel trapped. *One more for luck*, but I've already lost.

Then I get up and out of that godforsaken structure for the very last time.

**I'M HOME SAFE, READY TO** restart my life again, to draw a line under all this. But there's no Felix. It's after 2 a.m. and his party must have finished hours ago. I get that familiar itch. The iPad is looking at me. Where is he?

I log in, wishing I'd wiped the password out of my mind, but glad that he hadn't changed it out of suspicion after I used it the last time. His messages bleep from four to five. And now to six. That familiar itch takes over, and my finger lingers over the button. Can't stop my hands.

> I'm sorry, Felix, I should never have done that. Please come back so we can talk?

My hands tremble as I resist the urge to throw the iPad across the room again, but this time shatter it like my splintered trust. Helena? Helena, his old boss Helena? Helena who there's a picture of in the 1980s at *The Times* where she still looks older than I am now? Helena who could be my mum? I check the associated email on the contact. She's nearly fifty . . . *Think about your own evening, slut.*

> I shouldn't have come. I was just drunk and miserable that my friends had gone home to their babies. You understand me, you don't have kids to go home to . . .

But I want all of that, you didn't. And while you're very attractive . . .

. . .TYPING

Thank you – so are you. Felix, you're a very sexy man and I know you're being under appreciated. I really wish you'd turn around and come back to mine. I can appreciate you

And you're really turning me on . . .

I can hardly type I'm so turned on. Only using one hand . . .

Oh my god, I'm remote log-in-ed to a sex chat between my husband and another woman.

I have a wife, and I love her. I can't do this. Doing this with you is only going to fracture it completely . . .

This might be your last chance though . . . I always knew there was something there when you worked for me and I thought tonight was our chance. But I see I was wrong. Good luck with it all, Felix. I hope Olivia doesn't ever find out about tonight. I'm not sure I'd want my husband doing what you did to me in the back of that cab

I'm vibrating with panic. I lie on the floor of the dining room, the truth heaped on me like heavy spadefuls of dirt on my coffin. What has he done? What have I done? Does that mean we're even?

My blood is boiling as I pace from the front door, through the dining room, the length of the kitchen and back again. I'm ignited with envy and greed, anger and lust. I'm rucking the hessian rug up beneath my thick slouchy socks. I'm half madwoman, half animal, dressed in Calvin Klein leggings and an indecent white vest ready to pounce. It's now nearly 3 a.m., and there's still no sign of him. He's left her or they wouldn't be messaging, but where has he ended up instead?

The hands of the clock are moving quickly now, matching my arrhythmic heartbeat. Should I check the iPad again? I'm effervescent with torment. Why can't he ever take it out with him? Should I try to track his phone? Or should I just phone Mads, like I really want to?

Bret and Jemaine track my steps from their perch on the stairs like umpires in a tennis rally. I pour blood, sweat, tears – and some grunting – as I hurl myself back and forth in the lamp light. I am worn into a simmering mess of rage. My phone sweats in my hand: call Mads and take the energy out on him. *FaceTime him and give him something to see while you berate him.*

Just then, as my finger is poised to dial, a car pulls up, idling in the middle of the road: a cab. The gate shudders and then thuds shut. Felix's footsteps assured on the path. He's in a hurry to get into the house, to me. I turn and straighten myself up, launching myself as I hear the key in the lock. I catch his eye as he clears the threshold but I say nothing at all. There's no need for words, the jealousy hisses

from me. I slam his back against the door and start unbuttoning his jeans.

Sad                       Heavy

**CHRISTMAS MORNING IS A TIME FOR JOY.** It's the
time for children getting you up at 5 a.m. because they can't
hold in the excitement for *this day* any longer. It's being
allowed to scoff buttered Panettone and a handful of Quality
Streets for breakfast while sitting on a cushion admiring all
the bounty beneath the tree. It's opening presents – a baby-
sized Head gym bag, a Take That pencil case, CK One – in
your pyjamas, and trying on clothes you never would have
bought for yourself but Dad picked in Next and you quite
like actually, or fiddling with the first CD player you've ever
owned. It's wrapping paper that's been sellotaped at eleven
on Christmas Eve only to be discarded seven hours later to
decorate the recycling bin. It's heaping all your gifts, as if
they're real happiness, into a pile in the corner of the front
room and saying, that's mine.

But what happens when you're not a kid, and you don't
have one either? Not even a tiny one, too young to covet
the Toys R Us catalogue and there to simply issue a baby
Jesus wail of life to wake you from your festive dreams?
What if the pregnancy test says no luck once again – just
to hammer it home – and the only noise to wake you at
5 a.m. is the cat scratching the side of your bed for food?
What if the room set aside for a baby has been still and
cold and silent for more than two years now? What if you
forgot the Panettone and the Quality Street because you

were too frantic trying to track down five turkey crowns after you forgot to order the bird? What if you didn't buy each other presents this year because you needed to pay off the credit cards? What if the turkey legs you eventually bought cost the same amount as a new pair of trainers each anyway? What if the only social media you did on Christmas morning was looking vengefully at what everyone else has? What if even the cats slunk off because there was no catnip under the tree and the tree lights have blown and now not even the Sky is working, but you don't have time to watch *A Muppet Christmas Carol* because you have to peel five kilos of potatoes to batch cook for thirteen people and the house isn't even clean yet? What if you couldn't even be grateful for that?

*What if you'd both been nearly fucking other people?*

'WHERE'S THE SODDING GRAVY?' hisses Felix, barely holding it together. He is clutching the bubbling kettle, his itchy acrylic Spurs Christmas jumper partially obscured by the food-stained tea-towel slung over his shoulder.

'It's fine, Felix, I made three jugs already!' shouts back his mum from the dining room. I tussle my way back through the seven family members lingering between the living room and our dining-room-cum-hallway to plate up another three dinners simultaneously from the turkey-potato-pigs-stuffing-veg production line we've set up along the work surface.

'Why did we ever agree to this?' I hiss over my shoulder, as I look out at Mona, John, Mum, Dad, Gracie, Henry, James, Isaac and Clemmie, all getting in each other's way as they make awkward small talk over Bucks Fizz beside our gloriously HYGGE-ed table setting.

'It's your fault – you invited them!' snipes Felix, using the kettle water to make gloopy bread sauce instead. 'This should be a one-family-at-a-time house . . .'

'But we couldn't have one side left out on *Christmas Day*, could we? It's too much pressure to choose,' I whisper across the sprouts, which have now gone a murky yellow colour from being left on too long. *Our timing is always off.*

'Why is it always on us though?' he moans. 'Why can't our families just relax and have a nice time on their own for once? That's all I want in life. Just to be left alone . . .'

I scowl at him. *You just want to be alone, so you can get off with your old crone.*

'Why doesn't everyone just RELAX in the living room while we get the dinner served?' I motion to the room pretty aggressively, my fringe sweated to my forehead from all the sprout-infused steam. No one is helping, just getting in the way and my mum's sole focus is on fussing around the newly repatriated Grace. We've realised, too late, that the oven seal is broken, so I'm wearing a new fragrance: Eau de Roast.

'I wouldn't say this in front of the kids,' my mum says, leaning dramatically to Mona, *and saying it right in front of the kids*. 'It's just not the same without a little one running around.'

I glance over to Grace who's placating Henry, in his chinos and a neat cream argyle sweater (smart dad-wear for someone that will never get to pay his kids' school fees). He's obviously in a huff that the baby pressure is rising again, and he can't have his way. This is a Christmas nightmare.

**REVENGE – AND CHRISTMAS 'LUNCH'** – is a dish best served cold: which is lucky, because it was 7 p.m. by the time we got the main course on the table. Both of our mums had helpfully brought a bolster dish with them – Mona's traditional Jamaican goat stew, and Mum's Irish boiled bacon – and spent the whole meal not eating their own food, but fussing over making sure the boys had enough heaped on their plates. At one point, when food was looking scarce, myself, Grace and Clemmie all eyed each other, shouted 'Feminism for food!' and made a break for freedom, piling seconds on to our plates. I marvel how my nan used to make catering for fifteen look so seamless.

And now, as John scrubs the pots, and my dad intricately stacks the dishwasher listening to Christmas tunes on the kitchen radio, my mum and Mona laughing over coffee and Gracie and Henry talking animatedly about which board game to start first with the Gyamfi brood, I look at Felix and all of them and think how lucky I should feel. The open fire flickers on our HD TV. There are Quality Street and presents under the tree now. And while there are no kids, we can go on into the night. 'Next year, we can do better,' I say, squeezing Felix's hand and standing up to reach for the bottle of Advocaat. 'Now, who would like another Snowball?' But he's already batted me away.

# Cycle 27

WE LIE SIDE BY SIDE but we're drifting further and further away. We're wrapped in our guilt, only half insulating us from the world like the duvets around us. I want to hold his hand, but I can't reach. Or can I just not move? The light from a street lamp slices the room neatly between us, but I haven't adjusted the curtains either. It's well past midnight on a new New Year, but I can feel that he's not asleep. I wonder if he knows I'm not either? A single thick tear trickles down my cheek, pooling in my hair and on to my pillow. My heart is boiling over: what happened, how could you, why? But I'm asking myself the same, and I can't reveal my hand. I can't suffer and *be* suffered at the same time. I need one of us to have a reason to go on.

I turn on to my right shoulder so I'm facing Felix, his body tense. I can see his eyes are scanning the ceiling in the dark, but he daren't breathe. The veins in his neck stand in anguish. And then a dread gulp of air, as he can't contain the emotion any more.

'Come on, baby,' I say. 'It's OK, talk to me.'

'There's nothing to say, I'm fine. Let's just go to sleep.' He's guarding himself from the truth, but does he know why I don't push him? Does he think I simply don't know? Are we supposed to pretend that we went to bed at 11 p.m. on New Year's Eve because of a little tiff over a takeaway?

That these days and weeks of hardly talking was because Christmas got in the way? This purgatory alone is penance enough for whatever he's done. I haven't served my time yet. Letting out the truth now would be like a deep slash to the wrists: we might bleed out.

There's something sublime about the amount of pain we're in. Like we're locked in separate boxes, side by side but always together. We're just on the precipice of having those coffins kicked off a cliff.

'Y'know what we need to do?' I say sitting bolt upright in the bed. I can't take it any longer. 'We need to go out!'

'Liv, stop it! New Year is gone. The festivities are dead. We've missed the party.'

'Not listening!' I say, switching on the dusty sixties lamp on my bedside table. 'It's only 12.30, we're not dead yet. Let's go to the pub at the end of the street. I can still hear it going. Irish pubs never close anyway.'

'Liv, you're acting mental! Stop it! What do we need to go out for?' He's still lying flat on his back looking at the ceiling. He's still locked in by his guilt.

'Because we can't go on like this, lying sombrely and moping about being "tired" or depressed at going back to work. We're still young. We've got no ties. Remember when our nights out didn't even *start* till midnight?' I'm pulling my jeans on over my pyjama shorts and smiling, beckoning him out of bed. I start doing his trademark bedroom dance to at least coax a smile out of him.

'But we won't know anyone . . .' he says flatly. I know he's laughing in there somewhere.

'I want to celebrate with YOU. No one else matters. Just me and you.'

**STEPPING INTO THE JOLLY HAY BALERS** at 1 a.m. on New Year is like stepping back in time. It's rammed with drunken locals in various states of dress (who knew Boohoo mini dresses could co-exist with Fair Isle knits). There's a live band playing Irish folk standards that neither of us know, and the narrow length of the neighbourhood den is hung with knick-knacks – relics and limericks, Guinness posters and shamrock stickers. It's a place my nan would have enjoyed a sherry at. A place unchanged in fifty years. Everyone is smiling, jubilant, celebratory at this new start ahead of them. Guts full of beer, heads full of insidious tin whistle. I start to do a jig through the crowd to the bar, arms pressed firmly to my sides like I was taught when I was seven years old. I still know a few of the old steps, maybe that's why people are turning to me and laughing, not because I've just dragged us from the grip of insomnia and thrown us out into the cold.

And even though Felix isn't smiling (yet), I know we've done the right thing getting up out of bed. It doesn't matter if we're still in our sleep wear, or that I've got not a scrap of make-up on, or that this place is at the end of our road: it's as anonymous as that random night out on holiday. Where no one knows your name, but everyone pulls you in for a dance. I grab Felix's arse (and catch a flash of his navy flannel pyjamas under his jeans, as well as the same white T-shirt he had on in bed), and kiss him deeply for the first time in what feels like months.

'This is where we start afresh, my love.'

**MY HEAD IS THICK** and my face even more blanched than usual. Whoever said Guinness was fortifying ought to be subjected to that yard of ale and those Jameson chasers as a sentence. I did it because it made Felix cheer and holler for me. He was excited to be with me, and I with him. But then it also made me vomit right in front of the bar stools as I tried to jig leglessly back out of the pub 'for some air'. At least there's now a Polaroid of me pinned up behind the bar by Padraig, the ruddy-faced landlord, to show I did it. And everybody knows our names. We're neighbours.

And as Felix tucked me under his arm and dragged me back up the road to our beds, peeling the jeans off my lolling legs to reveal the pyjamas once more, I caught him looking down at me with that same face he used to have when we were first together: endeared by confusion at my silliness. I'd won in some small way, even if now, I taste like I've been sucking a peat bog, and look like I've been sleeping in one too. He's not far behind (even though he always looks hot in the mornings), so we're even. *Even more even than before.*

And somehow, as I huddle in a ball on our old worn sofa with a colourful bobbly crochet blanket round my shoulders, there could be no better state in which to make the most holy of vows: my New Year's resolutions. The list most battled with. How long will I last this time?

---

Ⓔ Evernote ⌄

### THIS YEAR YOU'D BETTER BE BETTER

*Go about work with a modicum of mystery (stop drinking green juice in favour of coffee and cigarettes like sexy French insouciant)*

*Quit leaning in: you don't get paid enough for that shit.*

*Date my husband*

---

*Abandon dual identity – time to pick a side?*
*Am I disregarding feminism by going full*
*Gyamfi if I want to? (ask Lucy Eight Ball)*

*Volunteer with refugees (penance for heinous*
*Alternativity)*

*Stop trying . . . will have a baby once relaxed*

*No more Madsness*

Egg-White    Low Energy

**THE ACCUPUNCTURIST'S BED** looks wretched, the electric blanket partially exposed under the edge of a
brick-coloured towel. I said I'd stop trying, but not until
I've tried these last couple of things. But this box room is
the antithesis of feng shui. The shelved clutter – toys masked
in tatty stack'n'stores, books on war and music double
piled, ironing hastily collected in a basket hoisted up high
– impend on the small space. How did Orla, her body
gristly with anxiety, ever relax here?

Andy, the reed-thin, even reedier-voiced acupuncturist set
to 'right my xi, right here, right now,' leaves me to settle
in as he goes to check on his *FOUR* children playing downstairs. I remove my jeans; legs are as coarse as sandpaper.
I just assumed I could be needled fully clothed. As I mount
the decrepit table – will it hold my weight? – my leg hairs
stand on end, the room's unheated air attacking my skin.
I pull the thin white sheet over myself for warmth and to
protect what modesty I have left. I'm tenting myself off

291

like I'm about to have a Caesarean: he's going to have to see the legs, but I don't have to see him seeing them. *Spike him; he deserves it for being so fertile.*

Andy wafts in vaguely again. I guess this works for most people? A fertile sandy shadow man redirecting their energies and making them fall pregnant immediately? He grasps my feet ('god, excuse the bunions!' I blurt daftly) in some ritualistic patting sequence. My muscles tense as he starts to roll up the sheet. *Please have poor eyesight, even though you're going to stick me with hundreds of sharp implements,* I pray to whichever Chinese acupuncture god I'm here to supplicate. *He'd need to have blind hands too to ignore that stubble.*

'Sooooo . . .' he exhales, 'what are we here for Ooolivia?'

'I want *you* to get me pregnant!' I laugh. His thin lips stay flat. He's heard that gag before.

'Well, oobviously Ooolivia, I can oonly prepare you for pregnancy . . . To make your booody in sync with itself again.' He's moving around me now, prodding my abdomen with a finger, tapping on what I hope to be my hairless ankles. 'Acupuncture isn't magic. But it's clooose.'

I laugh a slow, disbeliever's laugh.

'What is sooo funny?' He's smiling now, ready to be brought in on the joke: that guy at university with his socks off at parties dying to 'play a little thing I wrote' on his overly stickered guitar. And there's that very guitar in the corner, next to his basket of needles. These are the guys who never grow out of wearing their scabby trainers from 2001, always primed for a Kill Bill samurai shakedown. These are the guys who prick people for a living and impregnate their chilled, harem-pant-wearing wives without fail, over and over ad infinitum, because they're so bloody relaxed. *Oooorla, what have you sent me to?*

'Sooo . . . What I'm going to dooo, Ooolivia, is concentrate the needle wooork around your abdooomen, and do some other healing techniques that I learned on my travels in China,' – *of course, on your gap-yah* – 'but if you have any other pain, or concerns, I can also wooork on thoooose tooo. We want yoooou to be in great coonditiooon for moootherhooood . . .'

I'm now mesmerised by his oohing. Perhaps this is a surreptitious mindfulness technique. Maybe I'm not even here for acupuncture and he's just hypnotising me.

'OOOKEY' I sigh, staring at the mildew-stained ceiling. 'My back is quite tense at the moment, but I think it might be stress.'

He lowers the lights, and wafts the sheet back down over my legs. His over-zealous eyebrows fade into view upside-down over my face as he begins to massage my shoulders.

'Lack of conception can be suuuper stressful. How long have you been trying fooor?'

I try to contain myself, but every word is making me want to wet myself laughing. It's like the trans-vaginal ultrasound with even skinnier probes. Why do women always need to get poked?

'We've been at it about two and a bit years now, but I'm not feeling that stressed about it really . . .

'OOOKEY . . .' he says, obviously disbelieving. 'Sooo what is the crux of yoooour stress? Wooork?'

'Work is pretty hectic, I just took on another job while my friend is on maternity leave, my family are pretty intense and we have stuff to do every weekend with them, money, keeping our heads above water. You know, the usual.'

*The heavy weight of guilt biting my ear like a squawling capuchin.*

'Well, there's nooothing like a cooomplex set of stresses to get to wooork ooon. Sooo, Ooolivia, I'm going to try a couple of needles here along your eyebrows to reduce those tension headaches.'

'I didn't actually say I had tension headaches.' I also don't want my eyebrows pierced.

'But you must get them with all those worries on your shoulders?' coos Acupuncture Andy.

'I mean, I'm stressed, but it doesn't necessarily manifest itself in my head?'

'Well where would you say it manifests?'

*In wanting Mads. In my vagina.*

'Probably in my shoulders?' I lie. 'I feel like my back is very tense.'

'OOOKEY . . . Sooo if I can flip you over and you put your face in that hooole right there – gooood – then we'll see what we can do for your upper back before we start on the reprooductive system.'

I turn over, as instructed, awkwardly trying to keep my legs covered.

'I'm just going to put some music on to get yooou nice and relaxed. It's a little song I wrote . . .'

I stare through the hole. Right there beneath me are his hairy toes.

**I SIT IN THE VOLVO** outside AA's house and dial Orla. I can't believe what I've just seen and I'm too light-headed to drive yet.

'Erm, Or, what is Acupuncture Andy all about? I'm so shocked you were into that!'

'He's an acquired taste,' she's laughing. 'But he's got a proper chill-out vibe to him. Did he play you his special song?'

'Oh my god, YES. At least his long ooohs come in to good use.'

'I downloaded it from iTunes to do my tax return to. It's quite therapeutic.'

'I think you've lost your mind,' I say. 'He's a maniac with effective sperm peddling ancient nonsense out of his box room. He wasn't wearing any shoes!'

'I thought that was all part of the vibe!' Orla loves a man in Ibizan white linen.

'And then he basically stuck needles into my (overflowing) bush . . .'

She's laughing her head off now. 'Oh I should have warned you to get everything in control because you have to basically be naked.'

'Yes, that was a nice surprise.'

'But imagine how much weirder it would have been if he was hot.'

'Or if he could say Oooo without keeping it lasting for two hours?'

'I bet he's into tantric sex.'

'I think you've got a thing for Andy, Or!'

'Oh, as if, Liv!'

'I'm telling Rich you're leaving him for the acupuncturist,' I cackle. 'You're such a clichéd banker's wife . . .' I put down the phone and imagine being pregnant after that. Maybe Acupuncture Andy is a magician. *Maybe I should set him on Felix too.*

Exhausted    Peak Fertility    Egg-White

I'VE WOKEN UP FEELING spookily different. Even Felix is reacting to me in a new way, kissing me more keenly. Maybe I'm one of those New Agers now. Which is why I'm throwing myself out in the cold January drear, along with all the sales maniacs, to meet Lydia who is taking me crystal shopping to top up my juju.

I can hear Sonny babbling away to himself like a drunk in the buggy as I open the door to the cosy confines of the Nordic Bakery on Neal Street. I'm going to do exactly the opposite of Orla and immerse myself in other people's children. If there's a baby rolling past, I'll help push it. Need one winded? Give me a muslin and watch it puke. Fancy palming off twins for a night? I might have to consult Felix after the last babysitting fandango.

As I unfurl myself from my giant neon-green blanket scarf in the doorway – hit by the café's deep warmth – out of the corner of my eye I spot a muscular arm reaching up to run his hand through thick brown hair. Despite how beautifully tempting it all looks, I'm nearly sick on the pastries, I'm so convinced it's Mads. The barista finally lowers his arm behind the counter and shoots me a confused glare. Definitely not a come on.

'I figured, you love HYGGE so much that it might be apt to check this place out,' Lydia laughs as she motions around to the simplistic woodwork and rustic woolly chair covers. 'Plus the cakes are immense,' she says, pointing over to the tiled counter topped with glistening cinnamon buns and snow-sugared date cakes that I nearly iced with fearful bile just seconds before.

'If we suffer glycaemic overload, and die suddenly, I believe they have insulin pens behind the counter to revive us . . .' I joke, trying not to keel over just looking at Mads II fingering the moist *skoleboller*. 'I'll go up and order . . .' – nice excuse to examine him further, really press on the bruise – 'What are you having?'

'I think it's only right that, as I'm still breast-feeding, I can still consider myself eating for two. So I'll take an apple tosca and also a slice of tiger cake?'

'I'm sure Sonny would be up for having a slice for himself,' I say, looking at her little red-headed offspring chewing his fist merrily in the stroller. He's going to be a proper bruiser. 'Are you sure that's enough?'

'Yeah, I'll think about sharing with him. I'm nice like that.'

I wander up to the counter, studying the oatbakes and pancakes so I don't have to look directly into Mads II's eyes (green), but only at his hands (tattooed), until I realise I'm being shuffled forward by a very insistent queue of one forming behind me.

'I'll take her buns please,' cuts in the voice, 'if she can't make a decision.' The cheek of it, ordering before me. I turn, incensed, trying not to catch a glimpse of Mads II and his arms in the black uniform on the way round.

But as I do, I realise, I needn't have bothered. He's handing the plate of sweet things over to his doppelganger, and they in turn are being offered to me with an exceptionally seductive smile.

'Have you got me fitted with a GPS tracker or something?' I say, as coldly as I can muster. Lydia is looking up from tending to Sonny's teething wails, her own mouth agog and slightly salivating. *I hope you're proud of yourself.*

'You're trampling on my turf! Who said you have any claim to London's best Scandinavian baked goods? I need my home comforts. I'm all alone in the big city.' Mads is mocking me now.

*You're in public, Olivia. This is over, Olivia.*

'So alone. I bet you're always here crying into your—' I look around frantically for a witty sounding food item '—*smørrebrød*' – I smug-face at my Acupuncture Andy-ish pronunciation – 'and *not*' – I'm whispering, hoping Lydia can't lip-read – 'luring married women into your lair . . .'

'Oh, Olivia,' he sighs, fixing his new, incredibly sexy clear-rimmed spectacles, 'you know full well that the HYGGExperience was your lair, and it was me that was lured, not you.' He's curt. I'm astonished. Lydia's mouth has fallen even further. 'Why are you even putting up a fight?' he whispers, grabbing my elbow. 'I wasn't putting any pressure on you. I didn't ask you to leave him. I just can't stop thinking about you. And I didn't chance upon you in here, I stalk your Instagram, just the same way as you stalk mine. I needed to see you.'

'Stop being such a fucking psycho, Mads! As if any of that's true.' He's reeling me in to drop me from a great height. I know what's at stake now. *You love his games.*

'It's the truth!' he's still whispering, but his voice is insistent. 'You pick me up and drop me whenever your guilt permits. But I'm hanging on every moment that I see you. Was it all to get on at work? I've been going out of my mind thinking it was just that heartless, but I know you better than that.' He's pacing slightly, shaking his head and disrupting his carefully swept back hair. 'You wouldn't want to think you got somewhere because of anything apart from hard graft.'

'Listen,' I say resolutely. I need to stop this dead in its tracks. He's not interrupting my New Year. 'You could have any woman you want. You're sexy, successful, intelligent, creative, well dressed, well travelled, you're even funny. And you're fully aware of all that too. The only reason you want me is because You. Can't. Have. Me. And you can't stand it.' He stares me dead in the face, his hair suddenly dishevelled, his face a shade pinker than I thought it would go. I need to say this now. 'You can't handle unrealised sexual tension. You can't accept that someone beneath you might turn you down. But I'm going to make it easy for you: there is no tension. We had a fumble, it didn't last long. Just look at it like we were stupid sixteen-year-olds – nothing really happened but it seems like a big deal. So stop it now. Don't act wounded. Don't pretend like I meant something to you.' He reaches out to grab my shoulders now, draw me to him, but he sees me bristle and runs his hands through his hair instead. 'You could never love me like he loves me,' I say, my final stab.

'But it was real for me.'

He's acting wounded, but smiling seductively now.

'You're mad, Mads,' I say, my blood curdling at his perseverance. 'It's all in your head.'

'Well it's in your husband's head too,' he says sniping now. Lydia is ready to start filming on her phone, and the whole café is staring trying to catch the key words from our hushed tones. 'He rang me to ask to take you away, but he was trying to mark his territory. Don't think that you've got us both duped—'

'We are not talking any more about this. You need to go.

299

I am with my friend and we're shopping for crystals. I don't need my work life interrupting my *real* life.'

'So this *was* all just work then?' He chuckles flatly, placing the cinnamon buns that had been lingering in dead air throughout our exchange, back on the counter. 'Sleeping with the boss doesn't count in people's favour these days.'

'And that is exactly why I didn't sleep with you, Mads,' I hiss.

'To think I was a little bit in love with you,' he says at a normal volume this time. I'm sure he's mocking me still, but his tone is lacklustre, broken. And as quick as he arrived, he turns his back on me and is gone.

'SO DO YOU WANT TO tell me?' Lydia asks as we wheel the buggy together across the narrow street through the heavy sleet and into the darkened crystal shop opposite, 'or am I going to have to get a lip-reading expert on about ten people's Facebook Lives just then?' Her whole face is raised like one big eyebrow. After the tension I'd unexpectedly created, we'd been forced to inhale our cakes in silence within two minutes and get out of there.

'He's my boss. And it's complicated.' I say. Maybe that's enough explanation.

'That's the understatement of the year. Does Felix know?' Lydia won't tell, she's only met Felix on a couple nights out; I'm not sure they're even Facebook friends.

'No . . . I'm not sure . . . It's complicated.'

*That word.*

'How complicated can it be? You've got a hot boss and something has happened. Is he a risk-it-all? It's actually pretty simple.'

'Don't, Lyds. It's not like that. I *want* him but I don't

want him.' I'm too revved up to cry. 'And there's stuff on Felix's part too.'

Lydia issues a sharp intake of breath, but I realise it's because Sonny is chowing down on a smoky quartz the size of his head.

'Sorry,' she turns back to me with the slobbery stone in her hand. 'So Felix is shagging someone? Are you all right, Liv? I didn't realise this was an intervention day out. I would have packed some tissues.'

'No, it's not even as straightforward as that. I saw some messages. He's not been telling me the truth about his fertility.' This inevitably sounds less dramatic out loud than it is in my head.

'Oh my god, you're shagging your boss because Felix lied about his sperm count? That's ice cold.' She's staring me down, concerned.

'No! It's not that! Felix and an ex had an abortion but he hadn't ever told me despite all our fertility tests. I've known about it for months, but I can't tell him I know. And we've just been drifting and drifting. He travels constantly. And I just wanted something for myself to cut through the boredom. But I'm not shagging Mads.'

'Liv, we really should have talked about this over the cakes. I think I need sugar and a sit down.' She rolls Sonny, now caterwauling for his £300 crystal teething ring, further back in the shop away from the prying ears of the witchy-looking shop assistant.

'Don't say that! It was a mistake. A couple of mistakes. And Felix did something with his old boss too. So now we're even.'

'So you've discussed it?' She's concentrating on the assortment of topazes and opals in the display chest, picking me out a raw salty block for me to hold while I get it all off my chest.

'No . . . I checked his messages again . . .' My face is contorted, but there are no tears with the confession. I'm actually controlling the urge to smile. 'I'm so guilty. I hate myself.' *I've not felt this good in years.*

'Well you won't need this for fertility then . . .' she says, holding up a giant iridescent moonstone, the reason we came here. The reason for it all: my bloody babylessness. 'Because you're not going to be having Felix's baby like this.'

WHY ARE THESE CONSULTATIONS always when Mads is in my head? I'm back in the waiting room – the latching video on a hideous loop again – but this time I'm alone. I'm not swinging my feet on the chair, not holding anyone's hand. I know this is going to hurt and I know that I deserve it.

As I lie on the X-ray table, legs apart – *you spread them for everyone* – I'm instructed to only cry out when I can't take it any more. That this is going to burn, but it doesn't last long. This is your penance: tubes that lead to nowhere, emotionally tangled, flushed through with acid.

The pressure of the dye flowing through me is blunt, intense. No funny tunes for this. No floppy sheaths. Just long needles and sharp pain into a fiery selfish womb. I didn't deserve a baby then, and I deserve it even less now. I squeeze my eyes shut. 'Can you take more?' the doctor asks in his gruff Russian accent.

'Yes,' I heave.

I twist my hands into knots by my sides. 'Please . . .' I cry, wanting this lead-lined man who's torturing me to offer me his hand to clench from behind the protective screen.

'Just a little more, that's not enough,' he says.

I let the tears fall, my face is washed twice daily by them now. 'No,' I say.

'No more,' he agrees.

My hands rise from my sides in protection. I cross my womb and hope to die.

I walk to the bus stop dazed, the dye fizzing like a battery in my abdomen. *Why couldn't you just jumpstart something?* The consultant's kindness still rings in my ears.

'Your tubes are clear/always were/clearer now/don't cry, dear/pop a pill/you'll be right as rain/nothing to stop you/try again.'

Try again. Try again. Try again. Try again.

**AND NOW ORLA IS CALLING.** Another Tuesday morning. I've got that dark feeling in the pit of my stomach like last time. Maybe she was right that it hasn't worked. She'll be so sad. But if it has worked . . . I'll be so sad?

'Hey Or, are you OK?' I try to judge the sound of her breaths on the other end of the line.

'Erm . . .' *Oh god, darkness.* 'It's good news! They said we're pregnant!' I inhale sharply, trying to keep the tears from falling.

'Oh my god! Oh my god! Oh my god! What did I say! I knew this would be the case! I'm so happy!'

'Obviously I'm only telling you and Mum,' she says, conspiratorially. 'No one else knew we were doing it and there's still loads of risks that it could go like the last time . . .' she's gone back to bleak now.

'Well don't be thinking that – just relax and celebrate!' I say, feeling the griping pain in my abdomen, my searing hollow.

'It's just not the same without champagne!' she cries.

'You're having a baby!' I exclaim, up-tempo. More mid-tempo, because everything is in slow motion, the low winter sun blinding me through the grimy bus windows.

'But it won't change anything . . . Promise.'

Orla rings off, and I keep my smile fixed until she's gone. But the tectonic plates of our friendship have already parted: we were a continent, locked together by childlessness and now, instantly, there's an ocean between us.

I can't go to work like this, in crippling pain in my head and in my womb. I call the only person who could raise a smile at this kind of news. The shadiest bitch I know: Margot.

'You all right, Liv? It's ten on a Tuesday morning . . . I can't even remember the last time we spoke on the phone.'

'Yeah, sorry, Margs, I'm just feeling a bit overwhelmed.'

'Oh love, tell me. What's up?'

'Orla's pregnant . . .'

'Ahhh,' she sighs supportively. 'Well, I mean, you expected it, right? The IVF, I mean, it was likely, right?'

'I guess I should have had time to adjust. But it's still a . . . it feels like a blow and I don't even know why. I hate feeling so jealous of people I love.'

'But it's not like you two are out raving all the time – nothing's really going to change?'

'But it's never going to happen for me, meanwhile everyone else has it so easy.'

Margot inhales sharply.

'Listen, Liv, I've wanted to tell you this for a while, but

I knew you had a lot on your plate with work and *stuff*. But myself and Trine: we've been approved to adopt.'

I only just manage to mute the phone before the wail perforates the air around me, expulsive tears tracking geysers in my foundation. An old lady on the row next to me pats my shoulder to ensure I don't need medical assistance. I unmute the phone, but not my tears.

'Liv? Where did you go?'

'I'm still here. Just me. I've got to go, though.'

'It's going to happen, Liv, keep going. I'm sorry I didn't pick a better time to tell you.'

'There's never a better time than now for good news,' I say, as I put the phone down.

*Try again. Try again. Try again. Try again.*

# INTERVIEW 5: MARGOT

As Margot ambles in, elegant as a gazelle, slow as a snail, I realise how different she looks since she confessed. She was so tense, so self-contained before, but now she raises her head as if the weight is off her beautifully broad shoulders. She contemplates my little studio, assiduously examining the design of the large standing lamp in the corner ('can I have one of these for doing this?') and playing with the buttons on the camera as she talks to me (I don't know how to fix whatever she's adjusting). But I know her shyness is drawing round her like a comforting coat, that she'll only do this because it's for me. Not because she knows I need this for my work, but because she wants us to talk about this finally.

When she told me she was on the precipice of adopting, I was floored. And, even though I'd gone to cry on her shoulder about the loss of all my friends to motherhood, I knew she was the one who needed me. It's not like I know what to say, but that's what friendship is about, right? Just being there when the other needs you?

We dance around each other in the space, trying to make one another comfortable in the confines of the confessional. I duck behind the camera so she can settle into her seat, so she can remember it's just me she's talking to, not however many other people might see this film (possibly none if Trish doesn't like it). She looks so beautiful in the frame: so still and so ready.

**Olivia:** So Margot, how long ago was it that you started the adoption process and when did you make the decision to go for it?

**Margot:** We started the process . . . well, we went on holiday a few years ago and we started talking about it seriously then, but we had spoken about it for a long time. I saw on Facebook that someone I used to work with had adopted and I messaged him to ask about the process. He replied straight away. He said it was super full-on, but so worth it. He sent me a picture of their two little kids and I felt the joy explode in my chest. It was the first time I thought, yes, we could do this. So I said to Trine 'We could actually be mamas' and that was it, the seed was sown. I thought there would be loads of children waiting, there would be no complications and it would be quite easy to adopt if you're a nice person. But then you go to the council, and to Barnardo's and you see it's going to be a long road.

**Olivia:** So how does the process work?

**Margot:** Well, we've been having counselling and training sessions for eighteen months. And now we're fully approved for one child up to the age of five. And then you work with the local authorities and charities who get to know you very well as a person before they'd even think of matching you with a child.

**Olivia:** What's been the toughest part of it all?

**Margot:** When we started, we went to all of these information days and it was pretty grim. It's really eye-opening. You're not going to get a child who isn't damaged and

307

doesn't have trauma. You're going to be presented with really difficult challenges. I'm not going to pretend that we didn't walk away a couple of times thinking, 'Can we actually do this? Do we want to unsettle our safe, easy life?' But we talked about it and started to meet up with other couples who had adopted, and seeing how happy their families were despite the challenges made us think, 'We need to do this.'

Olivia: What were the main challenges for those other families?

Margot: Luckily for them, their challenges were more just becoming new parents. Not having that situation where on a Saturday you can just get up, go on your laptop, go for a nice coffee, go to the cinema. Suddenly your life is no longer about you. They told us they didn't have sex for three months, didn't even look at each other they were so consumed. But I would imagine that's most new parents. We've all got to grow up some time haven't we?

They were very lucky they got very young children, who hadn't had a huge amount of trauma. But the social workers always tell you, they will *all* have experienced trauma, they might just not present it yet. Shouting, screaming, drugs, violence while they're in-uterus – it takes so much toll on the foetus.

Olivia: So what did you say you could and couldn't cope with?

Margot: When you're preparing to go to a panel of approvers, they go through a long list of things that you feel you could take on when you adopt. It's really harsh. You sit there and you say 'yes, no, yes, no'. 'Would you take somebody with HIV? Downs syndrome? They ask you about foetal-alcohol syndrome, which is very common in adopted children, learning difficulties, speech, behavioural issues, attachment difficulties. Some of those things you're like, yeah I could deal with that, that's probably part and parcel of adoption. It's a very hard thing to do because you're effectively doing a checklist of what you wouldn't want. What's good enough, it feels like.

**Olivia:** Did that make you feel emotional having to pick apart what it was that you could deal with?

**Margot:** It did. It makes you think about those children who will have so many things wrong with them that they will live for ever in care. And it's really sad to think of those kids because they deserve a home as much as anyone. Caring for a child with a disability is very, very different and it takes a very special type of person to do that. I think maybe we're not quite capable of doing that. We don't have the skills to do it, emotionally and time-wise. It has to be right for the child.

With adoption, they make it very clear, it's never about your fulfilment to be a parent, nothing is geared towards your dream child, it's about the dream parent for the child. It's all geared around that. And once you realise that, it really puts into perspective what adoption is. It's finding them a family.

**Olivia:** So how does it continue from there?

**Margot:** Then you go through this long approval panel process and once you're through, they have a website called Adoption Link and it's very confidential and all the children go up and you can have a look at it. It's very odd, it's like going on Zoopla. A child comes up, sometimes with a picture, sometimes not, and details about their medical history, their parents. And then you register interest and see if you're a match. We've registered interest with five children so far and four of them have come back and said 'Discussion has not been started' – that's the formal way of telling you you've not been considered. Very harsh. Sometimes it makes you think 'What, is it because we're gay?' You can't help but go down that route, I like to think it's not that. We do have an open conversation at the moment, where we've not had any feedback at all, with a little girl called Leila in Wales and it says on her medical records 'born addicted to drugs, at the moment displaying no health concerns, did spend the first two months of her life in hospital.' It is very harrowing reading and work seems very irrelevant in those moments and you think 'I don't give a fuck about office politics, this is so much more important.'

**Olivia:** How are you going to split the adoption leave?

**Margot:** The adoption leave at my job is really good, it's the same as maternity, so I'm going to take a whole year. But with Trine, hers is not good at all. She would have liked to have been off too, but her company only offers two weeks paid if you're not going to take the primary leave. Really bad. She's going to have to take a three-month unpaid sabbatical. When you adopt, they tell you to not meet anyone with the child for the first month. Not even your family or your best mates. So when it happens, you'll have to bear with us, OK? Because the child will be really desperate and unsettled. And it will need stability, and possibly find it really hard to attach to you. And if you have a grandparent come in, they might attach to them and it can be very upsetting for you and for the child. Separating from their foster parent, they might have lots of questions about birth mum, it's going to be a very emotional time. It just means for that first month we can knuckle down and get on with the job in hand.

**Olivia:** So what have you been told about the moment you meet your child?

**Margot:** According to everyone I've spoken to, it's a very weird feeling. Particularly if the child is older, because you'll have sent a DVD and pictures and information of yourself. And you could walk in and they'll be like 'Mummies!' and that is a real head fuck. We don't know you, you don't know me, they desperately want to love you, you desperately want to love them, but you don't have a clue who the other is.

So you take two weeks off work, and then you go for a couple of hours the next day, and then more the next, then they come over to your house for half a day, then they sleep over at your house, and this is all in conjunction with the foster parent so they feel like it's easy stages for them. And then eventually after two weeks, they move in with you. To me now it's so abstract I can't imagine it happening. When you're pregnant, there's no physical doubt that the baby is coming. When you're adopting, it's still like no-man's-land, we've been told we can, but who knows when. It's so exciting, but it also feels like a non-event, because you can't get excited about something you can't imagine. We can't even decorate because we don't know how old they'll be.

**Olivia:** Did you talk about doing it naturally and using a sperm donor?

**Margot:** We briefly spoke about using a sperm donor, and I made a few phone calls. I don't feel anti it, but doing the adoption process has made me reconsider and think very carefully about whether I feel the need to create another baby when there are so many who need a home. I don't think badly of anyone who choses to do it, I'd love to know what it's like to have a child that looks like me. I never fantasised about being pregnant though. So we briefly considered it, but I feel more passionate about adoption than I ever have about anything else. Those moments when you think 'what's the point in any of this?' – I think that's the reason I'm here. I know it's really over the top. Maybe that's the reason I'm here, is to help someone, and I hope I do.

By the end of the interview, I'm crying, Margot is crying and we're just hugging in front of the camera. It would sound condescending if I had a child, but I don't, so I can say it: I'm so proud of her.

'I DON'T WANT THIS TO SPLIT US UP.' I'm lying in my nervous-breakdown tracksuit (which also doubles as decorating wear) on the floral rug in the middle of Mum and Dad's living room, my arms splayed like a murdered snow angel. It's come to this: I'm in parental therapy. I'm also here to paint the wall. Fair trade.

'Sure now, Liv, you're being dramatic. It's not like you didn't know this might happen at some point. And you won't be far behind. What's good for the goose is good for the gander,' she says missing the irony of her incorrect use of the adage, placing a mug of tea on the floor next to my outstretched hand. I let out a dry tearless sigh-wail, which sounds more like a belch, then lean up on one elbow to have a sip of tea, before flopping back down again.

'I can't even cry right! I'm emotionally constipated! Not fit for human consumption.'

Dad, looking as if he wants to laugh at me, ridiculously prostrate on the floor, instead opts for a reassuring 'poor you' ruffle of the hair from the couch.

'I've been doing a mindfulness CD to help with my sleeping: do you want me to put it on for you?' says Dad, revealing his anxious millennial self. 'Orla having a baby was always going to be hard for you, but it's going to be much harder for her. She'll be having sleepless nights while you can still go out and enjoy yourself,' he says.

*I can't enjoy myself too much.*

'But I've had enough fun. I'm *supposed* to have a baby now,' I huff, playing perfectly into my mum's usual line of enquiry in the hope that it'll provoke proper pity.

'Says who?' asks my dad, meaning it.

'Says the media. Says my biological clock. Says Mum . . .'

She's pouting now, that angry pout she does when she's on the wrong side of history. He looks at her and laughs.

'I just came here so you could sausage roll me in the sofa blanket, brush my hair, bring me tomato soup and heavily buttered crumpets and tell me I don't need to get up for work tomorrow,' I say, as Dad looks at me pityingly.

'Do you want a crumpet then?' says Mum, a confused furrow between her eyebrows. 'I thought you'd gone off them.'

I ignore her, but she's ducked into the kitchen anyway. 'And instead,' I say, raising my voice for her benefit, 'I give it roughly seven minutes – the time it'll take for Dad to finish his tea and two hobnobs – before you'll give me the heave-ho off the cold floor and tell me to get back to priming the wall.'

'Too right, daughter!' says Dad. 'There's nothing wrong with your arms and legs.'

Mufti comes for a sniff of my head. At least he cares enough to give me a kiss. Ah, no, he's off again: I'm not food.

'It's going to happen, Olivia,' says Mum, plaiting my hair from the sofa. 'You might be getting on, but the doctors are seeing to you now' – *appreciate the age concern there* – 'and you could always look at adopting?'

'WAHHHH!' I fake cry, lifting my forearm to forehead in dramatic lament. *Give me sympathy with the tea, parents.* 'Margot is adopting! Even she's ahead of me, and she can hardly even commit to her girlfriend . . .'

*You can hardly commit to your husband who you vowed to love until death do you part.*

'Then you can just get on and do it too,' says Mum. 'Look into it. Do the reading.'

She's completely unsympathetic. If I didn't know them better, I'd think my parents were as sick of me as I am of myself.

'There are plenty of children out there who need good homes. And once you've stopped running so much, you'll be able to give them it.'

Always running. If only I was actually into running.

'And where is Felix in all of this, anyway? Feels like we've not seen him since Christmas. Is he all right?' Dad's been keeping check and I hadn't even realised. He's now demolished half a packet of hobnobs, sneaking one to Mufti over my head, so I am showered in crumbs and drool. Is he comfort eating on my behalf?

'He's at work, as per usual.'

Or did Felix want to be out of the house away from me so much that he'd prefer to get told off by an angry manager than me?

'I'm sure he's taking this stuff hard too. All of his friends have babies, don't they? Remember the pressure on him. It's not all just about you.' Dad is resolutely on Felix's side. I might as well curl up in a ball like a hibernating hedgehog and never unfurl.

'Let's just go and paint, shall we?' I say, draining my tea with sad resolution. I can smell the crumpet burning in the toaster. None of this went as planned, so I might as well do something productive with my time. Like covering myself in emulsion and stepping it all round the garden so I can always remember this shudder of pain when I see the marks.

Orla
Today 15:20

Hey my darling best friend, how are you today? Feels like ages since we've spoken. How are you feeling? Are you feeling sick? Or craving anything? Maybe we could have a night in with some ice cream (not Phish Food – you're not allowed that much chocolate now!) and watch Love Story? I miss you. xxxxx

Hey! Was worried when I hadn't heard from you all week. I'd been scared that my news was a problem . . . Not that I think it would be, but just wanted to check you're all right? I wasn't sure how to put it, but now I've put my foot in it, I promise, it won't change a thing, promise. I won't be a baby bore. I'm banning those 'I'm one month old' placards. What have you been up to? I really hope everything's all right, it's all going to happen for you next. Love you lots. Xxx

I begin my answer, allowing my darkside to type for a minute to declutter my thoughts . . .

*No I'm not OK, your news has been playing on my mind since you did your first injection. It is a problem. You should think that, I'm a duplicitous bitch who can't be trusted and I'm not all right. It will change things and you will be a baby bore. A baby bore with loads of money, which is even worse. I give you exactly one month until*

316

*you get those placards and re-emerge on social media with a #blessedmummy flourish. What have I been up to? I've been lying in a prison tracksuit on my parents' floor crying about you. Nothing is good. How can it happen when my husband isn't even talking to me? I used to love you, but I've stopped.*

That's not how I feel, is it? My eyes cloud with tears as I flash with all of our shared history: the taking our lives into our own hands on bungees and hitching lifts, the petty squabbles over outfits and boys we both kissed, the laughter at ourselves, the holding hands through weddings and wrongdoings. Always together. Rants aside, I could never feel anything but love for Orla. She's part of me, and this baby will be too.

> Don't be silly! Of course it's not a problem! I'm so happy for you, really proud that one of us has finally managed it! I'm all right, it has been a crazy week – I'm at my parents' helping with the bloody never-ending pub garden and then work's been too much. Wish Rachel could be one of those people who only take four weeks off after having a baby. I never thought I would miss her . . . So are you going to do a little announcement? Love you too. xxxxx

> God, do you think I should do an announcement? xxxx

Is there ever a good way to do an announcement? I need to stop this madness – she's not even on social media, there will be misplaced hashtags all over the shop . . .

Well, it depends. You don't have a dog, so you can't hang a chalkboard round its neck and write 'new addition coming summer', you've not got a holiday booked, so you can't write it in the sand. You could hold up a pair of sickeningly cute booties and let the photo do the smugging (translatable only by basics). Obviously if you wanted people to literally see inside you, you could post the ultrasound? Or you could just write it on your wall – nice and simple? I think that would be best, wouldn't it? People are still able to read without visual prompts. That won't last long though, so seize the day. Xxxx

Absolutely no smugging! Rich wants to do one. He can't be bothered to even set up a WhatsApp group to tell everyone. We're going simple – no pictures! Thank you for being so wonderful. I'm so lucky to have such an amazing best friend. xxxx

*I wish I could be better.*

**IF I WAS A GOOD WIFE,** I would be plotting. It's a week until Valentine's Day, and notoriously, Felix is always prize-winningly romantic. I, however, am award-swervingly forgetful and shit. One year, he scattered handwritten love notes all through the house and garden. Another, he booked out a whole cinema for just the two of us to watch *My Best Friend's Wedding* on a random Wednesday morning (where we sang along with all of the songs), because he knows I love it, even though boy doesn't get girl, and girl is a massive bitch in a heinous brown trouser suit for most of the film. In return, I have purchased him socks from

Urban Outfitters on my way home from work. In my defence, they were nice socks.

In a rare moment of reprieve from the Rachel-gap onslaught, today my lunch hour has opened up like a tear in time. Trish Chippenham is holding a feedback meeting with the PR and social teams in the studio downstairs, which I knew well to avoid because it was going to be a blood bath, so the office is expansive in its solitude. Nursing my bowl of insipid chicken soup, I open the browser as tentatively as if I was logging on to my XConfessions account. And, in a way, I hope the mini-break I'm looking for will be just as fruitful as feminist porn.

As I scroll through pictures of infinity pools overlooking azure horizons, cosy sandstone country hideaways and some pretty flouncy Euro boutique hotels, one left-field choice draws my eye. '*Olivia*,' it says, '*this . . . is your nanobreak destiny.*'

The mattress hangs on a wooden platform suspended by roughly hewn ropes, and the walls are an austere prison grey, covered in mind-bogglingly angled erotic modern art. The huge floor-to-ceiling windows look down from on high over a disused market square. It's un-HYGGE. It's anti-romance. It's sexy.

It's in Copenhagen.

I go back over old ground. Perhaps a twee cottage in the Lake District wouldn't be so bad? Perhaps Felix would actually enjoy a hotel in the centre of Lisbon that looks like a funky house nightclub from 1999?

*Or perhaps we just need to go to Copenhagen.*

The rumble of staff mounting stairs threatens: I need to act now, or there might never be another free moment to pay £500 for a night in a Danish conjugal visit cell. I punch in my card details as Trish Chippenham strides by my desk, as puce of face as she is of jacket. The e-tickets land in my email just as I'm shout-summoned. *Bitch, you just walked past my desk*. But I'm happy. I've done a Valentine's thing. I'm taking my husband to the birthplace of the man I'm 100 per cent *definitely not* fucking.

'WHAT A WONDERFUL SURPRISE!' I hear Felix say graciously. In my head.

Instead, in a comprehensive character about-turn from his usual delighted holiday demeanour, he's literally shouting at me.

'You can't surprise me like that! You've never once planned a Valentine's thing, why are you starting now?'

He's perturbed that I've made his team assistant rearrange his diary so we can take Tuesday and Wednesday off to go to 'freezing cold fucking Copenhagen'. He was supposed to glow, not glower. Does he not realise this set me back the best part of a grand? He needn't think it went unnoticed that my birthday destination – Soho Farmhouse – is where all the managers and agents meet to thrash out player transfers. I spy an expenses job. Or at very least a discount.

'Just give it a chance, sweetheart,' I simper, mainly to get him off the trail of questioning my intentions. 'You're going to love it. The hotel is off-the-scale cool. And you love Danish pastries.'

'All right . . . sorry,' he says. 'It's just you've blown my plan right out the water. I was taking you to see Drake.' He looks disconsolate, but I can tell he knows he can sell those tickets in an instant (and for a profit probably).

'Drake can wait. I just want to spend Valentine's with

the best *I've* ever had,' I say, handing him a copy of a Danish football book I'd procured in place of a physical ticket. 'You'd better get reading.'

BOARDING CLOSING
**05:50**

LONDON GATWICK
**LGW**

COPENHAGEN KASTRUP
**CPH**

FLIGHT
**F1455**

DEPARTURE
**06:20**

GATE

NAME
**Olivia Gyamfi**

SEAT
**22C**

CLASS
**ECONOMY CLASS**

**TRISH CHIPPENHAM SHITTED** up the flights. Well, she shit me up with her *shouty* recall of how idiotic she finds all of our young staff, and then I covertly – and erroneously – booked a 6 a.m. Gatwick departure to Copenhagen. Which means a four-hour hanging around time until we can check into the SexHotel. This is why my work computer should be reserved for work exclusively. *Mads is work.*

But thankfully, we're on our way: Copenhagen here we come! Felix has nodded off under the cover of *Danish Dynamite*. He looks so cute, gentle deep breaths giving way to peaceful snores, that I take a picture of him snoozing. I've missed watching him sleep. *Such a creep.*

The Norwegian Air flight is shoulder-to-shoulder Klauses

(in fact, is that Klaus?) all neatly tucked in with their identikit navy grocer jackets, round glasses and iPads, scanning the morning news before their return to whichever Scandinavian haven they've been deigning to spare themselves from for work. I look down at myself and Felix – 'rag bags' would be my mum's judgement now – in our scruffy half-slept-in nanobreak best. The crotch of his jeans is tatty and about to give way (lucky me), while I'm transporting most of my clothes on my person, because my weekend bag is just a modest silver rucksack with only space to accommodate my (ill-selected) tiny toiletries, a pair of midi-heeled patent boots, a backless (and virtually frontless) new dress and some entirely unwearable underwear. My massive powder blue fur coat is mushrooming over into the seat next to me – where a spiky-looking woman is tapping away on her laptop and trying her best not to bat my arm away like an impinging fairground teddy. I'm also on sneeze five, which gives me until the end of this flight before the full cold hits. I have not had annual leave flu-free in the two and a half years since joining HYGGE.

SOMETIMES I GET STUCK on a sentence. I'll go over it thousands of times in my head, as if I'm trying to unravel its DNA. It's not OCD, more of a linguistic calming technique I've been working on. I've been silently muttering 'the *flygbussarna* pulls into Ingerslevsgade' over and over and over for the *whole* uncomfortably hot bus ride, so much, that when the *flygbussarna* does pull into Ingerslevgade, I think I'm dreaming. I have not slept and my face is an emergency dinghy inflated with mucal puffiness. I am delirious with flu. We've got three and a half hours to kill with all our bags. But still, I cry: 'We've made it!' into Felix's face. He's seconded himself into the row behind me 'to give me (him) some space' and wakes fresh from the third leg of his now substantial sleep. A pile of my weekend clothes sits discarded on the seat next to me as if a passenger has melted out of them, and I'm down to my undergarments (OK, jeans and vest), and have tissues stuffed in every pocket. Give this girl a Valentine!

The bus stops, and we throw ourselves out into the freezing air. The only other passengers are being met by friendly faces with cars, engines running to create a welcoming heat. So, as Felix loads himself up like a zombie packhorse with our mismatched luggage and scarves, I look around the dim, completely still square for signs of life – and shelter. Every imposing door is firmly locked, every window shuttered against the cold. Wait, is that a glimmer of something open? I drag Felix and my pullalong case, Rolo, towards it, hoping for hot chocolate, sticky buns and free wifi. I squint to make out the letters on the black sign in the half-light:

---

**MUSEUM OF BROKEN RELATIONSHIPS**

---

*Of course.*

'In here then?' says Felix wearily.
'I mean, could there *be* a better way to start our Valentine's

trip?' I say, laughing blackly, humour still asleep, heart still aware of what I've done.

We curve up a sweeping ramp into a tower, the incline dragging as I attempt to unlayer again while stopping my case from rolling back down. In the gallery are dirty white tube socks of exes past, yearning letters pegged to clotheslines to dry off the tearstains, and loud banners of spurned lovers. It's an echo chamber of dissatisfaction and hurt. Felix stands glazed looking up at one yellow satin patchwork proclaiming:

> **I MISSED YOU**
> **AS I DID IT.**

He rubs his face as if he's just getting the sleep from his eyes, but I see he's missed a tear.

'Hey, lover, look at this!' I say. 'Do you think it's better than the sign I gave you?' I pull him over to a bright red neon – about the same height as me – of an anatomically correct heart gashed in two and bleeding in big lit droplets across the floor below.

'Isn't that what you've been working on in your spare time?' he says looking at me with a smile. But this time, his wet eyes are devoid of emotion.

IT'S 11.49 AND WE CAN'T bear it any longer. We've visited a museum, eaten cake for breakfast, and cajoled the luggage for half an hour across town while our fingers near splintered off like stalactites. They have to check us in now. Hotel Højt Tårn, aka SexHotel, aka Hotel Hot Town?, aka Hotel High Tower (according to Google Translate) threatens to perforate the sky like a multi-faceted shard of blackened crystal. It's hideously kinky. We find our way down the pitch-black corridor using a combination of our hands and a system of bashing our bags into walls and furniture. When the cold light washes over us as we open the heavy wooden door to our room, it takes our eyes a moment to adjust.

The room before us is less comfort inn than discomfort dungeon. The hacked up ropes hang like giants' torture implements, the flat grey light from the city skyline eats at your retinas through the wall of glass. The lamps offer only a candle flicker of warmth. The bathroom is a plain unpadded cell unsullied by even a white metro tile, the violent shower offering only a sharp blade of hard water. This room is a penance.

I down tools, unwrapping myself again from the layers of clothes I'd bundled myself back into after exiting the bus into Copenhagen's chill winds. De-tissued and back down to vest and jeans, I join Felix surveying the city below us. I wrap my arms around him from behind, and peer over his shoulder at the people making their ways to work below.

'Today,' – aachoo – 'is a really good day, if you fancied a little' – aachoo – 'morning wakeup call?' I say, moving my hands from round his chest to graze his crotch (nothing, the sexy sneezing hasn't worked. *Yet*.)

He turns to me with a smile, and sleepy breath from our long journey, and kisses me, breaking only so I can sneeze again, and pushes me backwards towards the rope bed. As we wrestle our clothes off ungracefully, the bed sways like a theme park swing ship. My already thumping head is now swimming at the motion, so I lie as still as I can, waiting for Felix to finish unsheathing his legs from those holey jeans at the foot of the bed. As we get down to business

325

(because baby business is what this is), the ropes jerk and pull with our bodies, well, Felix's body – I'm staying pretty still – and I look up to see a long grey crack across the ceiling where the rope is hooked. Was that there before? I fasten my legs around Felix's bum to slow his roll, but in doing so, flatten him against my chest, which suddenly feels overwhelmingly tight and constricted. I try to groan – to help him along with proceedings – but the sound catches in the back of my throat, and the gravelly yelp becomes a cough, and the cough builds to a croup. Felix's face is a mix of concern for my health, and concern he's going to melt in disgust. 'Keep going,' I wheeze, fearful for the all-important ovulation day payload. Sightseeing does not lead to fucking in my experience: we need to get this banked.

'Oh, that's good, keep doing that,' I fib to egg him on. Felix looks like he's hit his stride again (and the bed swing has settled into a bearable rhythm). What he's doing down there is nice. It's just that I feel like I'm about to die while he's doing it.

**STRENGTH RECOVERED** with two plopps and a nurofen from the minibar, we put on our best sightseeing gear. I'm in my blue fur, neon lime blanket scarf, and Nikes with two pairs of socks, while he's back in the jeans, this time showing off the holes with his red running tights underneath, double shirt, and Brokeback Mountain jacket and boots. We look hot. We feel hot.

It's now 3 p.m. and we're dog-tired and starving from taking in the hipster neighbourhood of Vesterbro, but we continue. We've heard there's a little hidden gem beyond this housing estate, and the spliffy graffiti on this side of the road suggests it's just around the corner.

'Welcome to Christiania,' says the sign. 'A place where the only rules are: there are no rules.' That sounds like a dream, right? No rules. Nothing to live up to, to stifle you. No expectations. No trying. And yet, as the mud path begins to smear up the sides of the yellow suede of my trainers and I can see plainly into the bowels of the free town, it feels like the stuff of nightmares.

We're entering a giant troll garden. There are toadstools sprouting at the bases of trees, the long disused army barrack buildings are a rainbow of anti-establishment paint and posters. There are signs saying no photographs (hang on, that's a rule) next to stalls selling weed through hidden hatches and curtains. There seem to be few locals here, so dense is the carpet of outsiders looking in. Is this what free love boils down to? A dog-eared curiosity beset by fungus and legal highs?

We wander up a wooden staircase that weaves along the side of a muddy escarpment (everything is brown and dirty here). As we reach the brow, we realise we're on the lookout over the river, which roils like bathwater the colour I imagine the residents would generate, and from the other perspective, a sea of corrugated roofs, painted tree skeletons and smoking chimneys – the kingdom of Christiania. Tourists are swarming, it's freezing and grey but the clouds are temptingly ready to part.

'Oh my god, is that Liv and Felix?!' I can see a little family of heads looking and pointing up to us, but I haven't got my glasses on so I can't actually make out any of their faces. Sightseeing is only for vague shapes in the dusk, I don't need details. That's what iPhone 8s are for.

'Hello! Liv!' The little head below is waving now. It's Rachel. What the hell is she doing in Glastonbury-on-havn?

I grab Felix's hand and tell him we need to go down and see them even though he's rolling his eyes deep into their sockets.

'What are the chances?!' says Chris drolly, proffering a handshake to Felix from beneath the sheepskin lining of the Baby Bjorn strapped tight to his chest.

'We might say the same of you . . .' I say, searching Rachel's beaming face for clues as to whether they were following us on our Valentine's nanobreak.

'Oh we decided to come and stay out here for the remainder of the mat leave,' says Rachel. 'Chris has just got funding from the National to finish a play he's writing about gentrification. We're basically mucking around here for research.' Beckett and Freja hit each other with sticks as they toddle around in the filth.

'Yeah, it's called *Gents*,' says Chris, plumped like a peacock. 'It's a two-hander about two couples on either side of the gentrification divide.' Us then. 'We'd seen enough in Walthamstow, so we thought we'd see what the Danes had to say about it.'

*You really are a cock, aren't you Chris?*

'Sounds divisive as usual, mate,' laughs Felix taking the words out of my mouth.

'Oh, it's full of diversity, actually,' effuses Rachel looking at Felix. 'One of the couples is mixed race and the other is gay!'

I literally cannot believe them. Felix squeezes my hand hard to say we need to go, but we're hemmed in by them with our backs against the escarpment.

'So we were just going to go for a coffee,' she says, leading me loosely by the arm. 'There's a little hut that does interesting brews over there, probably all laced with weed, but maybe that's a good thing! Fancy joining us?'

We would say no, but both Felix and I are flagging, so we grit our teeth and wander across what looks like a grave plot to the Te Butik, which is tattooed in menacing skulls on to a wooden shack with some words I can't make out. Looks like we're about to drop acid with the kids round our feet.

As we nestle into the trestle, a harassed but completely stunning woman (late thirties, I'd guess, although her skin is flawless) comes panting up the path, trailing a little girl – equally as naturally blonde and beautiful as her mother – covered to the waist in grime.

'So sorry, Rachel,' she says in a light Danish lilt. 'Grete decided to go pee pee in someone's, how you say, compost?'

Despite being obviously rattled by her daughter's misdemeanour, there's something harmonious about the woman, something I, now the Nurofen is wearing off, am not. I pop a couple more pills to fortify myself.

'I'm Agnes by the way – Rachel's friend from playgroup. Is there space on the table for a few more? My husband will be along in a minute . . .' she looks around behind her expectantly, and a contented smile creeps over her face. 'Our little boy was a bit upset so he's taken him for a walk.'

Rachel and Chris nod sagely. They know what it's like. I just nod in admission that yes, she can join us. I don't have a clue about being a hot Scandi mother. But I'll have whatever she's having, maybe she can rub off on me.

Rachel has already popped a boob out as Chris proficiently un-papooses the baby, so keen is she to attach it to her breast. Felix and I look off into the middle distance so we don't stare at her engorged and surely frozen nipple flying free at the café table. This is Christiania: I begin picturing what it might be like if we were just topless and free. At least my boobs would be the most intact, although Agnes looks like hers have survived perkily.

As I open my eyes, I see over Agnes's shoulder a tall figure making his way up the path with a small version of himself perched on his shoulders. A dark beanie covers most of his hair, but there's no mistaking the hang of that navy pea-coat and the confident stride coming towards us, even without my glasses.

It's Mads.

*You've manifested this. You've summoned him.*

Felix is busy duelling sticks with Beckett underneath the table: I've got time, perhaps I can drag him away in the opposite direction? Perhaps I can dig up a mud ball and throw it at Mads Jr and divert their course?

'Ha, you'll never guess who Agnes is married to, Liv . . .' Time is rolling in slow motion now. Every breath from everyone around the table is like a bull's snort. Rachel's jokey introduction takes an eon. And then time corrects itself. And he is upon us.

'It's Mads!' she says, delight spreading across her face, as well as Agnes's.

'Hello, Olivia,' he says, lifting his tear-stained son gently from his shoulders with his blood-red leather-gloved hands and placing him between his mother and sister at the table. His whole family directly in front of me. His family. He's a father.

'Oh, I didn't realise you knew each other, how funny!' smiles Agnes, genuinely happy to discover these new friends in a drug-addled mud-pit in the middle of their city.

And as she says it, Felix looks up from Beckett, and he catches sight of Mads and I see every emotion cover his face in a millisecond. Fear, anger, envy, guilt, worry, anger again. There's no happiness, but as he stands to pull himself out of the bench, and steps back into the mud, I see a tiny smile cross his beautiful mouth.

'The famous Mads . . .' he says, almost breathless with ferocity. Mads looks to me, and then back to my husband, and I can see – he knows.

*Felix definitely knows.*

I have never once in the entire eight years of our relationship seen Felix in a fight. He's got the physique of a middleweight boxer, but the combination of his gentle nature, Mona and John's strict house rules, and an ever-present albatross of racial stereotyping has meant he's never so much as nodded in the direction of an altercation.

But now, I see his fists straining, the vein on the side of his neck popping. And yet his face is calm, considered even. Maybe he's going to rein it in. Because I went low, he'll go high.

*Nah.*

He goes bundling over the trestle table like a big cat, not even knocking a hair on anyone's head, despite Chris's attempt to defend himself with the back of the Baby Bjorn. It happens so fast, Rachel doesn't even blink, let alone unlatch.

'You fucking prick. You think I don't know about you two? You greasy fucking Danish bacon prick . . . with your fucking hair and your fucking . . . gloves.'

The truth bomb hits, and there's no shelter. Mads moves in towards Agnes, trying to shield his wife from Felix's words, and himself from his fists. Agnes's face is twisted in pain as she surveys me: this frumpy lump in children's colours, the smiling assassin taking tea with her kids. She's not surprised though. There's precedent. I'm not the first.

The children are mute in their incomprehension of all but the change in energy. Chris is sandwiching the giggling Beckett and Freja's heads together with one hand on either ear. Rachel has collected herself enough to swaddle baby Keith's head to protect him from the outpouring of emotion, but doesn't break him from her breast. Nothing will stand in the way of her nursing. Not even civil war in a Danish free town.

'Look, it wasn't like that,' Mads says, attempting to placate the man who could be his killer. 'Agnes, please, it was nothing.'

Agnes shrinks from the hand on her shoulder, pulling herself free from the table and languidly collecting the children's things into her Fjällräven bag. '*Komm på børn, det er hjemme tid.*' The kids hold on to her legs and look up to their father with sadness in their eyes. He looks winded.

'Agnes, please, look at her . . .' he yells coldly from the other side of the table, Felix just beside him, temporarily restrained as the family exit the crime scene. I try to catch his eye, but he's looking seethingly at the floor. 'She's nothing.' He's striking a low blow, and one that I deserve. Felix, however, is having none of it.

'Nothing! You call it nothing, you fucking balsa-wood-peddling shit cunt!' He's right in his face now, screaming, but at a decibel still suited to our family-friendly surroundings. I can almost see Mads's cheeks move as if he's in a wind-tunnel at the onslaught. Agnes hurries the children, now both howling, down the path and away from us. Not even a look back. Such strength. I hate myself to my very core.

'She's just the same as all the rest,' Mads turns to Felix.

'I come in, and they're putty in my hands. I see them, terrified by what's going to happen to their lives once they settle down. How unexcited they are. Did you think you were different, Liv?' He looks at me now, with that terrifyingly handsome face, pulling off his murderer gloves and his beanie and shoving them in his pocket, raking his fingers back through his hair.

'You should be ashamed of yourself, with your wife and your family waiting there for you,' I say, looking at my husband, rooted to the spot, his fists pulsating with desire, waiting for me all along.

'Talk about shame? What about you?' He seethes.

'I don't need to explain myself to you. I only care about Felix and he knows why it's been complicated.' I touch his arm, but he refuses to look at me, biting the inside of his cheek in pain at my admission.

'*So complicated.* You think you're so special, don't you, Olivia? So different from all the other girls with your *don't give a shit attitude.* You think I didn't see through that front? You know, the only real difference between you and all the others? You were that desperate to escape yourself, that you were satisfied
with
just
the
tip . . .'

Time slows down as Felix's fist connects with Mads's jaw, knocking him sideways. Mads stumbles, but catches himself, nursing his face in *that* hand.

'Oh, I see. So you think she's going to want you more if you act the tough guy?' he says, dancing around like a Victorian boxer in a ring.

I'm mortified to my core by this fight – about me, not for me. I should be the one punching him, save Felix's fists. *But he's right about everything.*

'You need to just shut the fuck up, you fucking mug!' Felix shouts, going in again, this time running at his torso, catching Mads under his arms and shoving him to the ground.

'Not my jacket!' cries Mads as they fall to the floor.

'Olivia.' Punch. 'Used.' Slap. 'You.' Grapple. 'You're.' Wriggle. 'The.' Slap. 'One.' Nuzzle? 'Who's.' Grapple. 'Nothing.' Punch to the nose. Felix stands up and starts dusting himself down, nursing his fist, confident in his KO. Mads plants his hands on either side of him in the mulch and levers himself back to his feet. I can see out of the corner of my eye that Rachel and Chris want to help him up but hold back. *Better friends than I thought.*

'Well, what does that say about you then, you schmuck?' taunts Mads. 'Can't even get the girl pregnant, can you . . .?'

How does he know about that? Rachel turns away in embarrassment. *Informer.*

Felix spins like a dervish, the mean smile of triumph now reduced to a thunderous glare. 'What did you say, you fuck?' He's weaving with rage.

'I said, you can't even knock her up – of course she's going to pick another dick.'

Mads flashes Felix, and then me, the most dazzling shit-eating grin, which falls straight off his face when he receives Felix's mountain boot straight to the balls.

Felix reels around, dismayed at himself, at what he's heard. But he's the champion. He feels vindicated. But Mads isn't done. His precious balls won't be wounded without reprisals. Winded but wound up, he returns like a bull to a red flag,

334

pushing Felix from the coffee shack across the muddy concourse and through the ragged wooden doors into what looks like a barn. Before I can reach it, I hear loud clangs and dinks and when I finally catch up, I find them entwined in blue string in a makeshift general store, wielding a wooden mallet and a blunt-looking saw at each other.

'You think you're proving yourself as a husband by giving the good fight?' Mads says. 'I'm surprised you want her. You could do better, *mate*.'

That's it, I've had enough. Felix could do better, but I'm not going down without giving the good fight either. I jump on Mads's back and begin to wrestle the saw out of his hand, repeatedly banging it against his line-free forehead (*he must have Botox, the vain git*) and knocking those tendrils of hair all out of whack like a Rockhopper penguin in the wind. He's trying to set himself free of my thighs – something he didn't try to do the last time we were in this position – but I can tell he'd love to straighten his hair up more.

'See, she's still jumping on me, even right in front of your face! I'm fucking irresistible!' he dances around with me around his waist. Until I clonk him across the top of the head. He lets go of my legs. Rachel cheers as he stumbles around, dazed.

Felix rushes at Mads once more, taking his body through the ugly misshapen farm food supplies and into several bales of hay. I stand back and survey them writhing in each other's arms. *You'd join them now if you could.*

Eventually, after wearing each other out, they extricate themselves from each other's grips and climb back off the hay bales, giving me one last check of which arse I prefer. Always Felix.

'Fucking irresistible,' mutters Felix as I rush towards him, attempting to land a kiss on his still braced jaw, but he brushes me away and staggers off to sit on the hay.

As Mads skulks out of the barn, he presses past me in his mud and hay-encrusted coat to sully me as I've sullied him.

'So irresistible!' I shout. 'Now fuck off and don't come near me again,' I say, as he walks out the door without another word. But how can I ever go to work after this?

NO ONE EVER TALKS ABOUT the moment after an altercation. The bit where the family who've been fighting have to split the bill. Or who holds the door for whom as you exit under a cloud. My fight-or-flight mode has been tripped for the past fifteen minutes – as soon as I cottoned on that bloody beautiful Agnes was bloody beautiful, horrendous Mads's poor unsuspecting wife – but a combination of Lemsip Max Strength, fear of reprisals and plain stupidity kept me stapled to the ground. As the pair, exhausted, walked off their anger in different directions, wiping the mud off their favourite coats, I said a teary goodbye to the shell-shocked Rachel and Chris, and ran after Felix towards the exit. Leaving that place, that thing, feels like an epic journey out of Mordor.

'You KNEW?!' I shout as we reach the solitude of the canal, pulling him back to me so I can inspect the bruise sprouting across his jaw again. I don't deserve to be shouting now.

'It was in the summer, when you came home from that trip early. I knew you'd not ditch Paris if something hadn't happened. I thought if I let you do what you needed to do, that it would play itself out. That you'd come back to me.

Really come back to me,' he says, stopping to sit on the edge of the canal, then cradling his head in his hands.

'Then on your birthday I rang him to warn him off. Show him that me and you were still a going concern – even if you didn't agree. But he just wouldn't stop. I saw how he looked at you at the Christmas party and how you tried to keep us apart. I've seen the emails. I've seen it all along. How unresponsive you were with me. Do you want to be with that vain fucking dick, Liv? He wears fucking serial killer gloves . . .'

My world is crumbling before my eyes. My husband, his feet dangling into a canal, his head hung in sadness. 'I've been holding on for dear life. But I love you so much, and I need you to be happy. So if that means me letting go of you, then I will. Because whatever *this'* – he says, pointing at me, him, Copenhagen (Mads?) – 'is, it hasn't been making you or me happy for a long time.'

I always figured that these were the moments where you'd cry. When the realisation that the life you hold dear is going to change – or be taken away from you – that all hell would break loose from your face. But my whole body is paralysed. I just want to escape from the conversation. The consequences bear down around me like a cyclone, but I, in the eye of the storm, am numb to it.

'Isn't this what we signed up for? For better *and* for worse?' I say finally, not knowing where my train of thought is going to take me. 'I can't walk away from you, even though you know what I've done, and even though I know something happened with you and Helena at Christmas . . .' He shakes his head, so resigned is he now that this must be the end. '*And* that you hadn't told me that you knew exactly that you could get someone pregnant, that you *did*

337

– just not me. I saw those messages too. So no, I'm not happy. But that doesn't mean I want you to let me go.'

The blood is back in my face as I state my claim. Felix is silent as he contemplates the truths I've just laid at his door.

'I won't let go. You can drop me, but I'm not going anywhere,' I say, resolute. He remains still and cold as the smooth stone he is worrying in his hand.

'So you had all of this information, and you didn't think to just talk to me?' he says, skipping it into the canal and narrowly missing a swan. We momentarily forget ourselves in a united 'oooohhhff!' in terror for (and of) the now angrily arched animal. It settles, and we settle too, remembering to return to disquiet before looking each other in the eye again.

'It felt like we were past talking. I was trapped in my own stress, about work, about babies, about being past my best. You don't just talk that out – it simmers, then explodes. But it damaged you, us,' I say, my face still. 'I can't ever put into words how sorry I am. There will never be enough platitudes. I know you'll never be able to trust me again, but I honestly never meant to hurt you. I was selfish, and stupid, and I don't deserve a baby, and I don't deserve you.'

'Now you don't mean that, and it's not true either,' Felix says, looking me straight in the eye. 'I need to say sorry too. I buried myself in work to avoid processing what was going on. I didn't want to admit that we weren't the united front we'd always been. That you might not love me if we couldn't have a family. So I just stuck my head in the sand and left you to deal with it alone. And then deal with it with someone else. So I'm sorry. Nothing really happened with Helena, she just made me feel better about not being the same as all my smug dad mates.'

'And you made her feel better *with some fingering?*' My face says I'm laughing, but in reality I'm numb. Maybe we've peeled away a barrier between us. The fog has lifted, but now everything's in ultra HD.

'I may have helped her enjoy herself in the back of a cab, by way of thanks,' he says, ashamed. 'I can't believe I'm telling you this. I can't believe what I've just heard, Liv. How could we do this to each other? I thought we were stronger than this . . .'

'We are!' I implore, the tears threatening now, me willing them on.

'I don't know. I think I need some space to think. We can't go on like we have been. It's obviously not making either of us happy.'

'But we can change. I have changed. It's done. I'm yours.'

'I'm not sure it's as easy as that Liv.'

And as we walk back, the wall between us is higher than ever.

# Cycle 29

I BURY MY HEAD UNDER THE EMBROIDERED CUSHION.

'No,' I utter, muffled by a mouthful of hempy Danish fabric and golden threads. 'I'm afraid I shan't be going to work tomorrow.'

Bret and Jemaine look at me with quizzical concern, because it's only them and the four walls that I'm protesting to.

It's been nearly three weeks. The house is colder and emptier than it's ever been. As soon as we returned, Felix took Rolo the rollercase and the dirty contents of his Copenhagen holdall off to his parents'. I console myself that he's being looked after by Mona: she'll make him tea and wipe his tears and tell him everything's going to be all right. Maybe she'll tell him gently that he should leave me behind. She'd probably be right. When I got back, I found his notebooks, sitting by our bed, ignored by me like he had been all these months. The pain I found inside tore my soul in half.

I'm gaunt, living on toast and tea, which all tastes like sand. The cats are so disturbed, they wake me at four each morning to beg for food when it's still dark. *Like babies.*

My eyes start to well, so I dab them by bashing my head inside my cushion cocoon. This Sunday night is different,

I'm more harrowed than the previous weekends. This week, I know *he's* going to arrive in the office, I just don't know when.

'What if he's had time to think and decides to have me arrested! I can't go to jail like this . . .' I poke my head out momentarily at Bret who's licking my hair tenderly (I'm making the gentle slide into being the woman in the attic with cat-spit dreadlocks). 'I always thought my extended reading break would be because of a white-collar jewel heist. And they don't even allow catty visitors.

'But, he threw quite a few punches himself, didn't he Bret? So I reckon he'd be locked up too.' Bret side-eyes my idiocy. 'Plus he'd have to be a sociopath to not be ashamed of himself.'

The problem is: I think he just might be.

Work has been hell these past few weeks – the shadow of Mads constantly threatening to return, every email setting me on edge – but home is harder. It reminds me that what I've done has lost the most important thing I had. Trust.

Now Felix won't even answer me.

Last week, I had to attend our IVF introduction evening on my own. I cried quietly as I sat on the floor in the crowded lecture hall, surrounded by Quaver-like wafts coming from the shoes of men who were with their partners in this depressing escapade. And yet I was alone as the doctor confidently revealed that our postcode, unlike all the others in the presentation, which receive three rounds of fertility treatment, gets just one go on the NHS. One chance and then you've blown it. And to get that one chance, you have to wait another six to eight months. I need Felix here to talk it through. I need him to hold my hand. But Felix might never set foot through these doors and do this by my side. And just as I let out a tiny cry of pain at the realisation, the doctor revealed his final slide: treatment for single women is not funded under the NHS. No man, no baby.

---

*New Year's Day*

*I thought I would be a provider. Everything in my life pointed towards it, to being that man who could look after a family. Not in the old-fashioned sense. Not hunting and gathering, or tying a girl to the kitchen sink, but being emotionally prepared for what it took. I wanted that so much with you, Olivia. I longed for nothing more than to be able to make strides to buy us a comfortable house in a place we wanted to be so you could have the freedom to do what you really wanted with your life. So that my dream woman could have her dream. Why is it us that has found it so hard to make that next step? Why are we trapped here in this mistake of a house? Working jobs that sap every morsel from us, making us grow apart? Are we doing it to ourselves, or are we pre-destined to toil like this while everyone else glides on? Is it selfish to even question it? Do we just deserve our lot? Did we wear out our luck in finding each other? But I know that there's more for us, my darling. I know that we can make a little family. I just wish I could reassure you of this so you wouldn't want to let me go like you seem to now. I miss us.*

---

**THE RAIN WAS SPARSE AT FIRST,** blurring the edges of my vision like Vaseline as I tracked the grey skyline of Parliament Hill. I couldn't lie there in a heap any longer. I called in the cavalry and now I'm outside, trudging the ridged pathways from Kenwood, Mufti snouting the surrounding grass and tree stumps. I think about how fertile it is underfoot despite the spiky dead trees swaying barren in the wind. Lying fallow for months through the cold, determinedly regenerating, ready to sprout and flower again.

I'm walking a pace behind, hanging my head in shame and watching them together: Mum swearing as her gumboot slides in the mud, yanked by Mufti's muscular neck, Gracie swooping in to gather her. They work as a duo, opposite marks. I fit neatly in the middle but have none of Grace's resolve, nor my mother's fire. Why have I let it all get so out of hand? When did I stop having my shit together?

They stop to let me catch up. I want to throw myself into the puddle that lies like a seeping wound in front of us and for them to leave me there to drown slowly in my own self-hatred. *Why can't you just start afresh? Why can't you just erase it all?*

'Sister, don't force me to waterboard you into talking to us . . .' says Gracie, taking me by the arm, while Mum tucks herself into the other. We're like a black marshmallow daisy-chain in our puffas against the downpour.

'Are you OK, sweetness?' asks Mum, taking an unfamiliarly gentle tone. They must have been discussing how to start this conversation before they ground to a halt.

'No,' I dry sob. 'I'm really not.'

'Then it's time you came out and said what's been on your mind all these months then, isn't it?' says Grace. *I wish she was here to protect me always.* 'Nothing can shock us, can it, Mufti?' Mufti looks up momentarily, then back to snouting the mud. He doesn't give a shit, for which I'm glad.

'I've failed . . .' I say slowly, a hot salty volcano erupting down my face. I can't see at all now, the rain and the tears melting my eyes into puffy slits.

'Sure now, come on, Livvie,' coos Mum, parting my matted wet fringe out of my eyes. 'Let's not be thinking that. You've got so much in your life. What is it that you've failed at?'

'Everything,' I wail. 'I've ruined it all. My career, my friendships, my chance of having a baby . . .'

'I've told you what I feel,' says Grace. 'The world's got plenty of babies, so stop putting pressure on yourself.'

'It's not just that. I gasp. 'It's also FELIX . . .' Although I can only make out their shapes, I realise Mum and Grace are now staring in fear at this last part, until Grace's firmness acts as a breakwater to stop me from drifting away.

'So what are the facts here, Liv?' she says, standing me still on the path and taking my shoulders in both hands. 'Because all I'm hearing are a lot of repercussions, but of what I don't know.'

'The fact is . . . I've done a very bad thing, and I don't think he loves me any more.'

Grace is having none of it. 'What are the facts, Liv,' she says sternly.

I'm trapped under a landslide of self-pity, but Grace is attempting to pull me out.

'I had a thing with my boss . . .' I say, unable to contain the terrible truth any longer.

My mother gasps, but it's not the slow judgemental noise I anticipated. It's recognition.

'Does Felix know?' she asks slowly.

'Yes. He found out in Copenhagen,' I say, although 'he found out' doesn't sufficiently encompass the Danish battle, or that he had known something was going on long before. 'Something happened with him too.'

Through my hot tearstained lids, I can see that Grace is

344

wearing the same pained expression as when she left for Syria after breaking up with Will. *My pain is her pain.*

'Do you love him?' asks Mum, more thoughtfully than I've ever heard her.

'Of course I do,' I say without hesitation, throwing my hands by my sides in anxiety that I've wrecked my love.

'Oh god, Liv,' she sighs, 'then we're in trouble.'

'Hang on,' I say, a crack of light creeping into my eyes. 'Do you mean Felix, or Ma— my boss?' Mum is searching my swollen face for answers. 'I love Felix. Mum, don't ever question that. He's the love of my life. Mads was just . . .' I trail off. What was he? A temptation. An ego-boost? An antidote? ' . . . a distraction.'

'Well then you have your answer right there,' sighs Mum again, lighter this time. 'You still love him.'

'But he won't love me again after this.'

'Want to bet on it?' She's back to being her brassy self. I haven't ruined her yet.

'To be fair, what do you know, Mum?' cuts in Grace, perturbed at her advice.

'Just yous pair remember I told you this: marriage is a long road,' starts Mum. 'There will be times when you feel like running away. Times when things won't go your way, or plates get thrown across the kitchen, or life just gets mighty dull. Or indeed when *someone* might charm you into thinking that they might be the answer.'

'Mum!' Gracie and I chime.

'But if you have love, then you need to take stock, remember the road you're on and keep driving. Spend the energy you'd use dolling yourself up for a night at am-dram – or whatever it might be – and use it to fuel your relationship.'

345

My eyes have completely dried and my mouth is open. *This is a genetic affliction.*

'So what Mum's trying to say is,' cuts in Grace again, laughing now, 'you've had enough fun for now, *Princess Slaggypants* – now get on and get your man back.'

'And don't either of you ever breathe a word of this to your father,' says our mother, gathering us back into a chain.

**MONDAY, YOU UGLY OLD DOG.** I can't go on like this. Every morning for the three weeks since I was inevitably forced back through those doors, the acid has risen in my throat at the prospect of walking into the office, and he'll be there in my seat, waiting to confront me. My face is painful with hard red lumps across my jaw and chin: an external punishment for what I've done. My sleep has been fitful and I wake up sweating in my own self-written nightmare. How will Felix ever love me again? It can never be a clean, simple love again. He might be willing to work it through, but could he stay knowing I nearly didn't?

So, here I am, sat on the train, clutching my water bottle for dear life in case I heave again and can't make it to fresh air in time. The anxiety twists the knife over and over again. It's been nearly three weeks since *the incident* and yet every day I feel worse not better. As if the physical manifestations of what I did are getting stronger.

I check my phone every minute like a tick. Felix has not contacted me once. My messages float delivered but unanswered on our previously boring iMessage trail. Instead, I scan his social feeds like a covert agent, tracking the clues of his days. There have been few crumbs. Clemmie posted a cat video on his Facebook wall, which means even she's noticed how sad he is. One football conversation invited his opinion on Twitter, but he didn't partake. I've ruined his enjoyment of even his most sacred things.

Twenty days since that day.

The train lurches, and I only just hold on to my stomach. Twenty days since we had sex. Twenty days since we had sex on ovulation day. Which means I'm four or five days overdue. The train jolts again and I feel a dry wretch rise in my throat. Overdue.

The day glides by in a new haze: life takes on new meaning. The stress cloud has parted with a single ray of light. I go about my morning tasks – which have suspiciously dwindled in the past weeks – unable to force down even my usual green juice. I need to leave this place, but I can't afford to walk out on my maternity leave, not after I've slaved to keep things afloat while Rachel's been in and out on hers. But can I last another eight months of this anxiety? Of the truth watching my every move like the grim reaper? And will there ever be a baby to take it for anyway? No, I deserve to get what's owed to me by the place that threatened my marriage. I need to get what's mine.

## P +5 DAYS

'OH LIV, HOW ARE YOU?' Orla sounds measured but glowy on the phone, picking up my call at 10 a.m. on a Tuesday, like I did with hers. I'm pacing the graveyard behind St James's church. This is the first time I've set foot in here in months, but now it feels like the right place to hide in plain sight.

'Orla, I don't know what to do . . .' I'm already on the verge of tears.

'It's going to be OK.' She's my stability in all this. My constant. 'Has something happened? Have you heard from him?'

'No, still nothing,' I say, mordant. 'I just feel like such a fraud . . .'

'Liv, it's going to take time. You'll feel low. But you've got to trust that if you put the work in, it will come back. You guys can sort it out, you're so wonderful together.'

Not as wonderful as we needed to be.

'I hope so. I really do. But he won't answer any of my messages. I've even tried calling his mum but she just said I need to give it time.'

'She's right, you know, Liv . . .'

'I just feel so tense, wondering if *he's* going to come sauntering into the office and then everyone will know. Maybe they already do. What if it changes things again?'

*What if you can't control yourself.*

'It won't. You've been through so much now with Felix. You've been to relationship ground zero, you just need to rebuild. You aren't just going to suddenly fall back on to Mads's dick because he's in the building.'

'But what if I can't stop myself feeling something for him?'

'Just remember what a vain psychopath he is – you just have to. You showed very little restraint before because things were wrong. You were both pulling away from each other. But now they're not. You love Felix and you want to be with him. That's all that you need to know. Everything else is irrelevant.'

'Thank you, Or. I'm sorry I need you now.'

'Love means never having to say you're sorry,' she dead-pans, taking me back to those late nights at university where we'd phone each other to cry along to *Love Story* on our portable TVs, then dissect how long it'd take to grow out our over-plucked noughties eyebrows to Ali MacGraw splendour.

'I love you, Orla. But I am still sorry.'

'Now I feel like that wasn't really what you called me for. Has something happened?' She's always been able to spot me. To know when I'm off-balance.

'Well . . . I don't know anything yet – there's no news! – but do you ever wish that you had just walked out on Children's Circle when you had the chance, instead of sticking around now until your maternity leave?'

'Oh Liv! How late are you?' She's breathless with anticipation. 'How exciting will it be for us to take our babies out in their prams for coffee and to go to little baby theatre shows. We can dress them up in matching outfits and they can snog each other awkwardly when we go on family holidays together when they're teenagers . . .'

'Not that you've been planning?' I smile for the first time in weeks.

*This isn't real, don't get too used to it.*

'Oh, not in the slightest,' she laughs. 'And going back to your point: yes, if I had known I could escape the drudgery for a better job, I would have, I still hate it. But, I've only got to last another four and a half months and then I get my money and most of that is Jemima's trial anyway which I'll revel in. And believe me, when it gets to my time to go, I am walking out of that door and never coming back.'

'You're right. It's not worth giving up over this. I'm just freaked out.'

'Maybe it's your hormones?!' she says. I've excited her too much. 'Stick in there. You deserve some recompense for all the hard work if nothing else. Plus, just think of all the stuff they'll give you for the nursery!'

## P +6 DAYS

'TO TEST, OR NOT TO TEST?' That is the question. I'm perched on the toilet, holding it in as I toy with the stick. My hope weighs heavy on that first morning pee, and I'm bursting. I'm not sure I can take the heartache if it's negative. I'll just allow myself another day of what if. Release the floodgates. *That's better.*

## P +7 DAYS

'YOU'VE BEEN A NAUGHTY GIRL . . .' Margot laughs good-naturedly, giving my arm a jovial punch. 'I can't believe it's you and not me!'

Ada pulls me closer on the booth and squeezes me tight to her so my face is partially sandwiched to her bosom. I can't believe I've kept it in so long: I couldn't face anyone knowing what I'd done. That Felix was gone. I was half expecting my confession would result in a naked walk down Oxford Street with my friends in command of the shame bell. I'm ringing it for myself.

'I'll get us some drinks,' Margot says. 'Pint for me, gin and tonic for Ada, are you on the water now as a penance?' she says, looking at my lime and soda.

'Yeah, I've got a presentation in the morning,' I lie, hoping they don't recognise the foundation caking on my chin is to hide the hormonal spots.

'I think it's better that it's all out in the open now with Felix. I mean, it's not like you actually went the whole way anyway, is it?'

'Are you trying to make out that unless you reach full penetration it is not sex again?' shouts Margot from the bar, grinning, ready for a tussle.

'Oh, stop with the preaching, Margs, it's different girl on girl. The first rule of dickonomics is: just the tip doesn't add to your tally,' says Ada, self-righteously.

'He told Felix that I was satisfied with just the tip,' I say, mortified.

'That must have really been some penis then,' says Ada. 'I wouldn't even be able to feel the tip of Jack's!' Margot lurches my lime and soda across the table, she's laughing so hard.

'It was below average. *He* is below average. Felix's is much bigger. He was just good with his hands . . .' I'm cringing. 'I know I had lost my mind, but I was only on board for the fingering. If he did slip the tip in, he shouldn't be boasting about it, the rapey motherfucker. Because it must have been that insignificant, I didn't feel a thing.'

'And you wonder why I'm a lesbian?' says Margot, her laughter dead in its tracks. 'At least now it's all over and you can go back to being the good wife that we all know you are.'

'I've never been so dutiful. I'm even considering going full Gyamfi. Not that Felix would ever know, because he *still won't take my calls* . . .' My eyes are welling again. I didn't know I had this many tears inside me. I take a sip of my boring drink to replenish them.

'But you've still not escaped Mads, Liv. What are you

going to do when he comes in to the office?' asks Ada. 'Surely you need to report him for gross misconduct?'

'I attacked the man with a hacksaw. Surely he could do me for the same?'

**NO SIGNAL.** I'm sober and without any kind of amusement underground, and now the train is stuck just before King's Cross 'because of passenger action'. Bloody passengers. Don't they realise I need to be at home in bed now? Don't they know my eyes, or at least my ears, need amusement every second of the day or else I feel like crawling the walls with nervous energy? *Zero missed calls from Felix*. I flick through my phone. My period tracker wants me to give it a clue as to why I'm so many days overdue. I wonder if the little AI inside it is willing me on: 'Do a test! Do a test!'

I open my photos. I can't remember the last time I posted anything on Instagram – a forgotten relic of when I had something to be proud of. I flick through my photo album to see if I can find my last good day. I skip back past 13 Feb: Copenhagen, truncated to only half a day's worth of images. Me looking doped up with my red nose, posing on the rocking boat bed. Us wrapped together against the cold on the top of the hill in Christiania just before my life fell apart. The screenshot of Orla and Rich's sweet baby post on Facebook – like a *Times* wedding announcement in its formality. Felix and I looking sweaty in the kitchen at Christmas as we took a flustered selfie with the burnt turkey legs, our paper crowns slipping down over our eyes. Those hideous costumes at the Alternativity, with at least thirty children attached to us. My proud look as I lean on the HYGGExperience with Felix and Orla in my sparkly jumpsuit bathed in purple light. Felix and I looking sombre in the grounds of Soho Farmhouse on my birthday. Ada, Margot and I feeding pigeons at midnight, our make-up all smeared round our chops on our night out in south London. I can hardly remember what summer feels like. The whole combined clan looking windswept up on our favourite cliff: Felix had worked out how to use the timer on my phone and set it up on a bench just a little bit too low, so we're all thighs, Felix and Isaac with their foreheads chopped off. Me smiling and patting the baby piñata that I later decapitated. A year has gone by so quick. We tried so hard.

## P +8 DAYS

'WOULDN'TCHA JUST LOVE it if we were *all* off to 'merica?' asks Mum to the car, as we run into a sea of red lights on the North Circular.

'Mum, it's stressful enough just getting me on a plane now, without thinking about what it'd be like to have all of you boarding with your masses of bags. I mean, look at this traffic, we're obviously going to be late. And I'm going to get held up at the other end for hours too because of all the Middle Eastern stamps in my passport.'

Gracie is unusually nervy, given we've seen her off on a total of twelve much more dangerous secondments over the years.

'Is Henry excited about reporting from the Capitol?' I ask, trying to pick the mood back up. Good old sensible Henners managed to swing himself a matching press corps job and went ahead to make sure the house was all set up for when Grace lands to start her job. So grown up.

'He says he was hoping for it to be like *House of Cards* – but it's actually just like *Veep*.' She's laughing, as I picture my sister in the actual White House taking pictures of that famous hair flapping in the wind of Trump Force One. I know there's something holding her back, something much more serious than fear. Gracie's sad to be leaving us.

'Are you going to miss us then?' I can't help but pick. Might be interesting to see some real unbridled emotion from my big sister, just this once.

'Well . . . I have to admit, it's been nice being back with you all. I didn't realise how much I'd missed out on over the years,' she's keeping her face neutral, but I can see the tears are welling in the corner of her eyes as though there's a speck of dust irritating her. 'So yes, sister dearest, I will miss you all.'

Mum bursts into a wail and flings herself back through the gap to cuddle her daughter, leaving Dad desperately wrangling to keep the old BMW in lane against the path of a passing articulated truck.

'Sure, you can't be gone long . . . OK? We can't *not* see you like we did with all the other jobs. Please promise you'll be back more often this time?' Mum can't control her tears and is talking through the guard of a pack of car tissues.

'I hear POTUS has great unrestricted Wi-Fi for all our Skype sessions at least!' I laugh, and Gracie puts her arm around me and kisses me tenderly on the forehead like she used to do when she was eight and I was five and she'd read me a bedtime story. And then the tap opens and I'm crying chubby tears too. *I can't be without my husband and my big sister.*

'I'll be back more this time. It's only a few hours on the plane (if you don't count what I'm going to go through at border control). And this time, perhaps you'll at least fancy coming to visit me.'

'Don't go pushing it too far,' says Dad, now recovered in the slow lane. 'If Liv tried to emigrate as well, we'd be on the plane behind yous, wouldn't we, love?'

'You just try and stop me,' says Mum, with a big old pantomime wink.

## P +9 DAYS

I AM ABSOLUTELY BURSTING. I've come in extra early, holding in my first morning wee in the hope that it will give me a result to *make* Felix talk to me. But getting from home, to Boots, and into the office toilets has been as arduous as walking with a water balloon perilously dangling between my legs. Actually, no, don't think about that.

As I step victorious into the lift in the office (nearly there), I hear two pairs of footsteps hurrying to join me.

'Don't worry, I've got it,' I say, prodding the door-open button for the other early birds trying to show me up with their morning diligence.

Crossing my legs inelegantly to stymie the flow for just a little bit longer, I'm joined by the most exquisitely edgy woman, a Jane Birkin five years my junior, who is – judging by her 'sank you' and general air of give-a-shit insouciance – from our Paris office. Why she's here when there's no one to meet her yet, I don't know. But I'm too busy clenching every pelvic floor micro-muscle to care.

And then Mads. The heat in my face rises.

'Very kind,' he says, smiling broadly at me, as if I was just any other elevator operator about to give a couple a golden shower.

*If only I'd let the doors close on that arsehole's face.*

He leans across me to press the button, lightly brushing past my right breast with his arm. I know it, he knows it. And, just as I am about to pull his hand into the air to announce to la hot Parisienne that he's arm-assaulting me, I feel a wetness between my legs. Oh, no, please don't lose control here, not now. Not when you're wearing acid wash jeans.

I scrunch my eyes shut furiously and think of anything I can to stop the flow. Dams. Deserts. Camels. But this isn't a Tena Lady situation. This is hotter. Thicker. NO.

*You still can't help yourself around this awful shit of a man.*

I hear their laughs fading as I sprint out of the lift doors and across the office as quickly as my three-inch flatforms can carry me, throwing my Burberry-ish trench at my desk as I go. I need to be away from him (and whoever she is) and I need to get acquainted with a latrine post-haste.

As I get in the toilet door, I'm already half way through unwrapping the piss-stick with one hand, pulling down my too tight mom denim with the other. *Hold it*, I tell myself, wait. And as I finally free the test, and lower my knickers, and my bum, I see it clear as day.

Blood. Only a little dab, but unmistakable.

The toilet cubicle becomes my padded cell as I toss the impotent pregnancy test at the door, incensed with my body, incensed with my decisions, incensed with my life. I'm caged here with my rage as a bunkmate, and Mads is standing a blind-eyed guard. How did you not know? As if pregnancy wouldn't feel different from PMS. *As if you'd be that lucky.* I can't carry on without Felix and I can't carry on in this place. *Maternity leave is wasted on you.* What do I tell Felix? *He'll love you even less.*

Coming to from my delusions, slumped on the toilet in a pool of sweat, bladder thankfully relieved, I unlock my phone to confess my imbecility to Felix. To add another unread message to the downpour of *delivered*s. But instead I open Instagram, as if calming my mind with a never-ending slew of lithe bodies and other people's children will fortify me to make that call.

BABS KRISTOFF

> Olivia,
> Thought I'd connect. Dezeen has been raving about the HYGGExperience and I'm looking for an assistant. Are you familiar with my work? Are you ever in the US? I really love your response to brief. Let me know if you're ever in town . . .
> BABS.
>

*The* Babs Kristoff? Am I familiar with your work? Babs, why are you familiar with my work? I probe my hideously mottled face in the dim toilet mirror for clues as to why I'm being catfished. The Hollywood set designer, my inspiration since my teens, the reason I studied visual communications, is inviting me to become the sorcerer's apprentice, apropos of nothing, in the moment I need it most. The world's most influential design blog carried a review of a snuggly marketing spaceship that I poured my blood, sweat and tears into (and yet did not create). Is it illegal to accept a job off the back of someone else's plans? Babs would be the creative brains, I'd just be the organiser. Rachel wouldn't mind, would she? *Rachel wouldn't need to know.*

357

Alive with a sudden flash of serendipitous force, I splash cold water on my face, tousle my hair to look like I've been doing something in here for half an hour – and because I need to look strong, big, powerful – and step out into the now 10 a.m. full office. The silver leather of my ridiculous brick shoes squeaks treacherously as I tiptoe to my desk. Mads and 'Jane' are half-masked by frosted glass, but the dance of their shared laughter garrottes me.

I pull my chair towards the desk with an awkward clunk, firing up my Mac, the fury fetid from every pore. Do work, stay low, bide time.

The Friday marketing report is a behemoth capable of obscuring even the most intrepid Internet searches. *I'm not actually going to update you, old friend, but you just sit there, open like my thighs, living a lie for a while.* Around it, I build miniature windows of covert research. Partner working visas, cat passports, rental values for our house, a reply to Babs. It takes me all morning to do all the relevant registrations – I daren't look up from my screen, let alone take a lunch break, but I do sequester one item from my desk each half hour to my silver tote in preparation. I look like I've laid out strategy for the company's entire fiscal year, when I've actually made a fool-proof plan to get the fuck out of HYGGE.

I check the top left corner of my screen – 15:15 has to be an auspicious time for the call. I rise to stroll slowly, avoiding eye-contact as I walk the gauntlet to the fire escape. As I shove the emergency bar, feeling the catch release, the cool air soothes my murderous face and I clatter down the dark staircase in momentary peace. Just one phone call.

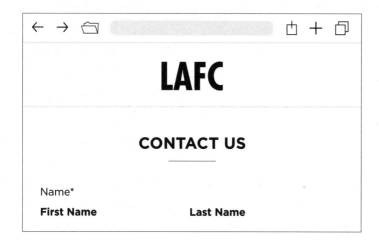

# LAFC

## CONTACT US

Name*

**First Name**                    **Last Name**

Please let it not be too late – or indeed, as it's only 7.15 a.m. over there – too early for this call. I hear the foreign dial tone, as I pace frantically down towards the pub on the corner. The temperature has dropped, but the low sun casts a beautiful glaze on its golden signage. I should have brought my coat.

'LAFC, how may I help you?' says a lively California girl's voice on the other end of the line.

'I'm sorry it's early, but would it be possible to be put through to Syd Chambers please?'

'I have a feeling he may not be in yet, but let me give his line a try.' Felix had boasted that Syd must have wanted him bad, or else he wouldn't always try calling him at 3 p.m. in the UK.

'Maybe they make you get to work that early every day!' I'd countered, talking him down from the ledge that I am now planning to push him off.

'Hullo, Syd—' cuts in a gruff Southern accent.

'Oh, hello Mr Chambers, I'm sorry to be calling so early. I'm Felix Gyamfi's wife Olivia.'

If there is even a modicum of charm left in my body now, I need to summon it.

'Good to hear from you Olivia . . .' he says warmly. 'Felix told me a lot of nice things about you.'

No wonder Felix was a fan, he's absorbing.

'Now Mr Chambers—'

'—Call me Syd, please. Mr Chambers was my grandpa,' he chuckles graciously.

'Syd, then. I have a very difficult question to ask . . .'

I anxiously debone a leaf I've plucked from a branch hanging low over the church fence next to the pub. It's too late. I know it's too late.

'Well, Olivia, what can it be? Felix has already turned down the communications director role . . .' he sounds concerned.

'That's why I rang. I wanted to know if you might consider offering it to him again? Our situation has changed and I know he'd love to accept.'

'Well, Olivia, I'm very sorry to hear that your situation has changed enough that you want to move halfway across the world. Because I can hear from your voice that it might not be a good thing that's prompted this . . .' He's one of those people who can read your tells even down a crackly transatlantic phone line. It warms me like putty.

'Well, between you, me and the ocean between, it's a few things, but, Mr Chambers – Syd – would you consider it? Or have you filled the position already?'

'Filled the position? I'm still looking. I had someone else in mind when he said no, but if you can get him here in front of me and the shareholders next week, we could meet again and see?'

'Oh, I don't know how to thank you, Syd—'

'Don't thank me. I haven't done anything yet.'

'You are so kind, Syd.'

'Like I said, don't thank me yet!' he chuckles, which I know is a good sign. 'And I look forward to meeting you when you touch down in LA, Olivia, and hearing the story of what the hurry is.'

I have never looked forward more to a meeting.

---

Olivia Galvin-Gyamfi
15 Beaumont Drive
Borehamwood
WD6 7QP

Friday 9 March

Dear Ms Chippenham,

    After three years at HYGGE, please take this note as my resignation from the post of Marketing Manager (UK). I have enjoyed my time working with you greatly, but due to unforeseen personal circumstances, I regret to inform you that today will be my last day. I will therefore be unable to serve my notice. Please instruct payroll to deduct any days this will leave me owing. I would like to thank you for your management and mentorship during my time working at the company, and best of luck for the future of the role.

    Yours sincerely
    Olivia Galvin-Gyamfi

PS. I deserved a lot more pay for the two jobs I was doing, and you know very well that you were drawing up the rope ladder behind you.

PPS. Mads is a psychopathic shagger, who I really should be reporting to HR. You need to watch out: he likes his women bored at home with lots to lose. Or maybe he's got to you already?

OK, delete that last bit. I can whistle-blow when I'm safely on another continent.

'OLIVIA, CAN I HAVE A WORD?' Trish says, speaking suspiciously quietly. Perhaps she saw what I was typing and is feeling dejected at losing me?

I enter Trish's office and can see Mads in the opposite meeting room, perched on a table with his arms crossed jauntily, laughing with the new girl – who has pulled her chair back from the conference table so her tanned tightless legs are angled towards him. Every so often he looks up in the direction of my desk to check I can see as he touches her shoulder and laughs at her jokes. I see you *very well*, Mr Rasmussen.

I close the door behind me and sit fake confidently in the chair opposite Trish's desk, clutching the plain manila envelope of my future in my whitened knuckles.

'Olivia . . .' she starts slowly. 'The reason I'm bringing you in here now is because, head office have decided to make some structural changes. Unfortunately, your role has come into question as to whether it's an effective use of funds.' I'm deaf to her preamble, still catching glimpses of Mads's overblown body language in my peripheral vision.

'So, with that in mind, I'm afraid, I've brought you in here to tell you this is the start of your consultation period.'

Distracted, I cut across her: 'I quit, Trish. I came in here to tell you my position here is no longer tenable.'

The weight of anxiety dissipates into a warm glow across my chest.

'No, Liv, well yes, that's the reason . . . but, you don't understand. *We're* making *you* redundant.'

I've confused her. Trish Chippenham always wants to feel

362

like she's the idea originator, so she's taking the words out of my mouth.

'No, Trish, I quit. It's my decision.'

'But Olivia . . .' she says, clearly confused now. 'You can't quit, because *we're* losing *you*.'

'Yes, I know you're losing me, because I'm leaving.

'We will miss you Olivia, I was shocked – but the decision was made for me.'

'By me.'

'No, not by you, by head office.'

'I only just quit, so how could they have known?'

'Because they have been planning for some weeks to make your position redundant.'

'But you can't fire me, because I already quit.'

'We're not actually firing you—'

'Yes, because I am no longer in your employ.'

'Look, Olivia, don't make it hard for me to give you this severance package – it's very generous. Six months' full pay with shares, effective today. We're very sorry to see you and Rachel go.'

'Rachel as well? Can you even do that while she's on maternity leave?'

'Well, she'll have a consultation period just the same as you where she can apply for the new role which is being created to fuse both of your positions. But between you and me, I think they're looking to take that department in another direction, and I think they have someone in mind,' she says, surreptitiously nodding in the direction of Jane Birkin.

'Oh, he really has done a number on me,' I say, baring my teeth in disgust briefly, then returning to a serene smile, when I remember what a touch this is.

'Who, Liv? Who's done a number on you?'

'Oh, no one, Trish. God. I'm talking about God, *OBVIOUSLY*. It's just not my lucky day.' I raise my fist, now crunching the manila envelope, flapping it to the sky with a pseudo-*why-I-oughta* grimace. 'OK, so I haven't quit, but I am off, right now, and I can have the money and not come back on Monday?' I say, raising myself off my chair, careful to look as pensive as someone who has just had their life's work bashed from their fingers with a wooden mallet, *not* someone who's just been gifted half a year's pay to bugger off to LA.

'And what about the films I made? Did you ever look at the rough edits?'

'I did watch them, thank you, Olivia. Management felt they weren't quite HYGGE enough for the brand. So I guess they're yours if you want to take them elsewhere. I certainly won't be tipping anyone off.'

*Which is lucky, because I'd already packed the camera and SD cards in my tote.*

'Thanks, Trish,' I say, suddenly sentimental towards the pastel-haired disciplinarian. 'Your shouting has been nothing but a pleasure. Please watch your back, because "God" might be after your job next.' And then I (and my envelope) get the fuck out of HYGGE.

'You're just not allowed to tell . . . anyone . . .' she shouts, as I exit her office, quietly this time, because this is *private* business that has in no way been affected by a *personal* vendetta.

I pull on my trench, more seamlessly than usual, sling my silver tote over my shoulder, smile at my desk mates who are all wondering why I'm the lucky one who gets to walk out at 3.47 on a Friday, then turn to the glass office opposite me, and give that smiling assassin a wink and a wave as I stride right on out of my past with my head held high.

**THE SUN BLAZES** sideways through the blotchy train window, and there's not a soul to be found on the prompt non-stopping 16:02 service. So this is my last commute. No jostling for oxygen in the face of a halitosis monster, no race for a seat against a woman weighed down by half of Topshop. It's almost an anti-climax. But as the sun continues to beat through on to my face, I can't help but smile. There's not even anyone around to see how it highlights the hairs on my chin.

**'BRET, PRESENT. JEMAINE, PRESENT.'** It's a cacophony of mewling as the cats glare through the mesh panel of their carry case. They narrow their eyes: I am the child catcher and one day soon they will grow up to avenge their kidnap by slaughtering me in cold blood. Except they're perfectly safe and just going on a jaunt to collect their doting cat father from his office. As soon as I let them out and give them some Dreamies, they'll be back on side. Just imagine what they'll be like on an eleven-hour flight.

I dial my parents' number as I run out to the Uber idling outside our gate and wonder if driving into the rush-hour traffic to give my husband a grand surprise is actually that good an idea? With the cats? At least I had a chance to take my squeaky shoes off.

'Liv? Are you OK? Is it Grace?' Dad has answered in one ring, and is on the verge of a heart attack on the other end of the line. Not over me. Over Grace obviously.

'Pa! Calm down! It's all fine . . . I haven't even spoken

to Grace. Is Mum there? I need to talk to you both.'

I can hear him flapping about, calling her in from the garden and putting her on speaker phone.

'What is it Liv?' cuts in Mum, breathless from her little sprint to the phone. At least the pub garden is finished before we go.

'So, I'm not sure how to tell you this, but—'

I can hear them both excitedly holding their breath in the background.

'You're preg—'

'We're moving to LA!'

'Congratulations!' they scream.

'Hang on, what did she just say?!' Mum immediately bursts into another wail, and I hear the phone rustle, as Dad attempts to put it back on handset mode and fend off her emotions.

'Liv, what? When? Where are you going to live? This is big news, how come you've not spoken to us about it before?' There's not a shade of anger in his voice, only concern over the logistics. I love how sensible he can be in the face of terrifying uncertainty, like the time when our boat capsized on a trip to Derry, and he told us all a fairy tale about a mermaid while we desperately trod water in the air bubble waiting to be rescued. He told me later he just thought at least we'd have a nice story in our minds when we all perished like Jack in *Titanic*. Misguided, but calming.

'We're going on Sunday,' I say resolutely, still not fully absorbing the ramifications of what's coming out of my mouth. 'It's something we need to do. I haven't told Felix yet, so you're the first to know.'

The tears are pouring down my face now, knowing that

I have to hurt them to save myself. But isn't that the first rule of being a child?

'*See*, Maeve – we're the first to know!' says Dad, trying to desperately find the positives, although I can hear him choking up. 'Hang on, what do you mean you've not told your man Felix? How are you taking the decision to move to *El Hay* without consulting him?'

Mum's sobs cease momentarily as she seizes an idea.

'Well, sure you can't go that quick then!' she says, dragging the phone away from Dad's hands. 'It's impossible! See, Billy, they can't go! Felix won't have even handed in his notice yet. And neither have you?'

'Oh, about that . . .' I say, taking a deep gulp of air. 'I got fired for having a fling with my boss! Surprise!' I'm really trying to sink myself in the parental opinion polls.

'OLIVIA GALVIN!' I can feel the veins popping in Dad's neck down the line as Mum stays silent in her knowledge. '*As if you did.*'

'I meant to tell you, I really did' – *I didn't* – 'but Felix and I were going through a rocky patch. Which is why we need this new start . . .' I'm rambling now, needing their seal of approval. 'Don't we, Dad?' Deferring it back to Dad draws him on to my side and helps him make sense of why I have to go for Mum when she comes out of her red mist.

'That's it, Billy, I'm booking our tickets now . . . There's no use being here if the girls are in America. No point at all.'

I can hear Dad in the background muttering, 'But what about our friends? What about the pub? What happened to us living our lives?'

'Don't you worry, Liv, you won't have to miss us for long. I know you'll be homesick. Won't you miss us? I know Gracie does, even though she doesn't let on.'

'You know we'll miss you, Mum. But we're adults now. We need to get on with our lives. And it won't be for ever.'

'A year it is then. I can take a year. But I'm still coming out to see you! I can't believe you fly on Mother's Day. I'll be a mother without children,' she cries again. And I start to cry now too: I know the feeling well.

Orla
Today 16:55

Hey, my love, I am so sorry to be writing this in a message, but I've just spoken to my parents about it and I'm exhausted. I'm also about to pull up at Felix's work to give him the shock of his life, so I need to keep this short. We're moving to LA. Felix got offered his dream job a couple of months ago, and like a bitch I made him turn it down. But today I found out that not only am I not pregnant, but also – as I went to hand my notice in in a fury – I've been made redundant! Mads brought in this super-hot French girl to move in on my desk while I was still there! But fuck 'em. I got an Instagram message from my favourite set designer saying if I was ever in the US she's looking for an assistant. That's got to be fate, right? So I just thought, fuck it, we're going this weekend. I'm sorry to go just when you need me, but I promise you can come visit whenever you like. Like, maybe the whole of your maternity leave? We just need this. I hope you can understand. xxxxxx

Liv! Love means never having to say you're sorry, remember? Please tell me you're flying first class. I could definitely fit in your luggage allowance even with my enormous gut. xxxxx

**\*\*\*SURPRISE 'WE'RE MOVING TO LA!'
PARTY\*\*\***

Apologies for the short notice, but we leave on
Sunday! Join us at our house (yes, that does
mean you have to come to Borehamwood) on
Saturday at 6p.m. to help us party and pack
before we bid you adieu for sunny California.

If you're feeling kind, please make a playlist and
bring a bottle, it might sound selfish, but we
don't have time for that sort of preparation.
Consider it a really cheap going-away gift!

Warning: no is not an acceptable reply. If you
don't say goodbye, we will never again say hello.

Love y'all xxxx

PS. DON'T TEXT FELIX ABOUT THIS. The main
surprise is, he doesn't know!

**I CLAMBER OUT OF** the prius dragging the cat carrier, remembering that I've just spent fifty minutes and fifty pounds on making this trip into Euston with them just to make some big song and dance of proposing this trip to Felix. I'd better make this good.

Two years ago, when he decided to give up on his dream of being the next Henry Winter and take this job so we could afford to start a family, I remember I came and stood in this very spot in the courtyard one afternoon to surprise Felix. A little romantic gesture to say thank you for the sacrifice. I threw a stone at every window on the

60s gold-trimmed four-floor block until he eventually cracked open the crittall window and stuck his head out to ask me what the hell I was doing. So maybe I won't do that now, but at least I laid the groundwork on which window might still be his.

I put the carrier on the ground momentarily while I flick through my Apple Music and ensure the iPhone speaker is on max volume. I then, like a girl scout, attach it to the sexy lanyard I've fashioned from one of the laces I grabbed from my silver flatforms as I jumped in the car. The other is stringing my ingenious sign from beneath the carrier. It's now or never.

I stand dead centre in the quad, hoping the acoustics will help, and hoist the cat carrier above my head and the sign drops down on to my forehead:

---

**COME WITH ME IF YOU WANT TO LIVE (IN LA)**

---

I press play. Serge Gainsbourg's cockish whisper rebounds across the courtyard.

I begin my patchy lip-sync, my pidgin French lagging behind every 'Écoutez', only to catch up loudly with the name-checks of Ms Bonnie Parker and her bit of rough, Monsieur *Clyde Barrooow*.

Passers-by – mostly advertising execs on their way to the pub – carry on with indifference, so many pop-ups and flash-mobs have they engineered in this courtyard themselves. They can see clearly that I'm just another arrogant idiot trying to market something shiny and shit to someone who really doesn't want to know.

The chorus kicks in. People are starting to cotton on to the tune now. I notice a few faces in the windows of the office above. Most wind their necks back in once they hear my largely tuneless and completely inelegant pronunciation on another verse.

*Bonnie and Clyde*
BOONNIE AAND CLYYYDDDE

Another chorus down and my arms feel like they're about to break under the strain. Bret and Jemaine, when did you get so fat?

I pretend to know the next bit. God, this song goes on. I feel like I can see his disapproving face peeping out on the third floor (not where he sits). No glasses again. He's disowned me completely. Maybe I'm imagining it.

Oh good, some more name-checking . . . Maybe Bonnie and Clyde would be cute as baby names. *That's not the point of this, keep your head in the game.*

Yet more chorus. He's not coming. I'm that contestant on *The Voice* eking out the final couple of verses with extra gusto knowing that no one is going to turn their chair for me. Please turn your chair for me, Felix.

*Another* bit I can't even pretend to pronounce. How can words sound so soft and yet be so difficult to get your mouth round. Ooh, I like this bit:

blah bla *TAC TAC TAC*

I can hear echoes of the lines. Am I delusional now? I'm not even pretending to sing along apart from odd noises.

No, people are around me, singing along. A couple see how much I'm struggling with the cats and come to support me on either side, swaying with me to the beat. I'm the marathon runner limping to the finish line with the crowd roaring around me, willing me to go the distance.

I've got a whole choir with me now, the couple have their arms wrapped around me, we're doing our best with the 'nous' and the 'fous' at the tops of our voices, practically yelping the choruses. The cats are joining in. I should be buoyed but I'm welling up. He hates me this much that he's going to leave me here on his doorstep. And I'll have to go away with my head hung in shame to LA with no job. Even the cats will disown me.

It's the last verse. My gusto for pretending I know what this song is about is all but extinguished. I begin the final mumble-sing at the top of my voice. I'm not hitting any of the right words now, but Felix knows even less French than me so I might as well just put on this final show for the crowd.

That's it. Like Bonnie Parker, I'm dead. I've got to give up.

Then, the mahogany and gold door flings open, and I see Felix bounding towards me. The couple step aside, allowing him to see the spectacle of me with the cats aloft in their boombox case, weeping like a widow in fear that he might not show. But here he is. I can finally put the cats down.

*Bonnie and Clyde . . .*

I run forward to meet him, our bodies and mouths colliding at full force, my arms like jelly draped about his neck.

'Felix,' I say, hoarse from all the singing and dry-mouthed as if I'm about to propose. 'I've been trying so hard to be so many things, that I stopped trying with the best thing I had.' He smiles his same goofy wounded smile as he did that first day I hit him in the face. This time, I get to jump on him and kiss it better. 'That's YOU.'

'But, if you can forgive me, I'd like to try again. *In LA.* We fly this weekend and it's all lined up. All you have to do is say yes.'

I hope that this really was his dream job.

'What?' he draws back from me so he can inspect my face, as if he needs to lip read what I'm telling him. 'Liv, this is madness.' Crazy fear all over his face like the cats in the basket. 'What about work? What about our parents? What about the house? What about IVF? What about the cats?'

But I can tell he's excited by what I'm proposing. He knows I don't take my chances lightly. And so, as I boost the basket on to my shoulder, take my husband by the hand, give the crowd a wave and as we run laughing into the distance together, I say:

'What about us?'

# Acknowledgements

If every cloud has a silver lining, then my empty uterus' is this book. No one wants to really try at anything; you want things to be effortless. But trying for a baby is a special kind of losing control – and in this book, I found an outlet for that. Laughter.

And so, the biggest thank you has to go to my husband Charlie Parrish, for trying so hard alongside me and always succeeding in making me laugh, even amid the tears. Through the innumerable bittersweet announcements, gut-punching delays and making injecting my bruised thighs a nightly comedic high, I couldn't have done this with anyone else. And for being my first editor in the middle of it too – especially that uncomfortable Heathrow-LA flight proofing 100,000 words in 5,440 miles – you are my champion.

In bringing the book to life, Kate Howard and the team at Hodder & Stoughton, I cannot thank you enough for taking a leap of faith on a couple of half-written chapters and trusting I could deliver. Kate, during a tough year you were a beacon of strength to me. To Veronique Norton for starting it all with an introduction and then finishing it off as an amazing publicist and friend. Thorne Ryan, for chasing Gainsbourg's ghost so I could write a singalong and Alice Morley for whipping the world into a floral frenzy. And then Sharan for being that early keen pair of eyes,

Justine for questioning the minutiae and Sarah for all those iterations of the blooming uterus.

To my agent Imogen Pelham at Marjacq, for 'getting' TRYING right from the start and being the ice-cool confidence to my blatherer. Now, hopefully everyone else will get it too. On that: a special nod to Sam Eades for making me feel that a funny novel about infertility could ever be a goer in the first place.

And then to my wonderful family, especially my parents Lucy and Patrick, my brother James and my lovely in-laws, I can never thank you enough for your unending support. You're nothing like the characters here, but I hope you love them as much as I do. Dad, you finally no longer have to tell me to 'write that book.'

To the friends who helped and influenced me along the way – Louise, Vic, Anna, Nathan – I couldn't have done it without you. And to Roisin for sharing the rocky road with me, it all came good in the end. To everyone who has confided their fertility journey to me along the way, I appreciate you sharing your challenges and allowing me to share mine. We're all in it together.

And lastly, to Ruby and Bella: the best furry writing companions a girl could ever wish for. May attempting to balance your whole bodies on a copy of this book bring you as much (uncomfortable-looking) joy as it will do to me watching you.

green
1

light green
2

yellow
3

pink
4

dark pink
5